BLADE OF DREAM

As Daniel Abraham

THE KITHAMAR TRILOGY

Age of Ash
Blade of Dream

THE LONG PRICE QUARTET

A Shadow in Summer
A Betrayal in Winter
An Autumn War
The Price of Spring

THE DAGGER AND THE COIN

The Dragon's Path
The King's Blood
The Tyrant's Law
The Widow's House
The Spider's War

Leviathan Wept and Other Stories

Balfour and Meriwether in the Incident of the Harrowmoor Dogs

Hunter's Run (with George R. R. Martin and Gardner Dozois)

With Ty Franck as James S. A. Corey

THE EXPANSE

Leviathan Wakes
Caliban's War
Abaddon's Gate
Cibola Burn
Nemesis Games
Babylon's Ashes
Persepolis Rising
Tiamat's Wrath
Leviathan Falls

Memory's Legion: The Complete Expanse Story Collection

THE EXPANSE SHORT FICTION

Drive
The Butcher of Anderson Station
Gods of Risk
The Churn
The Vital Abyss
Strange Dogs
Auberon
The Sins of Our Fathers

Star Wars: Honor Among Thieves

As M. L. N. Hanover

THE BLACK SUN'S DAUGHTER

Unclean Spirits
Darker Angels
Vicious Grace
Killing Rites
Graveyard Child

BLADE OF DREAM

BOOK TWO OF THE KITHAMAR TRILOGY

DANIEL ABRAHAM

orbit

orbitbooks.net

This book is a work of fiction. Names, characters, places, and incidents are the product of the author's imagination or are used fictitiously. Any resemblance to actual events, locales, or persons, living or dead, is coincidental.

Cover design by Lauren Panepinto
Cover illustration by Daniel Dociu

Map by Jayné Franck

Orbit
Hachette Book Group
1290 Avenue of the Americas
New York, NY 10104
orbitbooks.net

First Edition: July 2023
Simultaneously published in Great Britain by Orbit

Orbit is an imprint of Hachette Book Group.
The Orbit name and logo are trademarks of Little, Brown Book Group Limited.

Library of Congress Cataloging-in-Publication Data
Names: Abraham, Daniel, author.
Title: Blade of dream / Daniel Abraham.
Description: First Edition. | New York, NY : Orbit, 2023. |
Series: The Kithamar trilogy ; book 2
Identifiers: LCCN 2022042303 | ISBN 9780316421898 (hardback) |
ISBN 9780316421881 (ebook)
Subjects: LCGFT: Novels.
Classification: LCC PS3601.B677 B53 2023 | DDC 813/.6—dc23/eng/20220909
LC record available at https://lccn.loc.gov/2022042303

ISBNs: 9780316421898 (hardcover), 9780316421881 (ebook)

Printed in Canada

MRQ-T

10 9 8 7 6 5 4 3 2 1

To the audience
and other unacknowledged collaborators

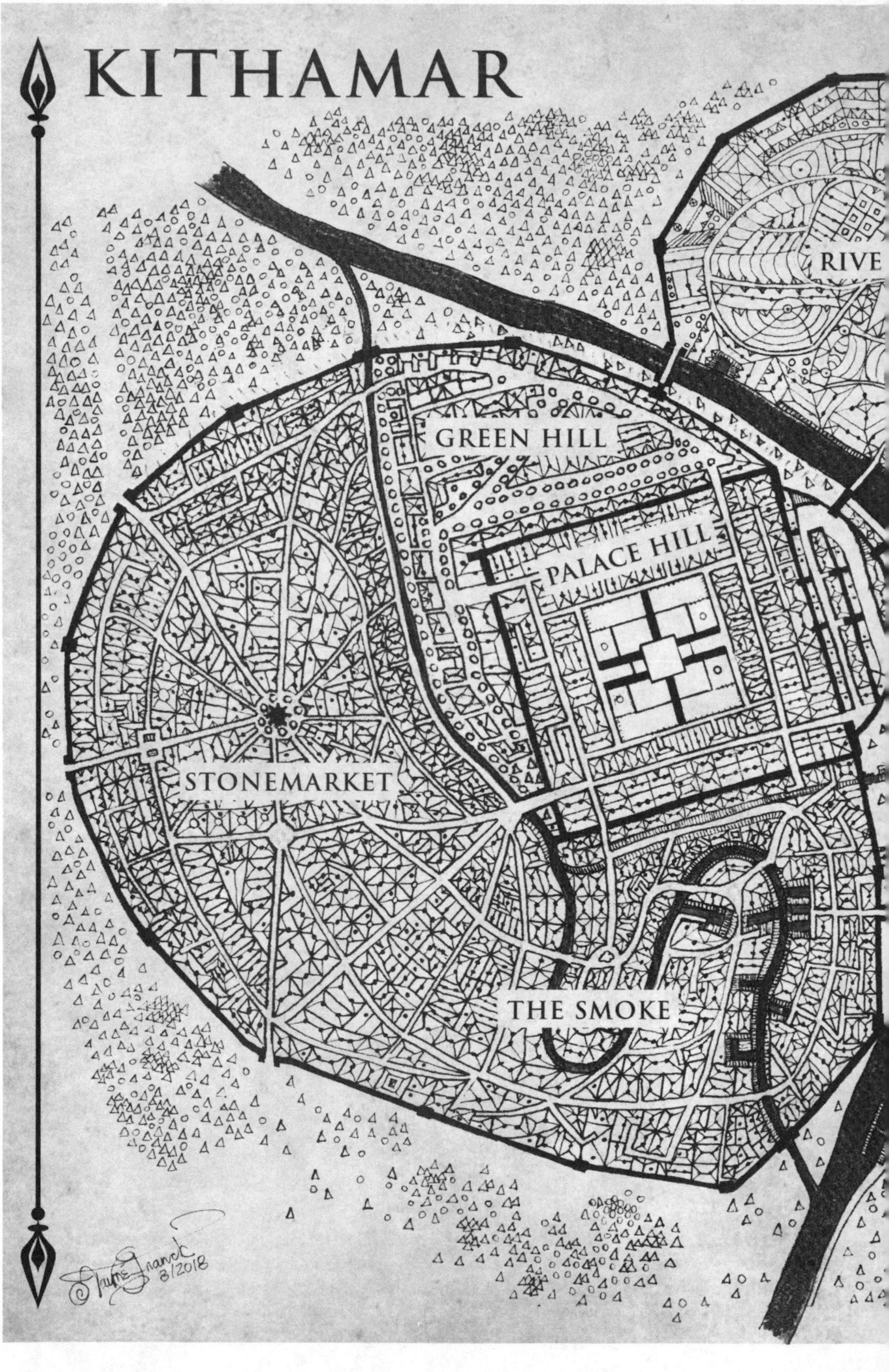
KITHAMAR
RIVE
GREEN HILL
PALACE HILL
STONEMARKET
THE SMOKE
©Tayne Franck 8/2018

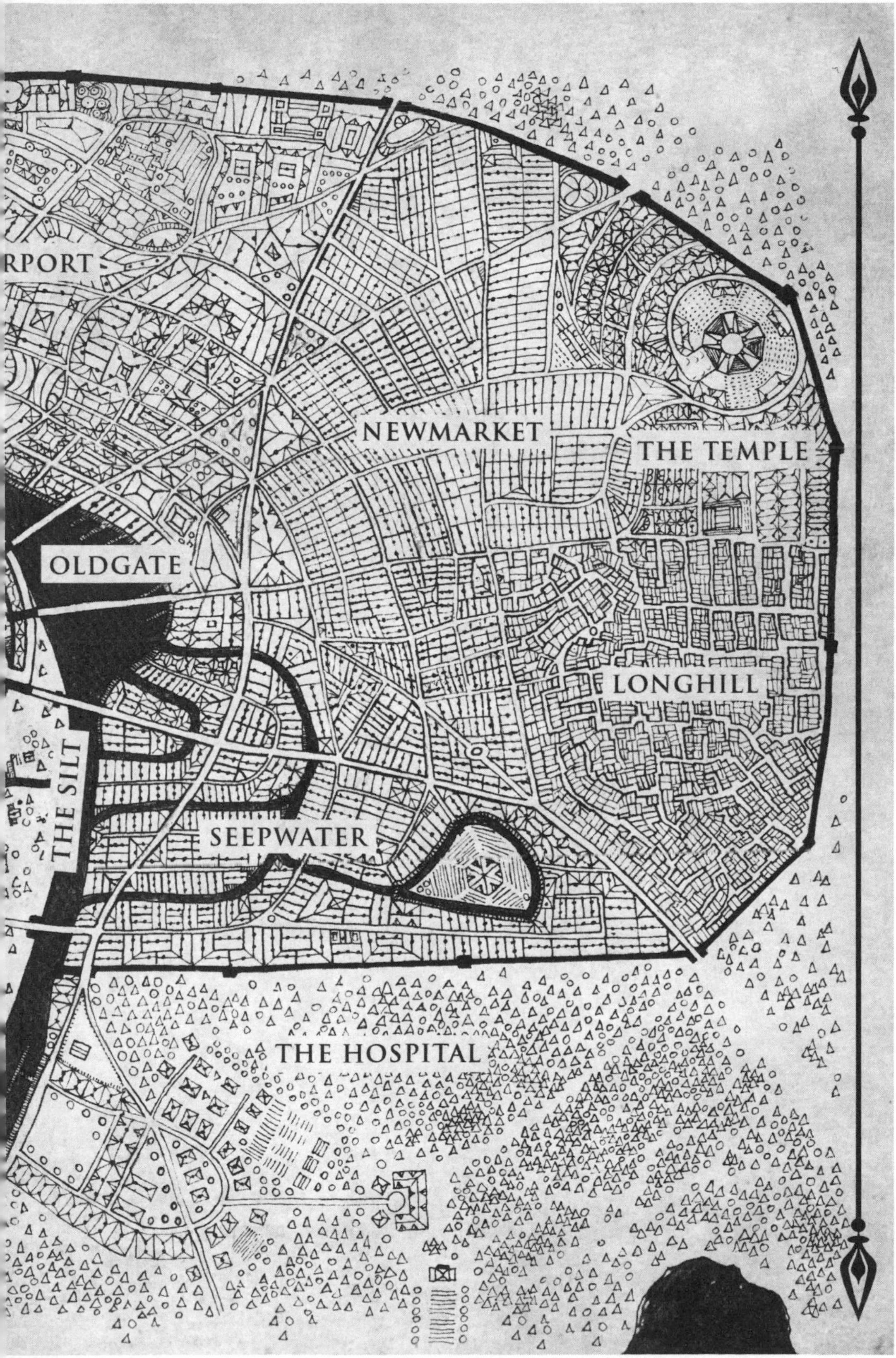
RPORT
NEWMARKET
THE TEMPLE
OLDGATE
LONGHILL
THE SILT
SEEPWATER
THE HOSPITAL

BLADE
OF
DREAM

In the course of a single life, a man can be many things: a beloved child in a brightly embroidered gown, a street tough with a band of knifemen walking at his side, lover to a beautiful girl, husband to an honest woman, father to a child, grain sweeper in a brewery, widower, musician, and mendicant coughing his lungs up outside the city walls. The only thing they have in common is that they are the same man.

These are the mysteries, and there is a beauty in them. In this way, Kithamar is a beautiful city.

All through its streets, Kithamar shows the signs and remnants of the cities that the city has been. Walls that defended the border of a younger town stand a dumbfounded, useless guard between the noble compounds of Green Hill and the fountain square at Stonemarket. The great battlements of Oldgate glower out over the river, the arrow-slits and murder holes used for candle niches now, and the enemy races who stormed or manned it sleep side by side in its armories because the rents are cheap. The six-bridged Khahon was the border between a great

Hansch kingdom and savage near-nomad Inlisc to hear it one way, or the first place that the frightened, violent, sharp-faced Hansch had come from the west if you told the story from the other bank. Now the river is the heart of the city, dividing and uniting it.

The ancient races killed one another and swore eternal hatred, only to bury their enmity and pretend to be a single people, citizens of one city. Kithamar has declared itself the subject of the one true god. Or the three. Or the numberless. For three hundred years and longer, it has been a free city, independent and proud and ruled by princes of its own rather than any distant king.

Only today, its prince is dead.

The reign of Byrn a Sal had been brief.

Less than a year before, the streets had filled with revelers and wine, music and joy, and more than a little imprudent sex to celebrate the great man's coronation. The months between then and now were turbulent, marked by ill omens and violence. A winter of troubled sleep.

Now, as the first light of the coming dawn touches the highest reaches of the palace towering at the top of its hill, the red gates open on his funeral procession. Two old women dressed in rags step out and strike drums. Black, blindered horses follow, their steps echoing against the stone. And all along the route, the men and women and children who are Kithamar wait.

They have been there since nightfall, some of them. They love the spectacle of death and the performance of grief. And, though few of them say the words aloud, they hope that the season of darkness will end and something new begin. Only a few of them ask their questions aloud: How did it happen? Was it illness or accident, murder or the vengeance of God?

How did Byrn a Sal die?

The black lacquered cart passes among the gardens and mansions of Green Hill. The heads of the high families stand at their entrances as if ready to make the dead man welcome if he should stand up. Servants and children and ill-dignified cousins gawk from the bushes and corners. Only the burned-out shell of the Daris Brotherhood ignores the funeral. And then the body passes into the city proper, heading first for Stonemarket and then south through the soot-dark streets of the Smoke.

Those lucky enough to have buildings along the route have rented space at their windows and on their roofs. As the death cart shifts and judders across the cobblestones, people jockey to look at the corpse: a little less than six feet of iron-stinking clay that had been a man. Behind the cart follow the highest dignified of the city.

The dead man's daughter—soon prince herself—Elaine a Sal, rides behind her father in a dark litter. She wears rags, but also a silver torc. Her chin is lifted, and her face is expressionless. The eyes of the city drink her in, trying to find some sign in the angle of her spine or the dryness of her eyes to tell whether she's a girl hardly old enough to be called woman drowning in shock and despair, or else a murderess and patricide struggling to contain her triumph.

Either way, she will rule the city tomorrow, and all these same people will dance at her coronation.

Behind her, the favored of the old prince walk. Mikah Ell, the palace historian in an ash-streaked robe. Old Karsen's son, Halev, who had been Byrn a Sal's confidant and advisor. Samal Kint, the head of the palace guard, carrying a blunted sword. Then more, all wearing grey, all with ashes on their hands. When they reach the bridge at the edge of the Smoke—yellow stone and black mortar—they stop. A priest walks out to meet them, chanting and shaking a censer of sweet incense. They perform the rites of protection to keep the river from washing away the dead man's soul. Everyone knows that water is hungry.

The rite complete, the funeral procession passes through the wider streets of Seepwater, past the brewers' houses and canals where the flatboats stand bow to stern, so thick that a girl could have walked from one side of the canal to the other and not gotten her hem wet. Midday comes, the early summer sun making its arc more slowly than it did a few weeks before, and the cart is only just turning northeast to make its way along the dividing line between Riverport and Newmarket. Flies as fat as thumbnails buzz around the cart, and the horses slap at them with their tails. Wherever the funeral procession is, the crowd thickens, only to evaporate when it has passed. Once the last of the honor guard rounds the corner, leaving Seepwater behind, the brewers' houses reopen, the iron grates on their sides start accepting wagers again. Delivery men spin barrels down the streets on their edges with the practiced skill of jugglers.

It is almost sunset before the funeral procession reaches the Temple. The bloody western skyline is interrupted by the black hill of the palace. The colored windows of the Temple glow. Full dark takes the streets like spilling ink before the last song echoes in the heights above the great altar and the body of Byrn a Sal, purified by the mourning of his subjects and the prayers of his priesthood, comes out to the pyre. His daughter should light the oil-stinking wood, but she stays still until young Karsen, her father's friend, comes and takes the torch from her hand.

The term for the night between the funeral of the old prince and the coronation of the new one is *gautanna*. It is an ancient Inlisc word that means, roughly, the pause at the top of a breath when the lungs are most full. Literally, it translates as *the moment of hollowness.*

For one night, Kithamar is a city between worlds and between ages. It falls out of its own history, at once the end of something and the beginning of something else. The skeptical among the citizens—and Kithamar has more than its share of the amiably godless—call it tradition and merely a story that says something about the character of the city, its hopes and aspirations, the fears and uncertainties that come in moments of change. That may be true, but there is something profound and eerie about the streets. The rush of the river seems to have words in it. The small magics of Kithamar go as quiet as mice scenting a cat. The clatter of horseshoes against stone echoes differently. The city guard in their blue cloaks make their rounds quietly, or decide that for one night they might as well not make them at all.

Under the northernmost of Oldgate's four bridges, a girl sits, listening to the water. She has a round face, gently curling hair, and a knife held in her fist. She is waiting for a meeting that she dreads as much as she longs for it.

Outside the city, the southern track where by daylight teams of oxen haul boats against the current is quiet and deserted apart from one lone, bearded man. He sits at the base of a white birch, his back against the bark. The small glass bead in his hand would be red if there were light enough to see it.

In a thin-walled bedroom above a tailor's shop in Riverport, a young man lies alone on a mattress. His right hand is bandaged, and the wound beneath the cloth throbs. He watches the moon rise over the rooftops, listening with his heart in his throat for footsteps on the creaking floorboards outside his door.

His name is Garreth Left.

PART ONE

MIDSUMMER

The city of Kithamar is its divisions. The river divides the old Hansch stronghold from the Inlisc township that it conquered and consumed. The buildings on the north side of a particular street are in Stonemarket, the south, in the Smoke. Within a single quarter, divisions are everywhere: the wealthy merchant halls of Riverport against those that are struggling; the sun-warmed wall of a house where the family basks and the shadowed side where servants shiver. Division and division and division until there are as many Kithamars as there are people that sleep inside its walls. And even a heart has chambers.

—From the Sermon on Integrity by
Avith Cerr, court philosopher to
Prince Daos a Sal

Ivy grew up the courtyard's northern wall, broad leaves a green so rich and dark they seemed almost black in lantern light. The day's heat radiated up from the stones, and the thick breeze was what passed for coolness in midsummer. It smelled like the river.

"Then five more came out," Kannish's uncle Marsen continued, holding up his splayed hand. "So there we were, me and Frijjan Reed and Old Boar with a full dozen Longhill thugs around us, and no other patrol close enough to hear the whistle."

Maur was leaning forward like a child, not a grown man with two full decades of life behind him. Garreth swallowed another mouthful of cider and tried not to lean forward too. Kannish, who had the blue cloak of the city guard for himself now even though he wasn't wearing it, crossed his arms and sat back against the wall as if by joining the guard, he'd made all his uncle's stories partly his own.

Marsen stretched his arms along the back of the metal bench, shaking his head at his own memories. He was halfway through his fifth decade, with grey at his temples and in his beard, and he wore the uniform with the ease of long familiarity. The uniform was so much a part of him that going shirtless like the boys never occurred to him, even in the heat.

"Did you get your ass split the other way, then?" Maur asked.

"No," Marsen said. "We could have, no mistake. These were all Aunt Thorn's knives, and she's a bloodthirsty piece of Inlisc shit. Our badges of office make us targets for her. But we were in Longhill itself. You boys ever go to Longhill?"

"Just on the way to the university and the theater," Garreth said.

"Well, don't. If you're going to Seepwater, stay by the river to get there. It's a maze, Longhill. The way the Inlisc rot out their houses and throw up new ones, the streets shift from week to week, and the new places are built from the same wood that the old ones were. That was what saved us." He nodded, and Kannish nodded with him like he knew what was coming next. "One of them had an oil lamp. Crap little tin-and-glass thing. So that's what I went for. He dodged out of my way, but I wasn't aiming for the meat of him. Oh no. I caught the glass and the tin. Shattered the fucking thing and got oil everywhere. Up and down my blade too. Looked like something out of a priest's story for a little bit. Gods with flaming swords, but it was just me and a bit of cheap oil." He held his right hand out, palm down, and pointed at his thumb. "You can see the burn scar from where it dripped right there."

Maur whistled low. The knot of scar was pale and ugly, and the pain of getting it seemed like nothing to the man who wore it.

"Point was, Aunt Thorn's boys saw the flame, and they panicked. Damn near forgot we were there. Started running for water. We had half of them dead or roped before they knew what was happening, and the rest scattered. They're dangerous, but they spook easy when you stand up to them. That's truth."

"What about the fire?" Garreth asked.

"The locals had it out before we had to turn to it. Longhill knows that if it starts burning, it won't stop. They've got hidden wells in some of those houses. There wasn't any real danger. But distraction? That's half of what fighting is."

"Outthinking the enemy's as deadly as speed or strength," Kannish said. "More, likely. That's what Captain Senit always says."

His uncle's eyes narrowed and he looked to his left. "He does say that."

A woman's voice called from inside. Kannish's mother, the host of the night's meal saying a wide, loud good night to some of the other guests. Garreth had spent time in Kannish's home since he and Kannish and Maur were all pot-bellied, unsteady boys playing swordfight with loose sticks, and he knew a hint when he heard one. The others did too. He and Maur pulled their tunics back on over their heads, and Kannish shrugged his blue cloak back into place. Kannish wasn't on patrol any more than his uncle was, but the uniform was a boast. A statement of who Kannish had become and his place in the city.

"Could head for the tap house," Maur suggested.

"It's a pretty thought," Marsen said, "but it's back to the barracks for us."

"I have patrol in the morning," Kannish said, "and Uncle's pulling tolls at the Seepwater gate."

Maur tried on a smile. "Another night, then."

Together, the four of them passed under the stone archway and into the house proper. The servants had cleared away the remains of the meal, and Kannish's mother and father were standing in the front hall along with their two eldest daughters. It was hard for Garreth to think of his friend's older sisters as anything but the agents of torment and objects of adolescent curiosity that they had been for him when he was younger, but they were women now, full-grown and ready to take their places in the family and business. The elder had just announced her engagement to the son of a magistrate, and the night's meal had been one of several meant to celebrate the coming union.

Garreth thanked Kannish's father and mother for their hospitality, as form required, and they laughed and hugged him. The merchant houses of Kithamar were at constant war with each other, but it was a war fought with favors and alliances and a firm eye on how to wring advantage out of every situation without quite crossing the law. That it was usually bloodless made it no less intense. The decision, made almost all of Garreth's lifetime ago, to have the three boys play together in the family courtyards had meant something, as did the choice to invite Kannish's friends to the meal tonight. That was the way in Riverport. Everything was something more than it appeared.

Kannish and his uncle turned south, heading toward their barracks. Maur and Garreth made their way west. It was the height of summer, and the long, slow hours left a touch of indigo on the horizon. Palace Hill was off to the southwest from them, Oldgate glittering with lamps and lanterns all down the left side, like the hill was a head seen almost in profile with the palace of Prince Ausai atop it like a crown. Kannish had been in the guard for almost half a year already, but it still felt odd to be walking through the warm, fragrant night without him. Like someone was missing.

At first, they didn't talk, just moved through the dark streets with their footsteps falling in and out of rhythm. At the little square by the chandlers' guild, Maur hopped onto the low stone wall and balanced on it like an acrobat with very little skill. When they reached the end, he jumped down and sighed. "You heard about Prince Ausai being sick?"

"I don't believe it. People like telling stories about how things are about to fall apart."

Maur made a little noise that might have been agreement or might have been nothing. He sighed again, more deeply. "I'm going to join too."

"Join what?"

"The city guard. With Kannish and Marsen."

"Oh," Garreth said.

"Don't."

"Don't what?"

"Feel betrayed. It's not about picking him over you."

"I didn't think it was," Garreth said. And then a moment later, "You know those stories the old man tells are more than half bullshit. All that about girls throwing themselves at bluecloaks and how the guard wins every fight? That's him on a stage."

"I know, it's just we're getting to where we need to find a place, you know? It's easy for you. You're the oldest, and only one brother under you. I've got six siblings ahead of me. My father had to make up a new position in the company last year so that Mernin could report to him straight and not to one of the other children. Saved his dignity. They're already spending half the time they should be working at plotting out how to run the business after my parents die."

"The eternal fight."

Maur nodded, squinting up at the moon. He looked like a sorrowful rabbit. "It'll be kindness to them and good for me if I find another path. And the guard's better than the Temple."

They were walking slower now. The corner where their paths

divided was coming up, and Garreth found himself dreading it. "You don't want to spend your days praying to the gods and scraping wax out of the candleholders?"

"I'm not the gods-and-spirits type," Maur said. "At least the guard has some adventure to it. And it's not as humiliating as taking hind tit in the family trade. Anyway, Kannish said there's an opening in his watch. One of the old-timers caught a knife in his gut, and it went septic."

"Lucky for you."

"Don't be bitter."

"I'm not," Garreth said. "I'm just... it's late and I'm tired."

The corner came, and they paused. Maur was shorter than Garreth by almost a head, thin across the shoulders, and with wide brown eyes with one a little higher than the other. They were the same age, except Garreth was born in the spring and Maur the autumn. How had it come that they weren't still boys digging in the mud and daring each other to climb the tile rooftops?

"Well," Maur said.

"Yeah," Garreth replied.

Maur turned north. His family lived almost against the city wall. Garreth went south, walking alone in dark streets. In Seepwater or Newmarket, a man walking alone at night could attract the wrong kind of attention, and he wouldn't have gone to Longhill even with friends and weapons. He'd only been across the river to Stonemarket and the Smoke after dark a few times, and then with company who knew the streets. But Riverport was home almost as much as his own family's compound, and its streets were as much a part of his place in the world as his own kitchen garden.

House Left had been part of Kithamar since before Kithamar had been a city, or so the story went. Back in the dim past when the Khahon had been a river border between the cities of the Hansch to the west and Inlisc hunting tribes to the east, a Hansch general had taken a merchant woman as lover. Their child, noble by blood but embarrassing to the general's wife, had been given favors of trade and custom under the mother's name. And so House Left was half merchant class, half secret nobility, and one of the founding trade families that had made Kithamar independent of the cities around it. Maybe it was even true.

Riverport was the northernmost navigable port on the Khahon, and the link between the farms and ocean cities to the south and the harder, wilder lands to the north and east. It was a key stop on the snow roads that went across the frozen deserts from Far Kethil to the Bronze Coast in the sun-drunk south. It was the first place that the cedar and hard oak floated down to from the logging camps in the north.

If you want to make steady coin, his father always said, *put yourself between something and the people who want it.* As wisdom went, that sounded less noble than stories of glorious war and forbidden love, but it had kept House Left in respectable buttons and warm houses for generations. And if Garreth's grandfather had maybe taken a few too many speculative shipments that hadn't paid out, if his father's plan to accept discretionary deposits had been foiled by the bankers' guild, if his mother's bid to regain the losses by shifting the family trade from wood and wool into more expensive goods like sugar and dye and alum hadn't made the returns they'd hoped, if she'd in fact been gone on secret business since late spring…

Well, no one knew that who didn't see the family's private books. At any time, a third of the merchant houses of Kithamar could be on the edge of collapse and keeping their plumage bright as a songbird so that no one could tell. House Left had weathered private storms before this, and they would again. That was what Garreth's father said, and he said it with conviction.

The compound they had lived in for the last three generations was large enough to be a little boastful. It didn't dominate the street the way the Dimnas or Embril families did theirs, but it had four white stories with shutters in the pale blue peculiar to House Left. The ground floor was for business and the entertainment of guests, the second for the family, the third for the handful of servants under the watchful eye of their head of house, and the fourth was storage for old furniture and generations of the family records and the unending battle against mice and pigeons who wanted to make it home.

Garreth walked down the moon-soaked street toward bed, his thumbs hooked in his belt and his mind lost in itself. He didn't notice anything odd until he was almost at the door.

The shutters were open, inviting in the cooler night air, but not only on the upper floors. The ground floor windows were bright with candles. Garreth's steps faltered. As late as it was, he'd have expected nothing more than a flicker in his brother's room or one of the servants' windows. The light spilling out to the street meant that something had happened. He told himself that the tightness in his throat was excitement, that whatever it was would be something good and not another setback.

The front door was latched but not barred. Voices came from the back. First, his father's low, measured voice, capable of cutting sarcasm with almost no change of tone and spoken too gently to hear the words. Then Uncle Robbson, sharp and barking: *Well, the old direction isn't working, is it?* Then his father again. Garreth closed the front door behind him quietly. The third voice was as unexpected as a snowstorm in summer.

"Mother?" Garreth said, already walking toward the lesser hall.

She sat beside the empty fire grate, still in a traveller's robe of leather and rough cotton, her hair pulled back in a severe bun that showed the grey at her temples. Garreth's father leaned against the front wall, his arms crossed over his chest, and Uncle Robbson—chin forward and chest puffed out like a rooster—stood in the middle of the room facing Father with anger darkening his cheeks. Mother ignored Uncle Robbson's tantrum with a calm she'd been practicing since she'd been old enough to change her little brother's diapers, turning her attention instead to Garreth.

"Where have you been?"

"Kannish. His parents had a dinner. I didn't know you were coming back."

Mother tapped Uncle Robbson on the leg and nodded for him to sit. He obeyed. Father remained where he was, expression placid as always. "I'm not back. Not exactly," Mother said. "Hopefully no one knows I'm in the city, and I'll be out again come morning."

"Why?" Garreth said, a little ashamed to hear the ghost of a whine in his voice. He was a grown man, not a child running after his mother.

"You know the policy on things like this," his mother said, and Garreth looked at his toes. For the family, policy was there to keep anyone from error. If the policy was to take debts to the magistrate after fifty days, it meant that even the closest friends didn't get a fifty-first. If it was policy to write family matters in cipher, even the most trivial house matter went into code. If the policy was that the secret business of the house was known only to those who had to know it, then the number of people who might let something slip was never more than it had to be. Judgment could be swayed by drink or desire, but policy was implacable.

Which was why his father's gentle, amiable words were more

shocking than a shout. "Now then, Genna. I think we owe the boy something, don't you?"

The emotions on his mother's face were too fast and complicated to read. She looked into the empty grate as if there were a fire there to gaze into. "The business... is worse than we let on. Over the last five years, we have lost a great deal of capital. More than we can afford."

"All right," Garreth said.

"There is a plan to put things right," she went on. "There's risk, but if it goes well, it will more than make up for our losses."

Garreth felt his heart tapping against his chest like it urgently wanted his attention. His parents had always been very careful to explain the workings of the house once a deal was complete. That was his training. To be told of something that was still uncertain in its outcome... Well, it was the ragged edge of policy, and it made him feel like a child in an adult conversation.

"How bad is it?" he asked.

"If this fails," his father said, "we will need to sell the warehouse."

Uncle Robbson slapped his thigh like he was mad at it. "You can't do that. If you start selling what brings the money in, you've already lost. It's like a farmer grinding his seed for flour."

"Robbson," Mother said. She shifted her eyes back to Garreth's. He didn't understand the hardness he saw there. She rose to her feet, walked to the door, and nodded for him to follow. The two older men stayed where they were, Robbson with his lips pressed thin, Father with a little smile that gave nothing away. Garreth followed his mother.

They went down the short hall to the dining room. He heard the clatter of the plate before they reached the archway. An Inlisc girl sat at the table alone, like a servant playing at being above her station. If someone had made an unflattering caricature of a Longhill street rat, it would have looked like her: plate-round face, curled hair, dark eyes. She didn't jump to her feet, though, or show any sign of embarrassment the way a servant would.

"This is Yrith, daughter of Sau," Mother said, "and you're going to marry her."

Elaine ab-Deniya Nycis a Sal, the only living child of Byrn a Sal and, at eighteen, the youngest and last of her diminished house, had three beds. One was in her apartment in the compound of her father's family, and it was dressed in green with a set of summer doors made from cedar slats designed to let in the breeze from a private garden. The second, in the children's salon in House Abbasann's family compound, where her mother had spent her childhood and her grandmother's family still lived, had a suite of pale stone polished within an inch of its life and decorated with pink-and-gold tapestries and pillows that had been in fashion a decade before Elaine had been born. The last was a cot in a simple cell of the Clovas Brotherhood with a washstand and a window of colored glass that looked out toward the ancient fortress that was the palace. The servants and guards in all three knew her by sight. Whichever place she chose would shift without comment to welcome and accommodate her, and she moved between them depending on her mood, the celebrations in Green Hill, and the demands of her tutors.

Of the three, she preferred her father's house and spent the majority of her nights there.

Which was how her cousin Theddan knew where to find her.

"Elly? Are you awake? Wake up! Let me in."

In her dream, Elaine was at a dressing mirror that was frustrating her by showing someone else in the reflection. She was trying to make it show her own face to her by turning and looking from the corner of her eyes, but she could only catch herself in glimpses. The thumping sound came from the glass like the reflected girl was trying to break through.

"Elly, I know you're there. I'm in trouble. Open open open open. *Please.*"

The mirror vanished like a snowflake melting on skin, and she was in her bed, her head thick with sleep. Her rooms. The dim, ruddy light of a night candle that was halfway burned down. She pulled herself up to sitting. At the foot of her bed, her servant girl was still snoring gently away. Elaine swung her legs over the side of the bed as the knocking came again, low and fast. Furtive. That was the word for it. A furtive knocking. She went to the summer doors, unlatched them, and let them swing open. Theddan swept in like a rainstorm. At nineteen, she was a year older than Elaine almost to the day, with long hair that would have been the color of caramel if there had been more light and a permanent smirk in the shape of her face that reminded people of foxes and mischievous ghosts. Elaine closed the summer doors behind her and latched them. The servant girl woke up, looking wide-eyed at the visitor.

Theddan started stripping off her clothes—cloak, robe, and shoes—and pushing them into the servant girl's hands. When she spoke, it was to Elaine.

"I was here all night. Just the two of us. We plaited each

other's hair and sang and traded gossip, and you tried to teach me that poetry thing you do, but I couldn't understand it. We fell asleep together, and I didn't go anywhere."

"What's going on?"

"Nothing," Theddan said, stripped naked now and going through to Elaine's dressing room. "We're asleep right now. Both of us. Where the fuck do you keep your sleeping shifts? This place is dark as a cave."

The servant girl, an Inlisc named something like Reya, looked from Elaine to the open door of the dressing room and back, her eyes so wide they seemed ready to fall out. Elaine sighed. "Hide those," she said, nodding at Theddan's cast-offs. "Put some lavender oil on them first, though."

"Yes, lady," the Inlisc girl said, and scuttled off.

Elaine yawned and walked across to the darkness that was her dressing room. The rustle of cloth came out of the shadows. "Do I want to know?"

"Yes," Theddan said. "Oh, Elly, my love, you want to know everything there and back again, but right now... Shit. They're coming."

Theddan boiled out of the dark—now in one of Elaine's sleeping shifts—grabbed her hand, and dragged her back into bed. Elaine pulled the light blanket up over them both and put her head on the pillows. Theddan's breath reeked of alcohol, and her hair smelled like a bonfire. And there was something else. A musky, animal scent deeper than sweat.

The knocking that came this time was from the apartment door, and Elaine waited until she heard the servant girl's voice asking who it was. The voice that answered was low and masculine and familiar.

"Wait here," Elaine said softly.

"Of course I'm waiting here," Theddan said. "I'm fast asleep.

Can't you tell?" She snored theatrically as Elaine got back out of bed.

Elaine hauled on a robe since her servant wasn't there to do it for her, and padded toward the main doors. The chief of her father's guard was there, lantern in his wide hand, glowering at the poor servant girl like she could have been responsible for anything.

"What's going on?" Elaine asked.

"Sorry to disturb," he said. "Theddan Abbasann's gone missing."

"No she hasn't. She's right there." Elaine gestured toward her bed and the motionless lump of girl under the thin summer blanket. "She's been here all night. Who thinks she's missing?"

The guard captain looked from her to the bed and back again. He didn't believe her, but she hadn't really expected him to. The calculation wasn't about truth, but about the advantages and disadvantages of calling out the lie. Elaine waited. The Inlisc servant shuffled in the background, trying to be invisible and failing.

"She must have forgotten to tell her people that she was going to be here," the guard captain said.

"Thoughtless of her," Elaine said. "Please let them know that she's with me, and she's safe." Those at least were true. Or as true as they could be with Theddan.

"I will," he said, then locked eyes with her. "You should make certain the summer doors are fast, miss. One of the guards said he saw someone coming through the garden that wasn't supposed to be there. Wouldn't want anything surprising to happen, yeah?"

"No surprises," she said, but she meant *I'll handle her,* and his nod meant he understood. The door closed behind him. Elaine nodded the servant girl back to her cot and climbed back into her now-occupied bed.

"He believed you. I can't believe he believed you. Men are so *dim*." Theddan giggled and then sighed. "Oh, you should have been there, Elly. You should have come."

"And where exactly was 'there' tonight?"

"A guild hall in Riverport. Right on the water. I took a boat to get there. There were so many people. More pretty boys with their bare chests out than stars in the sky. And some girls too." In the dim light of the night candle, Theddan's smile looked like an allegory of animal satisfaction.

"Riverport? You're going to wind up pregnant by some... wool seller."

"Some wool seller's son with a perfect round ass," Theddan said, and made a greedy, grabbing gesture. When Elaine didn't laugh, she said, "Don't be a prude."

"I'm not."

"Then I'm being a slut."

"I'm not saying that," Elaine said. "I appreciate a well-made ass as much as anyone. I just... You can't go on like this. It isn't safe."

"I wore a mask. Half the people there were masked. No one knew it was me. Don't be angry."

Elaine put her hand on Theddan's wild, smoke-salt hair, and her cousin pushed her head into the palm like a cat being petted. The wine fumes on her breath should have been rancid, but they weren't. They were like some exotic perfume that Elaine could have but never use. Something beautiful that didn't suit her. Elaine told herself that the tug she felt in her breast was concern for Theddan and annoyance with her, but she knew that wasn't the whole truth.

"I just worry for you," Elaine said. "That's all."

"I worry for you too. They want so much from us, you know?" her cousin said, her voice taking on a softness and drift.

"They take so much of what we are, and then tell us how to use the little bit we have left. And you *trust* them, love. It scares me how much you trust them."

"You're drunk."

"You're sober, and I'd save you from it if I could. You know I'd save you if I could, don't you?" A tear fell from Theddan's eye, the wet shimmering bright in the candlelight.

"We'll just have to watch out for each other."

"Always," Theddan said, and Elaine was almost able to believe she wasn't lying. "Always, always, always."

Her cousin smiled and settled deep into the pillows. Before long, Theddan was making small, soft noises—not quite snoring and not quite not. Elaine lay in the dim, trying not to shift and wake her. Sleep returned slowly, and it brought no dreams when it did.

Deniya Abbasann had had three children with her husband, Byrn a Sal. The first two, twin boys, died young. The third, Elaine, had been a difficult birth, and Deniya had lived long enough to see her daughter breathing and give the child her blessing. Or that was the story they told Elaine. Her understanding of her mother was made entirely from other people's words. Sometimes, she could conjure up a woman who looked a bit like her, but older, wiser, happier. Other times, she imagined a woman with dark hair and eyes, a cutting laugh, and a permanent, unresolvable disapproval of Elaine and everything she'd become. Her mother was a story in her own mind, and part of that story was that her daughter wasn't quite good enough because that was what Elaine feared about herself.

After Deniya's death, Byrn had chosen not to remarry. Elaine's great-uncle, Prince Ausai a Sal, had fathered no children.

When—if—Elaine had children of her own, they would have a Sal blood, but some other name. Even if her father remarried, Elaine would be the prince after him, and her children would take the throne after her, but they would not be a Sal. As it stood, House a Sal was the most powerful in Kithamar, and also it was fading.

It didn't matter. The powerful families of Kithamar shared blood and beds like a vast, complicated dance whose ballroom was history. The prince had been an a Sal for four generations, House Reyos for two generations before that, and House Adresqat half a dozen before them. Almost every time a woman took the throne, the name shifted, and the city itself was reborn in lineage if in no other way. It was a permissible kind of change.

The five great families had been seven and twelve and three, as the winds blew them. Families of great power faded, and there were minor houses—Erinden, a Lorja, Karsen, Mallot, Foss, and a dozen more—waiting to rise. But Kithamar was Kithamar, and all through its history, from its first founding to that day's morning sun, there was a thread that held it together. No usurper had ever taken the throne. No civil unrest, however violent, had split the city. If, in her studies, Elaine sometimes heard a drone of cruelty behind the symphony of her city's past, it was only the price they paid for peace.

Theddan, her face still and relaxed, was still lost in sleep when dawn drew its beams between the slats of the summer doors. Elaine watched her sleep until she was certain that she couldn't fall back into dream herself, then slipped out of bed without waking her wayward cousin and let her servant dress and groom her in silence. They could likely have sung tunes and clapped, as far beyond waking as Theddan seemed, but Elaine left her apartment quietly. The house itself was broad and grand, with room enough for a dozen to be kept in style, though there were only her and her father now. The guest house had been closed for years, and the south and east wings of the main house were shuttered. The north wing and its gardens were enough. More than enough.

She took her morning meal in the moss garden, sitting under a canopy of silk and iron with morning glories arranged around her table as if by chance. She was drinking cool water flavored with citrus when she noticed the carriage. It had the symbols of the Daris Brotherhood, and the man standing at its side wore the colors of House Chaalat. His face, webbed as it was with the scars of a terrible fire, was still handsome enough. She knew him by sight, if not by name. More than that, she knew what his presence meant. She ate the last few mouthfuls of egg and sweet barley, gestured for the servants to take the dishes away, and went to her father's rooms. She pretended not to be in a hurry, but the tension was already growing in her throat.

When she reached the great hall outside her father's private drawing room, she found her father's cousin Andomaka Chaalat coming out. Andomaka smiled her pale, kind smile, but concern was in the tightness around her eyes.

"Cousin," Andomaka said. "You're looking well."

"I appreciate your charity. I was up late with a friend," Elaine said, and laughed. "Palace intrigue, I suppose. Are things well with you?"

Andomaka paused the way she sometimes did, as if she were listening to music no one else could hear. "No," she said, then kissed Elaine on the cheek and went on her way. Elaine turned toward her father's drawing room. She didn't pretend to be relaxed anymore.

Byrn a Sal sat on a wide leather couch with knees apart and his hands clasped between them. The room was wide enough that she could cross halfway to him and still feel the distance dividing them. He lifted his chin to see her without quite raising his head.

"Andomaka was here," Elaine said. It wasn't a question, but it could have been.

"Not as our cousin. She's high priest of the Daris Brotherhood. She keeps the mysteries for them. And for Uncle."

"We aren't Daris."

"We aren't," he agreed, "but apparently they have a rite that calls for a bit of blood from the person's nearest relative." He held up his arm. A tiny scratch of red showed where he'd been cut. "It seemed rude to say no."

"A healing?"

"A death rite."

"Oh."

"He hasn't passed," her father said, looking down again. "But she says he will. That it won't be long." He shook his head. "Grandfather lived until he was a very old man. I thought there would be years yet. Decades, even. I thought..."

He looked around the room like it was a painting of something he'd already lost. He was about to become the most powerful man in the city, and he looked like a carter with a missing dog. She knew what he was going to say next and willed him not to. Just this one time, not to sound that same chorus.

"I wish your mother were here."

"I do too," she said, and her father didn't seem to notice the tightness in her voice.

"It hasn't happened, though. It's not yet. Andomaka might be wrong. He might still recover. I mean, there's no reason to give up hope."

Hope was such a strange word to hear from his lips, tied as the moment was to the death of her mother, the death of her granduncle, the life she had and the one she would be permitted. All she knew was that her father wanted the world to be something other than what it was, and that his wish enraged her. Everything she'd meant to tell him about Theddan and the night's adventure fell away, trivial. She watched her father retreat into his thoughts again, uncertain whether she wanted to go to him or leave the room.

A soft tapping came from behind her. An older man in a house servant's robe stood in the doorway. She raised her eyebrows, ready to send the man away with a snap and a gesture, but her father was already on his feet.

"Is he here?"

"Yes, my lord a Sal," the servant said. "Lord Karsen is in the morning garden."

"Thank you," her father said, already walking briskly toward the corridor. He paused, seeming to remember her, and stepped back. He kissed her on the forehead the way he had when she'd been a little girl and then took her hand. For a moment, she thought he would speak, but he only squeezed her fingers and released them before turning to his business. He bustled away, leaving her alone in the drawing room. Elaine stood silently for a long moment, then went and sat where her father had been, her own legs apart, her own hands clasped between them in the same pose of despair he had taken.

Her father was about to begin his reign as prince. He would leave for the palace, and the compound of a Sal—buildings, gardens, fountains, family temple, library, kitchens, stable, and all—would be her. Just her. Like a single seed rattling in a giant, dry gourd, she would be expected to fill the emptiness that her parents had left until one day her father died and the hollow houses were left empty even of her.

She imagined her mother—not her real one, but the ghost-image she'd cobbled together from other people's stories—standing where she had stood, looking at her as she'd looked at her father.

You expected something else? her not-mother said. *The great secret of noble blood is it gives you everything because it costs you everything.*

You're late in learning that, my girl.

The Khahon flowed from the north, fed by distant glaciers and the snows that gathered in the mountains. Thousands of brooks and streams found each other, growing wider and stronger as they came together like strands of thread weaving into rope. Lumber camps fed wood into the flow, but apart from a few stretches scattered along the river's length, the waters were too shallow and rough for travel by boat. The last cataract was just north of Kithamar. The cliffs were lower now than they'd once been, stone eroding under the constant, driving flow. It would be lifetimes before the river remade the land enough to flow smoothly, but the water was slow and patient and powerful. Given time, it would win its struggle against the land.

Nor was the cataract the only place the Khahon was making its mindless, eternal will felt. The curve of the river within Kithamar remade the city, but too slowly for any mortal to see it. The piers and docks of Riverport did what they could to break the power of the flow, but soil and stone washed away a finger's width at a time. Every few generations, the quays would be reinforced or rebuilt. And what the Khahon took from the cliff and the banks, it let settle in the slow water that eddied south of Oldgate and east of the Smoke. Soil and seed, timber and grass, old bones and things lost to the water; they all built up slowly into the strip of wild land within the city walls that was called the Silt.

In the height of summer, it was lush as any of the forests that lined the river to the south. Deep green leaves on the trees, and underbrush as thick and impassable as the bramble walls of a child's fable. An old Inlisc woman led a pack of ragged Longhill children as they scrounged for valuable trash washed up on the dirt and harvested wild blackberries from under the canopy of boughs. Barges made their way up toward the port and floated back down from it, the boatmen calling out to one another in a language of vulgarity and technique peculiar to this part of the river, their voices as lovely and impenetrable as birdsong. The river muttered against the bridges that ran to Oldgate and spun whirlpools on the southern side of the lichen-slicked stone stanchions. The traffic across the bridges looked like children's dolls come to life from the shore of the Silt: toy guardsmen in sweat-stained blue cloaks gathering taxes from toy carters while miniature horses and mules flicked away invisibly tiny flies.

The world smelled of summer, rich and verdant, with only a hint of the decay that autumn would bring. Two people sat in the shade under the trees, Oldgate to their back and the shifting surface of the water before them. The man had wiry white hair and an expression of broad amusement. The woman, round-faced and curly-haired as an Inlisc, had a scar along the side of her face and one milky eye. To look at them, anyone would have thought they were human.

"By now, it knows that the blade's gone," the man said.

"It'll have known for a while."

"I wish I could have been there. The greasy fuck going for his altar and finding nothing but mouse shit and air."

"A good moment," the woman said.

"Don't eat yourself over it."

"It lost the blade. I lost the blade. If one of us is a fool, we both are."

The man leaned forward, squinting at sunlight that blazed off the surface of the water. "In your defense, you're literally surrounded by thieves and criminals."

"But they're *my* thieves and criminals. When a dog bites the kennel master, it's always the master's fault."

"The dog's the one to get culled, though."

"That's coming," the woman said. Then, a moment later, "The blade's trying to get back where it's wanted."

"Well. I've called some things to me. Not that I'm sure what they are just yet, but he's not the only one who can play at this."

"And Shau's in the city."

"Is he?"

"I think so."

The man scowled. "Can't say I like that, but it might work for us. Too many gods in the streets these days. Makes things unpredictable. But as long as our Byrn a Sal is where he's supposed to be, we stand a chance."

"This is the closest we've been in generations," she said. "If we fail now…"

"We won't."

She turned her one clear eye toward him. "You believe that?"

At the edge of the water, one of the children shrieked and started digging in the pale dirt that the river put down. The man watched as the child lifted something over her head. A length of something metal. River trash, celebrated because it was more than they had.

The woman stood and clapped the dirt off her trousers. The man's gaze softened.

"When this is over," he said, "and it's the two of us again—"

"When this is over, we'll see whether we're both still standing," she said.

"Don't say that."

"Everything dies. *Gods* die. Otherwise, what are we doing here?" Her smile had a melancholy that didn't suit her face. She walked away, heading south along the edge of the trees. After a time, she started whistling to herself, a low, complex melody that belonged to an earlier age. She swaggered as she walked, and the woman and the children pretended not to notice her.

At the southern edge of the Silt, the land narrowed and the southernmost of the city's bridges stood above the smooth water, yellow brick and black mortar. Decades of land drift had put piles that had once stood in the river firmly on land, weed trees growing up around the dark arches. She didn't scramble up the side as others did or meet one of the little boats that rowed across the river. Instead, she stood for a moment, her one good eye sweeping the land and water as if she were reading it like a text. Then she stepped into the shadows under the bridge and didn't step back out.

Sometime later, in a brewer's house in Seepwater, she walked up a stone stairway and into the light. The bettors' window was covered by an iron cage, and she paused at it to look at the chalked marks. The man at the counter stiffened, but didn't look away. After a moment, he nodded.

"Aunt Thorn," he said by way of greeting.

The woman grunted in reply, turned east, and moved on.

In the end, Mother stayed for three days despite her best intentions. She kept away from windows, and Father avoided having guests come in past the front hall. He claimed that the servants were suffering a malaise, and wouldn't they please come back in a week when the house had been cleansed? Garreth's parents had his apparent new betrothed put in one of the guest bedrooms that looked out over the kitchen courtyard so that no one would catch a glimpse of her from the street.

The days were spent in close consultation. Sometimes Garreth and his younger brother Vasch were welcome to attend. Other times, only Garreth could be in the room as Mother, Father, and Uncle Robbson debated and chewed at each other. Sometimes even he wasn't welcome. The plan on which the family had bet its future was this: They would seal an alliance with an Inlisc tribe that worked the snow roads between Kithamar and Far Kethil. The wedding of Yrith and Garreth was the assurance that the alliance was real. In a perfect world, there would be children, but the balances of their accounts didn't leave time to wait. As a marriage gift, the Inlisc would take on a winter caravan for their new Kithamari cousins, the Left.

Winter caravans were desperate. House Cortan had hired one out eight years before with an experienced master and ten carts. When carts, horses, master, and goods had been swallowed up by a blizzard, Cortan had sold everything that remained to them and taken service where they could find other merchants to hire them. A broken house.

But with an Inlisc master, northern horses, and funding from a few carefully selected allies and investors, Left could pull the trick that Cortan had bungled. Spices, silk, alum, and medical herbs arriving months before their rivals. They could command the year's contracts, deliver goods that were already in their warehouses, and clear profits enough to settle their debts and fund their next year's investments besides.

And yes, they would have to be careful who they invited to help with the funding. Uncle Robbson wanted to approach Ocaso Durral, but Father refused. Mother argued for talking to Beris a Lorja, and Uncle Robbson called her an idiot to her face. No one took money from a priest and a nobleman and expected to come out the better for it.

When Mother finally took her leave, sneaking out in a deep-hooded cloak in the morning dark, the plan was still only half complete. But Uncle Robbson and Father had their tasks and negotiations clearly in mind. The stages of their plan were laid out and a timeline set. When the money would be gathered, when the orders would need to be sent to Mother and her agents in Far Kethil, when the caravan would arrive.

And among the dates and schedules, an entry for when Gareth would stand at the little family altar with a witness from the northern tribe and a priest Uncle Robbson would hire and bind his life to Yrith, daughter of Sau. It had as much weight as placing a loan or paying the boatmen's guild their fees. It was a matter of business.

"You're going to have to sleep with her," Vasch said. "You know that. They're going to want babies."

"I know," Garreth said.

Vasch had come into the world a little over a year after Garreth, but sometimes he seemed much younger. He had Mother's eyes and Uncle Robbson's jawline. He even shrugged the way Mother did. "Do you think you'll be able to do it?"

"What?"

"All your children are going to be half Inlisc. They'll look like Serria."

Garreth shot a look toward the doorway. They were sitting in the lesser hall. He hadn't heard anyone close by, but Serria—head of house and chief among their servants—was a quiet-footed woman when she wanted to be. "Serria's not half Inlisc," he said, but he kept his voice low.

"She's part Inlisc," Vasch said.

"Less than half. She's a third."

Vasch wrinkled his nose. "I don't think that's how it works."

"I don't know what she is, and it doesn't matter. She's a servant. This is . . . this is House Left. This is the family. Now. Forever. We're not going to be Hansch anymore."

"We will not," Vasch said.

"I don't have a problem with that," Garreth said. "I don't. It's just that other people will. And they'll look down on us."

"Think how she feels. Marrying into a weak city family like ours. We don't even milk our own goats."

Garreth's expression must have told his little brother that a line had been crossed, because Vasch lifted his hands, palm out in sign of surrender. There was something in his expression that Garreth couldn't read. Pity, maybe.

"We do what we have to for the business," he said.

"We do."

"So—" He didn't know what else to say. He rose from the table and stalked out. The tightness across his shoulders and in his jaw ached a little. The girl—Yrith—wasn't permitted to leave the house, and neither was the old woman who was her escort, but when he went to her rooms, the only one there was Serria. She had a stoneware vase and was arranging a spray of wide-petaled flowers in it. She raised her eyebrows when he stepped in, and Garreth had the eerie sense that she'd heard him speculating on the purity of her blood even though he'd been a floor below and across the house.

"I was looking for her," he said.

Serria turned back to the flowers and nodded toward the open shutters. "You'll find her there."

Garreth moved to the window. In the kitchen courtyard, Yrith and her chaperone sat on a low stone bench. The late morning sun was strong, and the heat and damp of the day were ramping up quickly. It would be a sweatbox of an afternoon. Yrith had something in her hands. Thin leather cords, maybe, that she was weaving together. He looked at the curl of her hair, the wideness of her cheek. There was a scar in her right eyebrow like someone had erased a bit of it. When sounds came from over the wall—the cartwheels clattering over the paving stones, the voices of men and women in the street—she looked up, searching around like she was expecting someone or something that she didn't find.

I will be married to you for the rest of our lives, Garreth thought. *When I wake up, you will be there. When I sleep at night, you will be there. Every meal, every meeting, every day, forever.* The idea bounced off his mind like a raindrop on waxed cloth. It didn't make sense.

"Can I help you with something?" Serria asked.

"No, I was just . . . I thought I should spend . . . I don't know what I thought."

"Should I have her called in?"

"No," Garreth said. "I can go to her there."

"As you like."

When he stepped into the courtyard, Yrith stiffened. Garreth walked toward her slowly, like he was trying not to startle a dog. Yrith's expression was blank and stony. The chaperone chewed her own teeth and focused on nothing, present and not present at the same time.

"I wanted to check with you," he said, speaking to Yrith slowly and nodding his head. "If there was anything you needed."

Yrith nodded once in return and said something he couldn't follow.

"I'm sorry," Garreth said. "I don't speak . . . um . . ."

The chaperone grinned and cackled like he'd told a joke, shaking her white-braided head. Yrith's cheeks flushed and she put her hands at her sides. Garreth didn't understand what he'd said wrong until she spoke again, more slowly so that her words weren't drowned by her accent. "Thank you, but I have all I need."

"Oh, yes. Of course. I . . . thank you." The chaperone laughed again, this time at his retreat. He made his way into the cool of the house. In the distance, Uncle Robbson and Father were talking. Or, really, Father was talking and Uncle Robbson was declaiming angrily.

He found Serria in the front hall. "I'm going out."

"Are you sure that's wise?"

"I'm not staying prisoner in my own house, Serria. I have friends. I have things that I do. None of this changes that."

The older woman—his mother's age, or a bit less despite the whiteness of her hair—pursed her lips. Garreth felt an apology pressing at the back of his throat, but he swallowed it. Whatever had his head stuffed with cotton ticking just then, it wouldn't let *I'm sorry* come out.

"I understand."

"Thank you," Garreth said. And then, "She needs a tutor."

"Sir?"

"Yrith. She needs a tutor. Someone who can help her... fit better. We can't bring her out into society the way she is now. It'll embarrass us."

"And it would be cruel to her," Serria said. "But I don't think your father will permit a tutor to know of her."

"We'll have to think of something," Garreth said.

"Of course. I will see to it."

The city guard had three barracks spread throughout Kithamar. The one in the Smoke was a wide, flat building of grey brick that overlooked a canal choked by ashes and the waste of the forges. The one in Stonemarket had been stables for the Hansch armies when Kithamar had been little more than a fording spot and favorite raiding grounds of the nomadic Inlisc.

The largest sat near the southern edge of Newmarket. Almost a block wide, it had a broad, dirt-covered training ground that punishment and discipline kept free from moss and weeds. The sleeping quarters themselves rose up three stories of off-white stucco and grey slate roof tiles. The stables held the carts that prisoners used when their guards, lash in hand, took them out to clean the streets and, presumably, their tarnished souls.

The barracks' yard opened to the south, like a priest glowering at the unclean of Longhill and Seepwater and the hospital to the south of the city walls. Guardsmen stripped to the waist trained morning and afternoon in the pressing summer sun. Sword and bow, whip and bare-hand brawling. The city guard was a constant show of violence because it was in a war that didn't—*couldn't*—end. The fear that the bluecloaks inspired in the lowest and most desperate of Kithamar was just as much a weapon as their swords and goads, and it was used to the same end: stability.

The city might not be fair, and it certainly wasn't kind, but it was itself. The streets that were safe for a merchant to walk down in his finery were always safe, and the ones that weren't were well enough known. The streetbound who died in the winter cold were cleaned away before they started to stink, just like the dead dogs and cats and rats and pigeons, the raw shit and rotting scraps. Those who feared the law always feared the law, and those to whom the law answered could rely upon it.

And when the city guard weren't walking the streets of the city or collecting the taxes and tolls that bought their food and firewood or training in the yard, quite often they were at the baths.

"What happened to *you*?" Garreth asked.

Maur looked up at him from the tepid pool, blinking like a mouse. The bruise across his chest was dark and angry, with dots of red where the skin had broken. "What, this little love bite?"

"Captain Senit decided to demonstrate a new fighting style," Kannish said. "And Maur volunteered."

The public baths were tiled green and yellow, and voices echoed through the rooms like in a cave. The men's section—the only one Garreth had ever seen—had a stand with cups of drinking water and a constant, low-level smell of bodies and soap. In the winter, the hot pool was always thick with the men of the city soaking and talking and keeping the cold at bay. In the summer, there were fewer, and those mostly in the tepid pool or the cold.

"I wouldn't say that," Maur said. "I was encouraged to show my fighting prowess."

Garreth took off his towel and settled into the water beside his friends. "How did that go?"

"I showed my fighting prowess," Maur said. "The captain suggested there might be room to improve."

"The good part was he used the flat of the blade."

"Yes," Maur said. "That was kind of him."

"What about you?" Kannish said as he leaned back against the tile, stretching his arms to either side like the pool was his private, personal throne. "You've been away for a few days."

Garreth leaned forward. "It's nothing. Just home. You know."

"You're a terrible liar," Maur said. "Really bad."

"All right," Garreth said. "It's a fucking mess. Every day under my father's roof feels like sleeping in a rainstorm, and everyone wants something from me and can't give anything much in return. And if I gave you the details, which I would dearly love to do, it would be breaking policy. So instead, I'm here to watch you get your skin split."

"It's not that bad," Maur said. "It looks worse than it feels."

"There's room, though," an unfamiliar voice said. "It could hurt until you were sick and still not be as bad as it looks."

The man who slipped into the pool beside Kannish was young-looking and a little doughy, with a beard that hadn't quite found itself. Kannish lifted a hand in greeting, and this new boy clasped it and let go with the ease of camaraderie. He lifted his chin toward Garreth. "Who's this?"

"Garreth Left," Kannish said. "He's an old friend of ours. Garreth, this is Tannen. He's one of ours."

"One of yours?"

"Brother of the patrol," Tannen said. "We watch each other's backs."

"Makes sense," Garreth said more sharply than he'd intended.

Maur leaned forward, looking from Garreth to the new man and back again. His agitation should have been funny, but it wasn't. "Garreth's been a friend of ours since forever. He's going to be head of a merchant company. House Left is a serious force in the market."

"You're being generous," Garreth said. "My family does well enough."

"I am being generous, but he's being modest," Maur said. "It's really something in between."

"Well, I wouldn't want to cross an important merchant," Tannen replied. "I promise I will do everything I can to keep Kannish and Maur from getting themselves gutted. Except by the captain. I can't do anything about him." He looked around like he was expecting laughter and was confused that there wasn't any. For a moment, the pool felt like someone else's place. Garreth wondered whether he'd made a mistake coming there.

"Not that it's likely we'll be doing anything exciting anytime soon," Maur said, filling the silence. "Not after..." He gestured to his wound.

Kannish picked up the thread. "It's true. We're on wine patrol until the captain's satisfied we can take on—"

"Anything at all," Maur said. "Until he's convinced I won't be mauled to death by a stray cat."

The words hung for a moment, like a ball tossed in the air that might or might not be caught. Garreth felt something shift in his chest and chose to ignore it.

"Wine patrol?" he said.

"Apparently someone's been staging orgies," Kannish said,

"which doesn't matter one way or the other to us, except they've been having them in other people's warehouses and boatyards and not cleaning up well."

"The captain thinks it's a band of the wealthy young with more money than sense," Tannen said.

"Sounds like the sort of thing you'd want an invitation to," Garreth said, and felt himself relax a little.

"Once it was true," Kannish said. "But I've taken my vows. My loyalty is to the city now. Which means finding whoever's doing it and hauling them to the magistrate. It's not the most glamorous part of the job, but we're relatively unlikely to get stabbed."

"You should come," Maur said.

From one of the other rooms, a splashing sound echoed, followed by the sound of laughter. Garreth looked toward the high, thin windows and the blue sky beyond them. "I can't patrol with you. I'm not the watch."

"For us, it's duty hours," Kannish said. "For you, it's taking a walk that happens to go more or less the same places we're going. No rule against that."

"Besides, you'll be perfectly safe," Tannen said, leaning back and spreading his hands. "You'll be with the city guard."

Garreth grinned, and wished that Tannen was anywhere in the world but there. The isolation and sorrow didn't belong to this new friend of theirs, though. They were Garreth's, and he needed to find his peace with them. Maur made a small sound under his breath. Impatience or encouragement.

"I..." Garreth said. "I don't suppose there's anything wrong with taking a walk. It's just I don't want to be where I'm not wanted." A sudden image pressed its way to the front of his mind. Yrith, daughter of Sau, her hard eyes and her tight, angry mouth. *I don't want to be where I'm not wanted.*

"You're always welcome with us," Kannish said, and splashed water at Tannen and Maur. "You're smarter company than these two. It'll be good to have some intellectual conversation for a change."

Tannen shouted, and splashed back, and they might almost all have been friends. Garreth let himself sink a little lower into the water. Maur tapped his elbow. "Really, though. Are you all right?"

Garreth smiled and shook his head, but whether he meant *No, I'm not* or *No, it's nothing* he couldn't have said.

Word passed through Green Hill like the breezes heralding a coming storm. Prince Ausai was dying, and an age was dying with him. And like any storm, crows flew before it.

The drawing room was dark, but it was hot. The summer afternoon offered a breath of sluggish wind, thick with the scent of cut grass, that seemed to bring in more heat than it blew cool. They sat at a little table of red-and-white inlaid wood whose pattern her father and Halev Karsen sometimes used for a game. It wasn't a game Elaine knew, and it wasn't the one she was playing now.

"When I came across it, I thought of you," Beyya Reyos said. Her smile was motherly and well-practiced. Elaine ran her fingertips over the needlework. It was hardly larger than her two hands together, but the craft was good. Silk and cloth making a tiny map of Green Hill. The compounds of the great families. The aqueduct that ran from the river above its cataract through Green Hill and down to the Smoke was iridescent blue and green. Elaine wondered what sort of thread they'd used to make it.

"You remember how we used to sew together when you were young?" Beyya asked.

"I do," Elaine said, because the truth would have felt rude and awkward. The matriarch of Reyos likely had taken Elaine in at some point, though Elaine very much doubted they had ever sewn together. More likely Elaine had been permitted to do some thread work with a servant or tutor of the house to keep her busy while her father met with the other adults. The little map had no more come from those pastimes than pigeons were born from dogs. The pretense was what mattered.

"I loved your mother dearly," Beyya said, perhaps sensing that her gift hadn't evoked the desired nostalgia. "She was a good woman. We all did what we could to help poor Byrn care for you when she was gone."

Elaine smiled while something in her recoiled. Beyya stroked her own papery cheek, as if lost in memory. And maybe she was. Beyya had known Elaine's mother in a way Elaine never did. Who was to say that this dried apple of a woman hadn't had some tender moments with the one who'd died when Elaine was born? But the threads of the map and the threads of memory were all meant to bind, even if just a little, and Elaine couldn't keep from resenting them. Beyya Reyos wasn't the first to drop by to visit Elaine, nor the first to bring some little gift to remind her that they had known each other. If Ausai a Sal were well, if his reign promised to stretch out for another decade or two, they wouldn't have come to her.

But when her father advanced to the palace, Elaine—his eldest and only child—changed with him. It became harder to ignore the fact that she would very likely ascend herself one day. Fevers came for the powerful as much as the poor. Men slipped and broke their bones. Princes suffered cancers and malice and ill fortune, just as anyone might. It paid to be on good terms with the girl who might one day be the city.

Beyya squeezed Elaine's hand and wiped away a tear that Elaine didn't actually see. The older woman wasn't going to mention that her grandson Forton was sixteen, and only two years younger than Elaine. Not today. And two years between sixteen and eighteen were a farther reach than eighteen and twenty would be when he was her age. Pointing it out now would be rude, but once Ausai's pyre was cold and her father comfortable in the palace...well, that would be a different world for all of them.

A servant girl knocked at the drawing room door, interrupting as Elaine had told her to. Annoyance flared in Beyya's eyes and was covered over, a fire doused by sand.

"The physician, Lady a Sal," the girl said.

"Thank you," Elaine said, rising and tucking the little map into her sleeve. "Tell her I will be there directly."

The servant girl backed out of the room. Beyya blinked a stage show of confusion and concern. "Physician, dear? I hope nothing's wrong?"

Nothing was wrong. Elaine had chosen an imaginary physician to cut her meeting short because it wouldn't give offense, but now that that moment was here...

"I have a boil," she lied. "So uncomfortable. Red and sore and the size of my thumbnail. I have the physician come and drain it twice a week. And it's right..." She squinched her nose and pointed discreetly toward her lap. The old woman's disgust was covered over as quickly as her annoyance had been. Let her take that image back to her sixteen-year-old would-be suitor.

"I'm so sorry," the older woman said, rising. "I hope...I hope it heals quickly."

"I'm sure it will," Elaine said. "But you'll understand. I must—"

"Of course, of course."

When the door was closed, Elaine dropped back into her chair. Regret was already setting in. That had been petty and mean, and probably would turn into gossip for the court before the night fell. She didn't know why it had felt so good to make the old woman uncomfortable, only that it had, and that was a vice.

A scratching came from the window, something moving through the ivy outside. A thick-bodied orange tomcat, one of the mousers that the servants kept, lumbered into the room.

"Oh, hello," Elaine said, holding out a hand to the cat. "Did you just run across something that reminded you of me? Did you, for no reason whatever, think, 'Oh, Elaine a Sal! How could I have let my friendship with her lie fallow so long?' "

The cat gave a little cough and trundled toward her outstretched fingers, sniffing uncertainly.

"What's the matter, Tom? Don't you want something from me? I may be prince of the city one day, you know? And prince of the city is so much better than being just me."

He reached her hand, considered it, and then turned his side and consented to her affection. His fur was rough and a little greasy, and she scratched his flea-bitten ears.

"Well, at least you're honest," she said as he purred.

The knock came again, and the same servant girl with it. Elaine lifted her brows.

"Your father would like to see you, when you're free. He's in his library," the girl said. "He said there wasn't a hurry."

Elaine rose. The tomcat, seeing that her attentions were off him, flopped down in the sunlight and started grooming himself. The servant girl stepped forward to wave him out, but Elaine stopped her.

"He's not hurting anything," she said. "Let him stay."

For most of her life, the library had been for show. There were books and a shelf for maps. A latticework holder with dozens of old scrolls that she hadn't been permitted to unroll for fear of cracking them. The way her father lived, libraries were drawing rooms for the times you wanted to look well-educated. Now and again, she'd snuck a volume out to read in her own rooms and at her leisure, especially the more entertaining histories and a couple books of erotic stories and woodcuts that her father would certainly have locked up better if he'd known they were there.

Today, however, the library was a workroom. Scrolls were opened on the table, held in place with polished stone weights where they had split. Books stood open on the holders that had always been decorative before. A piece of slate leaned against one wall on an easel, and chalk marks showed a cascade of numbers and equations. And across the table from each other like thieves planning their crimes, her father and Halev Karsen. They were both in shirtsleeves with sweat staining their armpits. Karsen had straight brown hair and a nose only a little too prominent for his face. He nodded to Elaine as she came in, but didn't pause in the conversation he and her father were having.

"But if you drop the tariffs with one..."

Her father rubbed a palm across his forehead. "Then all the others will want it too. Couldn't it be done quietly, though? I mean it isn't as if the Hyian ambassador and the Iustikar are sitting at the same table."

"You could if you could," Karsen said. "But how many people would have to keep that secret?"

"Too many," her father sighed. "All right. So how did Daos deal with it?"

"First, why don't you..." Karsen nodded toward Elaine as

she sat on a divan and looked at the open scroll before her. It was a treaty written in three languages, only two of which she recognized. A copy, she guessed, of one of the peace agreements between the Hansch and Inlisc in the years around the city's formation. As old as the paper and ink were, they were still too fresh to be the original.

"Of course," Byrn a Sal said.

"Be well, cousin," Halev said, touching her shoulder before he walked to the door.

"You also," she said, and he closed it behind him.

Her father sighed and pushed back his chair, blowing out a long breath, looking at the field of books and papers. "Thank God that Halev understands all this mess. I've been studying it half my life, and I still feel like I understand a third of it."

"Better than understanding a third of it and thinking that you have it mastered," she said.

"Truth, truth, truth. It would help if we could use Uncle Ausai's study, but he hasn't offered. Seems ghoulish to ask. Where have you been while I'm stuck with my tutor?"

"Being suddenly and inexplicably popular."

"Ah, that," her father said. "Yes. That's part of the work, I'm afraid. It doesn't stop. It's a puzzle, isn't it? You can't trust anyone, and you have to trust somebody. I have Halev. We've known each other since we were babies. Sucked from the same wet nurse, one in each of her arms. But everyone that you know, you've known since you were a child. You're still a child now. Or almost."

"I won't take that as condescension," she said.

"You're a merciful daughter," Byrn said. "Better than I deserve."

He looked at the ground and smoothed his hands on the thighs of his trousers. Skin hissed against fabric. He was working himself up to something. She stayed still and let him do it. It took a few more breaths for him to find the words.

"I wanted to ask something of you. There was a thought. An idea. Once Uncle Ausai has passed, it would just be you in—" He gestured broadly, meaning the whole of the compound. "It seems like a great deal for one person. And sooner or later you'd be coming to the palace anyway. Not for a few decades, I hope, but... It's one time or another, really. The shift is inevitable, and..."

He waved a hand as if he'd made his point. They were all thoughts that she'd had—visions of the future that she had dreaded—but she knew her father well enough to know there was more waiting to be said. She cocked her head and waited. When his shoulders dropped, he looked almost defeated.

"Your mother's cousin Jorreg is expecting another child. His wife's just three months on, but it means a fifth baby in Abbas-ann's back house. We have all this going unused."

"They can have it," Elaine said, almost interrupting him, as if it wasn't her home. As if she hadn't lived there her whole life. Her memories of being a child at play were in these gardens, these halls. The home her parents had come to when they'd married. The nursery where her brothers died. If it didn't matter to her father, why should it matter to her? What was it? Walls. Doors. Carpets. Nothing. The coldness in her spine wasn't sorrow, and the fact that she had dreaded living there alone until the moment it was going to be taken away offered her no comfort.

"You don't have to answer now. You can think about it."

"I don't need to," Elaine said. "They should take it. Mother would want it that way. And that way I'll stay closer to you."

He glanced at her from under his brows like a little boy who'd been caught stealing sweets. It was the answer he'd wanted.

"If you're sure. I want you to be happy."

"I want to be happy," she said. "But this is what we carry. I have everything, and none of it's mine."

"You have your mother's wisdom," he said. "She saw things that way all the time. You're sure this is all right with you?"

"It's fine," she said, convincingly enough that he could believe it if he wanted to. Sharply enough he could hear the truth if he preferred.

"All right, then. I'll send word. Quietly, of course. Doesn't do any good for Uncle Ausai to see us rubbing our hands and planning for the day after his last breath."

"Ghoulish," she said.

Theddan was lounging in the gardens of House Abbasann when Elaine found her. The trees made a carefully sculpted pool of shade around a granite fountain that drew directly from the aqueduct, cold river water splashing endlessly over stone. Theddan wore a gown of linen that stuck to her skin, and sweat beaded on her lip. Elaine sat at the fountain's edge, untied her sandals, and put her feet in the water. The air felt thick to breathe.

"Why are you doing anything?" Theddan asked. "It's too hot to do things."

"I'm cooling off."

"You walked here in the heat so that you could cool off from walking over here in the heat? That doesn't make sense."

An Inlisc servant boy with a moon-round face and curling hair stepped out from the house, but Elaine met his eyes and shook her head before he could offer her anything. He faded back into the building as smoothly as he'd left it. Elaine dipped her sleeve into the water, then brought it over her head and wrung the cloth like a sponge. A cool rivulet ran down her neck and vanished into the back of her blouse. "Do you know why I like you?"

"I'm your cousin."

"Everyone's my fucking cousin. That's not special."

Theddan looked over.

"What?" Elaine said. "It's true."

"All right, then. Why do you like me better than all the rest? I'm quivering to know."

"You don't want anything from me."

"I want things from you all the time."

"No," Elaine said. "You want things all the time, and sometimes you get them from me. There's a difference."

Theddan nodded slowly. "Are you sure? Because they sound the same."

"Father's giving away our compound to Jorreg Abbasann. It's going to be an act of princely largesse."

"Oh," Theddan said. "I'm sorry."

"It doesn't matter. Nothing matters. Not much."

Her cousin shifted, stood, came to sit at Elaine's side. Elaine would have leaned against her, but Theddan put her head on Elaine's shoulder first. She smelled like sweat and lavender. "Then why do you work so hard?"

"I don't know," Elaine said. She kicked the water with her bare foot and watched the splash. Then, with deliberate violence, she did it again. "I wish I was like you."

"Oh, sweet. Oh no. Don't wish that. I'm a mess."

"You're your own mess. I'm someone else's, and I don't even know whose. My father's? My mother's? Maybe I'm the mess of the whole city. You do what you want to do. I do what I'm supposed to, and what do I get?"

"Power."

"It doesn't feel like it."

"You don't like power," Theddan said. "You think it's inauthentic. That's why you really love me. I'm comfortable playing the part of myself as if Theddan Abbasann was a role and I was really the least shame-bound actor in Seepwater. You're jealous of my talent."

Elaine laughed. It was ridiculous, except that it also rang true. That made it funnier.

"You don't have to be so alone," Theddan said. "You could have anyone you want as a friend or a pillow mate."

"I couldn't, though. Even if they were there, they wouldn't see me. They'd see her."

"Her?"

"Elaine a Sal, daughter of the prince-to-be, and someday Kithamar herself. I can't have anything. She gets all of it. No one can see me when *she's* in the room. Even I get lost in her sometimes. The story about me is so much more than who I am."

"That isn't true."

"The real reason I love you is you know how to lie to me."

Theddan waved a dismissive hand. "I knew it was something like that. Next time, come out with me."

Elaine shifted, and Theddan sat up straight. A little smile tugged at Elaine's mouth, but she shook her head. "No. Absolutely not."

"It is exactly what you need. I told you. It's masked. No one knows who you are, not for certain. Isn't that what you just said you wanted? It's like the gods put this here just for you. It would be sacrilege not to go."

"It's a mess of drunken merchants, and you playing dangerous games below your station."

"But with *masks*," Theddan said around a chuckle. "I feel like you're missing that point. Take something for yourself now, while you still can. There won't be any sneaking away when you're in the palace under old Kint's guard. And you'll have a memory to keep you warm in the cold, cold winter of your dotage."

"Stop teasing me."

"Ancient Prince Elaine a Sal, on her icy throne, lost to crippling isolation and . . . I don't know. Ague? Crippling ague, with only the memory of one warm summer night of folly to remind her what being alive was for."

"Oh, you are useless," Elaine laughed. The tightness in her heart was looser now. Her smile felt like a smile. "I am not going to some guild hall with a bunch of strangers and too much wine. It isn't going to happen."

"I understand."

"I'm serious."

"I know it. I respect your choice."

They sat for a while, the cold water gurgling and playing around Elaine's ankles. A squirrel bounded through the trees above them, leaping from branch to branch on its way from wherever it had come to wherever it was going. The shade made the buildings look brighter, like the pale bricks had been formed from fire.

Elaine sighed. "Fine," she said. "I'll come."

Divol Senit, captain in the city guard and warden of the Newmarket barracks house, wasn't one of the pious, but neither did he see what there was to lose from playing safe. If the Three Mothers didn't exist, he was out a few nuggets of incense and the handful of minutes he spent sitting before the little altar in his office each day. If they did exist, maybe he'd find himself on the good side of the fates.

His office was small. The stucco on the northern wall had cracked, and he'd never quite gotten around to repairing it, even though it annoyed him every time he looked at it. The window was small, and made from a dozen small scrap bits of glass held together with poured lead. He didn't have the budget for a full pane. The incident book was open on his table. He ran his fingers down each entry.

NT 3rd theft Huttin Cammer leather shears rem mag. On the third watch, Nattan Torr's patrol had detained someone named Huttin Cammer for stealing leather shears and remanded him to the magistrates. The full report would be with the magistrates' office and no business of Divol's.

LL 2nd toll evade 2s 5b. On the second watch, Ledri Laddat's patrol had gathered two silver and five bronze from people trying to slip past the bridge tolls. These were just the fines. The toll collection sums were in a different book. Tolls went to the palace. Fines stayed at the barracks or in the wallets of the men who collected them. He moved his fingers down to the next entry.

In just a few moments, Divol could catch himself up on the business of his patrols over the last day. If there was something that piqued his curiosity, he could follow up. If there wasn't, there were a thousand other things that demanded his time and attention. Running the city guard—even just his part of it—felt more like being caretaker for three dozen children than being the hand of law in Kithamar. Was there enough food in the group kitchen? If not, that was his problem. Were the recruits being trained to be men of law and not just thugs with the power of the magistrates for a crutch? If not, the failure was his. Were the swords sharp? Were the holding cells secure? Were the magistrates happy? Was his barracks getting its share of the coin that flowed down from the palace? Were the pensions getting paid on time? Were any of the men being tempted into sneaking a bit of tax coin into their own wallet? His, his, and all of it his to fix or else choose to ignore.

As a younger man, he'd walked regular patrol. He could see a pickpocket in a crowd like blood on a wedding dress. He could feel the shaved edge on dice by rolling them in his hand. He knew a false coin from true by the taste and the weight. He could talk a drunk man off the side of a bridge or fight a half dozen Longhill knives to a standstill. He didn't have to go into the city streets looking for trouble anymore, but some days he did anyway. Nostalgia, as much as anything.

A knock came at the door, and he realized he didn't know

what the last few lines of the incident book had said. He dug thumb and forefinger into his eyes, rubbing harder than he needed to. "What?"

The door opened and Nattan Torr stepped partway in. The scar on his cheek pulled at the lip and left him seeming amused even when he wasn't, but his eyes had a merriness that meant maybe this time he really was. "Something, Captain. Marsen Wellis brought a man in. They're in a holding cell."

Senit closed the incident book and stood, hitching up his belt. "I have the sense that there's something about this you're waiting to tell me until it's funny."

"Might be."

"It's funny enough now. Spit."

"Prisoner's a thief," Torr said.

"Yeah? What did he steal?"

"He won't say."

Senit scowled. "Who won't say?"

"The prisoner."

"And the one that got stole from?"

"Prisoner won't tell us that either," Torr said. "Says he only wants to talk with you."

Senit met Torr's eyes in silence for the length of two slow breaths. "Oh, for fuck's sake," he said, grabbing the oversized silver badge of office from his table and fixing it to his belt. "This had best be good for a laugh, anyway."

He marched out toward the stairs and the holding cells. A light rain was falling from low, bright clouds. It wouldn't last, but it broke the heat a little. If the clouds cleared too much before nightfall, the city would turn muggy as a hot towel over his face. The new recruits were drilling in the yard. Old Saal was showing them restraints. How to keep someone held down without hurting them, how to do it only hurting them a little or else a lot. How to make sure they never walked right again. The newest bunch wasn't particularly promising, but also not the worst he'd seen. One of them was Marsen's nephew.

Marsen had been with the guard for a decade and a half. He was better at telling legends of himself than he was as a guard, but every now and then, he pulled off a surprise. Senit walked down the stone steps to the holding cell with a hint of curiosity that he kept hidden under his annoyance.

The cell itself was small. The only light came from a thin strip along the eastern wall. Not even a window, just a row of bricks with a few missing, set high enough on the wall it would be hard to pass anything through them unnoticed. Not that people hadn't tried.

People, in Captain Divol Senit's experience, were idiots.

Marsen was leaning against the wall, his arms crossed on his chest. He stood straighter when Senit stepped in. The other man in the room was underfed at the ribs and hungry around the eyes. Sharp cheeks, but spilling, curled locks that came down past his shoulder and a neat, scissor-trimmed beard. Hansch cheeks. Inlisc hair. He wore a workman's canvas trousers and a vest of yellow cotton with carved blackwood hooks, not buttons. When he scratched his neck, Senit saw the tattoo of a spider across the back of the man's left hand.

"Captain Senit," Marsen said.

"Guard," Senit said with a nod. "I understand there's something that needs my attention?" He kept his tone mild. The prisoner wouldn't hear the threat in it, but Marsen did.

"I was on patrol in Seepwater, sir. This man called me over. He wanted to talk with a captain."

Did he say why? came almost all the way to Senit's tongue, but he stopped it. It was sharp and harsh, and more to the point, it was talking about the man in the yellow vest like he wasn't there. It was rude, and rudeness was like salt. Easy to put on, hard to take off.

"Well, I see you've arranged it." He turned to the man. "I'm Captain Senit of the city guard. Was there something you wanted to say to me?"

The man licked his lips. It was a flickering, lizard-like motion. It made him look cunning, but not smart. "I need protection."

"All right. Tell me about that. Who is it you need to be protected from?"

The man looked from him to Marsen and back, weighing something in his mind. Whatever the man's angle was, this seemed pretty damn late to start thinking it through. He was committed to his path, whether he knew it or not.

"I stole something valuable."

"Did you, now?"

"But"—the man raised a finger—"I stole it from a thief, so that's not the same."

Senit almost stopped it there. Taking sides in the petty squabbles of Kithamar's worst held less than no interest for him. The man had already confessed to theft, and even without the details Senit didn't need to bother with a magistrate for this one. A few weeks cleaning the streets by day and sleeping in gaol by night, then they'd release the poor fuck to the streets again and see if the experience had made him any wiser.

That was a joke. It wouldn't.

But...the holding cell was cool, and Senit was tired. He could give the poor fucker some more rope and see whether he wove it into a noose.

"All right. What was this thing you took from the thief?"

The man in the yellow vest shrugged. "A knife."

"Well, there's a lot of those out there. What happened to this knife? You still have it?"

The man chuckled like Senit had said something dumb. "I stole it because someone wanted it. It's sold and the money's spent. Three silver."

"Pretty good," Divol said, nodding. "All profit, I guess. Except that you're here looking for space under my wing. What's that about?"

"I stole it from Aunt Thorn," the man said with a flourish like he was delivering the end of a joke. Which, in a sense, he was. He looked so proud of it.

"Ah. You're fucked, then, aren't you?"

The man's face fell. Marsen shifted his weight. If this was really what it seemed, Senit would swap the senior guard for his nephew on the wine-and-piss patrol and let the whole barracks laugh at him. Marsen would have it coming.

"She's set her people to kill me," the man whined.

"I imagine she has. And when they do, we will find them and put them to law. You can count on that. I think we're done here."

He turned to the door, and the man leapt to his feet. He rushed forward, grabbing at Senit's sleeve. Senit shifted his weight, turning from the hip, and landed his knuckles on the bridge of the thief's nose. The cartilage crunched like gravel, and the man staggered back. A moment later, blood was dyeing his yellow vest a whole new color.

"Listen to me, you little fuck," Senit said. "I know what you're thinking. *Aunt Thorn's my enemy. She's your enemy too. So must be we're pals now, yeah?* Here's what you got wrong. My enemy is every self-centered lump of shit in this city who thinks that the law doesn't count when it comes to them. You put two rats in a bucket, and they fight. That doesn't make one of them my fucking pet. As far as I'm concerned, if she puts you in the river, that's saving me time and effort."

"I can help, though," the man blubbered through the blood. "I can help you."

Senit's scowl made his cheeks ache. "How is a cat turd like you going to help a captain of the city guard?"

"I can find her," the man said. A bubble of blood formed on his lips and popped. "I took the knife from the tunnels. The places she hides."

Senit flexed his hand wide and back to a fist. "Say that again."

"The knife I took. It was a special one. It was in her tunnels. In her *rooms*." His voice was tight as a plucked string. "I was part of her crew. I know all the ways in. I know all the signs they use. I'll help you get her."

Senit's knuckles were starting to ache. Truth was, he liked the feeling. And still. Aunt Thorn. That was a name to conjure with. She commanded her thugs and murderers the way he did his guards, and she held more sway in parts of the city than he did. If this thin, desperate waste of skin could open the door to catch her. Or better, *kill* her...

He looked to Marsen, who only lifted his eyebrows. *Up to you, boss.*

"Get me a stool and some water," he said to Marsen, then turned back to the thief. "You start from the start, and we'll see what's in it."

The summer ripened, the days growing shorter without any lasting break from the heat. Rainstorms came every few days; vast clouds darkened the tall air, washing the streets and filling the afternoon with steam and the smell of slaked stone. The leaves on the few trees that found purchase in the gardens or at the river's edge took on a deeper green that promised red and gold to come. The sun lay on shoulders with the weight of an unwelcome hand.

To the uninitiated, the streets and warehouses might seem filled by carts of goods and wallets of coin, the awnings and counting house tables peopled by ledgers and contracts and honeyed almonds with beer. Garreth saw what he'd been taught to see: the constant probing for advantage, the slow and civilized battle of money and time, the triumph at the ruin of a rival house or the despair of one's own collapse. Riverport moved through the hours of light and darkness with the deliberate, studied violence of a wrestler bending his opponent's leg until the joint gave way. That was commerce, and it ran its course without pity.

In House Left, an unspoken tension ran through every meal, every week's worship, every task. Garreth felt it from the moment he woke in the morning until he put out the candle at night. His jaw ached.

In the front drawing room, Vasch sat with Yrith, daughter of Sau, and a map of the world. Or the world that mattered, anyway. The Inlisc girl's chaperone dozed in the corner with only a tiny wet glitter under the heavy lids to show that she was watching even still.

"No," Garreth's younger brother said, "the city's not like an animal. It's more like...a clockwork." He interlaced his fingers in imitation of gears. "Everything fits together, each bit at its time and in its place. And fitting together like that is what makes the next bit possible. And on and on through the whole year."

From where he stood in the shadows of the hall, Garreth could see the furrows of concentration on Yrith's forehead.

"Right now, we're coming to the end of the season," Vasch went on, pointing to the map as he spoke. "All the goods coming in now are to get us through the winter. Salt from the Bronze Coast for the butchers to keep the meat from spoiling. Alum and dye for the clothmakers. Ore and coal and forge wood that they can use in the Smoke over winter, but those come by land from the east or float down the river from the lumbermen in the north."

"And sugar," Yrith said.

"Yes, that's right. We get our sugar from Caram. My father's cousin has field rights on a good stretch of land there. But House Reffon gets theirs from Imaja, which is a little bit closer, so they have an advantage."

"Advantage," Yrith echoed. Her accent was still thick enough to spread on toast.

"If we can get ours first, we can fulfill our obligations and sell the overage before them. If they get theirs first, we have to take whatever's left once they've sold out, and we might be stuck holding some in the warehouse until spring."

"And are bad."

"Well," Vasch chuckled. "It's not good, at least."

Garreth stepped quietly back. The windows were open all through the house in hopes that a breeze would pass through and cool the darkness. Some days that worked, but today the halls felt like a baker's oven. Garreth climbed the main stair, leaving his soon-to-be-wife behind to her tutoring, and stalked back toward the family's private office. It was a narrow room with a lattice of iron over the windows and a lock on the door that only his parents and Uncle Robbson could open. The door stood open now, and the low muttering told him that Uncle Robbson was there even before he looked in.

His uncle was at the little desk, his back to the window. The records were open before him and a small steel pen was in his right hand. A thin page was pinned to the cork of the desk, and without drawing close, Garreth recognized his mother's hand and the family cipher. Robbson looked up.

"News, then?" Garreth asked. It was a risk. Before the girl had arrived, policy would have kept him from prying. But his status within the family and within the company had changed, and if he didn't quite know what it had changed to, then neither did anyone else. The only way to know if he was ranked among the heads of the family now was to act as though he were and see what happened.

Robbson grunted and looked back down at the letter. For two long breaths together, Garreth thought that was all the information he'd get.

His uncle cleared his throat, coughed. "There's some trouble."

The rush of hope in Garreth's chest was like a fountain being turned on in springtime. "Maybe that's best," he said, trying to keep his tone sober.

"What's that supposed to mean?" Robbson snapped.

"Going through with this . . . it's going to humiliate us. I don't want it to fall apart, but if it does, and we have to find another way, maybe in the long term, that's better."

Robbson put down the steel pen, leaned forward on his elbows, and smiled. There was no warmth in his eyes. "I forgot you're still licking off your caul. When I say there's trouble, it means that the deal isn't closed yet. That's all. Trouble is normal. It's what we do. Sometimes they invite it, and sometimes we do, but there's always trouble."

"Oh, I didn't—"

"If there was a better way, your mother would have found it. She's doing this because it's best for the company, and the family, and because of that it's best for you. Show some fucking gratitude."

"She's not even Kithamar Inlisc," Garreth said. "She's Kethil. No one's going to take her seriously. They'll know this is all just part of a trade. They won't respect us."

"They'll respect the money," Robbson said, turning back to the page. "That's all they ever respect. In this family, we eat the shit we're served, and you're not better than us."

"I didn't say that—"

"I'm working."

Garreth took a step back, nodded to his uncle who made a show of not noticing, then turned back for the stair. The hope was gone like it had never been there, and he couldn't put a name to what was in its place. Or he could, but he didn't want to.

Serria was near the front door with a new house maid. As

Garreth passed them, the older woman turned, her eyes widening in alarm. "Is something wrong, sir?"

He didn't answer.

Elaine was in her cell at the Clovas Brotherhood. It made sense, as much as anything did. Her tutors and her father's guards had a story about where she was. The servants at Clovas weren't particularly used to her being there, so if she left, they wouldn't be as swift to alert to the absence. And meeting Theddan at House Abbasann was asking for suspicion to be raised. Or at least, she guessed it was. She sat on her cot, stood and smoothed her gown, sat again, stood, paced. She felt like she was on the top of the palace, looking down the vast cliff of Oldgate to the river below. It was the same vertigo, the same giddiness. She had expected that there would be some part of her—some echo of her imagined mother, perhaps—telling her to stop. There wasn't.

Theddan came an hour before sunset. She carried a leather satchel. Her gown was silk in all the colors of sunset from red to orange to grey, and it draped from her body like a promise. Elaine felt her eyebrows rise in shock and appreciation. Theddan lifted her chin and paused, looking for a moment like the statue of some minor fertility god. When Elaine started laughing, Theddan laughed too.

"You are mad," Elaine said. "Everyone is going to remember you."

"They'll all remember someone," Theddan said. "No reason to think it's me. I mean, some reason but no *proof.* That's what matters. Here, put this on over—" She gestured at Elaine's gown with two fingers, then tossed a cloak of brown plainspun on the cot at her side. It was a servant's robe with a deep hood, and a hem a little too long for her leg. Elaine tied the stays down the front while Theddan slid another over the glorious gown.

"This works?" Elaine asked.

"No one sees a servant girl except other servants, and they know to keep their tongues sewn to their teeth. You'll see."

I'll see, Elaine thought. *Yes, I will, won't I?*

They slipped out past the brotherhood's kitchens and into the ivy-choked alley. Elaine started turning to the east and the river, but Theddan took her elbow and steered her west.

"Where are we going? Stonemarket?"

Theddan didn't answer. Elaine thought she saw her smile, but with the hoods pulled forward, she couldn't be certain.

The aqueduct that marked the western edge of Green Hill had been built centuries before as a way to bring fresh water to the villages behind Palace Hill and as a barrier from raids by the enemy long since conquered. Wide as a canal, it was shallow at the edges and deep in the center. The granite blocks it was carved from were sealed with gum that was replaced every five or six years to keep the water in. At the footbridge that spanned it nearest the city's northern wall, Theddan paused. She took two masks from the satchel, one gold and black, the other white and blue. She held the second one out.

"Here?" Elaine asked.

"And now," Theddan said, fitting the black and gold across the bridge of her nose. The cloth draped her jaw, hiding her mouth, but she still looked like herself to Elaine. As Elaine put her own mask on, Theddan slipped off her sandals and stepped down into the shallow water at the canal's edge.

"Follow me. Be quick!"

Elaine grabbed off her own sandals and dropped in. The water was cool, but not numbing. The stone under her feet was slippery and green, and she pictured herself stumbling.

"It's too slick," she said.

"It's not," Theddan said, already moving north toward the wall. "Just don't fall in."

Elaine followed, careful with every step to put her foot straight down and centered before she trusted her weight to it. At the wall, an iron grate that the city guard used to take prisoners out to clear branches and trash from the water stood open and a young man gestured to them. He was short, barely taller than Elaine herself, with broad shoulders and thick, dark, curled hair.

"Who's this?" he asked Theddan as he took Elaine's hand.

"My cousin," Theddan said.

The man turned his smile to Elaine. "Well, her cousin. I'm Burr. Pleased to make your acquaintance."

"Same," Elaine said as she passed into the narrow darkness. The tunnel that passed through the wall was close enough that they could only go single file, and with Theddan before her, Elaine couldn't see the other side until she spilled out.

North of them, young trees rose like thin fingers toward the sky. Beyond them, the permanent roar of the distant river, and then past that, forest and gold-and-rose sky. It was only for a moment, but Kithamar was behind her. She was outside the city that she belonged to, and it felt better than she'd dreamed.

Burr—if that was his real name—led them along a path through the trash scrub and blackberry that grew outside the city until they reached the river. A little boat had been pulled up on the bank. Burr waded into the Khahon, pulling it with him, then steadied it as Theddan clambered in. Elaine followed. The boat bobbed and shuddered in the flow, unsteady beneath her.

"Where tonight?" Theddan asked as Burr slung himself up and in.

"Ummon has the keys to a boatmaker's shed and enough silver to keep the caretaker at a taproom until dawn."

"Seepwater?" Theddan asked, and Elaine felt a little bite of concern. Seepwater was a rougher quarter than she'd have picked, even if they were staying off the streets.

"Riverport," Burr said, pushing them out into the flow. The northernmost bridge of Kithamar appeared and slid quickly closer. In the falling light, Elaine could make out the rings where the chains would go to gate off traffic into the city in time of war. There were no chains now.

Theddan pressed something soft into her hand. A leather wineskin.

"If it seems a little murky, it's fortified with some herbs," Theddan said, and winked elaborately.

Well, Elaine thought as she undid the stopper, this was what she'd come for.

Night fell, but slowly. The sunset lingered behind Oldgate so that the lanterns and candles marking the switchback road up to the palace were like a brighter kind of star and the city a deeper darkness than the moon-greyed sky. The four of them walked in the gloom. Maur and the new one were a little ahead, Kannish and Garreth a little behind, but none of them so far removed that they weren't clearly one group. The other three wore their blue cloaks and short, brutish swords. The badges of office hung from their belts along with the whistles that would summon more of their new tribe. Garreth had a little knife in his boot, and the only thing hanging from his belt was his wallet.

"I'm not supposed to know about it," Kannish said. "No one's supposed to know about it, and nobody who does know is supposed to talk about it."

"But we're talking about it?" Garreth said.

"It's all anyone's talking about. The whole barracks is gossiping like my sisters having their friends over all night. They come to me because Uncle Marsen brought him in, and they think since we're family I know something."

"Do you?"

"Yeah, I do. But it's worth more than my job to tell it," Kannish said with a lift of his chin that meant he was exaggerating. Maybe even lying. Garreth felt a little rush of affection for the man, and for a moment he forgot the weight of his future, living a moment longer in his boyhood and the past.

"I'd hate to cost you your place. I won't pry."

They passed the ropemakers' guild hall and turned southwest, toward the river. Maur and Tannen were talking to each other, but with their backs turned to him, Garreth couldn't make it out. The scent of the river—rich and deep and clean compared to the streets—came on a cool breeze. A shooting star dashed across heaven, split in two, and vanished. An omen of something, but Garreth didn't know what. Before they reached the next corner, the silence grew too heavy for Kannish.

"Well, I can say a little about it."

"All right," Garreth agreed.

"In general terms, I mean. It doesn't take knowing secrets to see that it's a desperation play, coming to us."

"It does seem like a strange plan."

"There's a certain low cunning to it," Kannish said in inflections that echoed his uncle. "The one thing he can be sure of is that we aren't going to side with Aunt Thorn."

"Is she really that bad?"

"I think if Captain Senit had the choice of breaking her and dying in the same moment or else living a full, happy life knowing she was free, he'd open a vein. Aunt Thorn's behind half the crime coming out of Longhill. The crew that burned down Amman Pettit's shop when he didn't pay them? They were Aunt Thorn. That time three years ago that ten men with swords raided the Temple was her too. Captain Senit thinks she's trying to take over the slavers' trade. Force them out, and own it for herself."

"There aren't any slavers in Kithamar," Garreth said.

"There are," Kannish said, and he didn't lift his chin this time. The moonlight left pools of shadow around his eyes, and Garreth shuddered in a way that didn't come from the breeze. "I didn't think there were either, but there are. There are things that happen in this city at night that make me want to nail my sisters indoors at sunset. If people knew what the guard knows, they'd never leave their houses."

Maur and Tannen turned left, heading south along the water. If they went far enough, they'd find themselves in Seepwater. A prisoners' cart clattered past them, still stinking of shit and dead animals that the condemned had already thrown in the river. The men in the back of the cart were vacant as corpses, their eyes dull with exhaustion. The carter had a man beside him wearing the same blue as the others and a leather goad like a fist at the end of a rope that bounced against his side. He called out to Tannen and Maur as he passed on his way to the gaol, and they called back merrily.

"This city would eat itself, if it weren't for us," Kannish said. "Uncle Marsen always said that, but I see it now."

They came to an open square where two roads met by the water. A cistern squatted beside a low stone wall, and the buildings rose up like the shoulders of strange men. Maur stopped short, and Tannen took two more steps before he looked back. Garreth felt a little thrill of fear in his belly. He told himself it was only that Kannish's talk had spooked him, but he felt the night growing a little clearer, a little brighter, a little sharper at the edge.

Kannish grunted as they came to Maur. The smaller man had his head tilted like a dog hearing an odd noise, and he answered like Kannish had asked a question. "That's Ognan Grimn's boathouse."

Kannish looked toward the water. The boathouse was tall and wide, with one face to the street and the other in the dark water. Across the river, Oldgate rose like the city itself looking down at them. Like a god.

"Think so," Kannish said. "Why?"

"I heard a voice," Maur said. "And look at that window. There's a cloth over it, but..."

"There's a light," Tannen said, and drew his sword. The metal caught the moonlight. "Someone's in there."

Kannish put a hand on Garreth's arm. "You wait here."

Half against his will and half in relief, Garreth sat on the low stone wall, his back toward the darkness and his eyes toward the boathouse. In daylight, stevedores and carters and servants with baskets full of bread and vegetables from the market would sit on these same stones and feel no dread at all. In darkness, it was different.

"It's all right, Maur," Kannish said. "We can do this."

"I'll come with you," Garreth said.

Tannen turned with a sneer. "You want to help, keep out of the way."

"It's better if you stay," Maur said. His voice was trembling.

Garreth put his palms to the stone and watched with his heart in his throat as the three junior guards spread out and walked toward the boathouse and whatever was inside.

The boathouse was wide and tall as a ballroom, but there the similarities ended. A water-filled lock took up more than half of what would have been the dancing floor space. The river doors—wider than a warehouse—would have looked out across the Khahon toward Oldgate and Palace Hill at its crown if they'd been open, but instead they were just an expanse of well-sealed wood with the river flowing a few inches below the bottom. The roof, half hidden in gloom, was a webwork of pulleys, rope, and chain with catwalks and old iron tracks mottled with rust. A flat-bottomed boat hung in the darkness, its hull part open like a great dead fish halfway through being cleaned. The air stank of tar and varnish, and the fumes mixed with the fortified wine in ways that left Elaine lightheaded and a little nauseated.

Burr and his friends had tacked cloth up over the windows to hide the light of a half dozen lanterns. There were perhaps twenty people sitting on benches or dangling their feet into the river water. Most were young men of Burr's age who wore rough canvas work pants like costumes. Few of them had physiques that spoke of physical labor. Of the other women, one was masked and three weren't. The men milled around, slapping each other on shoulders and laughing and pretending not to stare at the women. The women stayed in a group, mostly, with one or two looping out and away from their coterie and then coming back. Except for Elaine. She'd taken up a perch on a thin wooden stairway that clung to the wall and led up into the darkness. She was neither in the group nor apart from it, but comfortably at its edge. Her mask hid a polite smile.

Theddan, talking to a very tall, very thickly built man, glanced over toward her. Elaine waved back to her cousin. She meant it as *I'm fine, don't mind me*, but Theddan squeezed the big man's arm and stepped away from him. The look of disappointment on his face would have been visible from across the river.

Theddan twirled as she walked, showing her dress to its best effect, and plucked a bottle of wine from one of the other men as she passed. He didn't object.

When she reached the stairs, Theddan poured herself down beside Elaine, draping her arms around her and leaning her head on Elaine's shoulder. "You're bored."

"I'm not," Elaine said.

"I made it sound too good, and now you're disappointed."

Elaine kissed her cousin's head. "I'm fine. I wanted to come and see. I have come. I am seeing."

"It's better if you're drunk?" Theddan said, and held up the bottle. It was black glass and clinked with liquid.

Elaine shook her head. "I'm queasy from what I had on the way here."

"But you're sober."

"If I get too sober, I promise I'll drink. I don't see how getting sick will make the evening better," she said, and heard how harsh the words sounded from her mouth. When she spoke again, she was gentler. "I'm hungry for something, and I don't know what it is. I want. I want badly, and I don't know what I want."

"But not this?"

Elaine shrugged. It wasn't this. It would never be this. She saw the joy, and she understood it. Breaking rules. Tasting freedom. But part of it was a loosening of self-control, and that sleeve would never fit her arm. Theddan could throw herself into the world and trust the gods to catch her. Elaine had no such faith.

But it seemed rude to say it, so she pretended instead. "Who knows? Daylight is a long way from now."

Theddan shifted down a step and laid her head in Elaine's lap. "I wish you were happy."

"I wish I were happy too," she said. And then, "Oh my... what is going on there?"

A half circle of revelers had formed at the side of the lock. The big man who Theddan had stepped away from stood with his back to the water and tugged at his pants.

"That's Eddik," Theddan said. "When he feels ignored, he likes to wrestle."

Eddik managed to solve whatever knot had been frustrating him, and stepped out of his pants. Elaine felt a blush rising in her cheeks, and laughter with it. The naked man raised his fists above him and gave a roar.

"I love it when he does that," Theddan said. "He's a beautiful man."

"He looks like a shaved bear."

Another of the young men started pulling off his own clothes, and Elaine shifted a degree to get a better look. The second man was thinner and softer, but made up in bravado where brute nature had failed him. The others in the half circle shifted, making a space for the coming violence. Eddik apparently found the whole proceeding exciting in more ways than one.

"Oh my God," Elaine said. "I take everything back. This is hilarious."

"Don't let him hear you. It'll hurt his feelings," Theddan said around a chuckle.

Elaine had seen nude men before, but always in the context of a celebration or a performance. A ritual with expectations and rules. This was something else. The two began to circle each other, arms wide, mouths set in grins. Elaine tried not to look at them too closely, then noticed herself doing it, and let go of her restraint. She stared at the bare bodies, the way their legs shuddered at each step. The violence and the vulnerability and the strangeness of the moment made them hard to look away from. She found herself leaning forward.

Something happened, some failure of technique invisible to her, and the two men leapt at each other. Arms flailed as they tried to find purchase on each other's skin. Eddik groaned and shifted his weight. His opponent leaned down and—back and legs and buttocks straining—tried to drive the big man back into the lock and the dark water. It almost worked too. The crowd cheered.

"Someone's going to hear us," Theddan said, and like she'd called it forth with her words, a whistle sounded. And after it, a voice.

This is the city guard! The first one that fights gets a blade in their gut!

Theddan spat an obscenity and turned. On the boathouse floor, the revelers became a mob, surging first for one door and then another. Theddan pushed Elaine, and together they went up the stairs, away from the chaos and into the dark.

More whistles. Elaine couldn't guess how many, but more than two. At the top of the stairs, a little platform of planks gave access to the chains and ropes. Below, two bluecloak city guards were shouting, blades drawn. The whistles were down to one, but it would call others if they were close enough to hear it.

"Be still. Be quiet," Theddan said. "They won't see us."

Elaine was fairly sure that wasn't true. She inched along the bare wood boards, looking down on the stones below her. The stink of dust and grease filled the air. Someone shouted. Someone screamed. She took a long, slow breath, letting it out between her teeth. The distance between her and the floor of the boathouse seemed much larger than it had when she'd been looking up. Below her some of the others were dropping to the ground and spreading their arms like they were hugging the earth. She moved forward slowly, half certain that every shift of her weight would tip her over and down. She'd come far enough that the lock was beneath her. The water shimmered with lantern light, black and silver.

"What are you doing?" Theddan asked, a little too loudly. One of the bluecloaks looked up.

"Hey! You two! Get the hell down from there!"

Elaine looked back. Theddan's eyes were wide above her mask. "Follow me."

Elaine jumped, or tried to. She slipped a little at the end and tumbled in the air. The river water rose up to meet her. The cold was like a slap, but she'd anticipated it. She forced her eyes open, found where the dancing shadows showed the stone side of the lock. And where they vanished under the river doors. She kicked and pushed the water, swimming out toward the wild flow and freedom. The wide wooden doors passed above her, and she was outside, in the river itself. She was elated for a moment.

Then the current caught her.

Even in the heat of summer, deep threads of the Khahon ran cold and cruel. They grabbed her, pulled her down. Something bumped against her face—eel or fish or water plant. She spun once, nearly losing her bearing, and kicked for the surface. Her head reached air, but the sodden mask choked her. She ripped it off, sank, kicked again for the open air, and started swimming as hard as she could for the bank. The river toyed with her, catching her in a wide eddy, tugging her down and letting her go again, like a cat deciding whether it was hungry enough for mouse.

Her lungs were burning and her feet and hands were growing numb. Her arms and legs ached with effort. A small, still part of her mind thought *This is going to kill me. I'm about to die.*

The bank seemed farther away than when she'd started swimming toward it. The impulse to rest, to give herself time to think, to reason some way out was tempting, and it was death. She pushed past pain, past planning. It was a raw animal fear, and she let it drive her. Slowly, tentatively, always ready to change its mind, the river relented.

A public quay appeared, and she caught its edge. Her fingers slipped on the algae-slimed stone, but she was out of the cruelest part of the current. The water chose not to yank her back. She paddled to the rough steps, dragged herself up over the worn, slick stone, and only then turned and looked back at the river. If Theddan had done as Elaine had told her, she was in there now. She might be drowning. She might die. She *would* die. The fear was like a vise around her heart. Elaine lifted the hem of her dress and ran.

The river had carried her several streets from the boathouse, but the moon and Oldgate oriented her. Her bare feet slapped against cobblestones. She didn't know where she'd lost her sandals. There would be bluecloaks at the boathouse. She'd get them to help. Yes, she'd be caught. Yes, she'd be humiliated. But it was the only aid that might reach Theddan in time.

Her dress felt like it was made from ice. It clung to her skin and chafed her as she ran. She felt her breath catching and didn't know if she was crying from pain or fear. She rounded the last corner.

An open square with a cistern and a low wall. A man was sitting on the wall, his legs out before him. Not a bluecloak. She followed his gaze to the street outside the boathouse. Three bluecloaks with weapons drawn had the revelers on their knees. The smallest of the guards was going to each of the new prisoners in turn, knotting their wrists together and putting them on a lead. Every one of them would be marched to the magistrate. Every one of them would pay the price of justice.

And at the corner of the group, head bowed and face streaked with tears, was Theddan. Relief and horror warred in Elaine's heart. Theddan was safe. Theddan was caught. Theddan was going to live long enough to be dragged before her father in disgrace and wish she hadn't lived.

One of the two larger bluecloaks looked toward Elaine and raised his sword, pointing it at her like an accusing finger. "Hey! You! Stop where you are! In the name of the prince!"

He started toward her, distracted from his arrayed prisoners. It was apparently the chance Eddik had been waiting for. With a roar, the large man jumped to his feet, barreled into the smallest guard, and sprinted to the north, still magnificently naked. His pale limbs pumped away into the moon-bright streets like some unlikely god, and his receding shout was joyous and animal. Other prisoners started to rise, and pandemonium threatened. The guard coming for Elaine turned back, and she saw her own chance. She sprinted, jumping the low wall and pressing herself against it like she was a little girl again, playing hiding games with her nurse.

The man sitting on the wall leaned back and looked down at her. He was her age, or nearly so. Sharp cheeks and hair that, with the moonlight, could have been any color. The vast amusement in his expression would have made him handsome in another situation.

She raised a finger to her lips—*be silent*—and then clasped her hands to her breast.

Please.

When the whistles sounded, Garreth stood and started pacing. The distance between the cistern wall and the boathouse was short enough he could have crossed it in seconds. Voices rose.

A woman shouted. Whatever they'd found, Kannish and Maur were facing it, and he was standing in the dark instead of being at their side. His fingers tapped against his thigh, drumming as fast as raindrops in a storm.

Two of the whistles went silent, and there weren't any answering calls. No other bluecloaks were in earshot. This wasn't going to work. He'd give his friends to the count of twenty, but then he'd go in. Staying in place was too much to ask of him.

A door opened in the boathouse. Light spilled out. Silhouettes moved in the frame, each dissolving into the other until Kannish appeared, sword in hand. His back to Garreth, he gestured with the blade, and a young man came out and knelt on the cobblestones. Then another. A woman in what looked to be an expensive dress. From inside the building, Tannen's voice barked something that sounded like a dog herding sheep. Kannish looked over his shoulder, a grin folding his cheeks. He lifted his sword to Garreth in salute. Garreth bowed and sat back down.

As Maur and Tannen brought the prisoners to the street and put them on their knees, Garreth waited and watched. It seemed to go on forever, but eventually the last emerged and Kannish shut the door behind them. Maur started binding the prisoners' hands while Kannish and Tannen walked with blades out, intimidating the prisoners into submission. Tannen said something, and Garreth's friends laughed.

The girl came up from the south, bare feet slapping the road. Her dress was wet and stained, her hair plastered to her neck. When she saw the prisoners, she seemed to soften. Lines of fear erased themselves from her mouth and eyes, and Garreth remembered an old story he'd heard as a child. The spirits who lived in the river and tempted boys out to their death.

"Hey! You!" Tannen shouted, turning to the newcomer. "Stop where you are! In the name of the prince!"

A roar came among the prisoners, spinning Tannen back around. A huge and vastly naked man had knocked Maur to the street. Kannish started toward the runner, but the other prisoners began to rise. It was lose one, or lose all. Tannen waded into the kneeling crowd, slapping at them with the flat of his blade as they rose. Kannish hauled Maur to his feet...

...and the girl bolted. At first, Garreth thought she was running at him, but she was only taking the shortest path to the wall. She cleared it as gracefully as a dancer, folding herself into the shadows on the far side. Garreth leaned back to find her staring up at him. The moonlight silvered the curves of her face, and he could imagine better how drowning spirits could lure boys into rivers. She put a finger to her lips, and then clasped a hand at her breast, begging his complicity.

"What is the fucking matter with you!" Tannen shouted.

Maur was on his feet now, but there was a smear of blood on his face, and he was staring down at the street in shame. When he shrugged, his lips moved, but Garreth couldn't hear what he said.

"That's a ripe turd of an excuse," Tannen said.

Kannish stepped between them, scowling, and said something to Tannen. Maur went back to tying the prisoners together, but Garreth knew him well enough to see in how he moved and the stiffness of his face that Tannen had humiliated him. Tannen muttered something inaudible but clearly obscene and turned back, his eyes sweeping the night street. He raised his sword toward Garreth in command. "You! Where did the girl go?"

The lie came easily. He pointed south. "Back the way she came. She was limping. Badly. You could probably catch her."

In the dark, Tannen's frustration and anger seemed to light him from within. "Kannish. You and that one finish here. I'm tracking the bitch that jumped."

Kannish nodded sharply and turned to the people kneeling in the street. "I can't kill you all, but I swear by every god under the sky that I will kill the first one of you that stands without my permission." Tannen ran south, his sword at the ready like he'd murder the girl if he saw her. Like she was a threat. Garreth leaned back and let what he'd just done settle into him. His chest felt wider than he remembered it feeling in weeks, and he had to fight to keep from grinning. After a few moments, he glanced down and to the side. She was still looking up at him. When he smiled, she relaxed a degree. He shifted his head to the side, pointing with his chin. She frowned her confusion.

"Hey," Garreth called. "I'm going to leave you two to this."

"Fair," Kannish replied. "Don't expect there will be much more to see tonight. Stay out of trouble, yeah?"

Garreth stood, spreading his arms like an actor. He turned north, which wasn't the fastest way home, but his friends didn't take notice. He walked slowly at first, and heard the scuttling following along behind. When he reached the end of the wall, he turned back. Maur had moved on to tying the second line of captives, and Kannish's whole attention was on keeping them from rising up. Garreth might almost not have been there. A narrow street led east, away from the river and into the quarter.

"Come to me," he said. "I'll see you safe."

He walked into the night, and for a moment, he thought he was alone. Then the slap of bare feet on stone pattered up behind him, and she was at his side.

"Nice evening for a walk," he said.

She looked at him like he'd grown another arm, then a few steps later, laughed. She had a good laugh. Complex, and deeper than he'd expected. "Better for staying home," she said, "but it's too late for that."

"I'm Garreth."

"Thank you, Garreth," she said. She didn't offer her name, and he didn't press.

Elaine understood intellectually that she was in danger, but it was hard to feel it. Yes, she was on the wrong side of the river with no way home. Yes, Theddan—the only one who knew that she wasn't safe in her rooms in Green Hill—was spending the night in gaol and facing the magistrates in the morning. There was nothing keeping her maybe-savior from slitting her throat and dropping her corpse in an alley except his amiable nature. She was cold, she was out of her element, and she had nothing to protect her but her wits and good fortune.

But she also wasn't drowning. She wasn't at the wrong end of a guard's sword. She was walking down the nighttime streets of Riverport with the sort of man Theddan would have called a wool seller's son with a perfect ass. The night was warm. Her clothes and hair were drying. The city around them was quiet and brighter in the moonlight than she'd expected. And, except for the soles of her feet burning and abrading from walking bare against the stone, it was pleasant. More than pleasant. As the panic settled, there was even a strange beauty to it.

One day, she would rule this city. The streets she was walking through now, nameless and in darkness, were her streets. They didn't know it yet, but more to the point, she didn't know them. She wondered if her father had ever found himself unguarded in Kithamar. If he had ever seen the shutters open to welcome the night breeze or the cats shifting in the midnight shadows. It might have changed how he saw his city. It might change how she did.

"Did someone know Ognan?" Garreth asked.

"Who?"

"Ognan. That was his boathouse."

"Oh. I don't know. Maybe."

"How did they get the keys?"

"I don't know how any of it works. It was my first time at one of these. My last too."

"Not impressed?"

"Oh, impressed," she said. "Not favorably."

His smile was easy, but there was a sorrow in it.

"Do you know him?" she asked. "Ognan?"

"He's married to my mother's cousin."

"Odd coincidence."

"Not really. Everyone's connected somehow. If it wasn't that, he'd be in a fraternal order with my father. Or my uncle. Or he'd go to the same priest. Or fortune-teller. Everyone knows everyone. We're all trying to destroy each other, and we all have each other's backs."

They turned east. The street was wider here, and the shadows in the doorways and alley mouths seemed not as dark. Someone had left a wooden chair leaning against a wall.

"Strange choice," she said. "Being loyal to someone, but not too much."

"That's commerce. Everyone wants to win. Everyone wants to have more power and influence. And we also all rely on each other. If everyone decided to stop taking contracts with a particular carter or wouldn't trade with someone's warehouse... It doesn't matter that you're hip-deep in Gaddivan silk and Omresh dye if no one trades with you."

"Was that what happened tonight?"

He looked over at her.

"You knew the guards by name," she said. "You fooled them because... there was something in it for you?"

He was quiet for long enough she thought she'd made him angry. "You mean why am I helping you."

"That, yes."

"Well, it was spite at the first. Kannish and Maur have been my friends forever, but Tannen, the one who came for you, isn't someone I know. And he was cruel to Maur, and... I don't like him."

"Well, I'll burn incense to the god of spite, then. I assume there is one. But once he was gone, your friends were still there."

"Yes."

"You didn't point me out to them."

"I wanted..."

Elaine felt a little twinge of anxiety and waited for him to finish the thought.

"I wanted something of my own?" he said. "I hear about all the events and adventures they have. Most of it's lies and the rest is exaggeration, but there's no space for me in it. I'm not a guard."

"Why not?"

"What?"

"Your friends are. Why aren't you?"

"Neither of them have a place in their family's work. Or not high enough that they could take it and still stand proud. The guard's an option for them. I only have one brother. I have a duty to my family... Did I say something funny?"

"No, I just understand that."

They walked in silence a little way more. They had fallen into step.

"Do they know you miss them?" she asked.

"Maur does," he said.

"Not the other one?"

"Maybe. I don't know. Maybe they're angry because I don't have to give up all the things they do. I don't answer to the magistrates or the guild contracts. I can sleep when I want to. Work when I choose. Eat something other than what they're serving at the guard kitchens."

"Take a wife," Elaine said.

"Guards can take wives. They can rent rooms outside the barracks. There's not enough money in it to buy a house of their own, though. Even the bribes aren't that good. It's stupid, I know, me being jealous of them... But I may be stupid."

"Incense for the god of stupidity too."

"What about you?"

"It's not wrong, wanting a moment that no one else has claim to," Elaine said.

"You're kind to say so," he said, angling them along another street. The moon had drifted while they walked. Not far, but enough that she could tell. "We're almost there."

"There?"

"My family's house. I didn't think you'd want to walk back across the river without some boots."

"What makes you think I'm from across the river?"

"You're not from Riverport or Newmarket. I'd know you. That dress is too well made for Seepwater or the Smoke, much less Longhill. That cloth and seam work? That's money. So Stonemarket. Am I right?"

"Yes," she lied. "Just southwest of Green Hill."

"It's too late to get a favor from a carter, so that makes a long, long walk. Tannen and the others probably won't be looking for you, but if they do, they'll be watching the bridges."

"I'll need a disguise. I had a cloak with a good hood on it, but..."

"We'll figure it out," he said, as if assistance in sneaking back home across a whole night-drunk city were the most normal thing in the world to ask. He touched her arm and pointed to a low wall behind a tall compound, four stories high. The shutters were all dark. "There's a place right here we can hop over the wall. Watch me, and I'll show you the trick of it."

He lifted himself up, swung over into whatever was on the far side. She only hesitated for a moment before she followed.

The girl landed gracefully in the kitchen garden, but he put a hand out to steady her anyway. The house was dark. The ground floor would be empty, and the servants were all two flights up. Yrith and her chaperone were in the guest rooms on the west of the house across from his father's. If they went up the main stairway, they'd need to pass the door of Vasch's rooms, but not Uncle Robbson's.

"Smells good," she said. And then, seeing his face, "It smells good here."

"Herbs for the kitchen."

"Oh," she said.

"There aren't kitchen gardens in Stonemarket?"

"I'm sure there are, but I don't see them."

He leaned over and started pulling off his boots. She steadied him, her hand on his shoulder. "We need to be quiet," he said.

"I understand."

He left the boots where they were. He could come get them in the morning. The servants' door was bright red in daylight. The moon made it darker. He opened it carefully. It creaked, but only a little. He listened for voices or the sounds of footsteps besides their own. The house was silent. He drew her in. Their bare feet made the faintest tapping against the stone floor. Any other time, it would have been silence, but his senses had all been sanded raw by the danger of being found. He moved slowly past the blue doors that led to the dining hall. Even the moonlight was gone now, and the darkness was profound. Her hand found his, and he held her fingers, guiding her through the house that he knew and she didn't.

At the stair, he slowed, taking the first step up slowly, and then the second. Showing her through his movement where the risers were, how high each was. This was no time for a stubbed toe. The slight shudder of her breath and the rustle of their clothes were the loudest things in the world as they ascended.

On the second floor, windows that looked down over the kitchen garden let in a spill of light that made him think of swimming underwater. The wood floors were solid, and creaked almost not at all. The pair moved past Vasch's doorway, down the hall a little. When they reached the door of his room, he squeezed her fingers in reassurance and let her go. With one hand on the handle and the other pressed against the wood to muffle any sound, he opened the door and stepped in.

Both sets of shutters were open to let in the cool night air and the moonlight. He imagined how she would see it. The four-post bed with the fly netting. The flowers painted on the wall, hardly more than complications of shadow now. His little desk. It was the room of a merchant's son: not cramped but small, not squalid but unassuming. The air smelled of the soap Serria's cleaning servants used, and of the street. The kitchen gardens had been better.

He closed the door behind her and lowered the latch. She moved through the room, touching one thing and then another with her fingertips—the wall, the desk, the window, the netting—like she was trying to decide if it was real or all of this was a particularly implausible dream. He went to his bed, knelt, and pulled open the drawers that were built there. His clothes were stacked, folded, and ready, fresh from the launderer. He started pulling out what seemed best. There was a shirt that had been his favorite when he was younger that had never been given down to Vasch. A pair of brown working pants that were a little too short for him. A cloak that was too heavy for summer, but that had a hood.

She leaned over him as he knelt, her wrist brushing against his ear. "What are these?" she whispered.

"Your disguise, I hope."

"Mine?"

"They're looking for a woman without shoes in a ruined dress. With any luck, they'll see you as a young man out on other business. The boots are going to be too big. I can't do anything about that. But we can put some extra cloth in the bottom and keep the laces tight. You shouldn't wind up with many more blisters than you already have," he said, tapping the bare and street-blackened foot beside his knee. "You'll want to wash those with good soap when you're safe."

"There may not be enough soap in the world."

He pulled the last of the clothes onto the bed. "Try these."

"All right," she said. And then a moment later, "If you don't mind."

"Yes. Of course."

He went to the window, set his back to the room, and looked out over the street. The familiar walls and roofs of Riverport looked like a painting of themselves done in blue and grey. From where he stood, he could see dozens of other windows that opened into other rooms, other houses. No one was looking back at him. The city was so deep in its sleep that it might have been empty.

He heard the sounds of her behind him. The hush of cloth. The creak of the bed frame. An exhalation with some effort behind it. He felt his body responding to the fact of her nakedness and fought to take his thoughts elsewhere. He put his hands at the small of his back, wrapped his right hand around his left wrist, and dug his nails in until it was distracting.

"Are you all right?" she asked.

"Fine," he said.

"Really?" There was a hint of teasing in her voice.

"I'm having a strange night."

"You can turn around. Modesty is preserved."

He shifted, trying to seem more at ease than he felt. She stood at the end of his bed. The ruined dress was a puddle at her feet. She lifted her arms, showing his sleeves on them, his cloak on her shoulder, his boots on her feet. "Well. Will I pass for a man?"

He tried not to laugh. "No. Not for a moment. Not from a street away. Not if they were blind. You look like a woman dressed as a man and nothing else."

"Maybe they won't think that's suspicious."

"Or maybe we need another plan."

"Or that," she said. "But I don't know what it would be."

He leaned against the wall and considered. "My family shares a stable with a couple other houses. It's just a street from here. We can go at first light. I'll say you're a courier who brought some contracts from Stonemarket and needs to get back. The first cart that goes that way, you can go with."

"First light."

"It's not that long from now. There are birds that start singing before there's any hint of it. When we hear them..." He paused, shook his head, went on. "When we hear them, it will be time to go."

"End of the night," she said.

"You can't be sorry about that."

She paused for a moment, like she was listening to something he couldn't hear. "You don't have any idea who I am."

"You're a girl who broke into a boathouse."

"Not my name. Not what my life is. Not if knowing me would be an advantage to you or a burden."

"No. None of that."

"Would you want to?"

"Want to?"

"Know."

He looked down. His boots on her feet. "I don't have room in my life for someone like you."

"You don't know what I'm like."

"I know what I would want you to be, and I don't have room to find out."

"I understand better than you guess," she said. She stepped out of his boots and leaned toward him. Cloth rustled.

His breath caught. "I don't think you should do that."

"If you don't want—"

"No, I could be dead and I would want. But my family... and I'm not..."

"You can't be part of my life," she said. Her breath was warm. "I can't be part of yours. All we have is from now until the birds sing. Maybe that could be for us?"

She rested her head against his shoulder. Her hair smelled like the river. She moved, but not away.

"If you," he began, and then lost his train of thought. "If you keep doing that, I won't be able to think."

He felt her smile.

Garreth didn't know at first what woke him, except that it was loud. He swam up from sleep, disoriented and confused. Light poured in through the unshuttered window. The sounds of cart wheels clattering against stones rose from the street.

The girl was sitting beside him holding his bedclothes up to cover herself. Her face was set and grim. Uncle Robbson stood in the doorway, his face pale with rage. Seeing him, Garreth remembered the shout. That was what woke him.

"What," Uncle Robbson said, "is this... *shit*... that I am looking at?"

Garreth's heart dropped.

"I think we missed our birds," she said.

Garreth was a year and seventeen days older than his brother, and it had defined who they were to each other from the start. When they competed as brothers will, Vasch lost. When they wore their best clothes to the guild meetings and celebrations, Vasch's were all things Garreth had worn the year before. At most, they were retailored or had a bit of ribbon replaced. When the boys' tutors came, Garreth's numbers and letters were a little bit ahead of Vasch's. Garreth went out to help his father oversee the shipments coming in before Vasch. He led the family's prayers first, he took the larger rooms, he attended the magistrates' sessions first. No matter how hard Vasch tried, Garreth always had the edge. It wasn't that Vasch never won anything, it was that he always lost more. And above that, they both knew that as sure as summer gave way to winter's cold, Garreth was and would always be a little better.

Vasch, for the most part, had learned to accept it as an unpleasant truth about life. The world had illness, injury, accident, and his brother. His tolerance of his own lower status took on a kind of morose good humor. It wasn't, Garreth was certain, that Vasch didn't care. It was that he had learned not to show that he cared. It was policy, and it worked for them.

Usually.

Once, when Vasch was eleven years old and Garreth twelve, someone gave Vasch a pomegranate. For reasons Garreth didn't know then or understand later, Vasch had been supremely proud of the gift. He'd strutted through the street with it in his hand like it was a magical orb made by the gods themselves, and he was the chosen. Garreth and two or three of his friends had made a game of it. One of them—he didn't remember who—snatched the beloved object out of Vasch's hand, and they'd started tossing it between them. Vasch had sprinted toward whoever had it and shrieked in fear every time it was passed to someone else. It wasn't particularly cruel as cruelties went, and Garreth and his friends had laughed at the younger boy's distress as boys had since childhood was created.

Garreth had been the first to hear the rawness in Vasch's cries and sense that they'd gone too far. The next time the pomegranate came to him, he held it out to his little brother. Vasch grabbed the leathery red fruit out of Garreth's hand, ripped it in two, and threw the halves to the cobblestones. He ground them into the stones with his feet, red juice streaming between the cobbles like blood, and screamed in animal rage. Though he never forgot it, Garreth hadn't seen that feral look in his brother's eyes since. Not until now.

"What were you *thinking*?"

Vasch leaned across the breakfast table, his weight on his elbows like he was one stray impulse from coming across the plates of eggs and fish like a belligerent drunk at a taproom.

"It wasn't like that," Garreth said.

The irony was that his father came to the same strategy he

had. The girl, dressed in servant's clothes and a hood, had been escorted to the stables by a quietly livid Uncle Robbson. The plan was to move her out as if her presence was utterly normal and hope that no one noticed or cared. That Robbson had gone an hour ago and still wasn't back meant he was running other errands of the house—checking the warehouses, delivering the schedule of boats to the port master's office, paying the access tax. Whatever little chores he had would keep him plausibly out of the house until he either assured himself that there was no trouble coming from Garreth's indiscretion or calmed down or both. Their father was in his private office with Yrith's chaperone and had been for most of the morning. Garreth didn't know where the woman he was meant to marry was, but she wasn't there for the morning meal.

"'It wasn't like that,'" Vasch repeated mockingly. "What's that supposed to mean? You weren't thinking? It wasn't a thinking kind of night? You took off a day from thinking? For fuck's sake, you brought a whore into this house with Yrith here!"

"She wasn't a whore."

Vasch pushed back from the table. "Oh, she's not a professional? Just an apprentice street fuck?"

Garreth put down his knife. A poached egg bled its half-eaten yolk onto the plate. "Don't try sarcasm. You're not good at it."

"Mother is trying to make an alliance. Yrith is here to marry you. She's your wife in everything but the ceremony. How would you feel if she were dragging strange men into her bed?"

Garreth took a breath. His cheeks hurt from keeping still. He locked his eyes on Vasch's, and there was the barest ghost of a flinch in his brother's expression. When he spoke, Garreth said each word on its own. "Get her some. We'll find out."

Vasch's face went dark. He snatched up his plate and threw it at Garreth. His speed and rage were greater than his aim. The plate shattered against the wall. A bit of fish lay on the table where it had fallen, small, shining, and absurd.

"Ah, boys," their father said, stepping into the room. He looked at the fallen shards like they were an unexpected and not particularly attractive blossom. Vasch sat, hands in fists between his knees. "Yes, well. I was hoping to take a moment of Garreth's time."

"Yes, Father," Garreth said, standing.

"Good, good, good. And, Vasch? That was the last time you will refer to this situation in any way. In the house or out."

"Yes," Vasch whispered.

"Yes?"

"Yes sir." His voice trembled.

Father turned and ambled back into the corridor, Garreth following behind like he was a child again. The corridors seemed unnaturally long, and the servants were all conveniently elsewhere. There weren't even the sounds of voices to accompany them to Father's private study.

The study itself was a modest room with a green wooden table that had once been a door and simple wooden chairs to match. Shelves lined the walls, filled with papers and ledgers. A window let in the fresh air, and decorative ironwork drilled into the wall kept out anything larger than a fly. A lock box of iron and brass held the family ciphers, or pretended to. Garreth was fairly certain that anyone who went through the trouble of stealing them would find only gibberish. The true ciphers were locked in his parents' heads. The chair creaked under Garreth.

"Would you like something? A cup of wine?"

"No," Garreth said, staring at his shoes. "Thank you."

"Well, I certainly do. And it's early to drink alone."

His father took two rude earthenware cups and a red glass bottle out from behind a pile of ledgers. He put one cup before

Garreth and the other near himself. The wine clinked as he poured it. His father sat, drank down half of his cup, and sighed. "I have consulted on the customs of Yrith's people. There's no formal loss of honor to her. So that's good. We will need to apprise your mother of the situation, though."

Garreth picked up the cup, hesitated, and put it back down. His father grunted and nodded like he was agreeing with something Garreth said. "My understanding is that the men take these things more lightly than the women do, and the caravan master we're negotiating with is a male cousin. But better that we be forthright, even if it is embarrassing."

He drank again before he went on.

"Of course, what we tell her will need to be true. So. Will this be happening again?"

"No," Garreth said.

"Is that you speaking, or the shame? The shame is going to say what it thinks I want to hear so that I'll end the conversation and let you go."

"I...I don't think it will happen again," Garreth said. "But I didn't expect it to happen at all. So I guess I can't be sure."

"Who is this girl to you?"

"I don't know her. I don't even know her name. I met her last night."

"Will she be discreet?"

"Yes."

"Because you want to believe she will, or because she will?"

Garreth lifted the cup. The wine was rich and astringent. On a night of little sleep and too many emotions, it sat uneasy in his stomach. "She made it a point that there was no room in her life for me and none in mine for her. She said that. Unprompted. She won't..." He gestured with the cup, trying to find what exactly she wouldn't.

Father let him struggle for a moment. "Well, that's as close to good as we'll get. We will put her out of our minds and hope she stays there. That only leaves you."

"Me?"

"You didn't trip and fall out of your clothes," his father said gently. "You misbehaved, and you know it. But again, put the shame aside and let's talk about why you did. What you gained from it."

"I don't know how to answer that."

"I'll start. You did it because you are angry with me and your mother, and you were able to feel that you hurt us. Or you did it because you hate Yrith, and this was a bid to sabotage the marriage. Or because you're afraid of her. Or it was a way of boasting to your friends so they'll think better of you and you won't feel as alone. Or you were feeling the itch and this girl was convenient. Really, it could have been anything."

"Then what does why matter?"

"It's a question of managing it," his father said. "I can't help you control it until you understand what's being controlled."

"I just needed to..." Garreth said, stopped, shook his head. His father refilled their cups. "I don't like being where I'm not wanted."

"Interesting point. You mean Yrith?"

"I don't know her. I don't know what she thinks or feels. Her people bartered her away to Kithamar for trade advantages, and we took her for the same reason. I'm the face of that."

"And your response to that isn't to know her better? Serria and Vasch tutor her. You could as well."

"They aren't going to be in her wedding bed. I am."

His father tilted his head. "Guilt? You did this from guilt?"

"I did it to be someone besides myself. To be in a different life than the one I have. Just for a little while."

Father sighed and leaned back in his chair. A smile touched his lips. "I remember when your mother and I married. It was similar to your situation now. My parents and hers saw advantage in the union. With the pair of us in control of both the Caram contracts and the warehouse, we remade my family business into something with much stronger footing."

"And yet here we are."

"There were some other factors working against us, and things have gone less well in recent years. But there were two decades of relative stability. That's to be admired."

"So it was worth it," Garreth said. "You and Mother learned to love each other and build a family, just as Yrith and I will."

"I've never loved your mother."

It took Garreth a moment to understand what he'd heard. Father watched him as the words sank in, and nodded when they did.

"I think she may have had some affection or attraction to me at the beginning," he went on. "It didn't last, of course. We did what we needed to do. You're here. Your brother. The house was strong for a generation. We are respected. That's victory."

"I don't..." Garreth began. In the street, someone shouted. His father ignored them both.

"Appearance is one thing. The...I won't call it truth. The situation behind the appearance can be very different. To the city, Genna and I are respectably wed. House Left is a machine of commerce, unified and strong. If we were anything less, we would be targeted. Weakness is opportunity. Within this house, privately, Serria and I have been lovers for the past, what, eight years?"

Garreth stared at his father like he was seeing the man for the first time. The dark hair turning to grey at the temples. The silver-and-black stubble that showed his morning ritual had been interrupted. His eyes were mild and sympathetic.

"I didn't know."

"You didn't need to. Now, apparently, you do."

He sat in silence as his father finished his wine, corked the bottle, and put it back in its niche behind the books. He took Garreth's cup and drank what was in it as well, then put both together at the edge of the table for the servants to take away. Garreth put his head in his hands, fighting something like vertigo. His father put a hand on his shoulder and shook him gently. It could almost have been mistaken for comfort.

"You need your outlets. That's fine. But you have to think about appearances, my boy, or you will embarrass the house. And you aren't to embarrass the house, yes?"

"I won't."

"I appreciate that. I do."

The hand left his shoulder. The door closed. Garreth sat alone in the study, waiting for his world to right itself again. Everything in his history shifted. Mother's travel wasn't that she loved the pleasures of the road. Robbson's grating anger came from living with the constant grit of bearing witness to his sister's humiliation. The iron control that Serria maintained over the servants, bringing in new help and releasing the old without consulting anyone, was appropriate for the de facto lady of the house. His family wasn't what he'd thought it was, and he felt like a fool for not questioning it before now. The love between his parents was a show played to the world like actors on a Seepwater stage. He didn't know why that hurt as deeply as it did, except that he had been fooled along with the rest of the city.

He rose to his feet, one hand on the table to steady him. When he was sure of himself, he walked out, down the hall. He heard Vasch talking to someone in a room nearby, and he turned away. He prayed silently that Serria wouldn't be at the door, that he could get out of the house without seeing anyone. Whatever gods were watching him took mercy.

The street was bright. The midmorning sun had already banished the cool of night, but it couldn't quite hide the end of the season. By reflex, Garreth noticed what the carts carried and which way they went. Rope and jute heading south, toward the port. Sacks of grain—the leavings of the last season—going east to the Temple to fill the public silo and clear out the warehouses for the crops that would arrive with harvest. As surely as leaves losing their green, the shifting of trade marked the change of the year. The end of summer was coming. The end of many things.

A boy chased a dog that was running south along the street, looking over its shoulder to make sure its pursuer didn't fall too far behind. A flock of pigeons rose and swirled in the high air until by some invisible consensus it chose a new place to land. Garreth walked without knowing where he was walking to. Without caring. It hadn't been a day since he'd gone out to find Kannish and Maur. In all the time since he'd met the girl, fallen into bed with her, and suffered the consequences of it, there hadn't been a sunset. He'd barely slept. If he hadn't felt punch-drunk, it would have been strange.

He tried to imagine the girl, what she would look like in the late morning sunlight. What she would say. He remembered what it was like, walking with her through these same streets when they'd been alone in them. What her skin felt like against his. He wished now that he'd pressed for her name. He wanted to be back in those hours more than he'd ever wanted anything.

A low wooden bench stood against the wall of the chandlers' guild hall. A little brass plaque dedicated it to someone he didn't know. Merrin Alliat ran by, his leather satchel bouncing against his hip, but he didn't stop to talk. Garreth sat, watching people and dogs and carts and birds with an equal emptiness. He felt like he should weep, but he couldn't. He didn't notice his uncle until Robbson sat down beside him.

"They told me you'd gone out. I was checking the taprooms."

"I don't think beer is going to fix anything for me."

"Well, that's something like wisdom. Late descending, but better now than not." Robbson laced his fingers together on one knee, then shifted to the other, then put his hands at his sides. "I got her safely on a cart for Stonemarket. Larel Pannish had a load of ground flour that was due at a bakers' collective, though the gods only know why they're buying from this side of the river. Anyway, even if they drop the cargo first, she'll be in Stonemarket by midday. No one seemed to think she was out of place."

"Good," Garreth said. "Did she say anything?"

"She made a joke about the carter's boots. Otherwise, she kept quiet. Best thing she could have done."

"Yes."

Robbson went silent. They sat. Garreth had the sense that his uncle was waiting for something, but he couldn't find it in himself to begin. Two bluecloaks passed by laughing with each other and watching the passersby, but they weren't Kannish or Maur. The sunlight was warm.

"I heard your father talked with you," Uncle Robbson said.

"He did."

"He told you, then?"

Garreth didn't answer. He didn't need to. Robbson cursed under his breath. "She didn't want that. Your mother was always very clear that you and Vasch weren't to be bothered with it. He shouldn't have."

"Did you always know?"

"From the first. Your mother confided in me when things

started going sour in the marriage. And the solution he proposed."

"It was his decision, then?"

"It sure as hell wasn't what I picked. I wanted to drop him on a knife and call it an accident. But they came to an agreement. I think there's an actual contract they drew up between them. The fucker made her sign it," Robbson said, and then seemed to remember himself. "Are you . . . I mean, you must be upset."

"I'm not anything. Not right now."

"We should go back to the house."

"No. I'm not going to do that."

"This alliance with Yrith's people? It *has* to be made. It will save the house, and for Genna to eat all the shit she's eaten these last years and have it come to nothing would be more than I could stand."

"It was punishment, wasn't it?" Garreth said. "He told me as a punishment."

"You made him angry." Robbson leaned back on the bench and spread his arms across its back. When he spoke, he sounded tired. "Your father carries himself very gently, Garreth. But he's the cruelest man I ever knew."

"Theyden Adresqat, on the other hand, had a very different opinion about the nature of gods," Elaine's tutor said. He was a new face in the eternal stream of experts flowing through her days in the effort to improve her. This one was an older man with wiry hair that stood out from his head like a halo, and his name was Goro. "She reversed the locus of origin."

"The locus..."

"Of origin," he said.

The drawing room shutters were open to the garden. From where she sat, she could see the orange tomcat stalking through the stems where the flowers had dropped their petals. She wished she could be outside with him. But the morning was already halfway gone, and she had no spare time for play.

Elaine had expected the day after her outing with Theddan to be uncertain and had taken the precaution of postponing all her duties. Her full day, she'd thought, could be devoted to recovering from her debauch. In practice, it had been a wiser choice than she'd expected. But there weren't many opportunities to add things into her calendar, and so catching up meant that four days later, she was still meeting with tutors and court followers, priests and etiquette masters, family and friends and people who wanted to make sure that she knew them. For later. In case.

"The traditional view is of gods as... nature, yes?" her tutor said. "They existed before humanity was formed, and they will exist after the last of us has passed. And so the origin of the gods must be in the distant past when the world was created. Or perhaps even before it."

"That would make sense."

"Theyden's philosophy inverted that. The gods did not—*could* not—exist before people did. She argued that gods find their creation in humanity, and in the collective spirit people create. The thoughts you have create a kind of current in the world, and that current guides your thoughts. So when the Rites of Adrohin have him say 'whenever the chosen call me forth, I am,' it's a description of a literal truth. She used an Inlisc term for it—*egrygor*."

"So the gods are all real to the extent that the thoughts of their worshippers evoke them."

"Not necessarily worshippers," he said with a smile that seemed to appreciate a joke she didn't understand. "It could be a congregation or a business or a nation or a tribe. It could be something smaller. Whenever even just two people come together, a third spirit is there. And the power of that identity—not any one person's, but the more they become when they become something more—gives the gods form and voice and influence in the world. Gods are thoughts given form, and form creating the rites, rituals, powers, and miracles that guide our thoughts. Aspects not of ourselves as individuals, but the guardians and guiding spirits of the groups that we create."

He made a circle with the forefingers of each hand.

"That can't have gone over well," Elaine said.

Her tutor's face fell. "She did die in exile, yes."

When Elaine had returned on foot from Stonemarket, wearing clothes borrowed from a Riverport servant, it had been almost midday before she crossed into Green Hill. The exhaustion of a near-sleepless night, of joy and embarrassment and the strange lifting defiance of transgression, left her nearly trembling. The closest of her rooms was in House Abbasann, but that seemed like a dangerous place to be seen, at least until she knew what had become of Theddan. Instead, she made her way to the Clovas Brotherhood and her cell there. She changed into her own clothes, and had a servant girl take away the ones she shed. No one had said anything to her about it, and if they spoke of it, they spoke of it in private. There was, Elaine thought, a great deal to be said for failing to see things that would bring trouble.

She'd tried to sleep, but as the day had stretched on, warm and bright, something in her defied rest. Whenever her mind began to wander, it wandered toward what she'd just done. Garreth, his name was. Instead of dreaming, she remembered. His uncertainty, his hesitance, and how he had shed them. The shape of his face, the hunger in him, and in her. And the satiety. And then she would find that her eyes were open, her mouth in a broad grin, and slumber escaped again through the little window.

In the days since, she had resolved to put it out of her mind. There had been a night, an indiscretion, and now there was her whole life ahead of her. Serious, meaningful, heavy, and dour. She'd dedicated herself to forgetting a thousand times, and then a minute later imagined running into Garreth at some function of the city. Of seeing his face in a crowd. Sometimes, she imagined his shock in knowing who and what she was and delighted in his surprise. Sometimes, it left her melancholy. She wondered if he was haunted by the same carnal memories and imaginings that interrupted her. She wondered if she wanted him to be.

It was childish of her.

It was also true, and she wasn't sure what to do about that. The one she wanted most to talk to was Theddan, and her cousin, the servants told her, had taken a fever and was too ill for visitors. It was a lie that could have covered anything. Elaine had sent a runner to the magistrates and the gaol, but there were no signs of Theddan. However her arrest was being handled, it was discreet.

"I'll leave this for you," her tutor said, and set a book down on the table. The cover was red leather. It was heavier than she expected it to be, and the pages were thin and soft as cloth. *On the Nature of Gods*. She worked her face into an expression of gratitude. She wasn't sure she managed it convincingly.

"We'll discuss the first section in our next meeting," he said. "Assuming that your duties allow it."

"I look forward to it," she said. That was a lie, but by saying it, she committed herself. To reading the book, to talking about the book, to engaging with the tutor and the process of her own education. There was nothing that tied her to learn more effectively than being reminded that she didn't have to. The court had any number of men and women of the highest station who chose to be ignorant out of sloth. Elaine didn't like to think she held anyone in contempt, but the truth was that she did. Nor was it her only vice, apparently.

For a moment, Garreth was there with her, his hand on the back of her neck. His breath in her ear.

"I will set aside time next week?" she said.

"That will be fine. Thank you," the tutor said, bowing himself out. She waited until he'd gone, then flipped the book open to a random page.

*If the gods are mutable, then stability itself becomes the metric by which they are judged successful. Kindness, justice, nobility, wisdom—all are secondary to brute endurance. That god which slices off the will to change remains, and that which chooses some other virtue—*any *other virtue—that might compete with this simultaneously dooms itself. Thus it follows that a god which survives unchanged is in its essence amoral, bestial, and cruel. And what we say of gods, we also say of guilds, brotherhoods, nations, and men: that which is eternal tends inevitably toward evil.*

"Well, I can see why you went into exile," she said as she flipped through the pages, finding the first section and where it ended. Seeing how much she'd doomed herself to. It wasn't as bad as it could have been.

She ate a small plate of fried trout and fresh apple, then put the red book in her rooms, had the girl help her change into a fresh gown with sensible shoes, and started out for the compound of House Abbasann again. She walked with her head high and her step certain. She could have taken a carriage, but she wanted to be seen on her errand. Every day she made an appearance and was turned away made the next refusal harder.

And in fact, this was the day. A door servant escorted her to one of the northern drawing rooms in the main building. That was a little odd. Elaine was a member of the family, and being treated as if she were a guest in the house, while not a slight, was a curiosity. Theddan was dressed in a gown of yellow linen, her hair tied back. Apart from looking a little tired around the eyes, there was nothing to hint at what had happened between the cobblestones of Riverport and now. She rose as Elaine came in. The servant retreated, closing the doors behind himself.

Theddan swept forward, wrapped arms around Elaine, and lifted her off the ground. "I thought you were dead! I thought I'd watched the future prince of Kithamar throw herself into the river to die! Don't ever do that to me again!"

"Sorry," Elaine gasped. Then, as her cousin put her back down, "It wasn't as good an idea as I thought it was. Even if it did work out."

"You were lucky. Or the gods were watching out for you. Or you were lucky the gods were watching out for you. People die in the river all the time."

"They swim in it too."

"Not that stretch of it."

"I know that now," Elaine said with a shrug. She sat, and Theddan with her. "I'm sorry I left you. I didn't want to."

"It was the only thing to do," Theddan said, waving the comment away. "You couldn't have done anything to get me out of that. It was my fault. Years of dangerous living finally coming due. But you have to tell me what happened! Where did you go, and how did you get back home?"

Elaine felt something release in her like she'd been holding her breath for days and only now had the chance to exhale. Everything spilled out of her. Hiding behind the wall, the night walk, sneaking into Garreth's home, the plans to get home, being discovered. The whole of it came like she'd rehearsed it, like it was Theddan telling one of her own stories, except this time it was hers.

Her cousin drank in the details with growing delight and clapped her hands together like a child at a puppet show when Elaine was done. "And then what?"

"And then nothing," Elaine said. "I came back, rested as well as I could, and started back to my life."

"You're lucky they didn't recognize you."

"Why would they? It's not as if we spend our evenings in company. And if they saw me at some formal event, I wouldn't look like a girl who'd half drowned herself in a river."

"Washing off the paint does change the shape of your eyes,"

Theddan said, then leaned forward and took Elaine's hand. Her voice was a whisper. "Are you pregnant?"

"No," Elaine said. "I mean, I don't think so. The timing isn't right."

"That doesn't mean anything," Theddan said. "My mother said she only ever took Father to bed the day before her blood came, and there's still six of us."

"Maybe she took someone else to bed the other times," Elaine said.

Theddan's laughter was delighted. "You are in a mood, aren't you? Look how bold."

Elaine felt a little blush rising in her throat.

"What else do you know about him?" Theddan asked. "You can't tell me that you didn't look into him."

"There's nothing that can come of it. We had a pleasant moment, and it's gone now."

"That's not an answer."

"I may have made a few minor inquiries. Just to assure myself that nothing of it could come back to haunt me."

"And?"

"He's the eldest son of a merchant family. House Left."

"Your bastard child will be better off than a wool seller's son. That's good."

"His family trades in sugar, alum, and spices. His father is Mannon, his mother is Genna. Her brother Robbson is part of the household. And there's a younger son who's either named Vask or Vasch. The record was smudged."

"You're thinking about him."

"It's strange. It's like when I was really young, and just losing my milk teeth? Do you remember what that was like? How it hurt, but it was fascinating too? I look back at it, and it's not exactly that I want it back, and it's not exactly that I don't. I just think about it, and everything else is a little—" She waved her hands, trying to find the words she didn't have.

"He hasn't taken your heart, has he? You can't just have the first boy you fall in bed with take your heart. You have to sample about first. Otherwise it isn't fair."

Elaine ignored the teasing. "It's not that. I didn't think it would change anything. And it hasn't, not really. But there's something about going through a day's meetings and tutors and garden parties and private audiences that... it doesn't weigh as heavy when I can just pause and remember it all. I'm reading about the nature of gods, and I'm thinking about his bed."

"Memory is a beautiful thing," Theddan said. "And they can't make you give it back, can they?"

Elaine frowned. Theddan's smile went stiff. It was only a little change. Barely there. The hair at the back of Elaine's neck rose.

"What is it?"

Theddan shook her head and leaned back on her divan. "Nothing I shouldn't have expected. It's fine, Elly."

"What happened with you?"

Theddan shrugged. "I was escorted to the private hall of the magistrates. I was entertained overnight by some cunning young guardsmen who kindly sent word to my father, and a carriage was sent to take me home."

"Was he very angry, then?"

"I am being noviced to the Temple," Theddan said.

The air went thin. Theddan's smile looked sadder now. Maybe it had been since Elaine arrived, and she only hadn't seen it until now. "Noviced?"

"I leave in three days to meet my new master. His name is Himenet, and I hear he's a very intelligent, patient, pious man who has a good career taking... unruly young men and women and showing them a better path. So, that's my life. No marriage.

No titles. No presence at court. No children of my own. I'm for the Temple."

"Your mother accepted this?"

"Her offer was a wallet with fifty silver and an invitation to the street. Father at least wants to see I have food and shelter. It's all right. I was warned and given chances and begged, and I am still what I am. I can't say I didn't know it could come to this."

"It should have been me," Elaine said. "They couldn't send me off to the Temple. I should have taken your place."

"I'm not as strong a swimmer. They'd be fishing my body up onto the Silt by now. Don't carry it. It's mine."

For a moment, Elaine saw her imagined mother, eyebrows raised in approval of Theddan's fate. She pushed the thought away. "I'll talk to my father. He's on good terms with House Abbasann now. He might be able to talk your father back to reason."

Theddan's kiss was quick and unexpected. It took Elaine a moment to recognize it had even happened.

"You're good to me, Elly. Better than I deserve."

A sudden pounding at the door startled them both. Elaine stood as the door opened. She recognized the guard as one of her own. He wore her father's colors.

"Ma'am," he said with a bow, then turned a second bow to Theddan without addressing her. Elaine felt a tightness in her gut like the start of an illness. "Your father sends for you."

"Where is he?"

"At your home, ma'am. The young Lord Karsen's with him. They ask you to join them. At once."

"Why?" Theddan asked.

The guard hesitated. "It's Prince Ausai. He's died."

PART TWO

HARVEST

Whenever two people come together in passion—the passion of love, the passion of lust, the passion of hatred—something is born of the union. Sometimes it is a child, sometimes it is a spirit, but there is always something.

—From the private journal of Ulris Kaon,
court historian of Daos a Sal

In ancient days, before Kithamar was what it became, the palace hadn't been a palace. The Hansch fort had been placed on the top of the massive stone outcropping because it was the highest place that would support it. That the palace looked down over the city like a magistrate over their court might seem like grandness, but it had been born in fear and violence. The first Hansch ground had been chosen as the most defensible against the Inlisc raiders whose descendants scraped for food and warmth in Longhill. The long switchback trails of Oldgate had driven back attackers with stone and pitch. The gentler western slope had walls and the canal to frustrate attack. Because the fort was secure it became the center of power. Because it was the center of power, it became the palace, the grit at the center of Kithamar's dark pearl.

According to the histories, generations of princes had lived there, died there, and been succeeded by their children or nieces and nephews and brothers and sisters, each with a remarkable reverence for the old, the familiar, the palace as it had always been. According to the occultists, priests, and cunning men, the stability was a strange and ominous sign, like the prick of a rose thorn that never stopped bleeding. According to Lemel Tarrit, it was a dim place but a safe job, and he wasn't looking for more than that.

The kitchens were Lemel's kingdom within a kingdom. The broad slate tables had been made to hold the butchered flesh that fed a cohort of warriors, but they worked just as well for a gaggle of courtiers. The ovens were wide and hot enough to bake waybread for five hundred war-weary men, but they were fine for cakes. The ice house set deep in the granite flesh of the hill had protected the bodies of the dead from rot while priests were found to protect their souls or else harvest them, but it kept peaches and apples fresh from harvest to Tenthday too.

If the bleak shadows of history haunted the palace, Lemel wasn't the man to notice them. He was concerned with more immediate and mundane hungers: his little army of chefs and prentices, bakers, butchers, sauce men, stewards, and the boys with the buckets of lye water who kept the floors clean. And today, with the old prince put to the pyre and the new one parading the city, his focus was on a hollow wax ox.

One of the kitchen prentices stood beside the wax shell with a look of distress. Her hands were pink and raw and covered with the coarse hair that only half covered the false bull ox's flank.

Lemel raised a palm to her. "No, I see the problem," he said. "Here, give me some of those whiskers."

She knelt below the table, scraped around for a moment, and came out with a simple wooden box filled with ox hair. The bristles shimmered in the lamp light. There were no windows in the kitchens and never had been. Lemel shook the box gently, letting the motion align the bristles, then took a pinch between his thumb and forefinger and rolled them into the wax flesh.

"You're pushing them in like they're real, yes?" he said. "But you don't need that. We're making an illusion here. The trick is to keep them sparse enough that there's space for new ones in between. The thing you don't want is a strong line where all the whiskers end at once. It's difficult to make something look random that isn't. That's where the art comes in."

The prentice came in close to watch. She was new, the daughter of one of the groomsmen in the palace stables who Lemel had known for years. She was very pretty and very young, and when she leaned close to him, he found himself prone to distraction.

"You try," he said, handing back the box and stepping away from her. The prentice turned toward the wax, pinched the bristles as he had, and rolled them against the false flesh with her thumb. She made a small sound of satisfaction.

"That's much better," she said.

"There's a different technique we'll use when we seal the seam, but that's not until tonight," he said. "And we don't need a full coat. The poor beast's supposed to have been slow-cooked down to the skin before he goes in there. Just enough to look authentic. A little texture. That's all we need."

The wax ox was always a favorite for the end of a great feast or celebration. Lemel scheduled it after a run of heavy dishes—beefs, venisons, duck in cream. The court would be thick and slow and ready for something light and brighter. And instead, he would bring in what appeared to be a whole roast ox on a frame. A wave of understated dismay ran through anyone who hadn't seen the trick before, and a wave of anticipation through the ones who had. Once the ox had been strung up where everyone could see it, whoever among the kitchen staff was the biggest and strongest-looking—Lemel chose who—strode in with a great axe and cracked the beast in two. Whatever light, pleasant palate cleanser they'd filled the wax hollow with spilled out. Fresh fruit or wrapped tarts or, once, brightly colored stone orbs that turned to bowls of sorbet. Something colorful that wouldn't be spoiled by hitting the ancient stone of the feast hall. Lemel always waited a few years after doing his little trick before he tried it again, and sometimes he'd roast an ox and serve it off the same frame just to keep the court on its toes.

Being the chief cook of the prince of Kithamar meant playing a very long game.

"My lord approaches." It was Jerrit, the bread baker's son and prentice, but it could have been anyone in the kitchens. There were rules about visits from the prince. Lemel had heard from a hunter about a kind of bird that would set sentries out around the flock and if any of them sang out, the whole flock would alert. Kitchens were much the same. Lemel turned away from the wax ox and the girl tending it and strode fast down the long tables, moving half a dozen other cooks and prentices aside as he went. His eyes danced across every surface and sack. There were things that happened in a kitchen it was just as well that no one on the dais ever saw. He was more than half sure of himself when Samal Kint stepped in with the new prince at his side.

Everyone in the kitchens went to their knee and bowed their heads except the prince and his guard.

Lemel had known Kint for the better part of a decade now. He was a grey-faced stone of a man who never ate or drank or laughed to excess. Lemel respected him as one master of his craft to another, but they'd never been close. Kint wore the red cloak of the palace guard with a golden badge of office at his belt and a sword with a single ruby on its leather pommel that reminded Lemel of a cherry preserved in brandy.

The new prince clapped his hands together. "Please stand. Go about your business. I am not here to interrupt."

Almost reluctantly, the kitchen staff rose. Prince Ausai had come to the kitchens only rarely, but when he had, the staff had stayed motionless with their eyes on the stone while he'd had his conversations, and hadn't stood again until he was gone. They'd burned a few chickens that way, but it was etiquette. The idea of working in front of the prince of the city seemed vaguely blasphemous. But not doing as he'd said was worse. Lemel motioned, and the kitchen lurched back to life.

He'd seen Byrn a Sal before, of course. Lemel fed everyone in Green Hill at least four times a year. Byrn was very nearly the last of the a Sal house apart from his daughter and a splinter of distant cousins who no longer lived in the city. He didn't like soft cheeses, and liked his wine dry but with body deep enough that other people found it blunt. He wore the crown now. The first time, and for the rest of his life. It didn't look bad on him, but seeing it over any face but old Ausai's seemed odd.

"Lord Prince," Lemel said. "My condolences on the passing of your uncle."

"Yes," Byrn said. "We lost him too soon."

Lemel couldn't decide if this new prince looked old or young. He was younger than Ausai, of course. And a very different nose. Ausai had a long, aquiline nose. It had given him a sense of gravitas. Byrn was too pretty for that. But he had a little white in his beard that Lemel didn't remember.

"The tasters are mine," Kint said, continuing, it seemed, some conversation. "Master Lemel permits them at every stage of the cooking. Nothing will come to your table without half a dozen men having made certain there is no poison."

"That's good," Byrn said with a nod that suggested to Lemel that he hadn't considered the likelihood of poison before now. "I appreciate your efforts on this. And yours, Master Lemel."

"My lord," Lemel said, sinking into a brief but abject bow. "Any desire of yours the kitchens can accommodate. I am very proud of my people, and I assure you that you shall be as well."

"Yes, thank you," the new prince said. "You're doing the ox trick tonight?"

Lemel followed the prince's gaze back to where the prentice was furiously rolling bristles into the wax. He felt a little pinch of annoyance that the prince had lost the surprise of it, but he put on a good face. "Indeed, my lord."

"That's good. I love that one. I remember hearing once that Beyard Reyos had that done with a likeness of his first wife's lover instead of a bull. But I don't suppose that's really true, is it?"

Lemel smiled and tried to divine whether the question had been rhetorical.

"If you'll come this way, my lord," Kint said, gesturing toward the door to the yard. "The stables next, as you like."

"Yes, thank you. Good."

The two men left into the light of the late afternoon. Lemel had, like any of the masters of the palace, been briefed as to the prince's schedule. After the coronation, he'd spent the day riding through the city, then a small lunch of a hearty leek soup with fresh bread and cheese. Now, the tour of the palace and grounds with Kint. Once that was done, they'd dress him for the feast. Fourteen courses with the greatest names of all the houses, the highest of the highest of Kithamar ready to welcome a new age, with the understanding and expectation that it would be much like the old age.

Except Lemel didn't turn back to his work as quickly as he'd expected himself to. Something about this new, younger a Sal itched. Lemel had only ever worked under Ausai a Sal, but he'd heard stories about Prince Airis before him, and Daos a Sal before that. The princes of Kithamar were cold, distant men and women. They had a lordliness. Ausai had been capable of a kind of contempt that didn't need words to carry it. Byrn a Sal seemed very different.

But perhaps it was only that it was his coronation day. It took everyone time to ease into a new role. That was likely as true for princes as it was for scullery maids.

"That was him, then?"

Lemel turned. Walson, the head dessert baker, was at his side, scratching idly at the birthmark that purpled his neck and cheek.

"The new prince," Lemel said. "Long may he reign."

"I heard he's Clovas Brotherhood."

"I think that's so."

"That means we'll be seeing less of that scarred-up fucker from Daris, then. Always coming through on errands for the prince and that priest of theirs."

"I like Tregarro. You don't because he's foreign and he didn't appreciate your hardcakes."

"They were fucking good hardcakes."

Lemel clapped the baker on the shoulder. "Well, you're in luck. Unless Prince Byrn a Sal has a sudden change of religious alliance, you'll be seeing some officious fuck from Clovas Brotherhood instead."

The baker laughed. Lemel was about to turn back to the wax ox—they were running out of time to get it ready for the feast, and there was still all the tricky seam work to go—but the baker's voice pulled him up short. "Does it worry you?"

"What?"

"That one had his own house. His own servants. His own chefs. If he picks it, we could all be looking for jobs."

"Never happen," Lemel said. "The new prince always keeps on the old servants and staff. Maybe a little shifting around of the topmost counselors, but the machinery of the palace? They always keep that in place. It's just the force of tradition."

If they had been able to hear him, the historians would likely have agreed. The occultists, priests, and cunning men might have thought it was something else.

It was the last time Elaine would ever be in the home she'd grown up in. Even if she did return to the buildings and gardens and fountains, they wouldn't be the last echoes of House a Sal. It would be a second compound of the teeming horde that House Abbasann had grown into. Generations of marriages and babies and nurseries and tutors had filled her mother's family until their cup ran over, and the overspill was washing away the living spaces that Elaine had called her own. But they hadn't been.

The bedroom that opened on the gardens. The drawing room with the wooden shutters carved into the shape of two dragons that interlocked when she shut them. The private altar with the statues of Lord Kauth and Lady Er that neither she nor her father ever spent time in. All of them had belonged to Kithamar itself, and she had been permitted use of them for a time, and that time was over.

"Elaine," Dimnia said, hurrying toward her across the wide central atrium of the north wing. "I didn't know you were here. They should have told me."

Jorreg Abbasann's wife had been a Chaalat before marriage let her switch houses. She had a hint of the paleness that sometimes appeared in that family, but it wasn't as profound as that of Durran or Andomaka Chaalat. Her smile was anxious, and following behind her on fat, small legs, a child hardly old enough to walk was running, his wide, wisp-haired head bobbling as he went.

"I asked them not to bother you," Elaine said as first mother and then child caught up to her. "I'm just making one last look through the rooms I used. In case anything was overlooked."

"Of course, of course," Dimnia said, hoisting the child to her hip.

"Don't you have a nurse for that?" Elaine asked, teasing but also serious.

"Nurses are overrated," Dimnia said. "That's not true. Nurses are a godsend, but I do like my time. Especially when they're small."

They walked together through hallways Elaine knew, and that now were decorated with paintings and sculpture she'd never seen. Dimnia had instructed the servants to put yellow ribbon at the edges of all the shutters, and even that small a change altered the nature of the space more than Elaine would have expected.

"You and your father have been so kind to us," Dimnia said. "I can't tell you how welcome it's been to finally have a house we can call our own." Then she grimaced, there and gone fast as a blink, out of fear she'd said the wrong thing.

"It's all right," Elaine said as they turned down the corridor toward her old bedroom. "I'll tell you the truth. I thought I was going to be angry. Leaving this place? I thought I'd feel like I was losing my home."

"You don't, then?"

"I don't," Elaine lied. The truth was that she did feel very much like she was losing her home. The surprise was that she didn't mind. Some part of her, all unexpected, had become ready to.

Her bed was gone and two smaller ones were in its place. The doors to the garden were thrown open and a breeze blew through them, heavy with the smell of late summer flowers and bright with just a hint of autumn's cool. The shelves were decorated with small wooden models of machines—pumps, catapults, a cunning wooden device that made a pale wooden puppet seem to walk. A glimmer of red behind the catapult caught her eye, and she plucked out the book. *On the Nature of Gods.*

"This is what I was looking for."

"Well, good we found it before Little Jerr took it apart to see how it was made. He's a terror that way."

Out in the garden, a boy of perhaps twelve years was drawing a peacock feather through the air. The orange tomcat was bent, ready to spring, following the end of the feather with the focus of a hunter.

"Your father had to move. He had no choice," Dimnia said. "You did. This could have been your house. I want you to know I see your generosity."

Elaine shook her head. "I was ready for something new. Hungry for it, even. I just didn't know that until it came."

For a moment, she imagined her mother standing with them. Not the real woman, but the construction she'd made. For once, the ghost didn't seem angry or disdainful, but considering. That was odd too.

The funeral of Ausai a Sal was almost a week gone. It had been a terrible day, marching the old man's corpse through the streets for all of Kithamar to witness his death. Her father had walked the whole path, from Palace Hill to the Temple. Elaine had witnessed the first part of the march, but as the procession moved through Stonemarket and the Smoke, she'd made her way down through Oldgate and across one of the four bridges there. There were several paths that could have taken her to the Temple, and the one she chose brushed past Riverport like knuckles grazing someone she was walking beside. She didn't see any faces there she knew, and was something between relieved and disappointed.

At the pyre, the final rites had been observed. Andomaka Chaalat, as high priest of the Daris Brotherhood, had made her pale and shaken way through the rituals, taking the name Ausai had carried in life and giving him a deathmark that would be his name in the mystery that came after it. She'd looked devastated—her already pale skin bone-grey with exhaustion and grief, her eyes bloodshot from weeping or sleeplessness. Elaine wondered how close she had been with the former prince.

Byrn a Sal had lit that final fire, and Ausai a Sal, Elaine's great-uncle and the only ruler she had ever known, began his long passage to ashes and memory. Elaine had kept a solemn face, but the truth was she spent half the ceremony scanning the crowd for Theddan.

Her father spent the night at the Temple in rituals of cleansing, which he described later as sitting in a hot bath while old men chanted at him and sleeping when he was supposed to be meditating. She had gone back to her rooms in her grandmother's house. Her cell at the Clovas Brotherhood seemed too austere for the moment, but the vastness of her father's soon-to-be gifted-away home with only her in it was intimidating. Instead, she chose the bustle and flurry and fullness of House Abbasann, even if Theddan wasn't there to make it feel quite complete.

She'd slept poorly, though. Her dreams had an odd quality

about them, vivid and unsettling and—she couldn't find a better term—somehow slick or oily. She'd been glad to wake up.

They'd left before the sun quite rose, tracking back to the Temple to stand witness as her father took the crown. The temple grounds were thick with bodies pressed shoulder to shoulder, all pushing to watch the moment as it happened. She'd been close enough to see the flicker of uncertainty as he rose to his feet as the prince of Kithamar for the first time. She remembered a little thrill of fear, then. She remembered wondering if her father had taken on more than he could do. Not that there was any choice. Fate, history, and the accidents of birth—or, phrased differently, the will of the gods—had given Byrn a Sal the city, and he had no power to refuse.

The rest of the day had been the joyous mirror image of the funeral's bleak passage. The streets, filled with merriment and revelry. Her father had spent a fair part of the day seeing the people over whom he now had the power of life and death, and being cheered by them as he passed.

He'd become something more than himself. Or been lost in a larger story than the man was. The Byrn a Sal who played flute sometimes, and badly, when he thought no one was there to hear it. The Byrn a Sal who still sometimes fumbled, starting to call her by her mother's name. The one who coughed and swore in the morning. That man had been swallowed by the princedom of Kithamar. Elaine scandalized herself a bit, wondering whether he'd ever spent an evening with some woman who didn't know his name, and hoping that somehow he had.

The palace gardens looked like practice fields with a few flowers and shrubs pasted on them, because that was what they were. Elaine walked among the flowers, the midday sun on her cheeks and the misplaced book back in her hand, and marveled that she found herself largely content. An older man in a gardener's leathers trundled quietly behind her, pouring water out of a tin bucket onto the lush end-of-summer bushes.

It had taken her all of her first day there to understand what made the palace grounds feel so strange and isolated. She knew that she was at the center of the city, as much the heart of Kithamar as she could ever be, and yet the air itself seemed different here, the sunlight like it fell from some other sky. She felt unmoored. And it was because all through her life, no matter where she was in Kithamar, from the Temple to the Smoke to Riverport, the looming presence of Palace Hill had oriented her. By its size and silhouette, it told her where in the city she was, which was the same as knowing her place in the world.

Palace Hill had vanished now. With it beneath her feet, she was never in its shadow, never saw its bulk, and so she had to find new ways to know north from east from south. She hadn't anticipated that, and the surprise was a gift.

She passed from the gardens into the low, thick-walled corridors that ate sound and radiated silence. Since she'd come here to live in the palace, she'd found herself spending a part of each day walking through the halls and corridors, going through rooms that sometimes seemed not to have been used in years, and following the thin stairs up to the old storerooms where the ancient Hansch warriors had kept the weapons and medicines and salt-packed meat that would protect them in wars that had been won and lost before the city was a city. And because of it, she could already find her way from the garden to her father's royal apartments by cutting through the thin alley-like path between the stables and the servants' rooms instead of going out to the main halls and back in. She felt a little smug about that.

The prince's apartments had been carved out of a much older

building. As high as his entry hall was, there was a clear line in the stone to show where a much lower ceiling had once been. As broad as the rooms were, the floor still had the patterns of old walls that had been removed to make it. Its divans were silk, its tapestries were bright, the fire grate looked like it could hold half a tree and keep the place sweltering through the worst winter night, but its grandness was the grandness of scars and history.

Three people were in the hall when Elaine passed by the red-cloaked guards at the entrance. One was Samal Kint, head of the palace guard. Another was an older woman with close-cut grey hair and an expression of permanent curiosity. Mikah Ell, the court historian. And the last, of course, was her father.

"I find no record, my lord," Mikah Ell said. "And to be honest, I don't recall coming across any mention of it in my readings. I've read a lot. The court is my life."

"There has to be something," her father said. "Please keep looking."

The historian bowed and retreated like it was a dance she'd learned young and practiced often. Elaine caught her father's eye and lifted her eyebrows in question.

"Uncle's private study," her father said. "My private study now. But I can't get into it."

"Can't find the key?" Elaine asked.

"Can't find the lock. Just a wide iron door with a thousand decorative carvings that might hide a switch, except none of them do. I've been trying to get in for two days."

"Should we hold off, my lord?" Kint asked. "Or would you like the masons to proceed?"

"Tell Halev there's no point waiting. He can have them start."

Kint nodded, turned, and walked off like he was going to make someone's day very unpleasant and he was pleased to do it. Elaine watched him until he passed through an archway and vanished from sight.

"He's an odd one, isn't he?" she said.

"I think he and my uncle were close. I mean as close as anyone was with Uncle. He was an odd one too. My mother said that taking the throne changes you. I don't know if that's true, but from everything I heard, it seems that it was for him."

Her father turned slowly, gesturing at the hall and meaning the palace. "I feel like I'm living in his corpse. All of this was his, and now it's supposed to be mine. But I don't feel it. Do you want something? They've put some food in one of the drawing rooms."

"I could," she said, and he smiled and offered her his arm. She linked elbows with him, and they walked together up a flight of granite stairs, down a short, soot-stained corridor, and to a surprisingly small drawing room with one window that looked to the south. There was a table of light wood with a silver platter on it with grapes and cheese. He sat in one of the chairs and tore a corner off the cheese. She sat across from him. Somewhere in the distance, a hammer fell on stone.

"Are you tunneling through the wall?" she asked, plucking a grape from the bunch.

"The wall is softer than that fucking door," he said. "Halev and I spent all this time preparing for the transition. I have a list. Things I meant to do the first day I took the crown. And instead, I've spent the better part of a week confounded by a doorway."

Then he laughed, and she laughed with him. When she bit down on the grape, it was tart and sweet and perfectly ripe.

Her father nodded. "I know. I was expecting them to be a little underripe too. But harvest festival's coming sooner than it seems. Something about Uncle's dying made me think time would stop. Slow down, anyway. Give us some breathing room. But it turns out a day's a day whether there's a coronation or not."

"Are you all right?"

"I'm fine. I'm frustrated. I'm overwhelmed. What else could I be? I'm fucking prince of Kithamar." He ripped off another bit of cheese. "I'll be fine. I just need to get my legs under me. I wish your mother were here. She had a better head for this kind of thing."

"You still miss her?"

"Some days, yes. It's not as bad as when she left, but... I loved her. She was..."

"I know," Elaine said, to excuse the fact that she didn't. Couldn't. "Can I ask? What was it like when you and she started? I know all the stories about the wedding and when she went, but before that."

"Courting?"

"Did you court her?"

"Old scandal? Really?"

Elaine plucked two more grapes and handed one to her father. "Scandal, was it? You have to tell me now."

"She was spoken for when we started. Set to marry Raddeth a Jimental. And then we were at a celebration together—"

"A celebration? Just any celebration?"

"We were at the first thaw celebration at Daos Adresqat's. Halev was there too. Your mother arrived late with her cousin... Marget. Marget Foss. She was wearing green, and the fashion that year was yellow. She didn't care. She knew what she looked good in. I knew her, of course. Everyone knows everyone. But she hadn't... there hadn't been anything between us. We were going to the back garden to look at a kite Daos had made, and your mother slipped. And I caught her hand. And..."

"And?"

"And there are some things that fathers don't share with their daughters. There was a great deal of outrage and hurt feelings. At one point, I had to fight Raddeth to address his bruised honor, but thankfully we used blunted swords—"

"But with her. What was it like with her?"

His face softened, like a year of worry being forgotten in a moment. "I would tell you that, if I could. Your mother was amazing, and I know that because I was amazed," he said. "Is that what's happened?"

"What?"

"With you."

"I don't know what you mean," Elaine said, but there was a taste of panic in her mouth.

"We've upended your whole life. Our home. Your friend who was noviced. All this. You don't brood. You don't pout. And I love you, daughter, more than I love anyone living, but you can brood a horse to death. Is it like that? Is there somebody that's..."

"No," Elaine said. "Of course not."

"Why 'of course'? You're human. You're alive. What your mother and I felt didn't stop after we felt it, any more than we invented it for the first time. It's natural. It's normal." He waved his hand. "It's inevitable, maybe. You tell me."

For a moment, she saw Garreth in his room, his body silhouetted against the moonlight from the window. "There's no one," she said through a smile.

"Can I ask who?"

"Who no one is?" she said, and pelted him with a grape.

"Well, who *your* no one is. Don't be ashamed of it. It's the joy of life. It's the part that makes all the rest worth doing. It's a dark world sometimes, and the sparks are precious. And I like it when you're happy."

"Don't be melancholy with me."

"Was I?"

"You were about to."

"I was. You're right. So who?"

Elaine looked out the window. Looking south, the Smoke would have spilled out below them with the black, polluted snake that the canal became as it passed the forges. Beyond that, the city wall, and the forests beyond. Where she sat, she could only see the sky.

"There are things," she said, "that daughters don't share with their fathers."

Byrn a Sal clapped his hands and laughed. "Good, good, good. Turn it against me. I deserved that."

Elaine hung her head to hide her blush, and a soft knocking came at the door. Halev Karsen peeked in. His hair was greyed by stone dust. "I'm very sorry to have missed the joke," he said, "but, Byrn?"

Her father nodded, gathered himself, and rose. "Well, if I can't march in through the doorway, I'll sneak through the walls like a rat. Tell them the rat prince will be there in a moment."

"I will not," Karsen said, and left again.

"Well," her father said. "I suppose I'm off. Hopefully we can open the fucking door from the inside, and I won't have to make them just build a new one."

"It could be a new tradition," Elaine said. "Every new prince pokes a hole in the wall."

"A building entirely made from doorways. It's a good thought. I'll sit with it." He stepped toward the door, then paused, about to speak.

"Not melancholy," Elaine said.

"Not melancholy," he agreed. "But serious, for a moment, yes? If you can be happy, do. They won't give it to you. Even if it hurts sometimes, and it will. It does. It's worth it. And I do like it when you're happy."

She woke sometime in the night. Her rooms in the palace were smaller even than the cell at the Clovas Brotherhood. She thought for a moment that the shape at her bedside was her night servant, but the servant's bed was in a separate closet here, and that door was closed. The only light was the glimmer that spilled in from the doorway to the corridor. She sat up, and the shape started back.

"I'm sorry," her father said. "I'm so sorry. I didn't mean to wake you."

"What's wrong?"

"Nothing, nothing," he said, but his voice was tight and high. He sat at the foot of her bed. Sleep and dreams receded, and she saw him more clearly. Even in the dim light, he looked pale. There was a tightness in his mouth she hadn't seen before.

"When you were just born?" he said. "After your mother died? I used to wake up in the middle of the night, certain that you'd stopped breathing. Sure of it. I'd lie in bed and try to decide whether I should go see the worst just then, or wait until morning for my life to fall apart again. I could never wait. I always had to go check. It got to where the night nurse kept a cup of wine for me, I went so often. And you were perfect. You were always well." He looked around the gloom. "Old habits, I guess."

"Was there something in the study? Did you find something there?"

"You don't need to worry about that," he said. "I'll take care of it."

"Take care of what?"

He stood, one hand on his belly like he was checking to see his wallet was still there. He nodded in her direction, but not at her. "Don't worry. I'm sorry I woke you. Everything will be fine."

The way he spoke made her think that it wouldn't.

Garreth woke up grinding his teeth. His jaws were tight up to his temples. The sound of servants talking in the corridor seemed louder than it should have, but that was likely just the headache. Sunlight pressed in at the cracks in the shutters, and he closed his eyes against it, willing himself back down to sleep for just a few minutes more.

The effort was wasted.

After a few more minutes of wishing, he got up, took the night pot from under the bed, and pissed until there was nothing left in him. Outside his door, a bowl of fresh water and a cloth had been set out. He brought them in, put them on the desk, and cleaned himself for the day like he was washing a corpse.

When he went to find a shirt, he paused at the old favorite. The one she'd worn, however briefly. He shoved it into the back of the drawer and picked out a more recent one that meant less.

In the corridor, Serria was sweeping with a wide broom while a boy hung fresh rosemary from hooks in the walls. Vasch's door was open, his brother already gone downstairs to breakfast. Garreth looked at his father's lover, the woman he kept in the house whether Mother was present or away. It was like looking at a fire. She glanced back and smiled. It was probably the same expression she'd always had. It was the change in him that made her seem smug. Or maybe she'd always been smug, and he'd never known to notice it.

"Is all well?" she asked.

"Perfect," he said. "It's a glorious day."

At the table, Father, Uncle Robbson, and Vasch were eating fresh bread with oil and salt, berries in tin bowls, and coffee. Every inch of the table that wasn't plates, bowls, or mugs was taken up by paper. The contracts of the whole year, laid out from end to end. Every contract, every letter, every deposit agreement. The whole of the family fortune in pulp and ink instead of silver and silk. That was the magic of it. Warehouses of cloth and grain, cartloads of salt and alum. Coffers of bronze and silver and gold. All of it could be reduced to a line of cipher and put on a table.

His father, vest undone and sleeves rolled to the elbow, had a page in his hand. Uncle Robbson stood behind him, leaning over his shoulder and pointing with a crust.

"That's the payment due, right there."

"Aren't we portioning that out with Caldon and Sitt?"

"They're making us whole when they take their goods. But we have to make the full payment to the dockmaster."

"We have it, though?"

Robbson grunted in a vaguely affirmative way. Garreth sat and took a bowl of berries, then leaned back, lifting the front feet of the chair off the floor. His father glanced at him.

"You slept well," he said mildly.

"Well enough," Garreth said. He tried to make his tone amiable. Being curt would have felt like he'd lost a contest. "Any word from Mother?"

"No, not yet, but I wouldn't expect it. Before the first frost, I think. But there's a great deal to be done between now and then. I'd like you to check the warehouse, if you could."

Robbson stiffened.

Father looked over at him, blinking. "You don't mind, do you, Robbson? I thought it would be better if Garreth were seen taking a firmer hand on the rudder. To soften things when news of the marriage comes."

"Where is Yrith?" Garreth asked. "Shouldn't she be learning the family trade?"

His father shrugged and considered the paper in his hand. "Once she's family, perhaps."

"She's near enough, isn't she?"

"The marriage hasn't happened. Even once it has, we'd be wise to keep her in the closets. It isn't a long jump seeing we've married our son to a northern Inlisc bride to wondering what we gained by it. What our brothers and sisters in the guilds don't guess, they can't counter."

"I should go too," Vasch said. "To the warehouse."

"No, I need you for Pattan Udrestin. There's a letter he needs to see. Today."

"Yes sir," Vasch said.

Harvest was one end of the great pendulum swing of the house business. The other was at thaw, in the spring, when the first boats could make their way back up the Khahon, or down it if any had wintered in the city. Then it was all a rush to take orders, make contracts, set the board for the great game. The scramble to see that all the contracts were fulfilled, the danger of paying defaults to the guilds or the palace that could wipe out a whole year's profit, the dance of keeping the taxman happy without making him too happy.

Other years, Garreth had felt excited by it. Walking through the streets, it was like the city itself had come alive. Like the carts and couriers were blood coursing through cobblestone veins. In the south of the city, there would be sacks of grain piled high as a man's head and baskets of fruit and berries dripping sweet juice on the filthy streets. In the north, the traffic of the river was a barely reined chaos. Dozens of boats jockeyed for their places under the cranes, with the dockmaster sending bluecloaks out in skiffs to maintain order by threat of confiscation and violence. The warehouse doors were open, carts running back and forth to the water, trying to get all that was meant to hold through the winter safely to shelter and all that was due in the south on the right boat with the right master and all the bills of lading and countersigned receipts in order.

It was usually exhilarating. The last stretch of a relay that would raise some families almost as high as the noble compounds of Green Hill and cast others down until a proud merchant family found itself in service to an old ally or rival, sleeping in the servants' beds alongside the maids and cooks and garden men. It was the promise of the leaves losing their green, of the river running dark as tea when they fell. And the coming ice and cold and rest until the next spring came and began the contest again. Garreth had taken joy in it. He could remember that he'd taken joy.

Their head overseer was a hulking brute of a man, a head taller than Garreth, with one of his front teeth grey as a tick. He went by Bug, though Garreth didn't think it was his original name.

"All the sacks were underweight," Bug said, shaking his head. "Not by much, but all of them. I told him he could put them in the warehouse if he wanted, but I wasn't signing shit until you or your papa cleared it."

"He must have loved hearing that."

"He yelled at me for a while," Bug said through a grin. "Last I saw, he was headed toward the dockmaster saying he'd have me fined for slowing his day."

"You did right," Garreth said. "Get me weights on the sacks."

"You want me to use the magistrate's scales? There's a line for those."

"Ours for now. If I talk him into another sack for every . . . ?"

"Eight."

"Eight? They're that light? All right. An extra sack for every eight he brought in underweight, we won't take it to the guilds."

Bug nodded once, then turned back to the vast, buzzing array of workmen in the warehouse and whistled a trill so complex, Garreth could almost hear the words in it. Three of the men stopped what they were doing and trotted out toward them. Bug strode out to meet them, and Garreth folded the unsigned agreement and turned from the pandemonium of the warehouse to the pandemonium of the street.

Carters shouted and waved whips in the air while bored mules waited for the paths before them to clear. Men and women and children slid through the gaps between carts, and dogs slipped through the legs of the people as they walked. A girl in pale plainspun sat on top of a wall and sold lamb and chicken tarts to the crowd that flowed by at her feet. Garreth knew the way to the dockmaster's offices like it was a hallway in his own house. He pressed his way along the streets, turning sideways to squeeze between a cart of lemons and the rough stucco of the tanners' guild hall.

Behind him, someone shrieked in pain or outrage, and he glanced back to see a woman sitting in the middle of the street, grasping her leg just below the knee. Blood was flowing over her knuckles as she shouted obscenities at a young man in the colors of House Udorma. A courier who hadn't paid enough attention where he was headed, most likely. A sharp whistle stopped the traffic and cleared a path for two swaggering bluecloaks.

Two swaggering bluecloaks that he knew.

Garreth hesitated. Policy was that family business came first. There would be time to find Kannish and Maur after the issue of the underweight bags was settled. Turning back was only a little rebellion, but he liked the feel of it.

"How does giving *him* a fine help *me*?" the bleeding woman demanded of Kannish as the courier slipped away into the press of bodies.

"Teaches him to be more careful next time," Kannish said.

"Give me a stick and two minutes, and I'll do it better than that."

Maur caught sight of Garreth and lifted his chin in greeting. Kannish held his hand out to the woman, but she stood without taking it.

"Do you need help getting that seen to?" Kannish asked.

"Are you going to fine me for bleeding on the street now?" she said, then limped away toward the river. As soon as she was gone, Kannish started laughing. The traffic around them began moving again, but the blue cloaks and bronze badges of office made a little circle for them in the center of the chaos.

"Where've you been keeping yourself?" Maur asked, clapping Garreth on the shoulder.

"Sorry," Garreth said. "Things have been busy at home. How much did you fine him?"

"That one?" Kannish asked, pointing in the direction that the courier had vanished. "Four bronze. Enough for a beer and some good fish."

"For your captain, maybe."

"No, little things like this, we keep," Maur said. "That's why tolls and taxes are the bad work. Those have to come back to the penny, or the palace guard gets involved. But patrol supports itself. That's how it's always been."

"Nice work."

"It gives us an incentive to be vigilant," Maur said. "Less slacking on the job when the job buys your dinner."

"Seriously, though," Kannish said, "where have you been? I haven't seen you since..."

"The boathouse," Maur said.

The thrill of guilt that ran through Garreth was unexpected and powerful. Shame at having avoided his friends mixed with the rawness that was the night and the girl and the consequences of it. The urge to change subjects was irresistible.

"Keep it to yourselves, but I'm to marry."

"The burdens of running a successful house," Kannish said, pulling a face.

"Laugh if you want, it's salt on a cut right now."

"Who's the girl?" Maur asked.

"Can't say. Sorry. Policy. Where's Tannen?"

"Gone," Maur said.

"Gods. I'm sorry. What happened?"

"Not dead," Kannish said. "He's just gone. Captain Senit threw him out of the guard. We're supposed to stay together, and stick to the quarters we know best. Well, on coronation day, he got happy. Went down to Seepwater on his own, got his wallet and his badge of office stolen."

"Damn," Garreth said.

"Got worse. He chased the thief into Longhill. Captain said it was just luck he came back at all. Anyway, he's out. Last I heard he was looking for warehouse work."

Garreth made a sympathetic noise, but part of him was weirdly pleased. He hadn't liked the new man and wouldn't miss his company.

"You should come by," Maur said, and Garreth had the sense that his friend had seen exactly what he was thinking. "It would be good to see you again."

"I will. I promise. Not tonight, there's a dinner. But soon."

"It'll be good to catch up. You left before the boathouse thing ended. You missed the best parts."

Garreth couldn't keep his grin down, but he could pass it off as something else. "That's worth coming for all on its own. But you're buying the wine."

"Of course. But we'll be fining you first."

"For what?"

"We'll think of something," Kannish said, and hugged him. For a moment, they were just three boys again, and only playing at being adults. It felt better than Garreth would have guessed.

He turned back toward the dockmaster and the problems of the day, but his mind was split. Part of him was tallying the lost goods, calculating the demands he'd make and what counters he'd likely hear. But a part of him was at the boathouse again, and walking through moonlit streets with a girl he didn't know. He'd heard stories of the spirits that lived in the Khahon, and without meaning to, he found himself weaving a story that she'd been one of those. A wild wraith that had taken on human form for a night. He could smell the river in her hair again.

It was fanciful and childish, but that didn't matter. He could make up any story he wanted about her. She was gone now, and not coming back.

Outside the dockmaster's offices, a line of people stretched halfway to the next square. Complainants and boatmen and guild representatives and unhoused labormen looking for a contract. He walked through the line until he saw the face he was seeking.

"Hey," he said, pulling out the agreement and holding it up like a threat. "You and I need to talk."

○ ○ ○

The sunset was gorgeous that night: red and gold and grey. The dinner was with Teres Swinart and her family, and the courtyard was open to the west. The great stone tower of the Temple stood black against the glory, and the sky made it small.

"I'm sorry Genna couldn't be here," Teres Swinart said. "I miss her."

"I do too," Garreth's father said. "But we suffer what we must. And I think she'll be home soon."

The two tables were long enough to seat twenty each, and they were full. Torches stood ready for when the sun failed, and already a hint of autumn chill touched the air. Garreth sat at his father's side. Uncle Robbson was too far down the table to speak with and seemed to have gotten into a debate with one of the other guests. He was pointing a chicken's drumstick at the man, punctuating whatever point he was making. Vasch was at the other table, one of the oldest of the children. Garreth could feel his brother's humiliation, but there was nothing he could do. Etiquette was etiquette. Rules were rules.

Policy was policy.

"And you, Garreth," Teres said as she gestured a servant to refill his wine. "I haven't seen you since this time last year. You're looking all grown up and good enough to eat."

His father chuckled, and it occurred to Garreth with a sick clarity that the two heads of family were using him to flirt with each other. It was no different from how they behaved anytime, but he knew his father better now. What had once seemed innocent never would again.

"Bitter as coffee," he said. "I'm sure you could find better than me."

"And humble too," she teased.

A dragonfly swooped past, its wings buzzing softly. Garreth watched it swoop up and away until it left the courtyard.

"Eat," his father said softly enough that the others couldn't hear it. "It's rude to leave so much on your plate."

"I'm not hungry."

"I didn't ask."

"Yes sir," Garreth said, and lifted a knife of chicken to his mouth. He chewed it until it tasted grey and swallowed it with wine.

"With Byrn a Sal in the palace, the city may change," Teres was saying. Garreth hadn't been paying enough attention to know the context.

His father laughed, leaned forward, his fingers touching their host's arm. "Oh, Teres, that's sweetly optimistic. Byrn a Sal will rule the way Ausai did, and Airis before him, and Daos before that."

"You're probably right," the woman said, and Garreth was standing without remembering having made a decision to stand.

His father looked up at him with mild eyes. Others at the table were turning toward them. Garreth put a smile on, and it was easier than he'd expected. Than he liked.

"I think I've drunk a bit more than I meant," he said. "You'll excuse me if I go address some of the consequences?"

"I don't know that we needed the announcement," his father said, chuckling, "but please feel free."

Garreth nodded to his host and turned to the house. He waved away the servant who tried to direct him toward privacy, and instead marched through the full house and out the door. The carriage that had brought them stood waiting, but he went past that too. It was a long walk from House Swinart to home, but he was fine with it. The movement gave him a way to release the storm that had settled in behind his ribs. Anger and embarrassment and something else. Hunger. Longing. Regret.

Night fell around him. The moon was a sliver now, and the air was cool against his cheek. As his legs worked, his mind and heart calmed, but slowly. Very slowly. By the time he reached home, his muscles were aching, but he was sober and more collected than he had been since the night Mother had brought Yrith to the house.

Serria opened the door to his knock and looked out past him, searching the darkness for the rest of the party. He offered her nothing, but stepped past her and into the house. The sounds of Inlisc being spoken led him like a light led moths. Yrith and her chaperone were in the dining hall together, playing some pastime game with cards and lengths of string. Her expression went as closed as clay when she saw him.

Garreth nodded to the chaperone, pulled a chair out, and turned it so that when he sat, his full attention was on the girl. She looked back at him impassively. Ready, it seemed, for anything.

"I don't love you, and I don't think I can learn to," Garreth said. "It's no fault of yours. Really. I think…I think I'm in love with someone else. And more than that, I think there's something wrong in this house. Not you. None of this is yours to carry. None of this is anything you did. But I cannot marry you. I can't. And I want you to know it isn't that you've failed anything. You're fine, and you'll be fine without me, I swear it."

Yrith, daughter of Sau, tilted her head a degree and furrowed her brow.

"I don't know you. Why would I mourn your loss?" she said, and her accent was much less than it had been. Her chaperone laughed.

"Fuck me," Captain Senit muttered to himself.

Across the street and five buildings down, the woman paused. She was short, with close-cut black hair that curled tight to seem even shorter and a round face with a scar across it. She paused at a wooden building. The door had red banners at its sides with Inlisc writing on them that he couldn't make sense of. When she turned to glance over her shoulder, he unfocused his eyes but didn't look away. Nothing made you stand out faster than looking away. Better to stare right at the mark and pretend not to be paying attention.

It was the messy space, not quite Newmarket, not quite the Temple, not quite Longhill, but something of them all. The streets were wider here, dirtier. The language of the architecture didn't know what it was, wood and stone and stucco walls all jumbled together until the street wasn't one thing or another. The traffic wasn't the press of main streets by one of the gates or the port. Not a place to be after sundown, for certain. Not a place to be at all, if it could be helped. Which meant it was a breeding ground for Aunt Thorn and her nits.

He wasn't in his blues. In the old canvas trousers and a workman's shirt with a stain down the side, he could have been anyone. Or that was the hope. A sword would have stood out, so he made do with a knife slipped down his boot and a whistle tucked in his belt. Just in case. All he had in hand was a cloth with some stewed chicken he could pretend he was eating. Take a bite every few minutes and chew big enough to give people a story to tell themselves about what he was doing there.

The doorway opened, and the woman—fuck it, call her what she is. Aunt fucking Thorn ducked inside. Senit watched the door close again and settled down to wait. It was just good practice, though. He was already sure the woman wouldn't be coming back out.

For weeks now, he and four of his best had been following the crumbs the spider-handed thief had given them. A cheap butcher's shop in Seepwater. A stall that sold old clothes in Newmarket. A door in a Longhill alleyway. A crawlway beside a quay along the Khahon. They were like the anchor points on a web. The entrances to an underground Kithamar that the daytime knew nothing about.

Except for him, now. And because of him, all the city guard, soon enough.

A tall man came out, and then three women after him. They didn't look like whores and they didn't look like hired knives. He wasn't certain what he was looking at, but he made a point to seem bored by it. They turned south, heading into Longhill proper. Toward the enemy's home territory. Well, fair enough. He wasn't going to follow them in. Not yet.

He dumped out the last of the chicken, stuffed the cloth in his belt, and started back for the barracks. He kept a scowl on his face, but on the inside, he was dancing. He'd seen Aunt Thorn in the flesh, and she hadn't known who he was or why he was there. A kiss from a new sweetheart wouldn't have felt better.

Not that he had a sweetheart. Not any longer. Divol Senit had been born in Kithamar, son of a woman who loved a guardsman. He and his mother had lived in Newmarket, north of the Temple in two rooms of a building almost against the city wall. His father had been a bluecloak. Senit spent his youth pretending to chase down thieves and killers. Sticks had been their swords and long grass their whips. His father, when he appeared, had laughed at the pretend play, but he'd also been proud of it. It showed in his smile and the way he'd called his son's name. He was an important man, high in the guard and respected.

So respected, it turned out, that he'd been taken in for the palace guard. The blue cloak turned to red. Senit had been ecstatic when he heard. His father, one of the prince's own guard. He hadn't understood why his mother wept. Not then.

The pay was better. They were able to keep more food in the house, and rent a third room. But the palace was farther from Newmarket, across the river and up Palace Hill. He'd watched his mother pine and wither. Not away, but when his father came by less and less and less, Senit had learned the hard lesson of the guard. There was room to care for Kithamar or a family, but not both. One or the other would always take first priority, and second priority was a long step down.

When his time came to join the guard, he remembered that. He remembered it every day since. He'd had lovers—men and women both—over the years, but no marriage, no children, nothing that he'd have to abandon in order to do his work. And his work was always there for him. Love could be fickle. Romance could fade. There would always be some jackass taking what wasn't his. Some dry turd of a human who thought it was funny to break or burn or steal what others had. Some petty justice he and his could mete out that kept the good people safe and the bad people frightened. Guard work was constant as the air and as certain as stone. It gave his days meaning, and he loved it more than he'd loved a person, and more than he ever would.

He reached the barracks near midday, and a carriage from the barracks in the Smoke was standing in front of the stables. Captain Senit grinned, seeing it, and stepped toward his office a little faster.

Captain Pavvis was a thin man with a mustache that didn't suit his face. Privately, Senit thought he was a dandy and not as serious as he should be. But he kept the Smoke in order, and they genuinely liked each other, for all their differences in style and tone.

"Out of uniform?" Pavvis said. "Or have you finally decided to admit that you're in over your head? There's nothing ignoble about hauling piss for copper. You'll do great with it."

"No, I'm just returning from your mother's house, Pavvis. She's a woman of tremendous appetites, and I was afraid she might tear my work cloak in the rush to get it off of me."

"Her eyesight has been failing her these years, it's true."

Divol laughed, sat next to the altar of the Three Mothers, and made the sign of obeisance to them, as mindless as reflex. Pavvis sat at the desk.

"What's going on that you need me for?"

"What do you know about Aunt Thorn?"

Pavvis shrugged. "Inlisc bogeyman. She's supposed to change shape and cause trouble, especially to us. Does favors for her people and fucks ours over."

"The way I heard it, every Inlisc gets to ask one wish from her in their lives, and half the time, they'll be sorry they did. And the actual woman?"

"Whoever she is, she took the name. So Longhill all suck her toes because they can't keep her straight from the folklore. And she's been slapping your ass for a few years now."

"What if I told you she's got a smuggler's cave from my side of the river to yours?"

Pavvis chuckled, then when Senit didn't, sobered. "A smuggler's cave under the river?"

"Over it. There's one inside the bridge between Seepwater and the Smoke."

"Yeah, pull the other one. It's got bells on it."

"I'm serious," Divol said. He leaned from where he was sitting and plucked a roll of parchment from beside the incident book. He unrolled it carefully, the streets and walls, gates and alleys and public squares of Kithamar appearing before him in ink. A god's-eye view of the city. He traced his route back, finding the corner where the door with the red banners stood.

"Hand me that pen," he said, and Pavvis didn't object. As Senit marked a small circle on the map, he said, "I have a source who's pointed the finger at how the bitch moves through the city. There's an underground. Streets, buildings, fountains. I've spent the last weeks tracing it. I can't get in there, but I can find the doors in and out."

He handed over the map, and Pavvis spread it on his lap. The little circles were like raindrops on a pond. Pavvis's eyebrows rose.

"This is . . . this is another city, Senit."

"It is. And this is only what I've mapped. It's centered in Longhill, no surprise, but the rot spreads. I'm certain there are tunnels under the Temple and Newmarket. There's reports of underground canals and rail carts like a mine. Smugglers' roads that lead out under the city walls. An inverted Temple for the old Inlisc cults. That may all be bullshit, but it may not. And I'd bet my left tit that it's not all on my side of the water. If this is here, it's under your barracks too."

"Well, all the gods know there's enough digging been done in Oldgate," Pavvis said, then frowned, realizing what he'd just said.

"Yes. This bitch may be digging herself passages from the Smoke up under Palace Hill."

"That means Kint. If that's the case, he has to see this."

Senit shrugged, and Pavvis handed him back the map.

"I'm showing this to you because you're solid. I trust you, yeah? Kint's been strange from the start. I trust him about as far as I can spit. I'll tell him, because you're right, we have to do that. But I'm telling him after the problem's solved."

"What do you mean, solved?"

"Aunt Thorn dead or in chains or both. Her crew broken. Her money in our coffers. Less what we owe the palace, of course."

"Of course."

"It's going to be dangerous. And it has to be done quiet. No one can know about the plan until we're ready to move."

Pavvis tapped the map with a forefinger. "Who knows about this?"

"Too many. The man who brought my source in? It was Marsen Wellis. He's been in the guard since before he could take his own cock out to piss, and he knows the city, but he's a blowhard. Likes showing off. And his nephew's just joined up. I can't think he didn't at least share it in the family. But all this work's mine."

"So we have to think it's gotten out that we have someone talking to us about Aunt Thorn."

"But not what he's said, and not what we've found on our own. I want your help with this."

Pavvis nodded, but to himself. Senit could almost hear him thinking. "Can I meet this source of yours?"

Senit rose to his feet. Pavvis followed him out.

The cell was small and dank. Before this, they'd used it for people who were too drunk or angry to let loose, but not serious enough to bother the magistrate with. These last weeks, it had had just the one tenant. His yellow vest was gone, replaced by a wool cloak and a cotton robe. When he'd complained about not being allowed to see a barber, Senit had sent the camp haircutter to see him. Now he looked like a recruit who'd done something stupid and paid the price for it.

"This is Captain Pavvis," Senit said as they walked in. The prisoner scrambled to his feet. "I want you to tell him what you told me."

"You can't hold me here. You were supposed to protect me."

"I am protecting you. Look, you're alive."

"I'm in worse than gaol!"

Divol sighed. "If you want to leave, you can always go. I wouldn't recommend it until I get Aunt Thorn into chains, but it's your city. Do what you want to with it. Just as a kindness, tell the captain here what you told me."

The fight went out of the man visibly. For a moment, Senit thought the poor fucker might start weeping.

"It's just... I only took a knife," he said.

Afterward, they walked back toward Captain Senit's office slowly. The afternoon was still warm, but the night was going to be cold. In the practice yard, Beren Laumas was drilling sword techniques for a good two dozen men. Some of them were the new recruits, but there were veterans in there too. Musicians played scales. Boatmen practiced knots. Guards drilled at the skills it took to kill someone instead of getting killed by them. If it was still going when Pavvis had left, Senit would go drill with them. It was good for the young ones to understand that this was their life now. It set expectations.

"He's a mess," Pavvis said. "If you took him before the magistrate..."

"The world would be a better place if his mother used her hand instead the night she made him, and that's truth. But I'm not taking him to the magistrate."

"You're trusting him. That's madness."

"I found the man he claims he sold his stolen knife to. They fished his body out of the river."

After a moment, Pavvis said, "You think Aunt Thorn—"

"Got her blade back. I do. If my friend here goes loose, he'll be dead in a night. He's meat on bone, and he knows it. He's got no reason to play false with me, and I'm not asking you to work with him. I'm asking you to work with me."

"I have to think on this one, Senit."

"Don't just think. Look. Get down on the Silt down by the bridge. Look at the piles where the land's spread out under them. You'll find that smugglers' tunnel."

"I believe you," Pavvis said. "But I'm also going to look."

"Wouldn't expect less."

The two captains shook hands and parted. All in all, Senit thought it had gone well. He was less worried that Pavvis would refuse his help than that he'd suffer a bout of politics and take the whole thing to Kint and the palace guard before it was time.

When he turned back toward his office, a man was sitting on the steps there. He was a young one, but not a child. Just at the end of his second decade or the bleeding start of his third, at a guess. Good Hansch features and a softness that said he'd lived a comfortable life. Captain Senit put his thumbs in his belt and walked slowly toward the man. Behind him, Beren barked out, his voice as bright as a spark, and the men he was training shouted back flame. The man on the stairs caught sight of him and rose to his feet, his face respectful. He knew who Senit was even without his uniform on.

"You seem to be in the wrong place, son," Senit said.

"No sir. I was hoping I could speak with you. Sir."

"About what?"

"My name's Garreth Left, sir. I grew up with Kannish Wellis and Maur Condol."

"I won't hold that against you. What about them?"

Garreth Left kept his arms tight at his sides, his eyes down in deference. "I heard what happened to Tannen Gehart. I hoped you had a space for a new recruit."

It's been so long since a new prince took residence in the palace. Even longer since a family," Erendish Reyos said as she walked at Elaine's side. "How has the transition been?"

It was a very polite way of asking what the hell was going on there.

The Reyos compound was one of the northernmost in Green Hill, and Elaine had been there many times. Celebrations, dinners, funerals, harvest festivals, Longest Nights, first thaws. Erendish was only a year older than Elaine, and they'd shared tutors and religious instruction when they'd been younger. Elaine neither liked nor disliked the woman, and if Erendish had any particular opinion of her, Elaine wouldn't know. Admiration or hatred, it would have looked the same.

"It's interesting," Elaine said, the way she'd said it a hundred times before. The same words, the same inflection. It was on its way to reflex by now. "There's so much history in the palace. And it's so large. Did you know that inside of the palace walls, there's more land than all of Green Hill put together? The oldest structures in Kithamar are all there."

She shook her head, as if in awe, and Erendish nodded as if in agreement. There was no way to push the real question without being obvious, and obvious was another word for rude.

The truth was Elaine couldn't have answered that question if she'd wanted to. She was as hungry to understand as anyone, and more than most.

The day after her father's ominous midnight appearance, he'd announced that everyone of noble blood was to gather at the palace. Each family was to select one of their own to meet in a private council with the prince, and all of the brotherhoods as well. It was an astounding command. No one knew why he'd called such a vast gathering, and he was in his private study with Halev Karsen and unable or unwilling to answer questions. Even her own. When she asked to see him, servants returned with promises that gave way to excuses when they weren't kept.

And then, with as little explanation or warning, it was all called off. Speculation burned through the court like fire through dry brush. Byrn a Sal was going to abdicate or he was going to announce his marriage. He'd fallen ill with the same malady that had slain Ausai. He was preparing to call for war, though against who was anyone's guess.

The few times Elaine had seen him, he'd looked pale and grey. And when she'd asked what was the matter, he'd tried to wave it all away. As if pretending things were right would make them somehow be so.

"I am sorry you couldn't stay for the meal," the woman said. "I know Father enjoys your company."

"I wish I could," Elaine lied. "But I'm meeting with the high priest, and just getting there's going to take most of the afternoon."

"I'm grateful for whatever we can see of you," Erendish said as they turned the corner. The Reyos family stables were on their right, and Elaine's carriage was there waiting for her as she'd expected it would be. She gave Erendish her farewells—not so short as to be insulting, not so long as to take more time than she had to—and accepted the footman's help up to her seat. The horses were restless, but the coachman seemed at ease.

She checked the seat. The red book was there, and the letter she'd written. She knocked at the panel above her, and the coachman appeared, looking down. He was a man in his middle years with a genial face.

"I'm ready," she said.

"Yes, lady. So there's three ways we can go. Closest is we head for the north bridge and across there. Fastest is we cut back through Palace Hill to Oldgate and go down the face there, but I'm always a little nervous going down. Makes the horses skittish. They're better coming back up. Or I can take us south through Stonemarket and the Smoke, cross the south bridge, and up Seepwater to Newmarket and over."

"That seems out of my way."

"Yes, very much. Some might enjoy the uninterrupted time. Whatever suits, of course."

When put that way, the longest path did have some charms. If the sudden flood of social engagements and recollections of the past had felt unpleasant with Prince Ausai merely ill, his death and her father's coronation had easily doubled it. And this new intrigue, even though she was at best peripheral to it, doubled that again. The idea of hours spent alone in a carriage with only the company of the street and the coachman sounded restful by comparison.

"North," she said, and he bowed before he closed the panel. The carriage shuddered, bucked, and fell into the steady, clattering rhythm of the road. She found herself stroking the red book like it was a cat she was trying to soothe. She traced the words—*On the Nature of Gods*—and tried for the hundredth time to decide whether she was foolish for trying to find a path to Theddan this way.

She didn't know quite how her debauched, exiled cousin had become one of the only people she trusted. But there were conversations she could have with Theddan she couldn't with anyone else, and her head felt like it was filled with wool. Her thoughts shifted from her father's face when he'd come to her that night to Ausai's private study to Garreth Left to the thousand eyes studying her at court and back again to the start without lighting on any one thing long enough to make sense of it. She thought if she could talk with Theddan, tell her the story of her life in the palace, she might by hearing herself speak come to know better what she thought.

They reached the bridge, and she leaned to the little window in the carriage door to look out. The river was dark as wine today, and wide. Looking south, she could see where it widened into something like a little bay, and the piers of Riverport with boats and skiffs as thick on the water as ticks on a dog. When she leaned close, she could see the Temple rising up in the distance, towering over the rooftops to the southwest.

The Temple had served many gods since it was built. Its architecture was the unyielding stone of Palace Hill and Stonemarket. Hansch design, Hansch materials, and raised up over the wooden stalls of Newmarket and the wooden slums of Longhill to make a statement more political than pious. The Temple was the echo of Palace Hill, a monument to the Hansch conquest of the Inlisc centuries before, and the mark of Kithamar's limit. In some places the city wall blended into the walls of the Temple itself, as if the border between Kithamar and the world beyond were the god it served.

It held the surplus grain that would keep the city alive in a famine year and keep the poorest from death at any time. It held the permanent cadre of priests to oversee the spiritual needs of the city. It stood between life and death, one era and the next, like a lighthouse before a sea of Inlisc roofs.

As she passed through Riverport, she watched for streets and faces she might recognize. It was a vice, but one she couldn't keep from taking some pleasure in. Once, she glimpsed a street that she thought she might have walked down that night, but they passed it and moved on before she could search it and her memory to be certain they matched. In Newmarket, the streets thickened with traffic. Harvest was coming. She almost regretted that she hadn't brought an escort of redcloaks to clear her way. But more eyes meant more eyes, and suborning the coachman had felt daring enough. The quality of the carriage and the coachman's amiable whip were enough to clear their path without too much delay.

When the stalls and houses gave way to little temples and candle shops and the mausoleums of the merchant class, she felt herself growing tense across her shoulders and in the pit of her stomach. She didn't know whether she was worried that her errand might fail or that it might succeed.

As they arrived at the Temple gates, she gathered herself. Stepping down from the carriage, she looked back to the west and Palace Hill. Oldgate faced her straight on, like the face of the land itself looking at her. That was why the Temple stood where it did. To make the connection between the palace and the Temple grounds explicit. Like two men, facing each other with the river between them.

The coachman paused at her side, and she pulled her letter out from between the pages of the book and pressed it into his hands.

"To her. No one else."

"I understand, my lady. I will do all I can," he said. His solemnity was ruined by a little wink at the end.

The high priest was the same man who had placed the prince's crown on her father's head and presided over Prince Ausai's pyre before that. Thin-faced, but with surprisingly merry eyes and a small tremor in his left hand that she ignored because he did.

The drawing room where they sat was small, but opulent. The walls were paneled in rare woods, and if the chairs weren't pure gold, it was only because that metal was too weak to bear a person's weight and still boast the almost diaphanous design. The cushions were silk and cloth-of-gold. The altar in the corner was a single block of malachite carved into a form that looked like smoke or water or something of both. There were places in Green Hill and the palace that matched the wealth and comfort of the little room, but she didn't think there was one that could exceed it.

"Such a pleasure to see you, Lady a Sal," he said. "It's so rare for us to have casual visits from the palace. I understand it. We are the two souls of the city, but the walk would be a long one, eh?"

"As a carriage ride, it isn't brief," she said with a smile.

"To what do I owe the honor?"

In truth, all she wanted was a long enough moment with the man for her coachman to find Theddan and slip her the letter. How long that would take, she couldn't guess, but longer was better. She lifted up the book.

"I've come across some theological writings that I found confusing," she said. "I was hoping you could help me put them in better context?"

"Oh," the high priest said, taking the book from her hand and paging through it. "That's really quite simple. Theyden Adresqat was mad, you know. She lost her husband and child to a fever that passed through the city, and it..." He put the book down and made a gesture like he was cracking an egg. "A pity, because she was quite an intelligent woman, and an excellent scholar. But she wasn't right after that."

He shrugged, and Elaine leaned forward. "But there must have been something in her writing that had power to it? I heard she died in exile."

"She was sent away for threatening to kill the prince. Daos a Sal, that would have been. She had the delusion that he was an impostor. It was an imbalance of the blood, I think. I'm sure her heresies would have brought some consequences if people had taken them more seriously. And the writing in them is exquisite. She was a poet, in her way. Is there anything else I could help you with?"

"Could you, perhaps, explain for me exactly how she was in error?" Elaine asked, and the little whine of desperation was clear even to her.

The high priest looked puzzled, but not upset. "If you like. Certainly. You see, she drew a distinction between gods and the divine. The divine, she said, was above gods, though she called it 'more real.' She also called it *the absolute*, which she goes to great lengths to point out is beyond morality and even meaningful awareness of us. She said that there was a great mystery that underpins the world, but that the gods don't know the answer to it any better than we do. In fact, she centered gods as we know them—the Three Mothers, Urubus, Shau, and so forth—in us. In people."

He was starting to warm to the topic, gesturing with his good right hand as he spoke. She felt herself relaxing a little.

"She said that by our thoughts, we called forth forms. And those forms are what you and I call gods. Not really divine, but rather an expression of the congregation who summoned it. *Summoned* isn't the right word. She uses *egrygor.* An Inlisc word that means 'reflected lights.' We focus and reflect these parts of ourselves into a thought that gains form and power. And that, she said, was what we worship and pray to, and what answers our prayer as well."

"So we're talking to ourselves?"

"No, no, no. We're talking to the thing that comes from us but is outside ourselves. The system of which we are part. It determines the nature of the god that is formed. So one of the brotherhoods builds and calls forth whatever god it worships by worshipping. And that god is a reflection—an *egrygor*—of those people at that time. And because of that, gods can change as communities do. They can shift and take on different aspects. One god can merge with another if the communities themselves merge. It's all very abstract, and in my opinion quite self-indulgent." He folded his hands on his lap, as if he'd come to the end of the subject.

"And the reflections have powers?" she said, jumping a little at the thought. Something to bring him back. Keep him talking. "You said they answer prayers?"

"That's what she believed. But as I said. Quite mad. The gods are eternal, and we respect and honor and fear them."

He smiled and nodded to himself, as if he were pleased with his own answer. Elaine sighed. Hopefully her coachman had been lucky. She tried one last stab. "Is that why the Temple is consecrated to all the gods?"

"Yes, yes, yes. All gods are worshipped here. Which means, in a sense, none of them are." His smile was beatific, but the words surprised her.

"I don't understand. If we welcome all gods and sects, how could there be none of them?"

"We are broad-minded and open so that there is room for all," the high priest said, spreading his arms. "But the function of the Temple isn't only spiritual. We hold the city together. If we said only the Three Mothers were welcome. Or only Adrohin. Only Lord Kauth and Lady Er. Whichever. Then all the people in the city who that left out would become a little bit less of Kithamar. They would be divided, you see."

"So you make them welcome."

"So we make them *us*," the high priest said, and his eyes seemed less merry than they had been. "They say there are gods in the streets here, and there are. But they are *yoked*. The Temple brings all traditions together and weaves them into one thing, and that thing is Kithamar. The thread that binds us all together."

His smile seemed less friendly now too. Like there was some part of him that was in pain that he'd chosen to ignore.

"That seems very wise," she said.

"It is necessary," he said, and then shook his head, returning to his former demeanor. Elaine had the sense that something odd had just happened, but she didn't know what precisely it was. "But really, Theyden Adresqat is best appreciated for her poetry, not the seriousness of her theological insights, yes?"

"Thank you," Elaine said. "I can't tell you how much you've put my mind at rest."

He waved the compliment away. After that, it was only a few pleasantries, and then a novice—not Theddan, unfortunately—led her back out to the gates. Her carriage was waiting, and her coachman with it. The sun was setting, and the ruddy light silhouetted all of Oldgate and Palace Hill. The city itself seemed to wear a dark cloak and turn its back to her.

When she climbed into the carriage, her letter was on the cushion. She opened the panel, and the coachman looked down to her.

"No luck, then?" she said.

"All the luck," he said. "And time for a reply. We'll take Oldgate home unless my lady prefers otherwise?"

"Yes, of course," she said, plucking the letter up. "Whatever's best."

Her own script filled one page, but only a single face of it. When she turned it over, Theddan's handwriting was there: wide, scratchy letters that seemed less constrained by form. Wild, lithe, and never quite where they were supposed to be. Elaine was grinning even before she read the first sentence.

Darling Elly—Yes of course, you must find me and TELL ME ALL. We can arrange a time through a priest-itinerant called Haral Moun. He works the grain handout to the poor, so he'll be easy to approach without raising suspicion, and he has an ENORMOUS COCK. It's so good here, Elly, I can't tell you. It turns out priests are just more people! Everything is so rotten, it tingles when you taste it. I love you. I miss you. I'm half mad at the thought of seeing you. Hurry. Hurry. Hurry.

She'd signed it with her own name and a cheerfully obscene sketch.

They drove home to Elaine's laughter. She didn't realize until the carriage was moving along the endless switchback path up Oldgate that she'd left the book behind.

Watch your *head*!" Beren shouted. Garreth hoisted up the sword, and Beren hit his ribs hard enough to knock him to the dirt. Pain bloomed up and down his side and he struggled to catch his breath. The old guardsman walked over and put a boot on his chest, pressing him down to the ground. Garreth stopped trying to stand up. The dirt was cool against his bare back.

"That's today's lesson," the old man said, looking up at the other guards on the training field. "When you're in the fight, you watch the other man's stance and his sword arm. Everything you need to know is there. Anything else is lies and distraction. Understand?"

The others all roared *Yes sir*, and Garreth wheezed it too. The boot stopped pressing down, and Beren held out a hand. Garreth took it, more than half expecting to be thrown across the yard or twisted into one of the submission holds Beren also taught. When the old guardsman only hauled him to his feet, he felt almost grateful.

"You'll get better," Beren said. "Now get your ass back into uniform. You're on duty."

"Yes sir," Garreth said, and turned to run back to the barracks proper. All he could manage was a limping jog. The other bluecloaks laughed as he passed, and he'd learned enough to know that grinning back at them and taking a bow was the best reply.

His barracks was only a little larger than his room back home had been, but it had bunks for six, each with its own locker. Maur and Kannish were waiting there for him, already in their blues. The other three bunks belonged to veteran bluecloaks—men as old as Garreth's father with scars on their arms and backs and an easy, violent banter. There were women in the guard, though fewer, but they shared their own bunkrooms.

"Come on, we're running late," Kannish said.

Garreth nodded, but didn't have the wind to speak. He only leaned against his bunk, stripping off the canvas trousers and tossing them toward Maur.

"That's going to be a hell of a bruise," Maur said, pointing to the blood-red dots along Garreth's side. "But I'm sure there's a deep wisdom that comes with the pain."

"I don't recall you talking about wisdom when you were in the baths after the captain half split you," Garreth said, pulling on a fresh shirt and pants, and the blue cloak over them. His skin was tacky with sweat, and the cloth tried to stick to him.

"That was different," Maur said. "Back then, I was in pain. It's much easier to see the finer philosophical points when it's someone else doing the hurting part."

"Sounds like a problem with philosophy. Where's my belt?"

Kannish tossed the brown leather belt, and Garreth caught it with one hand, fit his scabbard to it, fastened it at his hips, and hung the badge of office from it. As he tied his boots on, the weariness tugged him toward the bunk—one thin pillow and a blanket of sandpaper-rough wool. A feather bed and silk sheets wouldn't have looked better.

"We're late," Kannish said.

"This is what happens," Maur said. "Give a man a few months' head start, and he starts acting like he's better than you."

"I am better than you," Kannish said. "I was training for months before you."

Garreth stood. The world swam around him, but only for a moment. He grabbed his sword from its place on the wall, slid it home in the scabbard, and said, "Why are you two taking so long? Don't we have someplace to be?"

It was more than a week now since Garreth had taken his oath to serve the city and execute its laws. Other people had family and friends come to their inductions, celebrations, and cheers. For Garreth, it was just him and the captain with Maur, Kannish, and Kannish's uncle to bear witness. Garreth hadn't gone back home after. He'd just taken the bunk he was assigned, and slept there. In the morning, he wrote a note to his father and mother saying what he'd done and paid a street child a bronze coin to take it back to the house for him. When the boy came back, he'd said that a woman who matched Serria's description had taken it and read it. There had been no message in return. Every day since, he'd waited for some response from his father or Uncle Robbson or Vasch. None came.

Since then, nothing had seemed quite real. He woke before dawn, ate semi-palatable breakfasts of stewed grain and organ meat at the barracks, suffered through any chores or errands that fell to him as the newest recruit, and then the day was split between training to fight, lectures from the magistrate's assistant reminding him of the laws he was expected to uphold, and then duties in the city.

It surprised him to be in the street so quickly. But in truth, he understood the laws and customs of Kithamar as well as anyone who'd lived there since their first breath. Some laws were written, some were not, and the city guard upheld all of them. If he felt like he was taking part in some extended joke between him and Kannish and Maur, if the blue cloak and badge of office felt like a costume, if some part of him expected that it would all turn out to be a passing fancy and the demands of the business and family policy would pull him away from it, still he went through his day from first light to long past sunset acting as if it were all real. So far, no one had told him otherwise.

Harvest was under way, and the streets were thick. The trees and ivies were losing their summer green, and the hours of light were growing shorter each day. The afternoons were still hot, but the nights had a bitter edge to them. Or that might just have been the thin blankets.

As the senior guard in the patrol, Kannish got their assignment from the captain, and today, they turned north. There were four gates on the eastern half of Kithamar: the north gate, the Temple gate, the hospital gate in the south, and the towpath by the river. With carts pouring in from the countryside laden with the season's crops, gates were clogged and crowded. The voices of the people and the horses, the bleats of the sheep led on ropes for the slaughterhouses, the whines and shouts of the beggars and pickpockets working the crowds all fell together into the vast music of the city. Garreth had been at that gate a hundred times or more, fighting through the chaos of the days leading up to a celebration or market. He was used to struggling to make a path, one hand on his wallet and the other pushing against the people pushing back at him as they made their own ways through.

It was different this time. The crowd thinned before them like fog. Men and women met their eyes and smiled—sometimes nervously and sometimes not—or else looked away as if they'd embarrassed themselves. Garreth and Kannish and Maur weren't themselves any longer. They'd become the face and arm of Kithamar, and people respected the city or they feared it.

Kannish's uncle was at the gate with three other guards. Garreth recognized them, but he didn't know their names. None of them were the men from the other three bunks. Marsen caught sight of them and nodded, then gestured for the cart making its way into the city to stop. The ox that pulled it huffed and lowered its head.

"Change of guard," Marsen said. "You boys go get some food. I'll take care of the striplings."

The other three guards laughed and fell back into the crowd, moving with the confidence of a man walking down his own hallway. Garreth tried to stand in place with the same confidence, but it seemed ridiculous.

"You know how this goes," Marsen said.

"He doesn't," Maur said, pointing a thumb at Garreth. "It's his first time."

A flicker of annoyance gave way to a grin. "Fair point," Marsen said. "I figure the taxes. I collect the taxes. The money goes in there—" He pointed to an iron box with a slot in it. "You three keep your eyes open. Anyone tries to sneak past, you stop them. Anyone tries to steal from someone—takes an apple off someone's cart, plucks a wallet off someone's belt—you take care of it. Anyone starts a fight, you end it. Anyone decides to be too much of an asshole, I've got a length of rope and we'll march them to the magistrate at the end of the day and introduce them to the noble work of scraping shit and dead animals off the glorious streets of Kithamar. If anyone gets it in their heads that they want to steal the day's taxes, blow your whistles like you're waking the dead and try to kill two of them before they cut you down."

"That hasn't happened in years," Maur said. "I asked."

"Any questions, ask them while we're working," Kannish's uncle said, then turned back to the waiting ox, and the duty shift began.

At first, Garreth tried to watch everyone and everything. The farmers' boys carrying sacks of peas across their shoulders because they were too poor to have a mule. The woman in the yellow cloak who stood apart from the crowd, watching the men and mules and carts come through the open gate like she was waiting for someone and growing more distraught with every disappointment. The Inlisc boy with the bad tooth who was begging for work from every cart with a large enough load on it to want a spare pair of hands. It was exhausting.

The sun was high and warm, and the street stank of mud and vegetables and the thick press of bodies. Garreth's ribs hurt whenever he breathed in too deeply, and his back ached. Sweat was sticking his cloak to his skin, and every time someone came near, he remembered what had happened to Tannen that opened the place for him and put a hand on his badge of office.

The sun had moved the span of two hands together in its arc across the sky when Marsen stopped a wide cart with two mules and a pile of beets on the back still caked with the dirt they'd grown in. He walked over to Garreth and put a hand on his shoulder.

"Don't try so hard," he said.

"Sir?"

"You're staring at everything and everyone like they're a puzzle you're angry to solve. That's not how it works. Just let your attention drift. Notice what you're noticing, and when something stands out, then give it the eye."

"I'll try," Garreth said.

"Watch the boys. You'll get the trick of it."

And he did. Kannish and Maur seemed almost like they weren't doing anything, but with Marsen's advice to guide him, he saw it wasn't quite true. The pair of them walked apparently aimlessly through the press of the crowd, but always in a tight area around the mouth of the gate. They glanced around, looking at nothing in particular. Garreth tried to imitate them. The crowd slowly stopped being people and mules and handcarts and sacks. It shifted into something that lived like an animal and flowed like the river, and Garreth found himself able to move across it like he was skimming a contract just to get the sense of it.

And more than that, he found himself looking for one particular face. It was foolish, yes. Stonemarket was across the river and against the far wall of the city. There was no reason to expect that particular smile or those fox-bright eyes here. But there had been no reason to expect her before, and there she'd been. The impossible happened sometimes. She was in the city somewhere. With a lover, maybe. A husband for all he knew. Whoever she was, wherever she was, she'd made it clear there was no place for him in her world, but he still looked, still hoped.

"It's not so bad, is it?" Kannish said, strolling past.

"I like it better than the getting-beaten part," Garreth said.

"That gets better too," Kannish said, and something wrong happened, to Garreth's left. He couldn't even say what it was, except that the motion of the crowd felt wrong for a second.

"Hey!" he shouted, and the Inlisc boy with the bad tooth—the one who'd been looking for work since noon without finding any—bolted. Garreth was after him at once, racing through the crowded streets. The boy was fast and lithe, slipping between people, changing direction, trying to vanish. But every time he looked back to see if he'd managed, Garreth met his eyes.

Garreth's legs burned with effort, and his breath fell into rhythm, inhaling deeply for two steps, exhaling for the next. The pain in his side was gone, and he felt like he could keep the chase going all the way to Longhill if the boy didn't stumble. Somewhere behind him, Kannish was shouting and someone was blowing a whistle. The boy looked back again, and there was despair on his face. They reached a small square with a cistern almost together. Garreth reached out as they ran, his hand coming an inch closer to the boy's back, another inch. Another.

He grabbed the back of the boy's shirt in his fist and pulled down. The boy stumbled, tried to right himself, legs flailing under him, and then he tumbled to the stone. Garreth stood over him, hands in fists.

"What the hell do you think you're doing!" he shouted. "I'm the city fucking watch! You don't run from us. You do what we say!"

The boy was weeping now, stuttering out something Garreth couldn't follow except the refrain of *don't hurt me* that ran through it like a chorus. He was bleeding at the knees where he'd skinned himself on the filthy cobblestones. A pale leather wallet was balled in one of his hands. Garreth took it.

"This isn't yours," he said. "Now is it?"

"I'm sorry," the boy managed between gulps. "I was hungry. I shouldn't have. I haven't eaten in a day."

"Stand up," Garreth said. "And if you run again, I'll catch you."

"I don't want you to hurt me, sir. I'm sorry, sir. I was so hungry."

"Stand up."

The boy slowly rose to his feet. A crowd was starting to gather, making a circle around them like they were putting on a little play. Even if the boy ran, he'd be grabbed. Garreth looked him over, then plucked another wallet from his belt. This one was older and worn, but it rang when he shook it.

"Haven't eaten in a day?" Garreth said. "Now you're lying to me too."

Sullen rage flickered in the boy's eyes as Garreth opened the wallet and poured five bronze coins into his hand.

"This looks like more than enough to buy some bread and beer," Garreth said, and tossed the wallet back.

The boy's mouth was a little 'o' of outrage. "You can't do that. That's my money."

"That's your fine for stealing. Unless you'd rather go see the magistrate and spend the next week cleaning shit off the streets. I'll give the coins back if you'd rather that."

He held out the five bronze coins, and the crowd around them laughed. The Inlisc boy shoved his newly emptied wallet back into his belt and turned to walk away.

"Hey!" Garreth barked. "Where do you think you're headed?"

"I thought you weren't taking me to the magistrate."

"I'm not, but you're coming back to the gate with me and we're finding who you took this from. And you can apologize when you give it back."

The boy tried to walk away, but someone in the crowd shoved him back. The laughter had an edge to it now, and the calculations of odds and stakes wrote themselves across the thief's forehead as clear as if they'd been in the family cipher. Garreth stood to the side and waved the boy to lead like he was letting someone pass through a door before him.

"She probably didn't even need the money," the Inlisc boy said. "She was fat."

"She probably does," Garreth said. "But let's go find out."

They started back toward the north gate, the boy limping a

little with each step. With the heat of the chase past, Garreth's ribs were happy to let him know how little they appreciated his efforts.

His blood went cold before he knew why. There at the back of the crowd, his father was standing. His head was tilted a little to the right. His smile was gentle and benign. Their gazes met for a moment.

Without speaking, his father turned, spat carefully on the ground by his feet, and walked away.

All through the streets near the Temple, other temples grew like mushrooms. A small chapel dedicated to Oniya the Prophet with its gold-painted doorway. An altar of Mammat with strings of beads at the doorway and the smell of incense and old blood. Gods of the old Hansch and the Inlisc, gods welcomed to the city to please traders from other faiths, new gods that sprang up out of the common talk like they had been waiting for the words that described them to be coined. The priests and monks and self-sanctified prelates lived as little more than mendicants or else they died. Their gods rose and fell, depending on who they could comfort, how well they gave meaning, how artfully they took the facts of the world and wove them into something that could seem like justice.

Elaine knew about these lesser temples, but she'd never been to one. Between the quotidian mysteries of the Clovas Brotherhood, her tutors, and the occasional icon standing alone in a household niche, her hunger for deity was satisfied. It felt odd stepping into the temple that Haral Moun had told her about.

The low ceiling was dark wood, the beams exposed and blackened by decades of candle smoke. The walls were a dirty yellow, the floor bare wood, splintered where too many feet had worn it down. On the front wall, a fresco of Lord Kauth and Lady Er stretched from floor to ceiling. The male figure had a white halo around his stylized head. The woman's halo was black.

As Elaine walked forward, the temple priest rushed toward her, his eyes wide. It wasn't often, apparently, that the high nobility of Kithamar visited his little altar. Elaine returned his bow and then, before he could offer her anything, took a seat on one of the threadbare prayer mats and bowed her head. With her eyes closed, she could only hear his hesitant footsteps hissing around her uncertainly, before, defeated by her apparent piety, retreating.

Then other footsteps came, less hesitant, lighter. Familiar. Elaine opened her eyes, and Theddan plopped down beside her like the temple was her garden. Her hair was cut short as a thumbnail, and it stuck out from her head in uneven tufts and clumps. Her robe was plain grey and her belt a worn and woven leather. Somehow, she made the ascetic attire seem as voluptuous as an unmade bed.

"Elly," she said through a grin that showed her dimples.

"Theddan," Elaine said, leaned over, and wrapped her arms around her cousin. She'd forgotten how good and warm and honest a real embrace could be. She found herself fighting back tears.

"Oh, no no no," Theddan said. "None of that. No crying. You promised me mystery and intrigue. Not weeping."

"I will, I promise. But just let me drink you in for a moment. Have you corrupted the whole Temple already?"

Theddan clasped her hands in prayer and inclined her head. "I have merely practiced gratitude for the vice and debauchery which the gods provided me." She dropped her hands and leaned back against the wall. "Honestly, I could have more lovers here than Green Hill could have managed in a lifetime. They're all so worried about things."

"Be careful. You're going to end badly."

"I might," Theddan said, a shadow coming over her. "But if I did everything the way I was told to, would I be promised a good ending? That's not how it works. This way, at least I'll be damned for what I am."

"Tell me not the high priest."

Theddan laughed, and the shadow vanished. "Him? No. Even if he wanted, I don't think I would. He's too cerebral. But I know about me. I want to know about you. I heard that your father's lost his mind?"

"I don't know what's happening with him. Something is."

Byrn a Sal, prince of Kithamar, had been hard to find. The last time she'd seen her father to talk with had been two nights after her visit to the high priest. She had spent her day working with her tutors and being prepared for the grand spectacle that was the harvest festival. It left her weary, but the stars or the wind or the complications of her own mind had kept her far from sleep.

Palace Hill was more than the quarters for her and her father and their guards and servants. The treasury was there behind ancient black walls, and the halls where the noble houses gathered for Longest Night and Tenthday, high summer and turning, planting festival and harvest. There were apartments for honored guests and ambassadors. A conservatory where musicians and dramatists could try to amuse the prince or ambassadors or whatever honored guests the circumstances required. There were stores there with food and fresh water and wine enough that they could close the red gates and live behind them for a year without anyone coming in or out. At the top of the palace, the wide roof that looked down over Oldgate and the river and the eastern half of the city and looked up at the vast starlit bowl of heaven.

The days were still warm, but autumn surrendered at night. The cold of winter wasn't sure enough to bring frost yet, but she could feel that it would. And the walls of the palace had a cold in them that the most determined summer would never break. And the wind. On its high perch, Palace Hill had no windbreaks in any direction. No matter where weather came from, it scoured some part of the palace, and the old stones muttered with it when they didn't whistle or shriek.

She walked in the darkness, not bothering with candles or lanterns. The moon was over half, servants and guards carried torches and lamps, and as tightly fastened and protected as she was, she didn't expect anything dangerous in the darkness.

She came upon her father without seeking or expecting him. He was in one of the drawing rooms, alone. A silver plate on a low table had the remnants of a fish, the pale bones catching the light of an oil lamp. They glowed with it. He was looking at nothing. Just staring forward like a man in a trance.

"Couldn't sleep either?" she said, and he started.

For a moment, he looked genuinely frightened, but a smile came quickly after, like a door closing on something bad. "I guess not. I probably should be asleep, but…it was a long day. There's so much to do."

"Is there?"

"Tax reports. Petitions. Requests. Appeals to rulings the magistrates made. I could spend every waking hour at this, I think, and there'd still be more tomorrow."

She sat across from him. He looked pale, but it might only have been the darkness and the light. "What about your private study? The room full of doors?"

"That," he said, "proved less useful than I'd hoped."

"Disorganized?"

He shook his head, and his gaze went back to the same nothing as before. He laced his fingers together over his knee as if he were hugging it. "It wasn't what I thought it was. Uncle Ausai wasn't what I thought he was."

Elaine leaned back. She didn't know what to say, so she let the silence speak for her. Her father shifted, wrestling some thought or feeling. The white streaks in his beard caught the light like the fish bones.

"I think... I think he may have been mad."

"Mad?"

"I hope he was."

"What did you find in there?"

His eyes shifted to her again. The smile again. "I don't know. Halev and I are trying to make sense of it. It doesn't matter, really. I mean, the man's gone now. There's nothing to fear from him, even if he was... even if he wasn't what I thought he was."

The knock at the door was soft, but it startled them both. Samal Kint, his red cloak made bloody by the candlelight, bowed. "You asked me to find you, my prince."

"Yes," Byrn a Sal said, then three more times. "Yes yes yes. All right." He stood and wiped his hands on his cloak. Little smears of fish oil darkened the cloth. "It's fine," he said to her. "I'm the prince. And someday you'll be prince in your turn. It will all be fine."

He left quickly, his head bowed. The head of the palace guard followed him, leaving Elaine alone with the bones.

"Was it Kint?" Theddan said. "Did he stop telling you because Kint was in the room? I mean if Prince Ausai was mad, the captain of his personal guard would know, wouldn't he?"

Elaine lifted her hands in despair.

"Well, what did your father say the next time you saw him?"

"We haven't been alone since then," Elaine said. "There was something in that study that frightened him, though. I just don't know what it was."

"Maybe Ausai had been torturing girls to satisfy his lusts," Theddan said. "That happens sometimes. I've read about it."

"It's as good a thought as any I've had. In fact, I could hope for that. If he was, then it died with him. But my father? He wasn't disturbed. I mean, he was, but it wasn't only that. He seemed frightened. You don't get frightened of things unless they could still be happening, do you?"

The priest looked in, saw the two women talking, and retreated again. Theddan shifted against the wall.

"You have to find out what Ausai's dark secret was," she said. "And the good thing is that everyone will be scared of you."

"Of me?"

"Why not? You're the prince's daughter. When he dies—years from now, old, in his sleep," Theddan said, holding her thumbs to ward off evil. "But when he does, you're going to be Kithamar. You can use that. I'd talk to the historian. Mikah Ell?"

"Why her?"

"She's a historian. Ausai's dead. If she's not interested in dead people, she chose a strange job. And . . . Ausai was Daris Brotherhood, wasn't he?"

"He was."

"That's Andomaka Chaalat. She's high priest over there. You should cultivate her too."

"What about Kint?" Elaine said. "Do I talk to him about it?"

"I wouldn't. If there is something dark and dangerous creeping around your new home, he's sure to be part of it. He's the man with all the keys. Oh! He has all the keys. You'll need to bar your bedroom door. From the inside. Just to be safe."

Elaine wanted to scoff and tell her cousin that she was being dramatic, but she couldn't bring herself to say it.

"I'll see what I can do."

"And be careful," Theddan said. "I'm stuck out here in a cloister. I can't appear with a sword at the last minute to save you."

"I wouldn't ask you to. But I'm grateful you'd want to."

"You're teasing me now. Fine, fine, fine. You're going to find out what you can, and then you're going to bring it all back to me. I'll be your secret diary. Only..." Theddan took her hand.

"Only?" Elaine said.

"All of this. Is it real, or is it about the boy?"

"The boy?"

"Your secret merchant lover. Garten."

"Garreth. Garreth Left."

"Him."

Elaine pushed Theddan's knee like she was scolding a puppy. "I haven't seen him. This is more important than...that."

"That's what I mean. I don't judge. But sometimes when someone's heartsick, they see other things to pull them away from it. When Linnia lost Morson's attention, she convinced herself for weeks that she was being haunted by a spirit, but we all knew it was just the space in her life where he would have been."

"You were just saying that Ausai was torturing girls for the joy of it."

"I made that up. I'm bored. I want something exciting to be happening, but not if it hurts you. You've dreamed about him, haven't you?" Theddan demanded, and when Elaine hesitated, she clasped her hands. "You miss him."

"He's a pleasant memory," Elaine said. Then, grudgingly, "A very pleasant memory. But that's all."

"I've been where you are, you know. More than once. It's more my home than home was. There's the first part where everything's brighter and warmer and the world's a better place, but that fades. You know it does. And then there's a want where it was. Sometimes I grab at the wrong thing to fill it."

"There's nothing I can have from him that's better than what I've already had. He knew. We both knew. I'm not inventing all the rest of this over Garreth."

The light shifted, a body blocking the doorway in. A tight whisper. *Theddy, we have to go back. Now.* Elaine looked over her shoulder. Priest-itinerant Haral Moun was a broad-faced, soft-looking man. The anxiety in his eyes bought him her sympathy. Elaine loved Theddan, but she didn't envy anybody who was infatuated with her. Theddan hauled herself up, and Elaine stood too. This embrace was brief, but it was tighter.

"I know it's serious," Theddan said. "I know you're scared. Don't be mad at me for asking."

"I'm never mad at you for long," Elaine said, and then her cousin was gone and the allegedly endowed priest with her. Elaine sat back on the prayer mat, waiting until Theddan was safely away so that they wouldn't be seen together in the street. Oddly, her mind felt clearer than when she'd come in. Yes, something was wrong in the palace. But Theddan had a point. She was the daughter of the prince, and one day prince herself. There were people she could speak to, questions she could ask. And maybe, if she were careful, a way to get into Ausai's private study herself. When she got back home to the palace, she could start her own investigation.

On the wall, the pictures of the gods looked back at her with their stylized, abstracted, inhuman faces. She felt a pang of guilt at desecrating their temple with her intrigues. When the priest peeked in again, she waved him over.

"My . . . my lady," he said. "It is . . . it is such an honor."

"The honor is mine. Please, will you let me leave an offering? Out of respect." She nodded toward the fresco.

The priest bent himself nearly double accepting the silver coins from her wallet, and promised to speak her name in his prayers. Hopefully the gods would be as easily placated.

At the door to the street, she turned back, thinking to bow to the gods one last time. The gesture of respect was empty, but the habit was good.

It was a trick of memory and her own distraction that the female figure—Lady Er with her dark halo—seemed to have changed. It was Elaine's own shadow and the play of the light on the walls that gave the illusion of movement, and her misremembering that the god's arm had been at her side when clearly it was lifted, palm toward the prayer mats as if in farewell.

Or else in greeting.

In the first place, Finrar wasn't supposed to be there. His job was to take the sugar from Caram up the river to the family hold just north of Everenhom. After that, he was supposed to trade with Vivrin and take the last load of the season back south—furs and ironwork and weapons down from Kithamar. Only Vivrin had gotten pregnant again, and even though he'd argued that any number of perfectly fine people got themselves born on the river, Grandmother said no. She said that the river was hungry, and any baby born there would never come quite right. Which was a dig, because Finrar's own father had drawn his first breath on a flatboat outside Imaja. But never minding that, Vivrin wasn't taking the sugar the rest of the way north, and someone had to. So that was Finrar.

The north river wasn't his stretch. He didn't know it like he did the south. He didn't like it. But he'd hitched his boat to the tow line, and the ox men had hitched it to their beasts, and he started the long second half of the journey. When he got back, he'd have to take the load south, and pay the penalties for arriving late, all thanks to Vivrin and Grandmother.

When they reached Kithamar, he'd hoped to put in at the southern piers outside the city walls, but the dockmaster there said no. The sugar was for Riverport, and so he had to go through the bridges and the press of boats, find his place in line, and stay there.

So now he was, with his little crew, holding just north of the third bridge with the Khahon trying to wash them all the way back to Caram, three dozen other boats around them hooking to tugs or tow lines pushing farther north, or sliding away to the south. The dockmaster's skiffs darted between the boats, a man in Kithamari robes barking orders and gesturing at parts of the shoreline. The cranes at the docks creaked loudly enough that he could hear them across the water. He paced the little deck—three steps one way, three the other—like a dog in a kennel. The great cliff-face neighborhood they called Oldgate stared down at them. He didn't even want to find a taproom and a girl. He just wanted to get the delivery made and leave Kithamar.

One of the skiffs turned toward him, and Finrar went to the edge of the boat. The man in it was heavyset, with a beard like a bird's nest and a blue cloak.

"What's your load?" the man shouted over the rush of water and gabble of voices.

"It's for House Left," Finrar yelled back.

The man pointed at the barrels stacked on the deck. "What is it? What's your load?"

"Sugar."

The bearded man shook his head and turned away.

"Hey!" Finrar shouted. "Where are we supposed to go?"

The man didn't answer, busy as he was making his way to another of the boats waiting on the river. Finrar went back to pacing, faster now and angrier, but still the same three steps.

The minutes passed into another hour. Ussman came to him from the back.

"We're going to be here all damned night at this rate."

"Get the oars."

Ussman's eyes went wide. "We're going to row up there?"

"No," Finrar said, and pointed to the stonework where the river met the bridge. "Just tie up at that quay. I'm going to walk my ass over to the dockmaster and sit on his desk until we get our fucking place."

"You say it, we'll do it." Ussman shrugged. Five minutes after, they untied from the pile. At first, it seemed like it was going well. There was a path to the quay despite the cluttered water, the path to the dockmaster's couldn't be that hard to find, and the raw fact of being in motion eased his frustration, if only a degree.

He saw the other boat—a flatboat with cargo enough that the river water threatened to slop onto its deck—as they came around another lumbering barge. They were both heading for the same clear stretch of water. For each other.

"Hey! You! Veer off!" Finrar shouted as he waved his arms. "Veer off!"

His own boat lurched under him as Ussman saw the threat. A woman on the other deck shouted at him, her face red with anger, and shooed at him like he was a fly she could scare away.

"I am turning," Finrar shouted. "You turn too!"

He looked over his shoulder to where a handful of people on the bridge had stopped to watch. Their heads were like birds on a branch, all turned the same way.

"Ussman!"

"I see it."

Two men appeared on the other boat carrying poles. As they came closer, closer, closer, the pair set the poles, ready to push Finrar away if they could. He hoped they could.

"What is wrong with you?" the woman was shouting. "What are you doing?"

"Do something helpful!" he shouted back.

Their poles touched the side of his boat, and the men braced. They were shoved back across their deck, but they held steady. They didn't stop the collision, but they slowed it. The two boats drifted inexorably together until he could see the moles on the shouting woman's neck, they were so close. The impact was a low grinding, like a tree being twisted apart by a giant. Finrar stumbled, and the crowd on the bridge—larger now—cheered.

His boat rebounded, and the other angled away, moving down the river toward the bridge and the south with a different woman at the rails with her hands raised in an obscene gesture.

"Fuck this city," he said to himself. Then, "Let's get to that quay."

"How bad's the hit?" Ussman asked.

"I don't know. Not too bad, I think." And he kept thinking that until they had almost reached the bank.

He felt the pop under his feet as much as heard it. His heart sank. "We've got a problem," he shouted, but it was already clear. Water lapped up the deck like the river was rising up to devour them. In a moment, it was at his ankles. The cold had teeth.

"The quay's not big enough," Ussman said. "If we can't find land, we're going to lose the cargo. We passed a place coming up. I can find a sandbar."

"You can't ground us."

"It's that or sink."

Finrar looked around him, tracing the water with his gaze. Looking for a miracle.

"Turn us, then."

The boat lurched, and a tremor ran through it. The water rose up to Finrar's knee and the illusion that they could reach safety died. Two of the dockmaster's skiffs were coming for them, oars flogging the water. Finrar stood at the prow of his sinking boat, trying to think how he'd tell Grandmother what happened and letting the despair wash over him with the water.

For part of an hour, the river ran sweet.

Garreth ached, but less. He was tired, but less. He sat in a taproom with Kannish and Maur, and more than them. Hellat Cassen and Frijjan Reed and Old Boar, all veterans of the guard. Abbit, who had been a bluecloak until he'd caught an axe through his left foot, and ran this place now. In and out of the taproom, a dozen more. Men and some women whose lives were spent seeing that Kithamar ran as it was meant to run.

The main room was wide and low, with rooms above it for the family who kept the beer and bread and cheap, pepper-hot sausage coming. The opened shutters looked out over a street corner falling into the gold and blue of twilight, and if the breeze was nearer cold than cool, it still couldn't cut through the barn heat of bodies pressed close on the old wooden benches and the warmth of the lamps. The house dog—a wide-headed, thick-shouldered war dog—ambled through the press accepting scratches between its rough-cropped ears and smiling.

"So I say, 'Open the door in the name of the prince, or I'll open your asshole in the name of the guard,'" Beren—the same one who'd bruised Garreth's ribs not all that long before—said. "And I'm waiting there, ready for some vast fucker ready for blood. After all the shouting and screaming, I figure this has to be some kind of half bear, you savvy? Door opens, and it's this twig of a girl. Thin around as Garreth's leg."

The others glanced at him, grinning.

"Turns out she and her boy were freshening up the luck, only he's got a wife. So the wait was all her getting him time to run out the back."

Hellat Cassen lifted his massive hand. "Which is where I was. Poor fucker was pulling his boots on when I got him."

"How much was the fine?" Garreth asked.

Hellat shrugged. "How to put a price on love? I told him not to scare the neighbors next time."

The others laughed as the cook came through with another plate of bread and jam and onion. There was a rhythm to the conversations. Someone would start telling a story, and the other conversations would quiet to listen, then pick back up when it was done. Garreth had heard more than one of the tales before from Marsen, but recast with Kannish's uncle always in the central role. He had the sense that if he stayed in the guard long enough, he'd be telling the stories himself one day. He might even think they'd happened to him.

The house dog plopped down by the cold fire grate and began licking himself with a vaguely obscene gusto. Maur lifted a hand for a fresh beer. Garreth felt a wide, warm pleasure at being with his old friends and his new. There were times he missed his home and his family, but there were also times he didn't. He couldn't say which version of himself was more nearly real.

And then there were other times when he thought about asking to shift his service to the Stonemarket barracks. He imagined walking with men and women he didn't know, learning new streets and alleys and squares. And maybe, maybe in all that not belonging, finding a face with that familiar wry smile.

"There's something coming," Kannish said. "The captain's been meeting with the heads of the other barracks."

"Maybe they're just talking about budget," Maur said. "Or looking for a way to get us cheaper food."

"I don't think so," Kannish said, leaning close so that his words would reach Garreth and Maur and then drown in the cacophony. "I think he's getting ready to crack Aunt Thorn."

Maur sobered at that. "That's a heavy lift."

"And a lot of ugly fighting in hallways they know better than we do, from what I've heard," Kannish said. "If the captain asks for volunteers for something..."

Kannish lifted his eyebrows, but Garreth didn't know if he meant they should take the chance together or stand aside. The door to the street opened, and Uncle Robbson strutted in, his chest out before him like he was spoiling for a fight. As new as Garreth was to the guard, he could still see the subtle reaction of the others. Shared glances, a smirk, a general retreat from the good cheer that meant someone from outside had come in. Garreth felt a strange blend of embarrassment at his uncle's arrival and protectiveness on his behalf. He was halfway to his feet before Uncle Robbson found him and started over.

Beren brushed past Garreth as if on his way someplace else and murmured *Say the word if you need his ass kicked, kid* before he moved on.

"Boy," Uncle Robbson said. It was the same bark he always had, but Garreth could hear it with the other guardsmen's ears, and it sounded half an insult.

"Uncle," Garreth said, his tone light.

"We need to talk."

Garreth pulled out his wallet, found enough coin to cover his drinks and food, and tossed them to Maur. "Pay up for me, yeah?"

"Done," Maur said.

Garreth nodded at the door, then started toward it, leaving his uncle to trot catching up.

In the street, the twilight had come to Newmarket. The

streets were a single blue shadow. To the west, Palace Hill was just losing its limn of red-gold and fading into grey. Garreth slowed, letting Robbson catch up to him and setting an easy pace.

"You have to come back," Robbson said. "I understand this rebellion of yours. And I'll tell you this, I respect you for it. I haven't seen your father have something thrown in his teeth like this in decades, and it speaks well of you. But you've made your point. The family needs you now."

"It's not rebellion. It's a choice. I took an oath."

"There's a hundred ways out of the guard if you want it. We'll make the captain whole for your loss." They walked on for a dozen paces in silence. "You heard about the sugar?"

"I heard a boat sank," Garreth said. "Was it ours?"

"It was."

Between one step and the next, Garreth felt his mind shift. It was as if he were standing in his father's office, the family's books open before him. Garreth the bluecloak was the merchant's son again, at least for the moment.

"Can we buy from someone to make up the loss? Vinant and Gastar both have contracts in Imaja."

"We have offers to both of them to buy as much of their overage as they're willing to let go. Even if there's enough to avoid penalties on our contracts, we'll be selling at a loss. Your mother's plan was our best hope before this. It's our only hope now. That's why you have to come home."

A boy of no more than eight ran out of an alley to their right. The deepening night took the colors from him, painting him all in greys. His whooping stopped short when he saw Garreth, and something part respect and part fear filled his eyes as he backed away. Garreth ignored him. Down the road, a woman stood at an open baker's shop, selling the last of the day's bread cheap. A half dozen men with dirty clothes and workman's hands were joking with her. Farmers who had come to the city for the harvest and were making a celebration of their own. He half wished that they'd try to run off with her bread or her coin, just to give him a way out of the moment.

"I have to think about that."

"There's nothing to think about," Robbson said. "Genna has put her whole faith in us to see the Kithamar end of this. She's done too much, *sacrificed* too much, for us to do less than every damned thing we can to make this work."

"I said I'd think about it," Garreth said.

"Fine. Sleep on it. But then of your own free fucking will, get back and marry that girl. Because if you don't, she'll lose her trust in us. If she loses trust in us, the winter caravan falls apart. And if the winter caravan falls apart, there won't be a home for you to come back to."

The palace, like Green Hill, like Kithamar, was in the thick of preparations for the harvest festival. In years past, Elaine would have been part of it. Especially when she'd been young, her father would make an event out of the preparations that was almost more than the event itself. There were costumes to be made, decisions to make about what food and wine to give out to guests who were making their way through the houses and brotherhoods, dancers and artists and poets to commission. Harvest was a time to be grateful for the food that would see the city through another winter, another spring. It was also a time to boast how much your family could give away and how beautiful a spectacle it could fashion. When she had been eight years old, she'd decided—only the gods knew why—that they should have a real dragon. Her father had hired a sculptor from the Smoke to cast a set of interlocked iron ribs twenty-five feet from nose to tail and a troupe of dancers to inhabit it. There had been a metal seat on the great beast's back just for her, and she'd ridden the dragon up and down the streets of Green Hill until she was too tired to see.

This year, the first of his reign, he was putting together a huge cart. It was meant to be like a great sailing ship with the high priests of the brotherhoods riding it through the city. For four days, the courtyard outside the stables had been filled with carpenters and wood and barrels of paint as the huge thing came together. Gigantic wheels were fitted to axles made of tree trunks reinforced with metal, and twice she saw men arguing about what route the massive carriage could take without binding against trees or buildings when it tried to take a corner.

If home had still meant the compound of House a Sal, someone might have noticed how little she took part. Home was the palace now, and so there was no precedent. Nothing was strange because nothing was normal. She could be any version of herself, and no one would think anything amiss, except possibly her father, and he was too preoccupied to notice.

And so she was free to do what she chose.

Halev Karsen sat in one of the libraries, an ancient book open on the stand before him. He looked up when she came in, and his expression was dour until he saw who it was. He softened. It looked almost like relief.

"Good morning," he said.

She sat on an old divan upholstered in red silk that was starting to shatter. "The guard says I can't go into Father's private study."

"Well. I suppose that's why they call it private."

She'd thought about how to approach Karsen. He'd been her father's nearest friend for as long as she could remember, eating meals with them, sleeping at the compound on the nights when his own father's failing health drove him from his home. Old Karsen was lost in delusions and dream now, and had been for almost five years. She'd heard her father trying to comfort Halev on some of the worst nights. He was as near to family as anyone besides her father.

He looked over at her, caught by her silence.

"What did you find in there?" she asked.

Halev bowed his head and turned away from the book. His long, aquiline nose made him seem like some kind of sorrowful bird. He didn't sit, but he stepped to the wall and rested against it.

"All we found were Ausai's books. Journals. Records. Observations and court documents. His and Airis's before him and Daos's before them, on back to the founding of the city, as far as I can tell."

Elaine stayed silent, her arms crossed.

"There were some things about it that were... It's nothing you need to worry about."

"There was something wrong."

"There were things about Ausai and the books that were odd."

"Meaning?"

"Meaning, we don't know. Not yet," he said. "I'm sorry that he went to you. It has to be worrying."

"It would be less if you told me about it."

Halev opened his hands in a kind of despair. "If I knew, I would. I don't understand what we're looking at, but we are looking. And when we know what it all means, you're the first person we'll tell. Until then, don't let it bother you. It may just be ravings about nothing. Probably it is. And if there's anything more than that, we will take care of it."

"Is Father in danger?" she asked. "Am I?"

"Everyone who wrote in those books is dead," he said with a finality that meant the conversation was over.

"Becoming prince of Kithamar changes people," Mikah Ell said. "It always has."

"You knew my great-uncle well, then?"

"I think no one knew Prince Ausai well, but paying some

attention to him was my role. I saw what he did, I think, as clearly as anyone could who wasn't his intimate. His heart? Well, hearts. What can you do with them?"

The court historian's apartments were on the northern edge of the palace, almost against the old wall that had once kept Inlisc raiders from pouring into the little fort on the top of the hill. The woman herself might have been grown there. Her skin had the papery quality of the very old, but her eyes were lively and bright. Elaine had never sat with her before, and she found herself liking the historian more than she did many of her relations and partners at court.

"Did he have many lovers?" Elaine asked. "I know he was married, but there were no children."

"Or else you might not be here. You'd still be at your old compound and not in line to rule a city of your own at all," the historian said, pouring a little more tea into their cups. "Ausai was not lucky with love, I'm afraid. He was married to Ulke a Jimental for twelve years. Monthly blood as regular as sunrise, poor thing. After she passed, he was set to wed Carrin Foss, which was a bit of a scandal, because Foss isn't one of the great houses, but nothing came of that either. What about your father? Was there a reason he didn't remarry?"

Elaine sat back in her chair. "Um," she said.

"As the future prince, he must have had some interest, yes? Women who were looking for an alliance, even if it wasn't a heart-match." The historian sipped her tea. "The assumption, of course, is that Old Karsen's son is his lover, but you know, I don't find that as convincing as some people do. There's a certain way men are with each other when they're sexually bonded, and I've never had that sense from them. Have you?"

Elaine felt a blush coming up her neck and laughed to hide it. "I haven't. But I hadn't really considered the question either."

"What about you? You're more than old enough to marry, and you're in the same position as your father. You've been approached by someone, yes?"

"I . . . I have, I suppose."

The historian's eyes opened a little in pleasure. She smiled encouragement. The memory of Garreth Left standing by his window looking out at the city as she stripped behind him intruded, and she pushed it away.

"I mean, there are always people who want to propose alliances in the court," Elaine said, maybe a little too quickly.

"And it will end there, at some point, won't it? But the main bloodlines are so woven together already. If it wasn't for the occasional Reyos or a Jimental woman taking a moment with her tailor or master of house, the great families would all be like those horses where they breed siblings together until their legs all get brittle and the knees fall apart."

Elaine found herself taking a long time drinking her tea because it gave her an excuse not to speak. The historian was in her own thoughts too, and so for a moment, they were silent.

"This is why I love my work," Mikah Ell said at length. "History is everything. It's the grain production and the reforms—or really lack of reforms—that shape the city and lives of everyone in it. The grand pronouncements and political theater pieces. But it's also the deeper, more human side of everything, isn't it? Who falls into bed with whom can change the fate of a family. Jealousy starts big wars and small ones. And the chance acts. Abelin Reyos was the most accomplished artificer the court has ever seen. He choked on a bone when he was twenty. The things he might have invented if he'd lived could have changed the nature of the city, but they didn't."

"I hadn't heard of him," Elaine said.

"He was before your time, I suppose. He was nearly before

mine, and mine goes back a way. But you were asking about your great-uncle. Who his lovers were?"

"I just... Now that I'm in the palace, I think maybe I didn't know him well enough."

"Ausai was a fascinating man. When he was young, he was so *funny*. He wrote a play once and had it put on at the university in Seepwater. He even put on a disguise and took a role for himself. Airis was livid about that. But once Ausai took the chair, that part of him just... He and his brother—your grandfather, that was—fell out soon after he took his seat. And now that I think of it, there was a rumor that Ausai had been secretly in love with someone before Airis died, and then fell out just after as well," Mikah Ell said, and her gaze shifted. Her smile faded into something like a scowl. "And yet here we are, and your father has remained close with Old Karsen's boy."

"They've always been close," Elaine said. "They've known each other forever."

"Forever's an odd thing. You know, I think history is like... sparring. It's a kind of fight. You have your blade, the other fellow has his, but it isn't really about the swords, is it? It's about the patterns. The things that always happen. The way he, maybe, always turns a bit to the left before he strikes. Or the way he closes his eyes after a blow. All I do—all we do, really, because of course I'm not the only student of history—is spar with the world. Look for the patterns and try to understand what they mean." She smiled. "And it's always interesting when a pattern changes, don't you think?"

"I suppose so."

"The things we can change, and things we have to live with. So interesting to see which ones are which."

Elaine felt a shudder pass over her that had nothing to do with the temperature of the room.

○ ○ ○

Elaine hadn't understood how oppressive the palace had become until she stepped out of it. The walk between the palace proper and the Daris Brotherhood wasn't a long one. Strict etiquette was that she should take a hand carriage or palanquin to save people in the street from having to bow. She made do with a cloak with a deep enough hood that anyone she walked by could pretend not to notice her, even if they did.

And the streets were full. All of Kithamar was to be decked out for harvest. Not just Palace Hill and Green Hill, but Stonemarket and the Smoke, Riverport and Newmarket and Seepwater. Most of the decorations in the carts or being lifted up the sides of the buildings—cloth and leather banners, garlands of silk roses or real ones, platforms on which singers would sit for three long nights, filling the air like birds—were for Green Hill. Carts with colored lanterns and banners would be rolling from the palace down to the river and across it, out from the palace to Stonemarket and the Smoke, north from the palace to the bridge to Riverport. From and from and from, like someone had upended a cup of wine at the top of Palace Hill and the red ran down everywhere.

The Daris Brotherhood was one of the three largest compounds. Even though her grandfather had changed the mysteries they followed to Clovas, Elaine had been to dozens of public events at the Daris. Feasts, mostly, but also a few rituals that the brotherhood put on to entertain the children. She could still remember hunting for golden acorns hidden in the courtyard where she and her cousin Andomaka now sat.

Andomaka Chaalat was a shockingly pale woman with a sense of being always a little apart from the world, like a mother watching children gambol in a nursery. Indulgent, amused, and also preoccupied with thoughts of her own which she didn't share.

They sat under a wide cloth banner that was strung between a ring set in one wall and an ironwork scaffold. It gave them both shade, and if there was a hint of chill that came with the shadow, it was a small price to pay for such easy company. It was hard, in the end, to want to turn the conversation toward the dead prince and his mysterious study. Elaine did it anyway.

"Now that I'm in the palace," she said, "I think I didn't know Ausai as well as I should have. You know? It just... everything feels like him."

"You feel like an intruder in someone else's house," Andomaka said, nodding. "Like you don't belong there."

"That's silly, isn't it?"

Andomaka's smile seemed like half a dream. "You feel what you feel. No one can judge your heart except you. And, I suppose, the gods."

"I talked to Mikah Ell. The historian? She said that being the prince changes you."

"Did she? Well, she's a very clever woman. I suppose it would have to, wouldn't it? A city is like a body that we're all part of. If a finger woke up one morning to discover it was a toe, that would feel odd, wouldn't it? Poor finger."

"You knew Ausai well, didn't you?"

"I did," Andomaka said. "I still do, I hope."

"Was he happy?"

"Hm," Andomaka said, her attention turning inward. After a moment, she shook her head. "I was just thinking. My cousin, daughter of the prince, one day prince herself, comes to sit with me and ask if the old prince was happy. The prince that was, the prince that is, and the prince that will be. And me, of course, who would be in danger of the palace if you fell."

"Yes?"

"I was thinking what it would mean if I'd dreamed it."

A bird flew past, a small rush of brown wings that bent up to the sky and was gone. From one of the upper windows, a man looked out at them. Andomaka's head of guard. The one who'd been burned. He stepped away into the building like a fish sliding deeper into a murky pond.

"I think it would mean I was frightened," Andomaka said, and her focus returned to Elaine. "Are you frightened?"

Elaine tried to smile, tried to laugh, but the effort was more than she could manage. Instead, she leaned forward, clasping her hands together. Tears came to her eyes, and her pale cousin put a hand on her shoulder.

"You are, then," Andomaka said. "Is it your father? Has something happened with him?"

Elaine coughed out a laugh, because that was why she had come, and now that she was here, Ausai and his books and her father's unease weren't what pressed at her heart. Around them, birds sang, and she wished they would be quiet.

"No, something's happened with me," she said. "What do you do when you think that maybe the best thing that's going to happen to you already has?"

"You're young," Andomaka said.

"That doesn't make it better. What if, in your whole life, there's only one moment that's really your own, and all the rest belongs to other people. You have to think about them, and how you're supposed to be."

"Then at least you have one moment."

"And after?" Elaine smiled, and a traitorous tear slipped from her eye. "What about when the moment's gone. How long can you live on memory?"

It gives you everything because it costs you everything, she thought. *It doesn't love you, and it isn't fair.*

Andomaka drew her nearly invisible eyebrows together and

gently touched her forehead to Elaine's. It felt warmer than an embrace. She was ashamed that she was weeping, and it was all she could do to manage not to sob. The sorrow was a shock to her. She'd thought she was happy. And she was. It was only that the joy hurt so much by being over.

Andomaka took a deep slow breath, and then another. Elaine took the cue, matching the older woman breath for breath. In, and pause at the top of the breath, release, and pause at the bottom when there was nothing left inside her. And after a few cycles of it, she found herself growing calmer.

"Being young is terrible," Andomaka said. "Some days, being young is like having your skin come off. Even the air hurts."

Elaine wiped her tears away with the cuff of her sleeve. "Does it get better?"

"Sometimes. For some people. Sometimes it's just the way things are. But I would be surprised if a woman your age could become a woman my age and not pass through some moments of real joy along the path."

"It doesn't feel like that."

Andomaka sighed. "If you saw the way out, it wouldn't be despair. When you do see it, no matter how bad the pain may be, it won't be despair anymore, will it?"

"I'm sorry. This is silly of me, I suppose."

"No," the pale woman said. "It isn't. Despair and joy and becoming who you're going to be. This is serious work. I'm flattered that you came to me. I will be here whenever you need whatever you need."

"Thank you," Elaine said. And then, more quietly, "Thank you."

When the time came, Garreth wasn't asked to volunteer. None of the new recruits were.

It was two days before harvest festival, and Garreth was getting ready for his next patrol. Each day was growing noticeably shorter than the one before, and the nights were cold in a way they hadn't been since the cold spring before. This was the first shift Garreth wasn't guarding the tax station at the gate or collecting tolls at the bridges, and he'd be going with Old Boar and Kannish's uncle Marsen. Maur had warned him to expect some pranks and hazing, so at first he thought Hellat was joking.

"Your patrol's off," Hellat said.

"Sure it is," Garreth agreed, still tying on his boots.

"No, seriously. You're here for the day. And the captain wants you out on the drill ground. Now."

Garreth finished his boots, still half expecting to go out to find Old Boar and Marsen pointing and laughing at his anxiety, but the captain was, in fact, pacing the yard. Half a dozen of the new recruits were with him, and more running up to join the little crowd. Garreth thought there was something odd, but he didn't put his finger on what until he was almost there. Captain Senit wasn't in his blue. He had on a brown cloak and pale yellow shirt. When Garreth pushed in beside Kannish and Maur, he saw that there was a shirt of thin mail under the yellow and a short scabbard at the man's hip.

"All right, listen here," the captain said as the last of the new recruits arrived. "Everything that was going to happen today, won't. I've put scant groups at the gates and bridges. You lot are to be here. You're covering the whole fucking city this side of the river."

By the main entrance, Beren and Old Boar were laughing and sharing a pipe. The smoke came out of Old Boar's nostrils like his head was a forge. Neither of them were in blue cloaks either, and they weren't wearing their badges of office. Garreth shifted from foot to foot.

"Marsen Wellis is taking command while the rest of us are gone. You do as he says. If something happens that needs us—and when I say needs, I mean a fire, a riot, or an attack by a foreign fucking army—Marsen decides which of you bastards has to go take care of it. Do your best. If Kithamar hasn't burned to the waterline by the time I'm back, you'll have done well enough."

"What's going on?" Maur asked for all of them.

Captain Senit's grin made him look younger. "Coordinated operation. Don't worry yourselves, children. We'll be back before sundown," he said, and dismissed them with a gesture.

Garreth turned and started back toward the barracks with a sense of disorientation.

"This is it," Maur said. "We're taking down Aunt Thorn. We're actually doing it."

"They're actually doing it," Kannish said. "We're actually

sitting on our hands while they do it. And Uncle Marsen too. That's crap. He's the one who started this. He should get to be there at the end."

"You know the end is a lot of fighting in very close quarters with people who know the lay of the land and like killing bluecloaks," Maur said. "Anyone you lent money to, you should get it back before they go. Some of them, we won't be seeing again."

In groups of two and three, the veterans made their way out to the street. To someone who didn't know better, it might almost have seemed casual. Garreth knew enough to see that each departure was planned, coordinated, and set to a schedule too important for him to know. The blades they wore were short and brutal, more knife than sword. It was going to be close work for them. He imagined himself running down into a dark hallway underground. He felt relief at knowing it wouldn't be him down there, and shame at the relief.

When the last of them had gone, Marsen called them out to run drills. It was late morning by then, but the sun wasn't punishingly hot, and Marsen seemed more intent on giving the barracks an appearance of normalcy than taking out any frustration on the new guards. There was wisdom in it. If any of Aunt Thorn's people came by, they would see the barracks very nearly as peopled as usual. There wouldn't be any reason to wonder why things seemed sparse, and so less reason for any alarm to be raised. He didn't like thinking too much about how different a surprise attack on the underground city would be from one with Aunt Thorn forewarned.

"Garreth Left," Marsen shouted.

Garreth fell out of the drill and ran to the for-the-time commander. "Sir?"

"You have someone wants to talk with you. Keep it short,"

Marsen said, and nodded toward the main gate where Vasch stood waiting.

Divol Senit walked through the open streets of Kithamar like he was stepping onto a battlefield. It was hard not to swagger. He'd been sending his best men to the entrances he'd mapped out. Without perfect knowledge of where Aunt Thorn's tunnels lay, he'd had to make guesses, but they were educated guesses. He'd been over the plan with Pavvis and Laufin. It was going to be the largest single action the city guard had ever coordinated. Come nightfall, Aunt Thorn and everyone who answered to her would be in the gaol or the river, and he didn't much care which.

The intersection where he'd seen Aunt Thorn hadn't changed much since the day he'd seen her there. The same door, the same red banners. But where there had been nearly empty streets before, now there were handcarts delivering wine and bread and fruit to the houses. Three of his men were in the street hanging the colored lanterns for harvest festival while a local woman with a round Inlisc face and curling Inlisc hair criticized them. Beren and Nattan Torr sat on the cobbles playing at dice and passing a wineskin back and forth between them. A young girl squatted beside them looking bored.

Senit leaned on the wall behind Beren where he could seem to be watching their dice and still keep a clear view of the door. "Hey there, little one," he said, and the girl looked up at him. "You're my runner?"

She nodded.

"You know your job?"

"When you say it, I go to the square next to Jamme Cortonn's shop, and the man with the red vest gives me a silver."

Senit nodded. "That's the heart of it."

Each of the apparently innocuous doors and gates that he'd put his men at had runners like this. At his word, they'd trip through the full city, and every time one appeared, they'd set two or three more running. Even with crossing the river, he figured he could send the signal to attack from here to the western wall of Stonemarket in under an hour. Two-thirds of the entrance points, they'd storm with blades and fire. The other third, his people would wait in ambush for the rats to run. He felt thirsty, but not for water or for wine.

He had to force himself not to stare at the doorway. He imagined Aunt Thorn on the other side of it.

"Boys," he said as Nattan Torr rolled three dice and pretended to have lost the throw, "if this goes bad, it's been an honor serving the city with you."

"Won't, though," Beren said. "We'll hang these bastards up by their tendons and let the cats eat whatever falls off."

"Leave a few for the magistrates or they'll be angry we had all the fun," Nattan Torr said. Senit felt a moment of vast affection for his guard. Not just the two at his side, but all of them.

"What's your name, little?" he asked.

The girl squinted up at him. "Mir."

"Well, Mir. Why don't you run and get yourself some silver?"

On any other day, there would have been people in the common room eating or drinking, gathering before their patrol or coming back from it. The pegs along the east wall all had the oilskins for the patrols to take on the wet days. The fire grate was cold and clean of ash. Garreth sat on one of the worn benches and his brother stood, hands clasping and unclasping the way they always did when he was anxious. The emptiness of the room made it seem larger, and the space that divided them, more.

Vasch breathed in deeply, like he was standing on the edge of the bridge and daring himself to jump. Garreth's jaw ached, and he realized it hadn't in days. Maybe weeks. Maybe since he left home.

"How are things at the house?" he asked at last, taking a kind of mercy on his younger brother.

"Tense," Vasch said. "Angry." He made an unconscious sweeping motion with his right hand, the same way their mother did. "You leaving changed things."

"I know," Garreth said. "I'm sorry for that."

"Uncle Robbson said he talked to you? About the sugar barge?"

In the training yard, someone shouted for the sparring to begin. The sound of wooden practice swords clacking together grated. "He did," Garreth said.

"They want you to come back," Vasch said, nodding to himself. "And I come here and . . . I mean, you're sleeping in a room with five other men. You're barely drawing enough in wages to feed yourself, much less find a house of your own or support a business."

"I'm fine," Garreth said. "The pay isn't the point."

"I've been tutoring Yrith. Telling her how Kithamar is, how it would be here, for her. She's not what you think she is. She really isn't."

Vasch wasn't looking at him. His brother's eyes shifted from the fire grate to the window to the floor. Anyplace but Garreth himself. His mouth had the thin-pressed look it got when he was nauseated. All Garreth felt was tired.

"I'm sure that's true," he said, but Vasch went on as if he hadn't spoken.

"She's funny too. You don't see it until you've spent time with her, but she has a wicked sense for a joke. And she's lonely. She gave up so much to come here, and we didn't even ask her. We didn't know." Vasch sank down on the bench across from him, his elbows resting on his knees.

"I'm sure that's true too," Garreth said. "I'm sure, given time, I could come to know her. And I'm sure she's a fine person."

"They don't know I'm here. You won't tell them I came, will you?"

"I know you want me back at home. I've let the family down by leaving. I feel the weight of that, I do. But who I am and who you want me to be? They don't fit."

"I don't know what I want," Vasch said, then looked him in the eyes for the first time since he'd come. "That's not true, though. I look at you here, and I see you making a mistake. No, let me finish. I see you missing your friends and wanting to still be who you were when you were a boy. I see you putting Father in his place for trying to tell you what your life would be. You're doing this from spite, and you don't regret it now, but in five years? In ten? Twenty? You'll be someone like Kannish's uncle, bragging about things that didn't really happen to him and making himself out to be the hero of the age when he's really just a hired sword who happens to get paid out of our taxes. I want better than that for you. I do. I want you to have the life you deserve, not this. But...but if you come back, I'm not sure I can stay."

Garreth felt he'd misheard, or misunderstood what he'd heard. He knew the words, but he couldn't put meaning to them.

"I don't think I can watch you marry her," Vasch said. "I think it would kill me. So I don't know what to do."

Garreth leaned forward, his posture matching his brother's

so closely that they were like different sides of a strange mirror. "You're in love with her."

"I haven't told her. I haven't told anyone. But when you left, I was so glad. And I felt terrible for feeling glad. I thought maybe I would step in. I'd be the one who married her, and we'd get the caravan and save the house, and I'd . . . I'd be with her. Then Father and Robbson started planning ways to bring you back, and I've been so frightened. And I'm so sorry for wanting you to never come back, because I also want you home." A tear ran down his cheek, and he ignored it. "I'm a mess, brother. I'm at war with myself and with you."

As if in response, the shouts from the training yard changed. The wood-against-wood clatter gave way to the sharpness of live steel. And then a whistle, sounding the alarm.

Garreth was up and moving to the doorway before he knew he meant to. The rush of blood in his ears was almost deafening. He had a short sword at his belt, and he put his hand on the pommel.

"What's the matter?" Vasch said.

"Stay there," Garreth said.

Senit was the first man up to the door with the red banners. He didn't pause to knock or call out, just strode across the busy street, drawing his blade as he went, and kicked the door at the latched edge. Wood splintered under his foot, but it took a second kick to open it. Before the street noticed anything odd was happening, he was pushing inside, ready for the fight.

The interior of the wooden building had burned at some point. The bare studs and rafters were old char and ashes. Beams of light cut down from holes in the roof, and the floor was debris and pigeon shit. Senit moved forward quickly, blade at the ready and teeth bared. No enemy leapt at him.

"All right," he said. "There's a way down in here somewhere. Let's find it."

He moved forward, following the footprints in the dust and shit. They led toward the back of the structure, and then to the right, where they seemed to delta out, following no particular direction. Like people had stood milling about in the space before turning back the way they'd come.

"Right in here," Senit said, stamping on the floor, listening to how his footfall sounded. Behind him, Old Boar was prying up a loose floorboard. Senit gestured for the others to help him. It a few minutes they had a new hole leading down into a thin crawlspace. The thinnest of them was Daud Belling, and he snaked down into the dark with a dagger between his teeth. As soon as he was gone, Senit squatted at the entrance.

"Look for where there's a structure. A hidden stair or an old well. Knock on the floor beside it and we'll find the way down or we'll make one."

Silence lasted longer than he liked, but he could hear the scraping and shifting as Daud moved beneath them. When his head reappeared, he was covered in dust.

"There's nothing down here, Captain," he said. "It's just dirt."

"Fuck are you talking about?"

"There's no passage down under this building, sir. It's an open crawl. There's just dirt and rat shit."

"Open that fucking hole wider. I'll find it my damn self," Senit said. But the fear was already in him.

The attackers didn't run. It would have been less frightening if they had. In the training yard and by the stables, they walked. A dozen of them at least, and likely more. Garreth drew his sword. There was a scrap in the training yard: three guardsmen falling back as five intruders closed on them. At the stables, four men had blades drawn—two in blue cloaks, and two in rough leather that didn't belong. Whistles were blowing at the back of the barracks and in the street outside it.

It felt like they were everywhere. *They're going to kill us all*, Garreth thought. And then, *They're going to kill Vasch*. He turned one direction and then the other, looking for a place to take the fight that wouldn't overwhelm him.

"Hey!" he shouted, in aggression and fear. "Hey, get the fuck out of here, all of you!"

And as if in answer, Maur's voice, high and fluting with panic, called out from the kitchens. "Over here! To me!"

Garreth ran. Long, loping strides that felt like he could cover whole streets between one footstep and the next. The promise and threat of violence widened him until he felt like the whole barracks was part of his body. Like some spirit or small god had come into him with strength and sureness that was more than his own.

When he rounded the corner of the building, he saw Maur surrounded. Two Inlisc men and a Hansch woman, all with blades out, had put Maur in the middle of the open space where the guard hung their cloaks and blankets to dry. They circled him like wolves around a dog, patient and cruel, while Maur spun, trying to protect all sides at once.

Garreth didn't slow his run, but angled it toward the invaders, ready to crash into them with the force of his whole body. The Hansch woman caught sight of him, but misjudged his speed, scuttling back when he was already too close to her. He swung hard for her leg and pushed the blocking sword back, leaving a shallow cut by her knee. His momentum took him past her, but only just. He turned on her, striking as fast as he could think.

Thrusting at her face, then her foot, then her gut, driving her backward through fury and will instead of strategy.

On the training field, Beren said that the fight was won by the smartest, but Garreth didn't think. A blazing rage was lifting him up, and the idea that he might die in the next few seconds seemed weak and implausible. It wasn't that it was untrue, but that it was spectacularly unimportant. He swung down at her three times, as fast as he'd ever managed, and the third time, she cried out, stumbling. A movement to his right danced him away from a killing blow, and the larger of the two Inlisc men cut the air where he had been.

Behind the new enemy, Maur had improved his position and was driving the smaller of the Inlisc men back with careful, intentional thrusts. Garreth shouted, and his voice seemed louder than it could have been. The new man shifted, turning Garreth away from the woman, who took the chance to drop her blade and run.

"You come to *my . . . fucking . . . house*," Garreth said, punctuating each word with a thrust of the blade toward the man's eyes. "You hurt *my* people. You don't want to fucking *live*."

Maur glanced back at them, his face cool and composed. As Garreth's enemy set to counterstrike, Maur jumped back from his own opponent, safely out of the man's reach, and threw his sword. The blade spun end over end, striking the man's shoulder and distracting him just long enough for Garreth's next strike to take him in the throat.

Garreth had never killed a man before. He'd never really hurt anyone. The blade pushed into the hard cartilage of the man's windpipe with a crunch that was unlike anything he had felt. It was just a bit of vibration carried from steel to grip to hand to wrist, but Garreth knew that it was death. The man jumped back, striking at Garreth's blade in a late parry. Blood poured down his neck, and his eyes shifted from left to right like he was looking for somewhere to run. Maur slipped around behind Garreth, scooping up the sword the Hansch woman had dropped. The dead man swung at Garreth, and the strike had a surprising strength behind it.

The next one had less.

The man fell to his knees, his expression focused and angry as he tried to draw another breath. The blood at his throat bubbled.

"Just a thought," Maur said, his voice conversational. "You should probably leave."

The last of the three wolves, suddenly alone and outnumbered, turned and ran. The dead man tried to rise to his feet, but failed. He knelt on the stones where the drying lines would have been strung, and died kneeling.

"What the fuck is going on, Maur?" The incandescent rage that had lifted Garreth up was passing, and he felt a trembling in his body like the whole world was shaking and he was the only thing standing still.

"It was a trap," Maur said. "They got all the experienced guards out of the barracks so they could come for us."

"Why? Who are we?"

They looked at each other for what seemed like a long moment and was probably less than a breath.

"Fuck," Garreth said, and sprinted for the holding cell. Maur ran at his heels.

Three men were at the open door to the cell, and none of them were guardsmen. Garreth pulled up his sword like a mouse lifting a toothpick. "Get away from there. All of you."

Maur put his stolen blade at the ready, and a woman stepped out of the door. She was Inlisc, with close-cut black hair and a scar that crossed one milk-white eye. Her hands and sleeves were bloody to the elbow.

"What did you do?" Garreth said.

Aunt Thorn considered him like a fisherman deciding whether to keep a young fish or throw it back.

"He stole from me. He sold my secrets to my enemy. He broke the rules," she said. "I believe in rules, don't you?"

She walked away, not even glancing back at them as she went. Her three bodyguards fell back with her, their eyes on Maur and Garreth and their swords ready for violence. Slowly, Maur let the point of his sword sink until it was touching the paving stones.

After they were gone, Garreth went into the cell to see what was left of the man. It had been an ugly death.

The older, more experienced guards came back throughout the afternoon. Some hurried as if there were still a chance to catch the fight that was already over. Others came in slowly, and from farther. They had been spread as far as the hospital outside the city walls, and they returned with the quiet anger of a team that has given its best and been humiliated.

Vasch had come out of the common room to the carnage with wide eyes and ashen cheeks, safe enough but shaken. Garreth had seen him leave, but didn't speak to him. The intrigues of House Left seemed to matter less now, and perhaps his little brother had understood that too.

Four guardsmen had died in the attack, and five had been wounded. Three of the enemy were dead, including the man Garreth had ended. And the prisoner. The thief. The man who had stolen from Aunt Thorn and paid the price for it.

Captain Senit came in almost last, arriving at sundown. He took the report from Marsen Wellis: the names of the dead, the damage done to the barracks, the price they'd been able to make the enemy suffer. He listened to it all like he was reading through the incident book in a normal morning. When he'd heard everything, he just nodded and gave the order that they'd be back on regular patrol come morning. He went to his office, returning a few minutes later with a handful of maps and a lantern. While the guardsmen watched, he took his burden to the center of the training field, doused the maps with lamp oil, and set them alight.

The smoke rose up like a dark pillar until it reached some invisible current of high air and was gone.

"And what did you make of them, then?" Theddan asked, leaning forward like a child anticipating a bit of honeystone.

They'd met at the Temple itself this time. The vast stone tower rose above streets teeming with the harvest festival. The poor of Longhill and Newmarket were lined up for blocks to accept the charity of Kithamar, and the priests and acolytes and novices had their hands more than full keeping order. Even though Elaine and Theddan were sitting cross-legged in a storage shed at the back, between the Temple proper and the city wall, the sound of voices was like a storm without the wind.

"I don't know," Elaine said. "Halev told me the most, but he also made it very clear he wasn't going to tell me all that he knew."

"Condescending," Theddan said, dismissing him with a wave of her hand. "The others?"

"I can't tell how well Andomaka Chaalat actually knew Ausai. I mean, yes, she's head of the Daris Brotherhood, and Ausai was Daris, but I can't tell how pious he was."

"Did she say he was distant? Strange?"

"She said she knew him well and that she hoped she still did, but then we found ourselves on other subjects. She's...I like her. She's easy to talk with, and she listens, and she sees the world in a very different way. Like she's looking at everything from the side."

"She's the next in succession," Theddan said. "If you and your father catch the same fever, she's Kithamar."

"I don't think she cares."

Theddan shook her head. "No feast that great goes without caring. She might be hungry and want it, she might be sated and dread it, but she cares. Count on that."

Elaine leaned back against a pile of crates. Something in them clanged with the sound of tin against tin. "The historian was strange. She talked and told me things. At the time, it felt like she was answering my questions, but in the end, I think she learned more than I did. I didn't come away understanding Ausai any better than when I went in. I know he had some strange books. I know he had lovers, and that he was married but without children."

"Well, that's certainly ominous," Theddan said. "A man with a wife and no children must be a font of evil."

"Sarcasm? Really? That's what I came here for?"

"What about Kint?"

"You said not to talk with him. And that I should be barring my bedroom door in case he tried to kill me in my sleep."

"Did I? Well, I was probably very wise. But if there's nothing and no one, maybe it's time to take the chance."

"Or maybe I'm jumping at shadows. They all say that becoming prince changes you. Maybe that's all this is. My father is learning what his life is now, and it's not what he expected. The people he knew had secrets. The world wasn't quite what it seemed to be."

"And so you're learning that too, but at a remove. All the distress and none of the details," Theddan said. "That could be. Well, and if someone tries to murder you for asking questions, then you'll know it was more than that."

"So comforting."

"My turn now," Theddan said, and Elaine relaxed back and spent the better part of an hour hearing about the intrigues of the Temple. Which priests were meeting outside the appointed ritual times for sex or heretical conversations or to funnel stolen relics and artifacts out to accomplices in Seepwater and Longhill. The crossed loyalties, the passions both pious and otherwise, the proxy wars fought by men on behalf of gods. Theddan wove a tapestry of conspiracy and honor and magic as rich and full as anything in Palace Hill. And when she was done, it was past time for Elaine to go.

Her carriage waited for her on the street, and she hurried to it with her cloak's hood raised to hide her face. Not that many people outside the Temple proper would have recognized her on sight.

"It may be a long ride back, my lady," the coachman said. "The streets are full. And without the palace guard to clear the way..."

"I have to be back to the palace by nightfall," she said. "We don't need to run anyone down for that, do we?"

He chuckled. "We do not."

He closed the carriage door and she latched it from within. Not that she was afraid, but it was the third and final day of harvest festival. There would be many, many people in Kithamar who'd had too much wine and too little sleep. The scraping sounds of the coachman taking his place, his voice gently commanding the team, and the carriage shook under her as she started the long journey through Newmarket, across the bridge to Oldgate, and then the vertiginous rise toward home. The clatter of wheels on cobblestones was a bright, percussive music of its own for almost five streets before they came across a crowd and had to slow.

Harvest festival was an ending to the year. A celebration of work done and also a vast communal bracing for the long, cold nights to come. By the time spring returned, they would all have forgotten what heat felt like, what a river was when you couldn't walk across the ice of it, that the trees were sometimes green. Knowledge was one thing, but experience was something else. She could know that days grew long, and the sun grew warm, but in the darkness and the cold, it was like knowing a song and not singing it. What was true for her was true for everyone.

The faces she passed as the coachman picked his way through the streets were merry and jovial and relieved, but she imagined she saw the shadow of dread behind them. Women wore wreaths of bright autumn leaves—yellow and gold and red. Not green. The knowledge of what they would all have to endure when the winter that was only threatening arrived drove the exuberance and joy. A last dance, a last drink, a last kiss before the long duration began.

There was, she thought, a great deal to love in Kithamar. Her city could be grey and cold and distant, but she also drove by doorways where men served out soup by the steaming bowlful to anyone that passed. She saw fathers carrying children on their shoulders to give the little ones a better view of the sea of their fellow revelers. She stopped at a square where five roads met and had to wait for a great dance to finish—men and women in their brightest clothes moving together while an old man with a beard that touched his belly sang out instructions and beat a melodic drum.

Newmarket was neither the wealthiest nor the poorest quarter of Kithamar. The people dancing in the street were neither fighting to live nor trying to outdo their neighbors with vast spectacle and shows of wealth. They were taking a moment together, sharing food and a day and a ritual to remind themselves and each other that another year had passed, that they were still here, and still together. A memory stirred. The nature of gods. The creation of something when people came together. Watching as the street dance ended in embraces and laughter, she could wish that gods really were made that way. She could hope.

Once the way was clear, the coachman took them through smaller, emptier streets, travelling farther from their usual route but faster. The carriage hummed with the textures of the pavement, swaying when they turned. The hoofbeats of the team took on a hypnotic pattern, and Elaine found herself drifting into thoughts that had no coherence to them. A song she'd sung with a tutor when she was young. The view from the window of her cell in the Clovas Brotherhood. The high priest of the Temple saying that there were gods in the streets, but yoked like the horses pulling her. Constrained by the coachman of the city who had been her great-uncle and was her father. On the edge of dream, she imagined a giant form sitting on Palace Hill with its legs dangling down the face of Oldgate, a great whip in its hand...

The coachman shouted and the carriage shuddered to a stop. Elaine came back to full wakefulness and looked out her window. They were stopped on the bridge between Newmarket and Oldgate. The carriage was high enough that she could look out over the Khahon flowing down at her from the port. Dark water shimmering gold. She was reaching up to open the panel when the coachman's muffled voice came through, but not speaking to her.

"What the fuck are you doing?"

"I'm collecting bridge tolls," a man's voice answered from ahead of them. "That's what we do here. Or is this your first time crossing a bridge?"

"Do you see this carriage? You see the side? This is a palace carriage. I am carrying Elaine a Sal. Prince a Sal's daughter. So the tolls you're collecting are going pretty much straight into her pocket. We don't pay tolls."

There was a pause. Softer voices, conferring.

"I didn't know that," the man said.

"Your first time on a bridge?" the coachman asked.

"Sorry. Go ahead."

The carriage shook and started forward when between one heartbeat and the next, she knew the voice. She burst up, slamming the panel open. "Stop the horses! Stop!"

The carriage juddered to a halt again. They hadn't gone more than two or three lengths. She opened the door and leaned out. The three bluecloaks they'd passed by looked toward her with dread. Two of them might have been the ones from the boathouse. The third certainly was.

She let herself down to the pavement. Her heart felt like it was tripping down stairs, but she kept her steps even and calm. He was in a guard's cloak with a sword at his side and a badge of office hanging from his belt. She saw when he recognized her. The other two knelt, and the smaller of them tugged at Gareth's hem, trying to get him to do the same. Instead, he took a step toward her and they both stopped. He was close enough she could have reached out and touched his arm, but she didn't.

"New job?" she said.

He glanced uncertainly over her shoulder as if he was still waiting for the prince's daughter to look out of the carriage door, then turned back to her. His confusion wasn't enough to drown his smile. "Yeah. Some things happened. It's kind of a long story."

She lifted an eyebrow, gave him a half-smile. "I'd like to hear it sometime." She nodded once, turned back to the carriage, and lifted herself into it. The air on the bridge had gotten very thin, somehow, because it was hard to catch her breath. She opened the panel and said *We can go* before settling back in her seat. The carriage clattered and swung. She put her hands to her cheeks, and they were warm. They ached a little from grinning.

She'd found him. She'd seen him again. He knew who she was now.

Slowly, the grin faded with the joy and something unexpected and sadder took its place.

He knew who she was now.

Garreth leaned against the stone wall and sank slowly to the pavement. His mind felt like there was a wind blowing through it. The carriage reached the far side of the river and turned up the switchback that would take it, if it went long enough, to the top of Oldgate. To Palace Hill.

He rested his head on his knees.

"Garreth?" Kannish said. "What just happened?"

PART THREE

WINTER

A city without desire is not a city, nor will lust alone suffice to make it one. Desire, jealousy, triumph, spite, solace, rage, forgiveness, hope. The passion of a mother for her child. The need of a child for honest food. The longing of a man for a woman or for another man or for a past he can never reclaim. Without all the thousand hungers that our artless souls are born to suffer, a city is only a complication of wood and stone.

—From the pillow book of Anayi a Jimental,
poet to the court of Daos a Sal

The first snow came early that year, white flakes bundling down from a grey-white sky that seemed almost low enough to touch. It began just after the first light of dawn, and by midmorning the streets outside House Left were bright with it. It piled onto the tops of the houses and added an inch of perfect, fragile white to the wall at the edge of the kitchen garden. All that was dark in Kithamar became for a moment softer, lighter. The shadows lost their edges, and Kithamar seemed to lean back into itself like a cat among blankets. Here and there, some small bit of color stood out, the whiteness around it making what had been there but unseen suddenly visible. The saturated redness of a fallen leaf, the yellow of a merchant's sign, the rich brown coat of a spring-born pup discovering snowfall for the first time.

And even though the sounds were all there—horses and dogs and cartwheels and men—the snow quieted them. Vasch, standing at the front of the house and looking out at the sudden winter that had come upon them, could imagine himself removed from the world. As if his home, his little corner of warmth, had retreated from Kithamar and stood now on some other street with the same neighbors, the same landmarks, the same place on the map, but also more removed, and everywhere the sweet, bright smell of pine sap and smoke.

Vasch Left wore a high-collared black robe with silver buttons polished until they were as bright as the snow. A twig of evergreen was pinned to his breast. His breath plumed in the cold.

Down the street, a figure in black hurried toward him. The other man's head was bowed, and flakes of snow caught in his hair. Vasch took a step toward him as if he could bring him closer by mere force of will.

When, at last, the priest reached the doorway, his cheeks and the tip of his nose were red with cold. The leather cloak that he wore against the wet was black with snowmelt. His smile was wide as the street.

"Vasch Left," he said. "Well, what a day for you. For both of us, really. I remember your induction."

"I've gotten a little better with the rites since then," Vasch said. "Thank you so much for doing this."

"I'm honored for the chance."

Father stepped into the doorway and waved them in. "Please, both of you. Come in. No reason to inspire speculation, is there?"

Vasch and the priest stepped into the warmth of the house. Fires were burning in every grate, and the lamps were lit, and the glow from them seemed buttery and rich after the snow light. Father closed the door and bolted it as Serria helped the priest take off his cloak. Beneath it, he wore the blue and gold of the Odimin rites, and the jeweled silver torc reserved for the great rites: birth and death and marriage. Vasch's father flinched when he saw it, but it was such a small gesture and so brief that it escaped the priest entirely.

"I am so glad you could come," Father said. "You do understand that this needs to be very discreet. For the moment, anyway? It's important that any public ceremony come later."

"I know, Mannon. You may rely on me. I won't say a word to anyone."

"Good, good," Father said, but Vasch could hear the concern behind it. "Before we start, why don't you come have a cup of wine. Serria's heated a pot."

"Oh, is that what I smell? Well, I don't see why we shouldn't."

Father steered the priest away with only a glance over his shoulder that said *Don't worry. I'll take care of this.* Vasch went to the front door and checked again that it was locked.

The dining room had been emptied of its table and chairs, and an altar put up in their place. It was wide and low with a statue of Reyek-Ano, god of peace and commerce. Also, in some traditions, of liars. Yrith stood before it, considering the god with quiet amusement. She wore a wedding gown of deep blue and bright white, even though there wouldn't be anyone there to see the preciousness of the cloth. Vasch moved to her side, aware of her breath and her body like all his senses had been polished.

"Do you have Reyek-Ano? In the north?" Vasch asked.

"No," Yrith said. "You have many gods here. It is strange to me. Do you believe in this one?"

"He's the god of our house and our guild. What? Was that funny?"

"I ask if you believe, and you give me his label. It is a strange answer. Do you believe that this one is listening to your prayers? Is moving the world for you?"

Vasch shrugged. "Like the way I think the sun will rise in the morning or that there'll be mice in the grain if you don't catch them? I guess that way I don't. It's more like an agreement."

"You make a contract with your god?"

"I make a contract with the people around me that we will all agree to believe something together. There are hundreds of gods in Kithamar, and all of them have someone who follows them. Or some group of them. But believing in any of them too strongly is . . . well, it's rude."

"Rude?"

"If someone is too pious or celebrates their house gods too much, it starts to feel like they're saying their way is better than everyone else's. I mean, there are some people who will anyway, but everyone else looks down on them. It isn't like that for you?"

She turned toward him. "Do you have marriage the same way? Never too real. There, but not too much there?" And before he could answer, she went on, "I am not of the city. I only want to understand."

"Well, um. There's more than one answer, really," he said, but even as the words came, he knew there was only one that mattered.

Her chaperone stepped into the room and said something in her native language that sounded, if he understood it, like *The mice are wet and the cats have the fire*, which didn't make any sense to him. So either it was an idiom or he'd misunderstood.

Yrith fluttered her hand the way she did when she was looking for a word she didn't know yet or couldn't recall, then laughed at her own distress, and said, "Forgive."

He watched her leave. The chaperone paused in the doorway and pointed all four fingers of her hand at him, bobbing them rapidly in a sign that was supposed to reassure him. It even did, a little bit. For the next hour, while his father took measure of the priest, Vasch paced the house like a dog in a new kennel. He wished his mother had come back to the city for the wedding. And that Garreth could be present for it. And that it could be done in the Temple instead of making do with the thrown-together altars and ceremonies here in the house. But he understood the need, and it was policy.

When his father found him, he was sitting by the fire in the front drawing room with a split log of pine ready to go on the flames. Vasch looked up, and his mouth was as dry as sand.

"I think we can proceed now," his father said.

Vasch reached into the grate, placing the log gently on the charred, glowing embers. Flame licked up around the rough bark at once, and sap hissed as it burned away. He stood looking into the fire and tried to find something calm in his heart. It was all elation and fear and guilt and hope, and none of it still between one breath and the next.

"Vasch," his father said. "It's time."

The firmness of his tone meant he was afraid that Vasch would follow Garreth's example. Maybe bolt out of the house and run down the streets to escape. He loved his father, but sometimes he wondered whether they really knew each other.

The group gathered before the altar was pitiably small. The priest and Yrith. Uncle Robbson scowling in his formal robe, and Serria smiling and taking the place of the lady of the house. The chaperone and Father took their places as well, and that was all.

The priest closed his eyes, lifted his hands. "We call upon you, Reyek-Ano, and the spirits of your house beyond the world. Witness now the union of these two, your servants in this house at this time."

Vasch had been to weddings before, and though this one was small, the form was more or less the same. The calling of the gods. The blessings of the two families—in this case performed by Father and Yrith's chaperone. The breathing in of smoke and the washing of each other's hands. When he'd watched other people performing the rites, they'd seemed deep and resonant. Or at least meaningful. Now that it was him and it was her, he couldn't help imagining how they would seem to Yrith. A series of actions and words, strung together in an order with no inherent meaning apart from the completion of a contract. If he had harbored any doubts about his own plans and intentions, the hollowness of the wedding ended them.

Half an hour after he'd stepped in, the priest put his hand and Yrith's together, and set them to look into each other's eyes as he waved a censer over them and stroked the smoke over them like he was petting a cat. They were married. He had a wife. She had a husband. To Robbson and Mother and Father, it meant they had a winter caravan and hope for the house to regain its footing. He looked into Yrith's eyes for some emotion—amusement, anger, fear, pleasure, anything. Anything at all. Yrith's smile was small and polite, and when the ceremony was over, she didn't try to keep hold of his fingers.

Father and the chaperone signed the wedding vows, with the priest and Serria making witness marks. "Be sure the date is clear," Father said. "It's very important that it be legible."

"Mannon, old friend," the priest said. "This is a joyful day." As if by saying it, it would be more nearly true.

"It is," Father said. "And when we are called before the magistrate to justify our caravan's arrival under guild rules, it will be joyful if we can answer clearly and in full."

If the priest's eyes betrayed a little pain, if the sacred nature of the rite seemed a little cheapened, if the celebration of love and union and all that it implied stood a little back from being sure all the copies of the marriage contract were identical, signed, and dated, still it was done. Father blotted the inked signatures with sand, and seemed to relax for the first time in weeks.

"There," he said. "All in place. I will take these to my office.

One for us, one for darling Yrith's family, and one for storage in the Temple until it's called upon. While I do that, Serria has prepared a little feast for us. Please don't wait for me."

The food was in the back drawing room, since the dining room had been taken up with the altar. Ham and beef and sweet potatoes. Seared spinach with cream. Blood pie. Everything heavy and rich, and the fire grate smoking just enough to flavor everything. Uncle Robbson and the priest talked over small things. Serria brought Yrith and her chaperone water flavored with lemon when they'd had enough of the wine. Father came in when they were half done to present leather scroll cases sealed with wax and handed them one to the priest and the other to Yrith's chaperone. When he started eating, it was with enough gusto that they all finished their meals together.

The snow was still falling, though less heavily, when Vasch and Robbson saw the priest off. Serria brought him his leather cloak, and Vasch noticed that the silver torc had come off before he stepped into the street. Twilight was a dimming of the clouds. A darkening of grey.

The door closed. The sounds of Serria overseeing the servants as they broke the altar down for storage and returned the dining room to its more usual function took the place of conversation or song. A less secretive wedding would have had speeches and gifts and all Vasch's friends playing pranks on him and Yrith and their families, and then making amends in the form of wallets of coin. There would have been wine and dancing and merriment until late into the night. Instead, it was just over. No one in the house but the family. Yrith still hidden from the city until the caravan arrived.

Uncle Robbson seemed to sense the oppression. "Don't suppose you and your lady wife would care to join me in a game of cards?" he offered with a forced jollity.

"Actually, I was hoping we could spend a moment alone, if that's all right."

Uncle Robbson coughed and reddened. "Of course, of course. I'll...ah...you...yes."

Yrith was in the hall by the kitchens, speaking to her chaperone in a liquid spill of syllables too fast for him to decipher. The chaperone was weeping and kissing Yrith's hands. Vasch didn't need to know the language to recognize a farewell. The older woman was leaving at once, going back by fast horse to her people and Vasch's mother with confirmation that this part of the bargain had been kept. And there was no need for a chaperone any longer. He made himself wait until they were done before he approached his wife.

"I have something I'd like to show you," he said.

Yrith nodded and took his hand. He led her up the stairs to the family's rooms and down the hall to the bedroom that was supposed to be theirs. When she saw what he had made, her eyes widened.

The bed was covered by a bright quilt with a hundred different swaths of fabric in a complex pattern. He had arranged a circle of stones on the floor in imitation of a fire pit, and four lanterns burned within it. A tin pot hung over the flames, and a silver cup waited beside them. Yrith walked into the room slowly. He couldn't tell if she was offended or amused or something else entirely.

When she put her hand on the quilt, he said, "It's all scraps from my family. My grandparents. My uncle. My parents. My brother too. I took one of the shirts he left behind. I didn't sew it myself. It wouldn't have been any good, and I wanted it to last. It's for you. It's yours."

Yrith plucked at the stitching. "It's good. You chose your stitcher well." She stepped to the false fire pit, looked down at it, and then up at him. A mischievous half-smile touched her lips. He sat beside the stones and she arranged herself across from him, spine straight and eyes forward like the floor was more comfortable and natural for her than any chair. Vasch poured the dark tea from the tin pot into the cup. It smelled pleasantly like turned earth. His hands were trembling.

"I'm sorry I don't have a seer or a bluestone man," he said.

"You've heard of bluestone men?"

"I asked around," Vasch said. "I did have something that I wanted to say, though?"

Yrith put out one hand, palm up, giving him permission. Vasch took a deep breath and let it out slowly. This had all seemed like such a good idea before, and now that the moment had come, he felt like an idiot. If he'd stripped to the skin, he wouldn't have felt more naked than he did now.

"I think about how I would have felt, coming to your people," he said. "Even if what I found there was wonderful, I think it would be...I'd feel like I'd lost something. I'd feel...sacrificed. Exiled. I'd feel I wasn't home. And so I imagine that's something you feel too."

He paused in case she wanted to say something. Hoping that maybe she'd interrupt. She waited, and he went on.

"We are doing something here for our families. And I hope it brings fortune to both our people, but that's for out there. That's the altar downstairs and the contracts and the business. That's not in here. And we're going to be doing something in here too."

Her eyebrows rose and he felt himself grinning back at her. "That sounded less forward when I was just thinking it, but here's what I'm trying to say. I don't want the altar downstairs to be the only one. I never imagined marrying an Inlisc woman, because I never imagined being Inlisc. And I'm not, but now

I also am. I have family in the north and I didn't before. And you're not Kithamari, but you also are, because you have family here now. And we aren't going to fit with the world. Not your world and not mine. We're something new. Even if other people have done something like this, they haven't done *this*. They weren't us."

The words were coming more flowingly now. He still felt as exposed, as raw, as defenseless before her. But he knew what he meant, and he could feel her listening.

"You asked if marriage was like our gods. Not too much there. Real, but not real. That isn't what I want for us. I imagine how alone you feel. How alone you've been. And I want to be that alone with you. I want us both to be in a new place that isn't like where we came from, and where it's just us."

She glanced down at the cup in his hand. He lifted it to his lips and drank. The tea was peaty and complex, and the aftertaste had a bloom of sweetness. He handed the cup to her, and she drank too.

"That was a good blessing," Yrith said, putting the cup down. "You could have been a priest."

"I have my brother's bed. It's just down the hall. I won't... we don't need to..."

She pulled back, her mouth twitching into a scowl. "You don't want me?"

"Oh, I do. But I don't want to be your obligation. When you're ready—"

She waved her hand and the little flames shuddered. "You're doing it wrong."

"What?"

"This. You were doing so well, and now this. Your brother, I understand. He didn't want me. Good on him. You say you do, you do all this to seduce me, but you don't ask. You tell me it's my choice. It's whatever I want, but you don't ask me what I want, and you don't ask me for what you want. What does this start? Try again."

"If you aren't ready . . . if you don't love me—"

"We are a crafted union. I like you very much. You are good company, and you're pretty, and you're sweet and smart. You understand well. I am glad to be joined to you. The love will come. Until then, you are skin and blood and bone. Ask for what you want."

Vasch was silent. He could feel his heart in his chest beating not quickly but strong.

"Can I have you?" he asked.

"Yes," she said, and blew out the lamps.

Old Boar's face squeezed into a vast scowl. "Why would you care about those candy-ass fucks?"

Garreth tried to act casual about it, as if the question was just a passing curiosity. "I've never been to the palace. I know they've got their own guard, and I didn't know how that worked."

They were walking down a narrow street in Newmarket. Old Boar and Garreth were in front and Maur and Frijjan Reed behind. The air bit with cold, and the cobbles were slick with ice where they weren't hidden by grey snow. The cold was harder to bear because it was new. When the depth of winter came to thicken the city's blood, this same air would seem like a warm hug. Now, with harvest barely gone and memory of summer still not quite forgotten, people bundled into wool jackets and cloaks and scarves and rushed through the streets with their noses and ears and bare fingers red-bitten. Even the winter sun hurried across the white-haze sky like it was impatient to find some shelter for the night.

Old Boar shrugged. "It's a soft enough post if you like that kind of thing. It's just another barracks and a different captain. The difference is down here you do something, and up there your whole duty roster is clearing poor folks out of the paths of their betters, holding a stick between your ass cheeks, and pissing contempt down on the rest of us."

"Do people shift between them?"

"You want to work up there?"

Garreth heard the buzz in the words like a hornet coming too close. "No. But I wouldn't mind seeing the palace for myself."

They came to a smaller building. Iron brackets in the walls showed where an awning would fasten come market days, but now they were just the source of long streaks of rust. The windows were small and shuttered, and the door was painted a yellow that was likely meant to be cheerful. A stairway clung to the building's side like a long-dead vine. Old Boar held up a finger—*Hold that thought*. Frijjan Reed and Maur took places at their side—four men together instead of two and two.

"City guard," Old Boar shouted. "Open in the name of the prince." His boot hit as he said the word *prince*, shattering the frame and slamming the door open. He stepped into the gloom, drawing his blade. Garreth followed with his own sword at the ready.

The interior of the tailor's shop was grim and small. The only light was the glow that leaked through cracks in the shutters. A long table had bolts of cloth and thread and long woven leather thongs ready to be crafted into shirts or cloaks or gowns, but the air smelled of sour wine and dust. A thin Hansch man whose hairline had retreated up past his crown stumbled down the thin stairway, rage in the shape of his mouth. If he saw the open blades, he didn't care.

"What in the shit is this? You can't come into my shop like this! I pay my tax. I've complied."

"It's not that this time, Josie," Frijjan Reed said.

A shadow moved on the stairway. Someone was at the top of the flight, listening, their body blocking the light. Garreth locked eyes with Maur, and they moved to be ready for anyone else who charged down while the older guards saw to the main business.

"You've been shaving coins," Old Boar said.

"The fuck I have."

"The magistrate's had complaints from ten people in the last three weeks," Old Boar said with a grin. "Not putting your fair dip to the tax count's not good. Scraping the edges off old Ausai's silver head? That's near sacrilege."

"Gods on a fucking string," the balding man—Josie—said. "All right. I'm not saying I did, but what's the fine that makes you bastards go away."

"We're past that," Old Boar said.

Josie's expression shifted between one heartbeat and the next. "You can't take me to the gaol. I've got to work the shop."

A shriek came from the top of the stairs. A woman came barreling down. She was in a plain cotton robe with a stain on the left breast. Her hands were bent into claws, and Garreth prepared to fight her back. Instead, she dodged between him and Maur and leapt for Josie.

"You said you'd stopped," she screamed as she clawed at the man. "You said when you'd paid your debts clear, you'd stop! You promised."

Maur grabbed her around the waist and hauled her away from her target. Garreth sheathed his blade and grabbed her arm. She thrashed like a snake while he tried to find a restraint hold that would stop her.

"I didn't do anything," Josie said, his hand to a cheek where she'd scratched him. "I did stop. I didn't lie."

"You always lie," the woman shouted. Garreth found the

lock, set her elbow against his forearm, and pushed her against the wall with it. He knew from when it had been used on him how much it hurt, but a deeper kind of pain had possessed her. She didn't fight back against him, just sagged and craned her head to see Josie. To show him her tears and her anger. "I wish I'd never met you. I wish I didn't know you."

"Love, no," Josie said, and Old Boar grabbed his arm, shifted it, and Josie fell to his knees with a yelp.

"Don't hurt him," the woman said. "Don't you fucking hurt him."

"We're just doing the job, Yan," Frijjan Reed said. "It's not personal." He gestured for Garreth to release her. She seemed to forget him as soon as he wasn't touching her.

"He'll walk. You don't have to tie him," the woman said, and punched Old Boar on the shoulder. It was like seeing a sparrow attacking an ox.

"Reed?" Old Boar said, and pushed the prisoner toward the street. The bound man was weeping.

Frijjan Reed took the woman by the shoulders. When he spoke, his voice was strangely gentle. "Don't get in the middle of this. Let him do what he needs to do, and stay clear."

"This is you!" she shouted. "Why are you doing this to me? It isn't fair."

"Josie's been shaving down coins again," Frijjan Reed said. "That's the only reason we're here. There's nothing more than that."

"You two," Old Boar snapped to Garreth and Maur. "Come on."

He pushed the prisoner stumbling out ahead of them. Garreth looked at Maur, and the two of them followed. When Garreth looked back, Frijjan Reed had an arm around the woman and she was sobbing into his shoulder. Josie walked with his head bowed, staring at the cobbles with emptiness in his eyes.

“They know each other, then?” Maur asked.

“Yan and Frijjan spilled a little salt when they were young,” Old Boar said. “Whenever we have to roust Josie here, he comes with us to help with Yan.”

“Help with,” Garreth said, wondering what the words meant. “Is he coming back with us?”

“He’ll catch up before we’re at the magistrate’s,” Old Boar said. “They don’t fuck, if that’s what you’re thinking. They got that done with each other a long time before now. But he still wants well for her, and she can get where she’s not thinking things through when she’s upset. It’s better this way.”

The prisoner turned his head a degree, but didn’t look back. “She’d be fine if it wasn’t for you.”

Old Boar took the rope that bound the man’s arms and yanked back on it like he was stopping a mule. Josie’s feet slipped out from under him and he landed ass-first on the cobblestones and snow.

“Your woman is weeping on another man’s arm because you’re a greedy fuck,” Old Boar said, speaking each word clear and loud enough to carry through the street. The soft clatter of shutters opening came first, and then a dark-haired head looking out of one window, a grey-haired one from another. Josie screamed in grief and humiliation.

“Come on,” Maur said. “I’ll help you up. We’ll get this part done and over with, yeah?”

Garreth went to the man’s other shoulder. Old Boar didn’t stop them, so between them they hoisted the prisoner up. Josie wasn’t wearing a jacket, and his nose was running from the cold. Old Boar flicked the rope like a coachman calling his team to the trot, and Josie stumbled forward.

“How often does he get in trouble like this?” Garreth asked as they walked.

"This one? Year or two, if he's on a good stretch. He gets a fine or gets hauled up to the magistrate, and he'll keep himself honest for a while. It don't last, though."

"Then why do we do it?" Maur asked.

"Not about him, is it? Josie was born bent and stupid, and there's no making him smarter or straighter than what the gods picked for him. It's all these other bastards looking out the windows and passing us in the streets. They see this, and they know that being bent and stupid's got a price to it."

"And that keeps them honest," Garreth said.

"It might, it might not," Old Boar said. "But imagine how it'd be if they saw there wasn't a price. And it makes them happy. Everyone likes seeing the other man punished. Makes them feel like, since we don't have them on a rope, they must be good. Or at least smart enough not to get caught. Public entertainment and moral instruction. That's what we do." Old Boar chuckled at his own joke, but Garreth wondered if what he said might not be true. Maur squinted up at the sky. When Old Boar spoke again, his breath was white as steam. "I can work something for you."

"Work something?"

"I know men on Palace Hill. You want to take a day's duty under Samal Kint, I can arrange it."

Maur made a small sound in the back of his throat like a man who'd just found something he'd been looking for.

"I would appreciate that," Garreth said to the older guard, ignoring his friend's knowing grin. "If you can."

"Oh, I can. No trouble for that. But it's a favor for a favor, and you'll be going first. It's just better that way. You can pick. Hand me over your fines for a week, or take my shit cart duty."

"Whatever you like."

Old Boar squinted up into the winter sky like he was looking for a sign there. "Shit cart, then. I've got four shifts of it this rota. They're yours. And you'll need to do your own work too. We're not trading. That fair?"

"I'll take it."

Old Boar grinned and cuffed him on the shoulder. "Damn right you will."

An older woman came out of a doorway to their right and scowled at the prisoner as they walked past. Her arms were crossed and her chin jutted out like a child spoiling for a fight.

"If you're the one did this, Mag, I'll know it," Josie shouted at her, and Old Boar kicked him in the small of the back. Josie stumbled forward onto the street, dropping to his knees. Old Boar swept down a hand, grabbed the back of the man's shirt, and pulled him up by it without breaking stride.

"It's not Mag's fault you broke the law," he said mildly. "You shouldn't blame her for what you done."

"You kicked me."

"Wouldn't have if you hadn't made threats. That's an offense, you know. I'd have fined you instead if your coin was worth piss. Trot now, or you'll get cold before we're at the gaol."

Josie tried gamely to trot, and Old Boar goaded him on. Maur leaned in to Garreth, speaking low enough the older man didn't hear him.

"Whatever it is that family policy's keeping you from telling, I respect. Just don't let the captain find out you're using your duty with the guard to help your family. He's touchy about that."

"I didn't say I was."

"No, but everyone knows your parents had a bad few years. And you just happened to be on a casual basis with the prince's daughter. And you were going to be married to someone you couldn't talk about. All totally unrelated."

Garreth didn't answer. The truth was that as long as Maur and Kannish thought Elaine a Sal knew him from some machinations of House Left, Garreth was going to let them. The falsehood was more plausible than the truth.

When Maur saw he wasn't going to answer, he sighed. "When you can tell us what this all was, I'll buy the beer to go with it."

The shit cart wasn't just for shit. Animals who'd been crushed by carts or frozen in the night or died of some illness in the alleys and cul-de-sacs of the city wound up there too. But between the horses and the dogs and the cats and the people, the bulk of the cart was filled with shit.

Garreth rode on the front of the cart beside the carter, an ancient man called Sooner, though that wasn't his name, who'd spent a life in the guard and retired to this when his knees went bad. The horse was a wide, patient beast with a wool blanket across her back against the cold.

With a team of four prisoners, Garreth was the only full bluecloak present. If there'd been six, someone would have come with him. The condemned had spades of blunt wood, and Garreth had a short sword and leather whip with a wide thong at the end, meant to sting more than cut. The whip was for encouraging anyone who wasn't enthusiastic enough about cleaning the street. The sword was to dissuade them from fighting back.

The little scrap of paper, the steel-nibbed pen, and the block of gum ink were peculiar to Garreth and the day.

It's been a long time since the morning with the birds. I understand better now what that was, and why I haven't seen you since. But I hope

"Fuck me! What is that?"

Garreth tucked the paper into his pocket and closed the pen

in the inkbox. It was too late to be called dawn any longer. Palace Hill was bright with the light, but Riverport was still in shadow. The cart had rolled out from the gaol before first light, and the cold had reddened Garreth's knuckles and numbed his feet. He had two Inlisc men, one woman, and a Hansch man with a missing front tooth and a limp. That was the one who'd cried out.

"What's what?" Garreth said, standing in the cart.

The Hansch man gestured to a lump in the darkness where the wall of the tanners' guild hall met the ground. Garreth swung himself down to the street and walked over. The little animal was dead, a black nose poking out of a knot of ice-hard snow.

"Looks like a fox," Garreth said.

"What if it's diseased? I don't want to pick up a plague fox."

The three Inlisc prisoners watched with a cultivated neutrality. Garreth grabbed the man's wood spade, set the point at the bottom of the little corpse, and kicked twice. The fox popped loose from the cobbles, frozen stiff. Garreth swept the spade up, launching the little animal into the cart where it landed with a thump.

"Like that," he said, handing back the spade. "If you don't like the job, stop picking fights with your neighbors. Now get to work, or we'll all still be doing this come nightfall."

The Hansch man scowled, but turned back to the street, sweeping his eyes over the cobblestones for the next bit of icy filth.

"You're too soft," the carter said as Garreth sat back down. "You should have whipped him until he did it himself. You get a reputation for being soft, and they'll take advantage of you."

"There's always next time," Garreth said, fishing the paper out from his pocket and spreading it open on his knee. The ink had smudged, but only a little. The letters were still clear.

But I hope your interest in my changes of life was sincere. The first time we met, you came to me. This time I will come to you.

He read over what he'd written with a sense of growing uncertainty. He wanted to say that he'd been thinking of her since their night together, that he had wished he were back in those dark, beautiful hours again a thousand times since he'd lived through them. If she'd been a Stonemarket servant girl—even if she'd been the daughter of some minor noble house—he could have. But he was writing to the prince's daughter, and he didn't know how to do that. He balled up the paper and tossed it behind him into the shit.

The cart turned slowly to the north, following a narrow street with windows that opened into the servants' quarters of House Reffon. Little black lumps and spatters of yellow fouled the snow. He'd been to dinners there with his parents back in some other lifetime. Baal Reffon dealt in spices and alum from the north. He was one of the people the winter caravan would ruin if it worked out well.

"Stop here," Garreth said. "This could take them some time."

One of the Inlisc men said something. The other laughed.

"Hey!" Garreth barked. "Get moving. This isn't going to get better when the sunlight warms it up for you."

"Whatever you say," the laughing one said. Garreth pulled a new piece of paper out of his pocket, wishing he had access to the little writing desk from his room. Finding the right words would be easier if he could be alone with himself, imagining her there with him. He could just think what he'd say to her, and write that down. Only here, he'd be saying things like *I hope we can get this cart full and dumped into the river before it warms up enough to stink* and *I am going to spend half a day in the baths before I feel clean from this* and *I'm starting to wonder if a life of beating shit cart prisoners was really the best choice for me.*

The sun peeked up over the roofs. Its touch was warming. He closed his eyes, imagining not Elaine a Sal but the girl from his room, from the street, with the smell of the river in her hair. He recalled how she spoke. How she carried herself. The undercurrent of melancholy and amusement that followed her like perfume.

I miss you. I barely know you, and you showed me so much about myself. I would be living a different life if I hadn't met you. Maybe a better one, maybe worse, but different. You have changed me, and I have missed you, and I want nothing more from gods or time or history than to see you again. I will come to you this time, if I can find my way.

That was better. That was a lot better. He wondered what favors he would have to do to get it delivered.

"Hey," the Hansch man whined. "These bastards aren't doing their part. I'm not going to do all this by myself."

The carter shrugged. "You don't have to like it, son, but it is the job."

"Seems like this is going to be a long, unpleasant day."

"Could be worse," the old man said. "You could be one of the men who enjoys it."

"Fair enough," Garreth said as he picked up the whip. He cracked it once for practice and climbed down from the cart again.

Week after week after week, she'd watched the guards around her father's private study, waiting for a lapse in their collective vigilance. Samal Kint's men were disciplined. The passage her father had dug through the stone flesh of the palace was under guard from one dawn to the next, and would be—it seemed—until rain wore away the mountains. According to Haral Moun, Theddan had been caught at something indiscreet at the Temple, and wouldn't be able to sneak out to speak with Elaine again until her penance was complete. Gareth, who was now apparently a city guard, hadn't appeared since the night she'd seen him on the bridge, and she wasn't sure whether she was more disappointed or relieved. Hours stretched into days with no possibility of change, of discovery, of progress.

Then everything happened in the same evening. Afterward, she hadn't been able to sleep. She rose in the morning of Longest Night with bloodshot eyes and a darkness under them like someone had punched her. The traditions of Clovas called for the day to be spent in contemplation of the year just gone by, and asking the spirits of her ancestors for guidance in the rebirth to come. Instead, she'd spent the first part of the morning trying to cover over the worst of her sleeplessness with cosmetics and tea.

She'd been more than half tempted to cancel her duties for the day: morning meal with Bel a Jimental, ceremonial observance at the Reyos compound with Dakke and Mayaral Reyos, Andomaka Chaalat, and an early evening feast with her father and a dozen or so of the heads of the great families. The decision to go ahead was part an unarticulated fear that changing her schedule would somehow expose her and part the dread of being alone. She didn't want to be with people, but she wanted to be with herself even less. And so fish and eggs in red sauce in the solarium of a Jimental, prayer and meditation at the private chapel of Reyos, and now lemon tea in a drawing room of the palace.

Of all her obligations, this one was the least odious. Andomaka Chaalat was an easy woman to spend time with, comfortable to talk with. Elaine didn't know her as well as she did Theddan, but she could imagine being close to her. Andomaka's almost eerie paleness made her seem like ice and snow in the form of a woman. The warmth of the fire and the brightness of the lemon tea were a kind of reassuring lie about the impotence of winter. Or maybe that was just her exhaustion talking.

She had meant to use the meeting to probe a bit more into Prince Ausai and the Daris Brotherhood. Background that might help her better guess what her father had found and the nature of Ausai's madness. She wasn't sure what she meant to do now.

"Thank you for coming," Elaine said. "I know this is a busy time for everyone."

"I'm happy for the distraction," Andomaka said. "And I was

sincere before when I promised to be here if you needed me. Is something troubling you, cousin?"

Elaine hesitated. What she wanted to say—what she almost said—was this: *Have you ever heard of the thread of Kithamar?*

The night before had been windy. All the nights seemed windy on Palace Hill, like the land itself had thrown the palace into an air higher than kites. Shutters rattled, eddies of wind muttered through the halls and passages like the voices of dead men who had forgotten to lie down.

Elaine had been walking the way she always did, finding her way through a home the size of a city's quarter, discovering niches and secrets that riddled the buildings. A basement by the north wall that was filled with musical instruments—lutes and viols and a great teakwood harp—covered in dust and mildew. A physician's quarters, abandoned generations before and simply left shut with diagrams of the human form and its lines of energy and vital flow marked in faded green ink. A closet filled with jars of medical curiosities preserved in salt brandy—a fetus with four arms, a lamb's severed head, a pair of thin-fingered hands. A storage room filled with vast dusty rounds of cheese that smelled ripe and deep and wonderful.

She was slowly coming to love Palace Hill not despite its odd corners and strange history, but because of them. The buildings were like a poem in a language she almost understood.

The new passage to the prince's private study was near the end of a dark passage. The door that Halev Karsen had ordered installed over the wound in the palace's stone flesh was simple: bronze and oak with a heavy bar and a lock for which only he and her father had the key. Guards stood by it day and night. She passed by often enough for her presence to seem as normal as mice, always hoping for some accident to open the way to her. It never did.

The old door was still closed fast, a puzzle without a solution. She stopped by it as well, probing the complicated ironwork in hopes of finding some hidden latch or keyhole. She never did. The decorations that covered the door were complex and beautiful and forbidding. She had to think it had been cast sometime in the ancient past of the city. The figures on it seemed to be telling a story.

A warrior with swords in either hand and a wolfskin over his shoulders appeared in several places. In one, he stood over a dead or dying man. In another, he was set in apparent battle against what looked like some kind of gigantic finch. He stood on the prow of a boat, or in the mouth of a cave, or before the altar of some kind of temple, though not one Elaine had ever seen. Dragons and monsters flew up one side of the door, angels and trees and naked men and women fell down the other. As a piece of craft, it was a masterwork. As an artistic work, it was incomprehensible. As a puzzle, unsolvable. Over the weeks, she felt certain that she'd pressed every dragon's eyes, plucked at every hero's sword, dug her little finger into the hollows around every figure and filigree.

Tonight, she pressed a flat palm against it, and it shifted. For a moment, she was as disoriented as if the wall had moved instead. It was easier to believe that she was imagining things, but when she pressed again—a little harder this time—the door swung silently in. It was terribly heavy, and opening a crack wide enough to step through took effort, but she managed and slipped into the darkness on the other side.

She moved slowly. The sliver of light that spilled in behind her was only enough to show the barest outlines of a wide table piled with something. A bench. And on the side of the table nearest her, a lantern. Its shape was as unmistakable as the smell of its oil. She fumbled with the flint striker at its base, but only for a few moments. When the flame took, it was steady and strong. Light filled the room.

It was close almost to the point of being cramped. The walls were covered from floor to ceiling with shelves. The spines of the books were in sections. Two shelves of ancient, yellowed parchment sewn with thick black thread. A shelf of black folios tied with twine. Half a wall of decaying leather, flaking and falling off the volumes they were meant to cover. Another wall more nearly intact with bindings of brown leather, then of red, then of a glossy black as fresh as if it had been taken from the tanner's house the week before.

No book was marked. There was nothing on the spines to identify one from the next. In all, there were thousands, and bare space on the shelves enough for a thousand more. It was like looking at the history of a bookbinder's trade, from the oldest, earliest form to the newest. A dozen lay on the broad table in piles, drawn from all the different ages.

She opened one. The pages within were covered in a beautiful, flowing script, the written lines even and regular. Disciplined. Flipping through the pages, she found sketches and diagrams. The architectural plans of a tower. A complex design in red and green ink and marked with religious symbols. The sketched study of a woman's torso and hips without head, arms, or legs. She chose a page at random to read.

The river itself is a power. That original channel—that splitting of its flow—was a happy accident indeed. Would all that came after have done if we hadn't needed fresh water? I think about how delicate it was at the start, and it's like looking down a fucking cliff. Never let that happen again. Points to follow: More canals on the Inlisc bank of the river—ritual pollution of the flow—more bridges?—controlled dredging to shape erosion? Consult with Cabbian.

She didn't know what any of it meant, but the diagram beside it was the Khahon. The subject of the author's concern, Kithamar. She closed the book and opened another. The same beautiful, disciplined script.

Neither peace nor war but a mixture of both. Enough violence, hunger, misery, degradation to make people long for safety, but not so much that they seek it for themselves. Suffering is the medicine of order, and too little is as bad as too much.

I have been too lenient.

She frowned, closed this new volume. The spine was cloth-covered board with threads that had started to decompose. She couldn't guess how old it was, but much older than the first that she'd opened. She cast around the table. One of the oldest-looking, its pages folded and cut, its binding twine threaded through awl-punched holes, sat just beyond her reach. She walked around the table, her shadow gliding over the dark walls like it was leading the way and she was only following. The parchment creaked when she opened it. The edges of the page were yellowed until it was almost hard to make out the last letters on each line.

Something about it made her flesh crawl, and it took her a moment to know why. She put the ancient book beside the more recent ones, comparing the pages.

The handwriting was the same. They had to have been done centuries apart, but the same hand had made the marks. Beautiful letters. Regular lines. The same hand that had written the other pages, the other books. She pulled back like she'd touched a snake she hadn't known was there. Dread drew fingers up her neck.

When she turned back toward the iron door, she saw lines and curves worked into the stone and filled with gold. They formed Old Hansch runes. She hadn't studied the language since she was young, but some of the old knowledge was in her. Along one wall, they spelled out something like *The End of All Ending*. Or, maybe *The Death of Death*. Along the opposite side, *God Above Gods*. And in the stone above the door, *The Thread of Kithamar Will Not Sever*. She didn't know why the old words in a dead language felt like a whispered threat, but they did.

A living voice came from behind her, distant but familiar. Halev Karsen, talking with a low intensity that bordered on anger. *What are the options?* She didn't know Samal Kint's voice as well, but she was almost certain he was the man who answered. *South of the Stonemarket canal, anything, but Green Hill's its own beast. There's no law there until you're ready to spill some very noble blood.* The pause seemed to last forever. *Not yet*, Karsen said. His voice was closer. They were coming.

Elaine blew out the lamp, and the room plunged into blackness more profound than it had been before her eyes had adapted to the light. She went toward where she hoped the iron door was, rolling her feet from heel to toe so gently that they made no sound. The edge of the great door was barely more than a line of charcoal in the black, but it was enough to navigate by. She reached out her hands, feeling into the darkness. Her fingertips touched iron, and she rushed out into the corridor.

She tried to pull the door closed behind her, but there was no handle to use, and she was afraid that it might make some creak, some scraping that would call attention to her. The sense of trespass, of having been where she wasn't meant to be and seeing things she wasn't meant to see, was instinctual and overwhelming. She turned and walked away, fast and quiet. The almost organic maze of hallways and chambers, courtyards and storerooms that had enchanted her before now felt like a threat. She had the sense of being within an immense, malicious living creature. The palace was aware of her, and she wanted nothing more than to be in her rooms with the door barred and every candle she could find pushing away the gloom.

Ausai wasn't what I thought he was. That was what her father had said. *I think he may have been mad.*

I hope he was.

The words had been odd at the time. Ominous. She walked fast, her head down like she was trying not to meet the palace's gaze. Like she could will herself not to be noticed by it. She wanted to run.

Perhaps it was some sort of strange pastime of her great-uncle's. The books looked old. Maybe they were old, but that didn't mean the script was the same age as the books. Maybe Ausai had found them all blank and spent his years filling them in. Journals and notebooks that seemed to reach back through the ages, but were all written in the course of one man's few decades of life. Was that possible? Could those thousands of volumes be the work of a single lifetime? And if they were, how had he found time to do anything else?

Or might there be a tradition? Some kind of princely script where every generation practiced the same letters and spacing until it was perfect. Identical with all the men and women who had come before. But if that was true, no one had told her. Or her father.

If there was a reasonable explanation, her father would have it by now. And if there wasn't, the only things left were eerie and unsettling.

She reached her private rooms with the relief of a fish slipping off the hook and back into the pool. A little fire was already burning in the grate, and the room smelled of smoke and burning sap. Her Inlisc bed servant came in from the side room with an expression that was polite and subservient and practiced. "Can I help, miss?"

"No," Elaine said. Then, "Yes. I'll eat dinner in here. You could fetch that for me."

"Of course. What should I tell the kitchens you'd like?"

"Their best judgment will be fine," she said.

"Yes, miss," the Inlisc girl said, then held out a scrap of paper. "This came. One of the guardsmen said it was meant for you."

"What is it?"

The girl shook her head. "I don't have letters, miss. It's for you."

Elaine took it between two pinching fingers. She waited until the girl left to unfold the note. *I miss you. I barely know you, and you showed me so much about myself.*

Elaine sat on a little silk-upholstered stool beside the fire and read the message in full, then read it again. *I will come to you this time, if I can find my way.*

She tried to feel joy or elation or even pleasure, but all she found were deepening layers of dread that feathered into one another seemingly without end.

"I'm happy for the distraction. And I was sincere before when I promised to be here if you needed me. Is something troubling you, cousin?"

Elaine hesitated. Andomaka had been Prince Ausai's priest in the Daris Brotherhood. She'd known him better than Elaine or even her father had. Would she know about the notebooks? Would she know what the phrases worked in stone meant? *Everyone who wrote in those books is dead.* That was what Halev Karsen had said. She wished it carried more weight than his *Not yet.* He was planning something. Or frightened of something.

"You've been crying?" Andomaka asked gently.

"Things have been hard since we came to the palace. Father's been busy and... he's distracted. I think it's all wearing on him."

Andomaka settled more deeply into her chair. Her smile was an invitation.

"I have to break something off," she said, and as she heard it, she knew it was true. "There's a man who I…I had a connection with. And I can't anymore."

"A connection."

"He was…" *He was the only man who ever saw me and not her, not the daughter of the prince. Not the version of me that gets everything and leaves nothing past that.* "He was exceptional. For me, he was exceptional."

"Does he have a name?"

"I'm the daughter of the prince. He's a city guard," Elaine said, and scoffed, though what she felt wasn't contempt. "He's a bluecloak. How could knowing me end well for him? Or for me? We could never be together, and pretending anything else is a cruelty, isn't it? For him or me or both of us? I should never have let him know. I shouldn't have stopped. I wasn't thinking."

The words spilled out of her, the fears and grief she hadn't known she had in her. If she'd been able to sleep, if Theddan had been there to talk with. Or Garreth. Or her father. She was overfull and only half aware of all she was saying, flooded by the raw feeling in her gut and her throat and her vacant heart. And by pouring out one secret, she wasn't pouring out the other. Andomaka listened, and made soft, encouraging noises now and then, but Elaine was elsewhere.

In her mind, she saw Garreth in the cloak of the city guard, standing amazed on the bridge between Newmarket and Oldgate. She saw him the night they'd met, meeting her eyes as she hid behind the low wall. *Come to me. I'll see you safe.* She was weeping in earnest now.

"He asked me to come, and I went to him," Elaine said. And he'd meant it, but he couldn't. There wasn't any safety to be had. Not for them. Had anyone ever made a simpler, more tragic promise than that?

There was something wrong in the palace. Something wrong at the heart of Kithamar. It was tangled up with Ausai's notebooks and the runes and whatever else her father had seen that frightened him. She didn't know what it was. Garreth couldn't keep her safe any better than she knew how to protect him. Or what she would protect him from.

"To his barracks?"

"No. His family house in Riverport," she said. The hollow feeling in her chest deepened. "I don't know what to do."

The pale woman was quiet for what seemed like a lifetime. "Follow your heart. It's a better guide than I am." Andomaka took her hand, squeezed it gently, and then retreated, leaving Elaine to the room and the fire and the cup of tea that had gone tepid while she wept. She closed her eyes, and they felt gritty.

The Thread of Kithamar Will Not Sever, the wall had said in its golden runes. The city would endure, it seemed to promise, and leave everything that was gentler, kinder, more hopeful, or joyous broken in its wake.

Including Garreth and his quiet birds.

Including her.

There's a plague in Stonemarket," Abbit said.

Captain Senit's gaze swam for a moment as he found the taproom keeper, but when he spoke, his voice was steady. "That so?"

"Kint sent his boys down to shut off the streets. Quarantined. Order from the prince, is what I heard."

"Well, good on him," Senit said.

The taproom had closed its wide shutters for the winter. Where once the walls themselves had seemed to open to the street, now it was just old wood with bits of wool stuffed in the cracks to keep the wind outside. Mostly outside. On a night with a good, ripping squall, they'd all still feel it. Today wasn't bad, though. Not that aspect of it, anyway.

It was seven days since Longest Night, two more before Tenthday. How much that mattered measured how much wealth and time people had to piss away. Seepwater, Longhill, the hospital. They nodded to Longest Night as it passed and got their asses back to work the next morning. Riverport had its great celebration on the night itself, and it would have an echo on Tenth Night. All the guilds and merchant houses making a display of their generosity and wealth by serving the cheapest meat and plainest beer they could pass off as good. Green Hill and the palace were in the yearly orgy of celebrating themselves that would end in a few days with men and women reclining on silk divans, exhausted by the effort of putting together wine enough for their feasts.

Through it all, the guard would do what the guard always did: keep the good people of Kithamar from robbing and raping and murdering each other more than they already did by raining hell on the ones who'd already done it. There were no days off from that.

Abbit trundled through the place with a rag and a broom, keeping the tables and floors as clean as they were ever going to get. The smells of overspiced meat and heated wine made it seem warmer than it was. The fire in the grate turned good honest wood into ash and embers, eating log after log after log. Senit watched the flames play. At the far bench, Linton Coar, Marsen Wellis, and Marsen's salad-green nephew were all celebrating themselves halfway to drunk. Either the new boy didn't understand the jokes they were making at his expense or had the good sense not to mind them. Abbit's dog was asleep by the fire, his wide, greying flanks and muzzle twitching as he ran down some dream rabbit. Senit drank his sixth, maybe seventh, beer of the night. He didn't feel drunk.

Abbit lumbered back across the room with a tin plate in his hand, sat down on the bench across from Senit, and slid a dinner's worth of sausage and coarse mustard toward him.

"Didn't ask for that," Divol said.

"Didn't charge you for it," Abbit said.

"I'm not charity."

"Didn't say you were. It makes the beer taste less like piss."

Senit scowled. "This is your beer that you're talking shit about."

"Was once, but you're the one drinking it."

"I said I don't want your fucking food," Senit said.

"I heard you."

Senit turned his attention back to the fire, but the keep didn't go away. He just sat quietly, alone with his thoughts, until Senit couldn't stand it any longer.

"I'm fine, Abbit. Stop acting like my mother."

"Do I look like I'm offering you a tit?"

"Are you calling me a baby?"

Abbit shrugged. The rage that sat in Senit's belly all the time now flared up brighter than the fire in the grate. His scowl deepened until his cheeks ached. He planted his elbows on the table and leaned forward, chin jutting.

"You," he said, "are a crippled old fuck who got lucky the day they hacked your toes off. You never belonged in the blue to start with, and I know it because I was there. So take your judgment and your bullshit sympathy and your pus-stinking sausage and your piss beer and shove them all up your cock."

Abbit stretched his neck to the left and then the right like a showfighter readying for the pit. "You are a grown man. Captain of the largest barracks in the city. You're the lead for the guard, the example that all the others follow. You are the law in Kithamar. You decide who goes to the magistrate and who gets put in the river, who gets a fine or a warning or ignored from the start. And all the bluecloaks on this side of the river look to you so they'll know what they should be."

"Fuck you."

"Fuck you back, you sloppy-mouthed shit," Abbit said cheerfully. "And eat the goddam sausage. You haven't shoved anything but beer down your guts since you came in."

Senit wavered. The evening was about to go one of two ways, and he wasn't sure quite which he wanted.

"Do you remember Captain Sault?" Abbit asked. "He was the old one that Mad Perrin kept on when she took over the Stonemarket barracks?"

"I remember him. He had pock marks."

"When I lost my foot, I was down past the south wall in the hospital with the herb man trying to pull the dead blood out before I rotted. Captain Sault came and saw me. I was down at the time, you know. Looking at the end of my career in the guard, and no idea what was coming after, or if anything was. And him, he could barely walk himself, old as he was. I still don't know if he'd hobbled all the way down from the barracks or had someone carry him, but he showed up. He sat at my bedside, with this look on his face. You know what he said to me?"

"You're going to tell me."

"I am. He said *Well, shit.* That's it. That's all he said. Came halfway across the city, stood by while I watched the shape of my life killed out from under me, said *Well, shit*, and then he went back home. No idea what he meant by it, except…"

Senit shook his head. Then, against his will, he chuckled. Abbit's smile seemed almost shy. After a moment, Senit picked up the sausage with his fingers and swept it through the mustard. The meat had lost the warmth of the kitchen grill, but the pepper and salt made it seem hotter than it was.

"She broke me, Abbit. It was going to be my legacy. Their children's children were going to tell stories about how Captain Senit broke Aunt Thorn. About the underground criminal city that I turned into a grave of the worst thugs in Kithamar."

"You've thought about that story a lot."

"I did. That was my fault. I let myself want something. I've lost before. I let myself hope, and then I started living in the hope like it was already here."

"I hear you."

"Everyone loses, all the time. It's why succeeding's such a big fucking deal. I could stand the loss if I hadn't dreamed my way so far into where it had already happened. They laugh at me, you know. My people. Pavvis's. Probably Samal fucking Kint is up there in his clouds pissing down at me. Why shouldn't they?"

"Wanting is dangerous," Abbit said. "But what would life be without it, yeah? Who doesn't want?"

"She made a fool of me."

"And who's not a fool? Who gets from the birthing chair to the grave with dignity? What prize do the gods hand out to people who never let themselves care about anything enough to be disappointed by the loss? Look around you, Captain. Everyone who laughs at you or cringes away? They're all thinking of some time when it was them. Some race they ran and came in last, someone they wooed who didn't want them, some moment of glory they reached for and wound up with an empty hand for the trouble. We're all fools. Everyone. That's why we hate fools so much. They're the echoes of when we were vulnerable in front of the world ourselves, and that's hard for us to forgive."

"You've been keeping a taproom too long. You sound like a fucking priest."

"Hazard of the job," Abbit said. "Point is, we need you back."

Senit took another bite from the sausage. At the other table, Marsen was telling someone else's story again with himself as the hero. His nephew was listening with admiration in his eyes. Linton Coar only looked indulgent, like a man married long enough that his wife's vices had become endearing. Someday, the boy would figure out that his uncle was a blowhard and a bullshit artist. Senit hoped Kannish would also see that his uncle was a good man and a solid guard.

The barracks were his people. They hated and loved and supported and undermined each other like families did. That was what made failing in front of them so hard.

"I don't know if I have it in me," Senit said.

"Then come work for me."

"Fuck off. If I'm out, I'm out. I'll take a boat for the south and find honest fucking work. Not this shit."

"You say it, but you'd miss them. They've already forgiven what happened, and they'll forget quicker than you will. If you can't run your barracks, you have a place here. And if you can, then you better should. All right?"

"All right," Senit said.

Abbit hoisted himself up and headed over to get fresh beer for the others. He only limped a little, and if his half foot hurt him, he kept it hidden.

It was the late morning of Tenthday, and Garreth was exhausted and cold. Between taking his own shifts patrolling the streets and Old Boar's turn on the shit carts, he hadn't had time for anything much besides work and sleep. If he'd been back with his family, he would have been sleeping enough, eating better food, and helping to run the house. He'd have woken every morning in a comfortable bed and a room that he didn't share with five other men. Every detail about his life would be different, and many of them would have been more comfortable and less dangerous.

Sometimes he tried to miss the man he had been and the life he could have led, but the memory of who he'd been and how he'd lived his life had faded more than time alone seemed to explain. He remembered being the Garreth Left who drank tea with his father and ate fish in the dining room with Uncle Robbson. He remembered Serria bringing his clothes from the launderer and tucking them in the drawers under his bed. He could still close his eyes and make his way from the front door of his father's house up to the storage rooms on the topmost floor and count every step and stair. It wasn't forgetting. It was the immediacy of his life now, and the way that Garreth Left of the city guard simply existed in a way that his previous self did not.

And it likely helped that he was exhausted.

The cart carried ten kegs of beer from the brewers in Seepwater. It was pulled by two affable donkeys whose breath plumed white even in the midday sun, one with a dark coat, the other a light tan and otherwise nearly identical. Their path up the face of Oldgate tilted the cart up and he found himself picturing what would happen if the cart came free of its team, and how far he could tumble before he died.

"You'll like Ras," Old Boar said from his perch between the kegs. "He's a good man."

Garreth nodded. Looking up, the walls of Palace Hill were near, towering above him like he was the brick at their base. He tried to imagine what it would have been like, charging up the path and trying to overrun the fort at its top. Centuries on, and there were likely still bones in the Khahon of men who'd tried.

The carter guided the donkeys up the last stretch of road. The paving stones were broken and loose, ancient beyond Garreth's imagination and worn by rain and wind and history. Two guards in the red cloaks of the palace stood at the side of an iron gate, and a servant in a black robe with bone fasteners down the front waved the cart forward. They lumbered through a short tunnel and into a courtyard. The palace rose around them like a city of its own. The windows were thin and without glass. The walls were stone or stucco, and radiated a deeper cold Garreth hadn't anticipated, and he was glad he'd brought his own gloves and scarf. A huge structure reared up above them, looking out and down like a sentinel in stone, and past it the sky seemed too close.

The donkeys turned to the left, moving to a wide wooden doorway without the carter guiding them. When they stopped, Old Boar swung himself down, and Garreth followed. Old Boar set his hands on his hips and looked around, trying for a light cynicism that didn't manage to hide a sliver of awe. Palace Hill was the house of Kithamar, and the air felt different here. Thinner and more aware. In Newmarket or Riverport, the buildings were buildings and the streets were streets. The palace was neither its own quarter with streets and buildings nor a single great house with gardens and courtyards, but something of both. When he looked at it, he felt it looking back.

The servant with the bone fasteners came as the wooden door opened. The carter handed down a bit of paper and the servant started checking through the load, marking off all that was there. No one paid Garreth or Old Boar any attention until a gaunt man in a palace guard's uniform came through the doorway and lifted his chin in greeting.

"Pig boy," the gaunt man said.

Old Boar grinned. The two men embraced for a moment, clapping each other on the shoulders, then still each with an arm around the other, turned to Garreth.

"This is the new meat?" the gaunt man asked.

"This is how far the city guard's fallen," Old Boar agreed. "Garreth Left, this sad sack of shit is Ras Fireson. Until tomorrow, he is the god you worship. Embarrass me, and all the shit cart work you've done the last weeks will seem like a pleasant dream. We understand each other?"

"Do," Garreth said, and braced in salute.

"He kisses ass well enough," Ras said. "He'll have a career."

The last keg came off the cart, a servant spinning it through the doorway. The carter tapped his donkeys with his whip, and the team started its wide turn back toward the iron gate.

Old Boar trotted alongside and hauled himself up into the cart bed.

"Send him back intact, or we'll have to charge you," Old Boar said with a wave, and then he was gone.

Ras looked Garreth up and down, then gestured with his head for him to follow. Together, they stepped into the dark, narrow corridors.

"The Tenthday feast starts in a few hours. That's part of why you're here. This is your job tonight: Don't do anything. Nothing."

"I don't understand," Garreth said.

"Down in the city, the guard's the law. Up here, you're a party decoration. Your job is to keep the nobility—and above all the prince and his family—safe from Inlisc raiders and cutthroats, and there aren't any of those. So your night is going to be striding through the public halls looking serious and not doing a god-damned thing. If a door is closed, you don't open it. If a curtain is drawn, you don't peek past it. If you see someone stealing something, you make note of who they are and what they're taking and let me know at the end of the shift."

"If I see someone getting beaten to death?" Garreth said, trying to make a joke of it.

"You come let me know, and I'll handle it," Ras said. "There's some of those we stop, and there's some we don't, and you're not going to know the difference in one night. If you see a servant with a knife in her hand charging the prince himself, get in between them and call out. The rules in the city aren't the rules here. Nobles do things that would put a shopkeeper before the magistrate, but if you step in, you'll be the one punished. Which means I will. Which means don't."

Ras turned into a wide, low chamber with two dull windows as thin as arrow slits. Red cloaks hung from pegs in the far wall.

Ras looked Garreth up and down, then took a cloak and tossed it to him.

"This should be close to fitting. Leave the gloves here, and keep the scarf under the cloak if you need it. Palace guards don't wear decorations, but until there are people in the halls, it can get cold. If anyone asks who you are, the answer is that you're on loan from Captain Senit."

"On loan from Captain Senit," Garreth echoed as he pulled his own cloak off and started struggling into the red. The cloth was thick, and it smelled musty. He wondered whether they kept unwashed cloaks just for city guards like him to remind them that they didn't really belong. Not that he cared. He was here, where she was, and he'd swallow a few more humiliations if that was the price. Once he had the cloak on, Ras inspected him, tugging at the back and sleeve as if that would make the drape better.

"All right," the palace guard said. "Come with me. I'll show you which places you can be in. Welcome to the palace. Don't get used to it."

The feast started early; men and women in the best-made gowns and shirts and jackets Garreth had ever seen arrived and made themselves at home. The dark, thick walls were decorated with flowers and banners, ribbons and lanterns. Garreth found himself quietly adding up the cost of everything he saw as he walked somberly among the halls and corridors. The sum was high enough that he took himself around a second time to check his math.

A fire grate long enough, he thought, to burn a whole tree at once blazed in the great hall. Musicians with drums and mandolins and flutes played softly in niches like they were part of the wall. Jugglers amused whoever paused to watch them and bowed without dropping a glass-and-silver ball when their audience grew bored and turned away. Magicians and conjure men performed little miracles, summoning flames and butterflies and bits of silk that whispered people's fortunes, or maybe they just played at sleights of hand. Servants slipped in to keep the food and drink on the tables from ever seeming less than overwhelmingly abundant. Garreth walked through them like a man in a dream.

When he'd been a boy, his mother had read him a fairy tale about an elf market where everything was beautiful and pure, with baskets woven from silver and sunlight. All he really remembered of it was being too scared to sleep after the elf-merchant made the parents into houseflies, but the sense of grandeur and displacement were the same. Garreth had been to the best feasts and performances that the Riverport guilds could offer, and they were faint echoes of this. In his red uniform, neither servant nor entertainer nor guest acknowledged him. The other guards seemed to know he wasn't really one of theirs, but they tolerated him. He didn't even have to explain that he was on loan. He was invisible. Invisible at the elf market.

When he was hungry, he followed the servants back to the kitchen where he could have a bowl of beef soup and a hard roll to soak in it. Compared to the bright delicacies heaped in the public halls, it looked a thin, sad meal, but it tasted better than anything Garreth had ever eaten.

Wherever he went, he looked for her. Twice, he caught glimpses through the crowd—the curve of a cheek, the movement of a shoulder—that made his heart race, but neither one was her. He'd imagined that the feast would be something of the size and scale he'd known. He knew that all of Green Hill would pour into the palace, but he hadn't thought through what that meant. It was a failure of his imagination. He'd thought that by being here, he would find her. That he could spend a full evening there and simply not happen to cross her path hadn't occurred to him, and now it filled him with dread.

Ras had made a point, too, that Garreth wasn't to take his patrol outside the halls where the feast was being hosted, but what if there were tiers? What if these were where the lesser houses were welcomed, and there was some even more lavish, even more decadent place where the prince and his daughter accepted the adulation and praise of even more illustrious nobles? The longer he walked the halls and corridors, the more plausible that seemed. The weeks he'd spent working double duty were about to be wasted, and the disappointment was like a stone in his throat.

He started noting the other places that the guests and servants flowed—a thin stairway that led up, a pair of bronze doors that opened only a crack to let a few people pass, a tapestry curtain with men's voices behind it. None of them were places Ras had shown him. None of them were where he was allowed.

He went through the bronze doors first. The hall on the far side was filled with performers and acrobats in costumes so thin and tight they looked naked. They ignored him as they prepared some finishing spectacle for the end of the feast. The other side of the tapestry curtain was eight men sitting around a green felt table with smoke pooling above it. Gold coins and red dice shifted in a serious, joyless game. The two men who glanced at Garreth had expressions as flat as lizards, and the others didn't pay him even that much attention.

The thin stairs led up to the top of the palace. A bonfire roared, its light and heat trying to push back the cold and dark of the sky. A stone garden, with statues of gods and people, and abstract forms that were only boasts of a sculptor's skill. The ruddy flicker of the firelight and the steady cool glow of the moon made everything seem alive and breathing. Two dozen young men and women milled around with cups of hot wine in their hands. Redcloaks and chaperones kept to the edges of the group, present and not present at the same time.

He saw her before she saw him. Elaine a Sal in a gown of yellow and blue, her hair plaited back with silver. She wasn't smiling or speaking. The crowd around her might just as easily not have been there. Her eyes were on the fire, and they seemed melancholy. Garreth stood, watching her. The aches in his chest and throat were physical. In that moment, he would have pledged the rest of his life to her, if accepting it would have brought her just a little joy.

As if his attention summoned her, she turned her head. Her eyes only widened a degree when she recognized him. She turned her back to the fire and walked casually away from the crowd toward the eastern edge of the rooftop. He waited a moment—as long as he could stand to wait, and only a moment—before he followed her.

"What are you doing here?" she said, and her breath was a plume of moonlit white. Her gaze clicked to him and then away at the city spread out below them.

"Came to see you. I didn't get an invitation to the party, so I made my own way." The joke tasted stale as he said it. She didn't laugh. "I tried to send you a letter. A note, really, but—"

"I read it."

"Ah."

The stone garden and fire were behind them. Oldgate dropped away before them, falling to the Khahon. Dark water hidden by pale ice. The lights of Newmarket and Riverport, the Temple, Seepwater, and Longhill all spread out before them. Some of them were his old house, where Vasch and Father and

Uncle Robbson still lived. Some were the barracks where Kannish and Maur were sleeping even now. The Temple was a shadow looking back at them from the eastern wall of the city, lanterns at its top like candles on a crown. The lamps and fires and plumes of smoke were like a warm reflection of the stars. Garreth was aware of the distance between his body and hers. The city didn't seem farther.

He locked his hands behind him.

"Is something wrong?" he asked.

Her chuckle was mirthless and grey. "What can I possibly tell you?"

"If something was wrong?"

"I'm sorry I got out of that carriage. I wasn't thinking. I was stupid. I'm sorry that I'm not that girl from your room."

"I'm not asking for that night back," Garreth said. "I only wanted to see you again."

"And thank me for changing your life? See if I can change it for you again?"

She sounded angry, but he wasn't certain the anger was with him. It sounded more like fear or despair or hurt that was spilled on him because he was the one present. But knowing that didn't teach him what to say, and maybe he was wrong.

"You didn't actually change my life. I did. You were the occasion, but I made my choices, and I don't regret them. I came here because I wanted to see you again."

"You don't know me."

The ache in his chest was still there, but he could feel its nature changing, like a summer leaf curling green to brown.

"Well…so, there was this time I spent a very pleasant evening with a young woman a while back. She was brave and a little reckless. And funny. And weirdly shoeless and…I don't know. I liked her. You say she's not here. She's not you. I don't entirely believe that. I do know you a little. Not all of you, but part. And I don't think it's a part many people get to know."

Elaine a Sal, daughter to the prince of Kithamar, lowered her eyes.

Garreth went on, "I think what mattered back then was that you were her. Just her. And I like her. I like that part of you."

"You want to fuck me again."

"Well, I'm not going to lie." Her glance was disbelief and outrage. Maybe a little laughter. He hoped, and he shrugged. "It was fun. You were beautiful. It was . . . good. But if we don't, we don't. I want to know you. It's not what we said, it's not what we agreed. But I can't help it."

She was shivering. "Look at us. Look at where we are. *Who* we are. Nothing about this ends well. Nothing about me is safe for you, and nothing about you is safe for me. I can't protect you, and you can only distract me. You should go home."

But you said you wanted to hear the story and a hundred other arguments rose up in him. They were all desperate. They all hurt. The moonlight on her cheek was familiar. The shape of her eyes was right in a way he couldn't explain, except all eyes ought to look like that, all the time. Her lips pressed a little thinner.

"All right," he said. "If you need me, you know how to find me. I am literally yours to command. I took an oath and everything." Her laugh was small, but it was there. He didn't dare to trust in it. He pulled the scarf from under his cloak and handed it to her. "You seemed cold."

She took it and put it around her neck. When he touched her wrist, she took his hand in hers. For a moment, they were both still, then, looking over his shoulder, she pulled away. "Please," she said. "Go."

He turned away, walking back toward the fire and the

shadows. A pale woman passed him, and he didn't meet her eyes or anyone else's. He was just a guard and a party decoration and the kind of fool who fell in love with a girl who didn't want him and then still longed for her. Tonight, he was no one. Moonlight pale as milk water shone down onto the whole and the broken alike.

She didn't watch him leave. She'd done what she had to do, and it felt like the moment between being struck and the bloom of pain. She knotted her hands in the scarf and wished that she hadn't taken it. It smelled like him.

It hurt, but it had to be done.

Her dream-drunk older cousin came to her side. Elaine wondered what Andomaka would have made of Ausai's eerie books. If she had dreamed that she'd come to the prince's secret room and found centuries of books written in the same eerie hand, what would the dream have been trying to tell her? That the prince of Kithamar wasn't a person, maybe. That the title meant something longer and greater than any of the mere people who carried it. But also that giving yourself over to that greatness was an abomination and a loss. That power and privilege and the highest nobility gave you everything because it took everything from you. She didn't need a dream for that. She already knew.

The silence between them stretched too long. Elaine had to break it.

"Andomaka."

"Elaine," her cousin said. "How is your heart?"

It was a ridiculous question. It was the only question. "It's been better. I have..."

I have given up something precious so I can pretend the loss was my choice. I have thrown something away so that it won't be taken from me. I've kept him safe. I pray I've kept him safe.

She clamped her jaw hard against the words, but her traitor eyes spilled.

Andomaka took her hand. "It's all right. Whatever it is, it will be all right."

The little compassion was almost too much to bear. Elaine almost turned to her, almost fell into her arms. "It's stupid. I shouldn't be... I should be happy."

"Why?"

"Because I'm free."

Her cousin's pale eyes narrowed. "You've ended things with..."

"I have. It's the only way to keep him safe."

Saying it made it real. She'd protected herself from him, and him from her, hadn't she? Their night together, their moment outside of time and the flow of their lives, wouldn't be corrupted by all the messy rest of it. She wouldn't change him. Wouldn't be responsible for his change. And he wouldn't be caught up in the webs she'd been born to.

They stood silently, hand in hand. Andomaka sighed. Her attention was turned into herself, recalling, maybe, some moment of her own life. Someone she'd known once and didn't now. Everyone carried loss. Elaine felt a little rush of affection and squeezed her hand. "Thank you."

Andomaka's focus returned, and she kissed Elaine's forehead the way a mother might have. "Are you sure of this?"

"I'm daughter to the prince. What else can I do?"

"You wouldn't be the first person to have a lover," Andomaka said, and then laughed. "Ausai shared his bed with more women than his wife. Everyone knew."

"It's not the same."

"Because he's a man?"

"That makes it different."

"It does. But it doesn't make it impossible." Andomaka put a hand on Elaine's shoulder, turned her away from the vast abyss of the city, and looked into her eyes. There was a depth there that Elaine didn't expect or understand. When Andomaka spoke, there was an intensity in her voice that was almost anger.

"We give our lives to the city, you and I. We marry for the city. We bear children for the city. And our family, and our blood. It's the sacrifice we're called to, and it's our duty. But it isn't everything we are. You have to take the pleasures you can in this life. They won't be given to you." She paused, gathered herself. "What is his name?"

"I'm not..." Elaine said. "I don't..."

I can't, she thought. *How can I say his name while he's still walking away from me? If I talk about him, I'll think about him, and if I do that, how can I stand it?*

"Name him."

"Garreth," she said, and knew that she was doomed. All the pretty ideas about protection and distance, about keeping parts of herself separate, her fear of the strange books and Karsen's veiled threats and her father's silence, all of it shuddered down to the ground like a broken kite.

"Go to your Garreth. Not as Elaine a Sal, daughter to the prince. Go as a woman to a man. Show him what there is in your life that he can claim, and what there isn't. And find what there is of him that will sustain you." The words were like wine poured in her mouth. They had the same bloom of warmth in her throat, the same subtle release in the muscles of her back and neck and belly. She wondered if her mother would have said the same things, if she'd lived.

"You...Do you...?" Elaine said. "I mean, have *you*...?"

Andomaka's eyes flickered. A complication of sorrow or memory. "I'm a woman too."

"Elaine!" The voice barking her name was like an intrusion on a dream. Elaine felt a little rush of embarrassment or shame, like someone had walked unexpectedly into a private moment. Halev Karsen was silhouetted against the fire as he walked toward them. He seemed more shadow than flesh. His scowl was anger or fear or something deeper that Elaine couldn't quite read. "Kint's been looking for you."

Why? she thought. Had she done something wrong? Was it Garreth? The books? Did they know she'd heard them? "I'm sorry," she said, without knowing what she might be sorry for.

"Please attend your father now," Halev said, and it sounded like a command. A dismissal. Elaine nodded and turned toward the fire and the stairway down into the body of the palace. Her breath was fast and shallow. She should do as she'd been told, find her father, see what he needed and what she could do. She should find Samal Kint and learn how she'd caught his attention.

She wasn't going to do either one.

In her imagination, Garreth dropped away from her like a coin in the river. She could see him retreating down the face of Oldgate or passing through the red gates and disappearing into the shadows of Green Hill or else the white gates and the endless streets of Stonemarket. She took the stairs two at a time, rushing down to the great hall and her mind rushing ahead of that. The palace guards were at every door, every courtyard. He could have retreated down any of a half dozen corridors and hallways.

In the great hall, voices roared like a storm wind. A hundred conversations crashing over and against each other, echoing from the old stone walls, drowning in each other so that each person had to be louder to be heard. Her blood hummed in her veins and she looked for some sign of which way he'd gone. Beyya Reyos leaned close to Hurdid Mallot so the older man could shout some story into her ear. Cannina Chaalat, weaving a little and eyes glassy from wine, walked on Barasin a Jimental's arm toward one of the side galleries. An Inlisc woman swirled into Elaine's path, turned a red silk scarf into a gout of flame and a paper rose, and swirled back away. A shriek of frustration haunted the back of Elaine's throat. Dimnia Abbasann caught sight of her and waved a hand, rising from her seat across the hall as if she were about to navigate the press of noble bodies and make Elaine talk to her when there wasn't time to talk.

Her weeks of late-night wanderings served her well. Elaine nodded to Dimnia, and moved as if she were going to meet her, but slipped instead into a side gallery, and from there to a corridor leading past the doors to the kitchens, and then south. Away from the feast, the voices faded quickly. She ran to the courtyard and the open air. Carriages stood waiting. Teams of horses clopped their hooves and blew great, pale breaths. Servants of all the great houses and most of the lesser ones stood waiting. There were even a couple of palace guards glowering and pacing the pavement. The air was cold and harsh, and Garreth was nowhere.

He's gone because you told him to go, her unreal mother said in her imagination. *What did you expect of him?*

She strode up to one of the palace guard. He was a broad-faced man with a bit of grey at his hairline. He bowed as she came near.

"There was a guard," she said. "One of yours, but not the usual. A new one. He'd have just left?"

"No one's come this way but us, my lady," he said. She stood in the cold a moment more, willing Garreth to appear from the shadows. When he didn't, she turned back.

As she neared the great hall, the sounds of singing reached her. Not the clear, ringing voices of artists, but the roar and bumble of the guests belting out an old Hansch song accompanied by the beat of a single drum. It was only merriment. Joy. There was no reason that it should make her feel more deeply alone, except that it did.

It would be easier to go back to her rooms, and she didn't want that either. The quiet, the isolation, the growing sense of powerlessness and dread. More than anything else, she wanted an end to the uncertainty and fear. She couldn't imagine a way for that to happen.

She didn't want to rejoin the feast. She didn't want to find Kint or her father. She didn't want Andomaka to ask her how things had gone. The hundred people waiting to visit with her, to see her and be seen by her, exhausted her already.

A flash of red caught her eye. Another of the palace guard walking the side gallery, his hands at his sides. For a moment, he almost looked like Garreth. And another moment. She froze. The song ended in a wave of laughter and clapping, her father's voice rising above it with words muddied and drowned by the general din. She stepped toward the guard—toward Garreth—almost without willing it. It felt more like falling or being pulled. When he saw her, his face closed and he nodded as if they didn't know each other.

"You're still here," she said.

His hands spread in apology. "I have to finish my shift. I'd get in trouble."

Her laughter felt like the only warm thing in the middle of winter. She had been so certain that sending him away was the right thing to do, and now all she felt was relief that she'd failed. A woman's voice started a new song somewhere in the galleries, and the drum picked up her beat. A rumble of voices like the river breaking at thaw. Garreth looked over his shoulder, like there was something he meant to go back to. She took his sleeve, turned, and walked away, drawing him behind her like he was a puppy on a string. He only resisted for a moment.

Her mind traced a path through the palace. If all her wanderings were only for this moment, they'd been hours wisely spent. She plucked a lantern from its hook in the hallway and led him down an abandoned servants' stair to the old kitchens that had been changed over to storage. Beds and chairs, tables and statuary, altars to half-forgotten gods all covered in thick canvas against dust and mice and time loomed up gold in the dim light. The only footprints in the dust were her own from other late-night explorations. Garreth rescued his sleeve and put his hand in hers. His fingers were warm and strong, his hand wide enough to envelop hers. She found the side-hall, and led him down again. The walls were solid here, not built with mortar but hewn from the living stone of the hillside. A breath of viciously cold air drew her on.

The little room had been a defense once. From its shutterless window, a soldier of some previous age could rain arrows or stones or oil or shit down on the invaders coming up the path of Oldgate. Crows had built a nest in the window's corner—sticks and twigs and straw, and one incongruous faded green ribbon. There were no birds there now. No one but the two of them.

She put the lantern on the thick stone sill. From the river below, it would look like a single star glowing in an empty patch of sky. The air smelled of dust and cold and the musk of absent birds. Like a bit of woods, hidden in the heart of the city. She leaned against the wall, trying to think of the best way to begin. There was so much she had thought she wouldn't tell him.

His lips on hers were a surprise, but not a shock. The rustle of cloth was louder than the wind. He smelled of smoke and soap and something pleasant she couldn't identify. She felt herself being distracted, and pushed him back gently with one open palm. He resisted, but only for a moment. He stepped back with a rueful smile, like an apology.

"I just..." he said. "If you're about to tell me to leave again, I thought..."

"Something bad is coming," she said. "I think something bad's already here, but I don't know what it is."

Garreth sobered. "Are you in danger?"

"I don't know. I might be. My father's keeping something from me, and I don't know why. And I found some books in Prince Ausai's private study and I can't tell what they mean. Halev Karsen and Kint are talking about spilling blood in Green Hill, and I don't know why. There's no one here I trust."

Garreth leaned against the sill beside the little glowing flame. His back was to the city and the stars. A man silhouetted in a window once again, like an image in a recurring dream.

"Start at the beginning, then," he said.

"I don't want you caught up in this. I don't want you hurt because of me."

"I don't either, but it's a big world. A lot of things happen here. Start by you not hurting me, and then trust me to make my own choices. I'll do the same for you. It'll work out."

"Don't be noble about this. We aren't lovers. You don't get to put yourself in front of a knife because you think you're supposed to. I'm not that."

Garreth lifted his hand, palm out, asking silence. His gaze was on hers, and his eyes were calm and fearless.

"You haunt me," he said. "It sounds like something of me haunts you too, and honestly, I find that fucking joyful. We'll get back to it. Whatever else we can or can't be, I am someone you think this through with. I'm not going to be loyal to anyone over you, and I'm not going to tell your secrets. I'm too clear on policy for that."

"I don't know if I love you or if I just need you," she said. "I don't want you to trust me."

"Here's the thing. I worship the air you breathe. My worst dreams are the ones where I'm going to wake up beside you because then I don't. If you want that to stop, I don't know how to fix it. I didn't choose it. It's just the hand I've been dealt. But whatever we do, whatever we are, it'll be all right as long as we're us. In the world, we'll do what we have to, but when it's you and me, we're just us. All right?"

Elaine crossed her arms. The lantern flame shuddered once and then stood high and still. She remembered her tutor's voice as if he were sitting with them. *It could be a congregation or a business or a nation or a tribe. It could be something smaller.* Well, there was nothing smaller than this.

"When my father took the crown, Prince Ausai's private study was locked behind an iron door, and no one had the key. No one thought much about it at first…"

The cold of winter made it seem like the sun gave no warmth at all until Garreth had to stand in the shadows for a while. Then it got colder. The street they were standing on was in Seepwater and just north of the university and east of the public stage where they put on plays and acrobat shows when it was warmer. Marsen and Hellat Cassen were going in the front to take a man in for murdering his neighbor's child up in Newmarket. The house where he was hiding belonged to the same brother who'd sold his whereabouts to Captain Senit. Garreth and Maur were in the street behind it, in case the murderer fled.

Garreth's mind was elsewhere.

"Are you all right?" Maur asked again, then grimaced. "I know, I keep asking. But I keep wondering."

"I'm fine. Really."

"Because you keep moving your lips. Like you're talking."

"I am talking. To you. Right now."

"That's not what I mean. When you're thinking something through that's bothering you, it's what you do."

"It is?"

"Whenever you have a bad hand at cards too. It's why you lose so much."

"And this is the first time you mention it?"

Maur shrugged. "Sometimes you lose to me."

The dark bodies of a dozen or more crows passed through the white sky above them, cawing at each other or else the ground. At the far end of the street, a girl pushed a handcart, stopping at doors and trading coins for cloth bags of barley and chicken. Garreth squeezed his hands into fists, released them, and squeezed again, trying to keep the numbness at bay.

"Who makes books?" he asked.

Maur blinked. "Makes books?"

"Binds them. Is that tailors' guild because the spines are sewn? Tanners for the leather?"

"Some are bound with cloth," Maur said.

"Paper's a bit like felting, the way it's made, but it's not taxed the same, is it?"

"I think there was a papermakers' brotherhood once, but it got folded into one of the larger guilds," Maur said. "Why do you need that?"

"I want to find out how you'd know when a book was made. Like in history. If there's a good way to tell a really old book from one bound in the same style, but recently."

"Strange project," Maur said, and a whistle split the air. Then another.

The back door of the house burst open, and a huge man barreled out. His hair was wide and wild as an animal, and the blade in his fist was dull grey and long as his forearm.

"Hey!" Maur shouted, drawing his sword, and the man slid on the ice and stone, curving the path of his escape. Garreth was already running after him. The murderer's bare feet slapped the stone as they ran. If he turned south toward the gate and tried to flee the city, they'd have him, but he went north, toward Longhill. If he reached the Inlisc quarter, Marsen and Hellat might let him go. Garreth lowered his head and sprinted. Behind him, Maur was still shouting for the man to stop. That seemed optimistic.

His breath was warm in his lungs, and he fell into the long, deep rhythm of a hunter running down prey. He forgot the cold. As the murderer shifted, pretending to turn down an alley and then veering off at the last moment, it struck Garreth that he wouldn't have been able to run like this a year ago. Months in the training yard had changed his body and his mind. The man before him was desperate and violent and armed, and Garreth was running at him instead of away. He plucked the whistle from his belt, put it between his teeth, and let his breath announce where he was to the other guards. The murderer looked back at him, teeth bared in anger and raw animal fear.

Garreth saw the shift in the man's body, and knew that he'd given up flight for combat well before he turned. To his credit, it was a sudden break and well executed. The killer's dull grey blade flicked out toward Garreth's throat even before Garreth could haul back his own momentum. Garreth's arm parried without him, and he spat out the whistle.

The man spread his arms, the blade out to the side and high, ready to swing down. In Garreth's mind, Captain Senit said *That's the stance of a man who likes intimidating people more than he likes fighting. Looks like a fucking dancer.*

"Last chance," Garreth said, and before the murderer could reply, darted in low and hard. He felt his sword scrape deep against the man's shinbone almost as he was jumping back. The murderer yelped and swung, but with the blade so far out from his midline, he might as well have been shooing flies. Blood ran down the man's leg to the street. It steamed.

The rage in the killer's eyes was turning to fear. Somewhere nearby, Marsen whooped like a boy playing at ball-and-whip. The murderer gathered himself for a last, desperate rush. Garreth waited. When the attack came, he ducked the killing blow, kicked the side of the man's knee, and moved over him where he stumbled and fell to the filthy street. The grey blade went skittering away. Garreth had the point of his sword at the joint of the killer's jaw, just under his ear, before the man—now the prisoner—could get his hands under him.

"Go ahead," he said. "Keep fighting. Save us some time."

The man's mouth was a square gape of low, animal rage. "You think you win. I'll see you dead. I'm going to piss on your mother's corpse."

"Nice work," Marsen said, and kicked the murderer in the back. The man squealed and writhed. Maur trotted up, winded but not so much as he would have been before they'd joined the guard.

"Hellat?" Garreth asked.

"This one pinked him," Marsen said.

"Oh. That was a mistake."

"He'll come to regret it. Briefly," Marsen said, and dropped his weight on the prisoner, wrenching the man's arm back and preparing to tie it. "What of it, brother? The magistrate's gaol, or sew some rocks in your cloak and hack a hole in the ice?"

"Scriveners," Maur said between gasps. "It was the scriveners. The guild that took the papermakers in."

"Oh," Garreth said. "That makes sense. They've still got their guild hall in Stonemarket?"

"Last I knew," Maur said as he took a desultory kick at the murderer's side. "But that may have changed when Thin

Timmons died. He was the one who insisted on keeping it there."

Marsen looked up at them with an indulgent kind of disgust. "Would my lords be so kind as to do their fucking jobs for a moment?"

"Sorry," Maur said, and knelt to hold the killer's shoulder back while Marsen bound his wrists and elbows. The blood on the ice and soaking the murderer's leg seemed improbably bright, like the winter had turned it festive. Garreth kicked aside a turd and wondered what would happen if the killer's wound went septic. Sometimes the magistrates insisted on keeping men like this alive until the city could execute them, and sometimes they just let the world take its course. Either way was fine with him.

In the days since Tenth Night, Garreth had become two men. His life had divided into aspects that were related, that touched like a man and his shadow, but they weren't the same thing. He was a bluecloak serving under Captain Senit, friend to Kannish and Maur. Separately, he was something to a girl he'd met three times now and dreamed of more nights than not. Her danger and his hunger for her company—not only sex, though that was part of it, but the sound of her voice, the curl of her smile, the mordant bleakness that ran under her jokes like the river flowing under ice.

They'd spent the better part of that night talking—just talking. All the oddities of life in the palace, but how she'd come to lose her other home, how she'd lost her mother and nearly lost her friend Theddan. They'd ended the night almost too tired to speak, just leaning against each other. It had been the best night he'd spent since the last time he'd been with her.

That she was in danger was like sand in his bedsheets. He couldn't rest, and even when he was doing something else, he was also thinking of her and of anything that he could do to bring her back to him and keep her safe. Where to see her, how to breathe a little more of her air, was a puzzle he chewed at, and there was no one he could share the problem with. He found himself turning to the details of the problem: How books were bound. How handwriting could be matched to the scribe. What the guilds knew about Ausai and Palace Hill. What people were saying about Byrn a Sal. Anything. Everything. It was all his alone to carry, except if it was hers too.

His other life—son of a merchant house, brother now to a married man and his Inlisc wife—barely intruded on him. It was only months ago, and felt too distant to have any effect on his present circumstances.

They passed through a wider street. The Temple loomed up to the right, strong and solid as a mountain. Garreth's footsteps slowed. He caught Marsen's eye. "Do you need me for this bit?"

The older guard shrugged. "Marching the scum into gaol is the glory bit. If you don't want it, more for me and this one."

"You take mine, then," Garreth said, and turned to the east. "You can hand me some glory back another time."

"Where are you going?" Maur called after him, but he only waved.

The sun moved more slowly through the sky than it had just weeks before. The days were already stretching toward a springtime that wasn't here, but the cold of winter was at its worst. There'd be bodies of more than foxes and dogs to pry up off the ice and stone. Some of the people doomed to die of cold were waiting in the charity line at the Temple. They huddled against the wall in their rags and misery. The half-mad or wholly so, the men and women wasted and rheumy from their need for wine or something stronger, the simply unlucky: they all came to the Temple for a bit of food once a day. Not enough to live on, but enough to die more slowly. The mercy of a merciless god. They shied away from Garreth as he walked past them. He tried not to meet their gaze in case seeing him eye to eye would scare them away from the thin charity that was waiting for them.

The line ended at an open door. The smell of boiled wheat and barley carried to the street on a cloud of steam. Garreth pushed through and no one in the line objected. Inside, the desperate packed three thin tables shoulder to shoulder, eating mush from little tin bowls. When one finished, the priest-itinerant would take the bowl, usher the man or woman or child out into the cold, and bring whoever was at the head of the line in to take the empty spot. Garreth didn't think they'd get them all fed before the sun went down.

One of the priest-itinerants was a wide-faced man with unkempt hair and a soft chin. His priestly robes were plainspun brown, but he had a wool shirt on underneath them.

"You're Haral," Garreth said.

"Bless, my cousin," the soft-chinned man said. "Is there some way we can help the guard?"

Garreth stepped closer and lowered his voice. "You're *Theddan*'s Haral?"

The shock in his expression was more than enough. Garreth had seen the same eyes on a dozen prisoners when he'd come through their doors. Guilt had a language all its own.

"I just need you to pass on a message, yeah?"

"Yes, of course," Haral said.

"Her friend. The one who visits?"

"I know the one you mean," the priest said carefully.

"Can you get a message to her?"

"I will try. I will do everything I can." Haral nodded like he was agreeing with himself. "It may take some time. I don't want there to be any trouble, sir."

Garreth put a hand on his shoulder. "I'm not 'sir.' I'm Garreth Left of the city guard, and we're on the same side."

Haral's smile was slow, but real. Even with everything he'd heard about Theddan Abbasann, Garreth hadn't quite put it together that Haral was in love with her. It was clear as fresh water to him now, though. Two idiots in over their heads, the pair of them, and the women besides.

Elaine a Sal had her coachman wear plain clothes and borrow a carriage that didn't speak of Green Hill, much less the palace. She had him stop in a narrow street to the north and east of House Left as if by coming from the direction opposite the palace, she would be better disguised. She'd taken a cloak from the supply that the palace servant used. It was green with old, worn embroidery at the hem and a hood deep enough that she could hide in it. She'd thought when she chose it that it wouldn't stand out in a Riverport street. Now that she was walking there, she wasn't sure.

The cold was sharp, but it didn't empty the street. The bitter chill of winter didn't stop the errands and chores and daily business of Riverport. From what she could see past the dim tunnel of her hood, it didn't even slow them down. Carts piled high with grey wooden crates rumbled down the street beside her. Two men in thick leather coats crossed in front of her, their voices raised and talking over each other about compensation rates for a lost toe. An older Inlisc woman with a wicker basket in her arms passed her, and Elaine hadn't known she was there until she brushed past close enough to cast a shadow on her.

Elaine turned into a stonework niche where a statue had been once but wasn't anymore. She pulled her hood back a little and glanced up and down the street, more than half expecting to hear voices call her name. That was her nerves, though. The truth was no one in the street noticed her. She was another body in a city filled with them. No one expected to see the daughter of the prince here, and so no one did. For them, she was just some Hansch girl in an old-fashioned cloak. She pushed the hood back and let the cold nip at her earlobes as she walked. She only made it a few doors farther before she plucked the cloth back up into place.

It was only another two streets to House Left and the wall she'd climbed over in the night a lifetime ago. It pulled at her like the earth pulling a stone as it fell.

"Don't hurry," she said under her breath. "You'll only stand out more if you hurry." But she hurried.

The days after Tenth Night had been strange for her. Talking with Garreth, telling him all the ominous things that had happened since her father had opened Prince Ausai's private study, had been a relief she hadn't known she needed. She'd said all the same things to Theddan, but the way Garreth listened and the way her cousin did weren't at all the same. Theddan cared deeply, but keeping her attention could feel like work. Garreth drank her words in like they were water and he was dying of thirst. He'd asked questions that Theddan never would have thought to: Who built the iron door? Had it been cast in a single piece, or made in bits and assembled? Had the shelves the eerie books had rested on been new or ancient? Someone had made them, and if they knew who and when, it might tell her something. They were a merchant's questions, sifting through small signs for the implications she might have overlooked.

He'd given her another way of seeing. Even if it hadn't opened the mystery to her yet, she had reason to hope that it would.

They'd talked through all the rest of that night, the celebrations and feasting and intrigue rolling along without them. When the sky outside the little room had begun to shift from blackness to the deepest grey, Garreth had to leave or risk missing his end-of-duty call. She'd walked with him as far as they could go without risking being seen, and then a little bit farther. He'd taken her hand before he turned away, and she'd watched until he vanished down the corridor that led to the courtyard.

Afterward, she had gone back to her rooms, let the bedroom girl prepare her for bed as briefly as she could, and fallen into as deep a sleep as she could remember since she'd first come to the palace. The days since had been no easier, Halev and her father no more forthcoming, and the mystery of the books and the dead prince no less ominous, but she'd been able to bear them more easily. Each day she found herself wondering what Garreth was doing, what he might have found, and how she might see him again. Then a message came from the Temple, and she'd spent every day since planning for this walk, this moment. She told herself it was in service of her investigation, and sometimes—not always—she even believed it.

She passed by the door of House Left, her throat tight with the certainty that Garreth's irate uncle would storm out as she did. She could practically feel his hand on her shoulder, turning her toward the stables and another ignominious cart ride back across the river. In her imagination, she took offense, announcing who she was and watching the proud-chested man wilt. An idiotic fantasy that would bring more trouble than it saved, and anyway by the time she'd entertained it, she was at the corner, turning down the side street, and it hadn't happened after all.

She'd worried whether she would recognize the place where

she'd crossed this wall before. She'd seen it months ago, and in darkness. But as she plucked back the hood again, the stretch of stone and stucco was so familiar that she thought she must have been dreaming of it. She put her hand on it the way Garreth had shown her, then hesitated and glanced back. There were a few people in the main street. A couple more farther down the side street who didn't seem to be paying her any attention. Waiting for them to leave would be more suspicious than climbing the wall, but she still had to overcome the sense of danger. Danger of what? Embarrassment? Shame? Of being caught out and losing the chance to see Garreth? She was Elaine a Sal, daughter of the prince. What, after all, was the worst that could happen to her here?

She put her boot to the little toehold and hauled herself up and over. The courtyard looked more open and bare in the daylight than she remembered it. The door leading into the house was shut, and Garreth stood where he couldn't be seen if it opened. His cloak was grey and plain. Not the blue of the city guard or the red of Palace Hill. He grinned, and she felt herself mirroring him. He gestured toward the door and motioned her for silence. She crossed the courtyard in fast, low strides as he opened the door, slipped into the warmth of the house, and paused, listening. Somewhere not far away, someone was moving. Garreth seemed to judge the sound, then crept down the hall, heading the opposite direction from her previous visit. There was nothing to do but follow.

The stairway he brought her to was so narrow that her shoulders brushed the walls on both sides at the same time and so steep it was almost a ladder. The wood was old and black with use, but it was solid enough that it barely creaked. She followed him up, first in silence and then struggling to hold back a mad, bubbling laughter.

"What are we doing?" she whispered as they came to a thin pair of boards that required an act of charity to be called a landing.

"It's a guild meeting. My parents and Vasch will be there, and the servants don't use these stairs when they don't have to."

"Why would they ever? These are terrible."

"It's just a little farther. Come on."

They rose, him first and her just after, until he pushed open a trap door, turned back, and helped her up into a dim storage room. Crates and trunks and old furniture wrapped against dust filled the awkward space. What light there was peeked around the edges of old shutters. The air was surprisingly warm, though, and the sounds from the street were audible, but softer here. Carts and voices and the cooing of pigeons. She thought of the little room where they'd spent Tenth Night, and this seemed like its echo. Another hidden place in another stolen hour. Seen that way, there was a melancholy about it. But maybe a beauty too.

"We used to hide up here when we were young," Garreth said. "Me and Kannish and Maur. When we were trying to avoid our brothers and sisters, we'd sneak up here and tell stories and play." He shrugged away some memory she couldn't share. "Are you well?"

"Frustrated," she said. "Confused. Thwarted at every turn. No worse than I was the last time."

"That's something. Not worse isn't worse, anyway. I don't know if I have anything to help, but I've been talking to people. Here, look at these."

He folded himself down to the floor, sitting with his legs tucked under him, and for a moment, she could see the boy he'd once been in the same place. As she sat beside him, he drew a handful of pages from his cloak and smoothed them out on the floorboards. They were covered in patterns and sketches of book spines and bindings with notes scrawled beside them in smudged ink. Garreth glanced over at her, half proud and half sheepish.

"It turns out there's a lot of history about how books get made," he said. "The three big questions are whether the pages are just stacked or if they got folded in bunches and the bunches sewn together, if the sewing was in straight lines or crossed like this one, and whether the threads were silk or not. If it's all lined up right... well, then it might be old or it might be faked. If they don't, though, you can be pretty sure that they were made recently and someone just wanted them looking old."

"And you found all this out?"

"I asked," he said. "Told the guild master there was a tax issue about whether an old book was real. Once I had her started, everyone in the hall weighed in."

"I'm not sure I can get into the study again."

"If you do, you'll be ready." He said it with a simple confidence that made her think it might be true. If she found her way back there, maybe she really would be ready. She wanted to think so.

She leaned against him, her cheek against his shoulder, and looked down at the pages. He smelled like salt and musk. "All right," she said. "Show me what I'm looking for."

For the better part of an hour, he did. And then, for a time, they did other things.

Captain Senit stood at his desk in his full coat and a thick cap of knitted grey wool with sides long enough to cover his ears. Each breath was a little cloud of white. A nugget of incense still burned in the altar to the Three Mothers, and the smoke smelled cold. He ran a numbed finger down the pages of the incident book. Theft, theft, assault, tax evasion, fraud, murder, theft. The steady beat of Kithamar's worst impulses, the same, he guessed, as anyplace that held enough humanity together inside a city's walls. A ledger of its sins more accurate and complete than any accounting the priests and temples could give.

A butcher in Newmarket had found his wife's brother contaminating his wares. A woman in Seepwater was afraid that her estranged husband meant her harm. A warehouse manager in Riverport was missing goods. Three corpses had been found under the northernmost bridge where they'd looked for shelter from the cold and didn't find it. It was easy to look at this face of the city and forget that there were others. Kithamar wasn't just crime and cruelty and violence, just the part of it that mattered to him. Senit paused for a moment, imagining some other incident book that kept track of all the good and kindness and charitable acts that took place within the city walls. It was a funny idea because it didn't exist and never would. The beautiful part about things that went well was you didn't have to do anything about them.

His stomach creaked. The morning sun was spilling itself over the training yard, and he hadn't had his morning meal yet. The hunger was a dull ache, and he relished it a little. He wouldn't be the man he was if some part of him didn't enjoy discomfort. He'd finish catching up on the book, then maybe make an inspection of the barracks. When that was done, he'd let himself eat.

The knock at his door was solid, but not loud. He turned his hand, pressing down on the page like he was pinning the words in place, and called back over his shoulder. Marsen Wellis came in.

"You wanted to see me, Captain?"

"Did. You've been working with our three new puppies some, haven't you?" Marsen crossed his arms and nodded. Senit went on, "What do you think of them?"

Marsen thought for a moment before he spoke. "I think Kannish has it in him to be a solid guard, but I would think that, wouldn't I? Ask someone else if you want a clearer view on him. Maur's smart. Sees things the others miss sometimes. Scrapping's not in his blood."

"Not every guard needs to be a pit dog."

"True. If I wanted someone to think a problem through, Maur's good enough. Not certain I'd want him at my back when the fight comes. That's all I'm saying."

"What about Left?"

Marsen's pause was long enough to be interesting. When he shrugged, it was half an apology, and Senit didn't think the apology was to him. "He's good. It's not that he isn't good. He shows up when he's called. Brave enough. Knows his way around a blade as well as anyone with his background and training would. It's just sometimes it's like he's thinking of something else, you know?"

"Not keeping his eyes on the work."

"It isn't even that, really," Marsen said. "He toes the mark. I've got no complaints on what he does. It's just that how he does it feels half-distracted some of the time."

Senit let that settle for a couple breaths. Then, "Time to snap his leash, maybe. Get his attention."

"Could be," Marsen said, but he didn't sound convinced. "Something in mind for him?"

"There's trouble on the far side of the river. The plague has people anxious, and Pavvis asked if we had any men we could spare, what with the quarantine."

Marsen's face fell. "The quarantine?"

"Kint's boys are walking the rope. Pavvis is looking for a few more patrols along his side of the river so he can free up some of his to send to Stonemarket. Show the rabble how we're taking it seriously."

Marsen was quiet. Senit knew all the things he wasn't saying. That taking on the territory on the other bank of the Khahon even just temporarily made it more likely they'd have to take responsibility for it more later on, and they were stretched thin already. Running patrol for someone else was showing his belly too. It said that Pavvis had other concerns more important than the scut work, and Senit didn't. And also that the fiasco around Aunt Thorn had embarrassed Pavvis along with him, and this was a way to ease that debt if not erase it. Sending the newest guards and not too many of those would salvage Senit's barracks some of its dignity. And it wouldn't alienate the senior guards any more than he already had. Garreth and Kannish and Maur might not even know enough to be humiliated.

Marsen scratched his ear, his lips twitching like he was having a conversation with himself. Senit leaned back against his table, his finger still fixed at the place where he'd stopped reading. Marsen glanced up at him, then down. "I don't know, sir. I mean, I see we've got to eat the turd. But…I mean, maybe it's better to get the big spoon and make the fuckers think we like it."

"Say more."

Marsen shifted his weight, his eyes hardening. "The plan didn't work, but we *had* a plan. The other barracks have a quarter each. We've got half the city, and Longhill in the middle of our ground like a splinter that never festers out. We saw a chance, and we took the fight to the bitch, and yeah we got our nose bloodied for it. Doesn't mean we were wrong to do it."

"We're talking about helping with the quarantine, Wellis. Don't overthink it."

"Give me the morning. I'll build up a patrol rota that'll make Pavvis think we're looking to take the Smoke by force."

Senit swallowed his smile, but there was a warmth that bloomed under his coat. "If you want to, I won't stop you."

Marsen braced, and Senit nodded his dismissal. When the door closed behind the man, Senit stood in the cold and quiet for a few seconds and let himself feel pleased. Not for long, and not deeply, but for a moment. The incense glowed orange as it reached its end, then faded to grey. The smoke thinned and stopped. Senit turned back to the place marked by his finger. A streetbound man had stolen a chicken and been caught starting a cookfire in an alleyway. A man had crawled too deep into his bottle, and the taproom needed help seeing him to the street. Half a dozen more little frailties and failures of judgment. He got to the end without finding anything that needed his attention, and he closed the book.

On sober reflection, maybe he'd get a bowl of eggs and mash before he made his inspections after all.

The brief, dark days of winter slowly grew longer, but the grinding cold didn't break. The frozen river made bridge taxes go down, the deep water covered over by ice as solid as stones. The celebrations of Longest Night faded into memory. The promise of thaw remained only a promise. The city pulled into itself, retreating from the cold like a snail folding itself into its shell. Only not entirely. People skated on the river, sliding across the white expanse for the simple joy of the movement. Little stands set up in the squares with iron stoves like tiny forges made to warm cider and wine at three coppers for a mug.

In a different year, Garreth would have been sleeping later and waking in a room that didn't smell of other men's bodies. He would have eaten at his family table beside a fire that Serria or one of her staff had set before he'd come down the stairs. The work of the family would have taken him to their warehouses or meetings with their allies, or else left him to his own devices while Father and Mother and Uncle Robbson went to conferences with the magistrates and guild masters that youth and policy still kept him from. Vasch was living some version of that life now while Garreth dragged himself out on patrol before the sun had come up and afterward sat in the baths until the heat made its way back into his bones or trained with Beren or Nattan Torr or Kannish and Maur until he was sweating despite the cold. The comforts of his old life weren't forgotten, but they also weren't entirely remembered. It was like he could recall that he'd lived more softly once, but he couldn't summon up the experiences themselves. He knew that he'd slept in a soft bed with three blankets, but the sleep he longed for at the end of his day wasn't that. He'd eaten rich foods prepared by an experienced cook, but his hunger now was conquered by thick stews from old pots with more salt than savor, and the honest fullness of his belly now was more compelling than the best of memory's echoes.

When he wasn't thinking about the work before him, he was thinking of Elaine a Sal. Sometimes of the mystery and threat she was picking apart at the palace, sometimes of the simple, authentic fact of her, and always of how he could find his path back into her company, if only for a little while.

For a while, it seemed like it could go on that way. He'd found his place, and nothing would have to change.

Coming back from his morning's patrol, Garreth knew that something was wrong by the way Kannish walked: long strides, arms swinging at the shoulders but solid at the elbow and wrist, hands in fists. His scowl could have cut glass. He marched across the training field toward Maur and Garreth, clearly coming to them. Something had upset him, and Garreth genuinely thought he was going to unburden himself and tell them what it was right up until the blow landed.

The world rang. Somehow, the training yard had swooped up behind him. The cold dirt pushed against his back like it was urging him forward, but there was nothing to stand on. His jaw hurt, and the sky swam above them. Maur was holding back a red-faced, raging Kannish who was shouting something about peppercorns.

A half dozen of the older guards were running toward them as Garreth found his feet. His balance was wrong. Kannish surged toward him again, fists ready. Tears of rage filled his eyes.

"You knew! You knew the whole time!" he shouted. "My sisters are *ruined*!"

Oh, Garreth thought. *The caravan's arrived.*

Captain Senit stood. Garreth and Kannish sat. The little iron brazier gave off enough smoke to give Garreth a headache and enough heat to keep the room from feeling like it was carved from ice. The captain's arms were crossed, and his mouth was a smear of impatience and disgust.

"My sisters have peppercorns coming from the Bronze Coast next summer," Kannish said. "With the market already flooded, they're going to lose on the trade. It's money they were counting on."

The captain passed a palm over his eyes. "Is there a law was broke here?"

"Yes," Kannish said in the same moment Garreth said, "No."

Kannish's jaw jutted forward and he turned toward Garreth. "Winter caravans have to be licensed by the guilds, and their contents listed before they're cleared. You cheated, and the magistrates are going to take every fucking coin you've got."

"Trade is always permitted within a family," Garreth said.

"So these Far Kethil fucks are your cousins now? They're *Inlisc*. They aren't even Kithamar Inlisc."

"By marriage," Garreth said.

Kannish's face went pale. He understood now what Garreth had joined the guard to escape. It wasn't a betrayal of their friendship, not really. He'd followed family policy the same as anyone of their class would. But it was true Kannish's family was going to suffer, and Garreth couldn't help feeling the shame of that.

The captain clapped his hands. "I apologize," he snarled. "I phrased that poorly. Let me try again. Is there anything in this that we need to go haul someone down the streets in chains over?"

They were quiet.

"I didn't think so," the captain said. "So given that, what the fuck business is it for either of you? You're not them anymore. You're us. You know that. The guard doesn't take sides, and if you do, maybe you aren't guard."

Kannish shot a glance at Garreth. The anger was gone, and only misery was in its place. Garreth lowered his head. The captain went on.

"We aren't House Left or House Wellis or House fucking Senit for that matter. We're city guard. Ours is to keep the thieves and the murderers and the rapists and the slavers from taking over the streets. If this isn't that, it isn't my problem, and if it isn't my problem, it isn't yours. The guilds are taking it to the magistrates, and I know that because it's my job to, not because I care. You boys are green. You still think you're both things, but you're not. I expected you at least understood that, Wellis. Maybe your uncle didn't teach as well as I'd hoped."

"I'm sorry, Captain," Kannish said. "I was . . . I was . . ."

"Damn right you were. Forget this rota's duty line. You're on the shit cart all day, every day until I say you aren't."

"Yes sir," Kannish said.

"Now both of you get the—"

"Permission to join him, sir," Garreth said.

Captain Senit stopped, fixed his gaze on Garreth, and hoisted an eyebrow. "You know he's being punished for trying to crack you open, yeah?"

Garreth's throat felt dry as dust. He swallowed twice before he spoke, but it didn't feel like it helped much. "If the guard's our family now, then the guard's our family now. Permission to join him."

"Some men come to like the shit cart," the captain said. "They're disgusting little perverts. Are you a disgusting little pervert, Left?"

"No sir. I hate it. But—"

"But," the captain agreed, and he almost smiled. "Fine. You're both off your regular rota. Be ready when the next cart comes back. You're going out."

They braced, and then walked out toward the barracks in silence. Maur, outside the door to their bunkroom, stopped pacing.

"I thought it was the prince," Kannish said. "Everyone knows your family's in trouble. Everyone figured they'd do something to try and dig out. After the prince's daughter knew you on the bridge, I figured it was something to do with Palace Hill. But it wasn't, was it?"

"No," Garreth said. "It was always the caravan."

They walked ahead in silence until Kannish muttered *Fuck*.

Maur went with them to change the duty roster. The most recent shit cart had gone out late that morning, delayed by a bad axle, and even if Frijjan and Ubrial Koke spent the whole shift whipping the prisoners on, it wouldn't be back for another hour. It wasn't enough time to get across the river to Stonemarket and back, even if Garreth could borrow a horse. But there was business he had closer in. He gave Maur a few coins from his wallet—enough to cover a plate of fish and cup of hot wine for him and Kannish both—before he started off to the east and the Temple with a message to pass up to Palace Hill.

There had been times—more as she grew older—when she could go days without seeing her father more than in passing. That had been when they only shared a family compound in Green Hill. Now they had a walled quarter filled with guards and servants, high functionaries and courtiers and all the human mechanisms of a city that he was meant to steer. It wasn't strange any longer for a week to pass without setting eyes on her father, and they were rarely if ever alone. She found herself awake at night, worrying about him and the city and the world, but in the mornings when she sought him out, he'd be in a meeting with some official of the city or in private conference with Halev Karsen or asleep and not to be disturbed.

And so when she came to the little gallery she'd fallen into using for her morning meal and found him already sitting there, it was a surprise.

He was by the window that had first drawn her to the space. It radiated cold, but the light was soft and beautiful. Decades of wind-driven grit had blurred the glass. The courtyard it looked out over seemed unreal: underwater or half in dream. A fire burned in the grate, and the stone flesh of the room held the heat even when the logs had fallen to ash. Like everything in the palace, it was thick and dark and brooding, but of the places Elaine had found, it brooded the least.

Her father sat on a stool, looking out the frosted glass. He looked not ill, but older and spent. Even in the soft light, there were new wrinkles around his eyes and mouth. A vein traced its path through the skin at his temple, more pronounced than she remembered it. There was a greyness to him that seemed as much spiritual as physical. It hurt her heart to see him, but she covered it over with a smile.

At first he seemed almost not to see her. His gaze swept the room, only pausing at her before moving on. Then, as if realizing what he'd just seen, he found her again and raised his hand in greeting.

"Ah, my darling child," he said, and the darkness in his tone might have been bitterness or anger.

"Is all well? I've hardly seen you these last weeks."

"I've hardly been." He looked back out the window, or maybe only at the glass itself. *Is he drunk?* she wondered. She looked around the gallery, found a footstool that she could pull to his side, and sat leaning against his leg like she was a little girl again and he was only her father. The sorrow thickening her throat was knowing that it wasn't true. She was a woman grown, and her father was more than that.

"What is it?" she asked.

"What's what?"

"What's really going on?"

She felt him tense, and then slowly, as if it took effort, relax. "There's a great deal going on. One thing floods into the next. That's all. I'm very busy. I suppose I should have expected that, but it'll get better with time."

"Will it?"

"I don't know," he sighed. "I love you. I loved your mother to the stars and back again. I thought I knew who we were. What the world was. How it worked. I didn't understand anything." He went quiet and still. When she looked up, his face was stony and his attention turned in on itself. She was afraid he wouldn't speak again, but then he did. "This city is a monster."

"What are Ausai's books?" She hadn't meant to ask, and knew as soon as she'd said it that she'd gone too far. Her father's sudden smile was like watching a door close. He ruffled her hair with his hand the way he had when she was younger.

"Nothing you need to worry about. The oddity of an odd man. My uncle was stranger than I knew. That's all. I should... I have..."

He stood, smoothing down his robe with his hands. He smiled at the window with the same mask-steady indulgence he'd pointed at her. Then the fire. Then the wall. He walked out without finishing his thought. Elaine swallowed twice to make the tightness in her throat release. The meal that she'd meant to eat seemed unappealing now. There wasn't enough space in her for bread and alarm both.

Outside, the sky was low and troubled. There was no rain, only a thin, gritty mist as much ice as water. The paving stones in the courtyard were slick and dark. Her carriage was waiting, the coachman rubbing down the horses on his team and cooing at them as he did. Elaine paused and looked back, half hoping to see her father coming after her. She only waited a moment.

"Some weather coming in," the coachman said.

"More snow," Elaine agreed.

"Rain, I'd guess, but that'll be bad enough. The old man never let us go down Oldgate when it was like this. We always had to take the long way around."

She heard the question in what he said, but it wasn't what caught her attention. "You knew Prince Ausai?"

"We all did," the coachman said. "He was the prince."

"What did you think of him?"

"I didn't. I did what I was told."

And what were you told? she thought, but there was no reason to give it voice. She squinted through the freezing mist at the dark shapes of the walls as if looking closely enough would reveal her great-uncle in their lines and corners. The old sense of the palace itself looking back passed through her, and she shivered. Everyone there, very nearly, from the lowest maid to the captain of the palace guard and the court historian, had served Ausai before they served her father. How strange that it had taken her until now to understand that serving one prince might not mean serving the next. How long could a man live someplace before that place—walls, windows, doors, gardens, and galleries—became an extension of him? How much of him could still live in that when the man himself was gone?

"Miss?"

"We can take Oldgate," she said.

"To the Temple?"

"No," she said. "The other place."

There were strategies to a decision by the magistrates. The arguments in a disagreement were heard in public with parties of interest—people, guilds, officers of the city—allowed to speak as the magistrates saw fit. It was also a kind of theater piece. Who was cheered and who was mocked wasn't supposed to have any influence over the law, but magistrates were human, and humans swayed. Who attended a judgment, how many allies and dependents and patrons they could muster up, how enthusiastically they voiced their support of an argument or derided the opponent's view was critical information for the officials of law. It spoke to the mood of the city, the stakes of the ruling, and how to know the path that led to peace from the one that led to riot.

Because of that, the practice of taking a full household to attend the judgment—from the head of the house to the newest servant—was so common that a whole genre of jokes existed about it. Garreth knew that with so much depending on the winter caravan's legitimacy, Father would have brought everyone he could. Everyone but Garreth.

He slipped over the garden wall and opened the servants' door with the same trick he'd been using since he was a boy. Inside, the house was quiet. The subtle scent of the lemon oil that Serria had the maids all use brought back floods of memories he hadn't realized were locked away until that moment. Being no taller than a table, stretched out on the floor while his mother hummed to herself in the next room. The one maid—Kayyla? Kavva?—who'd worked for them the summer Garreth turned fourteen and the doomed longing he'd developed for her. The sound of Vasch clopping down the hallways pretending to be a general leading a great army into battle in the lesser hall while he and a younger Kannish and Maur had tried to ignore him.

That the moments were lost made them sweet. Even things which had been annoying or unpleasant or even enraging took on a patina of melancholy because they could never happen again. There had been a last time for Vasch to interrupt Garreth's older, more sophisticated games, and it had already gone without anyone knowing that time had been the last. The boy who rested in the sunlight and his mother's unconscious song was gone. The maid with the sweet laugh and the little underbite who he'd tried not to stare at had some other work in some other house and likely a husband and children of her own by now.

Everything rose and was lost. Every decision ended the other paths that a different choice would have opened. Including all the lives in which this might still be Garreth's home.

He walked upstairs, noticing all the small changes. Someone—Yrith? Serria?—had installed little vases that hung from the walls with sprigs of pine and rosemary in them. The little tapestry that hung in the hall outside his parents' private rooms was gone, and a painting of a horse had taken its place. There was a scratch in the door to his old room that hadn't been there when he left.

His bed was still where it had been. His little desk. Someone had painted the walls with flowers. The room seemed larger now that he'd spent a few months sharing a barracks. The idea of so much privacy was almost ridiculously luxurious. But the air smelled like rain and dust. The scent of a room that wasn't lived in.

The winter shutters were up, inner frames covered by paper to let in light but keep the cold air at bay. He opened them, and the familiar view was less familiar now. Palace Hill was gone, smothered in cloud. The world felt small and heavy, the city hunkered down before the threat of the storm like a man braced against attack. The last time he'd stood there, he'd never killed anyone.

He heard her footsteps and closed the inner frames. The room grew only a little darker. She opened the door and paused before she stepped in. Her cloak was dark, and the gown beneath it pale. It made her seem thinner than she was, like the world had lessened her since Tenth Night. Her smile was complicated in ways he didn't understand.

"I wasn't sure you'd..." he began.

She stepped in like the words had broken a spell, closed the door behind her, and slipped off her cloak and let it fall to the floor.

"Well, thank the gods you're here. Otherwise I'd just be breaking into houses." The laughter in her voice was hard.

Garreth tried to gather his thoughts, but she crossed to him before he could, and then it was very hard to think.

"I'm sorry I couldn't find how to see you sooner than—" he began.

"Don't," she said. Her hand was a fist at the base of his spine, his shirt twisted into her fingers. She yanked the cloth up. The air was cold against his back. He started to speak, but she pressed her mouth to his. Her hair was damp against his palm as he tilted her face up to his, the muscles in her neck like ropes. Her hands fumbled at his belt. She found the sword at his hip and went still.

Some alarm within him, shrill as a whistle, found its way through the animal response of his body. He kept the embrace lightly and held himself back, waiting. The shudder that passed through her had nothing to do with desire.

"Can we . . . ?" she said. "Do we have to . . . ?"

"We're us. We don't have to do anything."

She stepped back. Her mouth was hard and joyless. Her eyes shifted like she was searching for something as she paced the room. "I'm sorry. I'm so sorry. This is humiliating. I thought that . . . It's not that I don't want to—"

"It's all right. It doesn't matter."

She met his gaze with her eyebrows raised, glanced down, then back up again. He considered himself and shrugged.

"That happens all the time," he said. "It doesn't mean as much as you think."

"Flattering."

"I'm just trying to—" He raised his hands. "I don't understand what's happening here."

She sat at the edge of the bed. "I saw my father today. I asked him to tell me what was going on. I asked him about the books, and he wouldn't tell me. Karsen knows everything, and I'm kept out." Her voice sang like a violin string, clear and high and beautiful, but taut with pain. "I hate the palace. I hate the princedom. I'm more than halfway to hating the city."

"I understand."

"How? How could you possibly understand when I'm the one going through it, and I barely understand it for myself? You mean you want me to feel better and be reassured. That's sweet. Really. But it isn't understanding."

"All right, I don't understand, but I'm trying to. And I'm trying to have your back. I'll help if I can."

"How charitable. Or is it loyal? Or worshipful? I don't know what word fits. What is it I'm supposed to expect from you?"

"Kindness and respect would be welcome," he said. "I mean, if you can bring yourself to them."

She closed her eyes. It looked like regret, but he wasn't certain. "I'm not... I'm not doing this well."

"You're carrying a heavy load," Garreth said.

"God, you're so fucking helpful and understanding and perfect. Do you ever get angry?"

"Oh, I'm angry."

"With me?"

"With you." The words hung in the air like smoke because they were true. "This much I do understand, whether you believe me or don't. You're not even vaguely who you were even this time last year. You're swimming in fast water, and it's too deep to stand. It's the same for me."

"Nothing is the same for us. It can't be. We aren't the same."

"That isn't what I meant."

"I know," she said, and there was sorrow in the words. She put a hand out. Her fingertips on his skin were an apology. He took a step toward her. "I know," she said again, more softly.

A whisper came, as unmistakable as it was out of place. A girl's voice, and close outside his door. Elaine looked up. She'd heard it too.

"What's that?" Garreth said. He had time to draw his sword.

The door burst open. The two thugs who boiled in had

weapons drawn. A Hansch knifeman with close-cut, greasy dark hair and a sword he held like he knew the use of it. An Inlisc girl with a lead-tipped club and teeth bared like a rat. Garreth felt a distance and calm falling into him. A roar came into his ears and the clear, animal need to kill both intruders before they could hurt Elaine.

The Hansch boy lunged, wrist-whipping his blade toward Garreth's ribs. It was an easy parry, and Garreth let the momentum carry him forward the way Beren had drilled him, taking him inside the enemy's guard. He had to end this quickly. Two against one was hard. If it had only been him, he could have looked for weaknesses in their defense. Elaine was the weakness in his.

Elaine stood off the bed, an expression of outrage on her face like the violence was less an affront than the interruption. The Inlisc girl swung her club, and there was no way to stop the blow. The impact had the sound of splintering bone. Elaine staggered and fell.

Garreth felt himself call out, wordless, as the Hansch knife tried to back out into proper range. Garreth wanted to go to Elaine, but the best protection was the fewest enemies, and so he was going to kill this one, and now. Then the Inlisc girl, and then anyone else in the house, or the city, or the world. His swing was tight and curving. If the Hansch man hadn't pulled back, it would have taken a slice from his side like carving a ham. Even as it was, Garreth felt the bite.

The eyes under the greasy hair took on a soberness. To Garreth's right, the Inlisc girl brought the club up, ready to crush Elaine's skull, but when the blow fell, Elaine was up and moving. The Hansch man's gaze flickered toward her, and Garreth thrust toward his face, pushing him back. If he could put the man to the wall where he couldn't jump back, it would be over.

"That's her. Don't let her get away!" the Hansch man shouted, but Elaine was almost at the door. The Inlisc girl tried to grab her and pull her back, but Elaine broke free. She was gone, and the Inlisc thug after her, shrieking as she went. Garreth swung hard and fast, five hard blows, his sword fluttering against the other man's guard. The fifth one got through. Blood soaked the man's side and bloomed on his shoulder. There was a glimmer of fear in his eyes now.

"You should go," the Hansch man said. "Before she splatters your girl's brains on the tile. You don't have time for me."

Garreth knew not to hesitate, but he did anyway. The other man thrust low, trying to cut his foot or his shin. Garreth danced back. He knew he'd been hit, but he didn't feel it yet.

"I'll do you a favor. Let you go," the man said. "She's dead if you stay."

Elaine's left arm was wrong. She reached the narrow stairs that led down, and the girl barreled into her. They fell down the wooden steps in a jumble, and pain bloomed through her shoulder and neck like lightning in a storm cloud. She landed on the stone floor of the hallway. When, by instinct, she tried to reach up and steady herself, bone ground against bone. She stumbled to her feet, sprinting for the back garden and the wall and the street and anyone who could help.

The Inlisc girl was close as a shadow and grunting with effort. They reached the kitchen garden with its bare earth and filthy snow. The low point in the stone was like seeing the surface of the river from below. Safety, breath, air almost within reach. Elaine dove for it, only flinching back at the last second by instinct. The Inlisc girl's club broke the stone where Elaine's back would have been. Elaine stumbled in retreat. Her arm was limp now, the burning in her shoulder and neck like a fire without the flame. A man's voice shrieked behind them, and an image of Garreth with a blade in his neck flashed before her like a vision from hell. The Inlisc girl took a grip on her club and waited. They looked at each other. The girl was young. Four, maybe five years younger than Elaine. Not an adult. Barely adolescent. She looked frightened.

Elaine's mind skipped and stuttered. The injury was worse than she'd thought. She'd seen hunting dogs accidentally trampled by horses, the way they tried to stand even with spines crushed. She felt like that now. If she turned her back, the girl would kill her, and the way forward was blocked. It was like a puzzle she couldn't quite solve. Thunder rumbled like a god clearing its throat.

The fear—was it fear?—in the Inlisc girl shifted, settled, became some resolve that Elaine couldn't fathom. The heavy leaden head of the club sank toward the ground. The girl stepped aside. The way to the street was clear.

When the girl spoke, her voice had the hard, percussive accent of Longhill. "Why are you waiting? Run!"

Elaine didn't need a second invitation. She ran.

The street seemed too normal to be real. Carts and mules. A man in a red shirt with unfashionably long hair pulled back in a braid. Elaine tried to hold her arm as if she were whole, and she walked. The coach was at the stables. The same one she'd gone to that morning in some other lifetime with Garreth's uncle and a cloud of disapproval. If she could just get there...

That's her.

She stumbled, caught herself. The man in the red shirt glanced at her with dim curiosity. She looked away.

The thug with the sword. He'd said *That's her. Don't let her get away.* They hadn't been sneaking into the house to steal. They'd come for her. They'd known she would be there. The coachman who'd brought her knew where she was, or close to it. Could he have told someone? Sold her to...someone? Or only been loyal to whatever mystery was on the other side of Prince Ausai's library?

The horror of the thought cleared her mind a little. She turned back, found a corner, and took it. Part of her wanted to go back to Garreth or call for the guard. Could someone in the guard be part of it? Had Garreth told any of them—some friend or confidant—where she would be, and when? The pain was turning to a numbness that was worse. She had to find someplace safe. No place was safe. She walked through the streets of her city, her father's city, her great-uncle's city, like a refugee in a foreign town.

A tap sounded on the stone beside her, sharp and sudden. A dark spot on the pavement. Then another. The rainstorm was here. It was going to soak her. Worse, it would make her conspicuous. A broken girl in an expensive gown and no cloak wandering through the streets like a ghost.

She had to do something. She didn't know what.

"She's dead if you stay."

Garreth shifted to the left, his blade trained on the enemy. Long smears of blood marked the floor. The dark-haired man quirked up a smile.

"If it's any comfort, the day's turned out poorly for me too. Go. I'll wait here until you're gone, sneak away, and get myself sewn up. We all live to fight another day. Even her. Fair?"

Garreth turned to the door, images of Elaine filling his head like smoke from a fire. He'd taken two steps when the Hansch man rushed at him. He turned in time to push the blade away, less a parry than a rough shove. The Hansch man's shoulder took him in the ribs, and they crashed into the wall together, both of their swords skittering away on the floorboards. A knife appeared in the other man's hand, driving toward Garreth's throat, but he caught the man's wrist, turning it. Breathing hurt. The other man's half-rueful smile had turned to the bared teeth of an animal fighting for its life. Garreth tried to remember what Beren had taught him, what Captain Senit had trained him in. The hours on the dirt outside the barracks had vanished from his mind.

His body remembered, though.

He twisted the man's wrist, pulling it straight and locking the elbow. When Garreth turned, the man had to go with him or break his arm. Either would have been fine, but the man turned with a cry of pain and despair and stumbled against the scholar's desk. Garreth kicked the side of his knee, the blow landing with a satisfying grinding sensation. The man tried to pull his knife arm free, wriggling like a fish. Garreth slipped in the blood. If he hadn't had his attention on the man, the knife, he might have kept his feet. All he could do was hold tight and bring the enemy down with him.

They landed hard, and the man let out a cough or a laugh or a sudden, powerful sigh. Garreth pushed away, reaching for his fallen sword, and the man didn't try to stop him. The knife was gone. Only the hilt was still there, protruding at an angle from the man's chest where he'd fallen on it. Garreth got a grip on his blade and tried to stand, but the pain that shot through his side with each breath was blinding. He bent forward, forcing the blade up to ready.

The man clenched his jaw and hauled himself to standing. His fists rose, ready to keep the fight going. Garreth shook his head.

"You lost. Let's get you . . . cunning man. For wounds."

The man swung, aiming a bloody fist for Garreth's left ear, and Garreth didn't have the power in his arm to stop him. The blow was like being hit with a cushion. The man raised his hands again, sank to his knees, and collapsed to the floor. The pool of blood spread around him, and he didn't try to lift his face out of it. Garreth tried to stand. He couldn't run. He couldn't reach Elaine, not in time. He dropped the sword, fumbled at his belt until he found the whistle. With what felt like the last of his strength, he pulled the shutters open, leaned out the window, and blew the alarm until he thought he'd pass out.

By the time Captain Senit arrived at the house, a hard, frigid rain had started falling. Frijjan Reed and three from his patrol had put up iron stanchions outside the house and roped it off. There was no sign of Elaine or the Inlisc girl. A crowd had formed in the street despite the foul weather. Something had happened at House Left, and they would all be wondering what it had to do with the winter caravan. People would never believe that two things might intersect by chance this way. Garreth knew from a life's experience that there would be a hundred different interpretations before nightfall, and all of them wrong.

"It would be useful for me to know what you were doing here," the captain said.

Garreth shook his head. "I can't."

The captain pursed his lips and nodded slowly. "I respect that you think you've got a choice. Let me rephrase that. Tell me what this is because you're city guard, I'm your captain, and I fucking asked, yeah?"

Garreth looked around the lesser hall like there was some

answer there. His ribs didn't hurt as much when he kept his breath shallow, and the cut on his leg had stopped bleeding. Captain Senit loomed quietly at his side like a landslide that hadn't quite started falling.

"I was meeting a girl," Garreth said.

"Who?"

"The prince's daughter."

The captain's scowl deepened. "Do you really think this is the best time to make fucking jokes?"

Before he could object, Hellat Cassen stepped in, a gust of cold, wet air with him. "Captain. The house owner's asking for you."

"We have everything we need from upstairs?"

Hellat nodded.

"Bring the poor fuck out, then," Captain Senit said. He turned back to Garreth. "Can you walk?"

"Out of here? Yes."

The old man cracked a smile that seemed nearly genuine and nodded toward the front door. Garreth steeled himself, stood, and made his way to the entrance. He told himself that Elaine was fine, that she'd escaped and gotten back to Palace Hill, but the knot in his gut meant he didn't believe it. The sooner this was done, the sooner he could get out and look for her. Images of the worst possibilities kept appearing in his imagination: Elaine in an alleyway with this same rain washing her blood into the cobblestones, or trapped under ice as the dark river pulled her corpse toward the sea, or locked in a slaver's cage. He didn't know if he had the strength to go searching for her, but he was going to do it anyway. There was no rest for him until he found her or collapsed.

His father stood in the rain. His lips were dark and blueish, his hair slicked back against his skull, but he stood as calmly as if he were still before the magistrate, as if it was beneath his dignity to acknowledge the wet and cold. Serria stood a step behind him with rage in her eyes. Vasch had a blanket someone had given him, and held it over himself and Yrith even though it was soaked. She was weeping, but it seemed more like exhaustion than grief.

"Ah, Garreth," Father said with a false mildness. "I am astonished. I thought the guard paid you well enough to hire rooms for the girls you picked up in the street."

Captain Senit coughed to cover a chuckle. Through his pain and fear and exhaustion, Garreth could still feel rage. "Is this really where you want to discuss the family's bed habits?"

Hellat and Beren emerged from the front door, dragging a handcart. The dead man was on it, his face caked in half-dried blood. They hauled the corpse in front of Father, and Hellat sluiced the blood away. Vasch flinched back, but Father leaned forward, paused, and shook his head.

"No. I don't know this one."

Captain Senit gestured, and the guards took the corpse away. "Make a mask of that one and put it in the storeroom, yeah?" he said, then squinted up into the falling rain. "Here's what happened, seems to me. Your son here got caught up in a bit of nostalgia. Knowing the house would most likely be empty, he stopped by to smell yesterday's daisies, as it were. He surprised that sad sack of meat who was there to rob the house. One thing led to another, and justice came out ahead."

"Is that what you think?" Father said.

"It is." The captain's smile could almost have been mistaken for genial. "And lucky for you. I'd say you owed your son here a debt of gratitude."

"Thank you, Garreth," his father said. "I am sure the whole family will remember all that we owe you."

"Oh for fuck's *sake*," Vasch snapped. "Are you all right? Did he hurt you?"

"I'm fine," Garreth said. "There's a mess in my old bedroom, though."

"I'd try salt and cold water," Captain Senit said. "Make it into a paste. Lifts the blood right up."

"May I enter my own home, then?" Father asked. Captain Senit waved toward the door, and Father and Serria marched inside. The guards were taking down the ropes and pulling the iron stanchions onto a wagon. The crowd was thinning, but only a little. They weren't certain the spectacle was done. Vasch put a hand on Yrith's hip, urging her toward the house, but she didn't go.

"Mother and Robbson?" Garreth asked.

"At the guild hall, finishing the papers," Vasch said. "We won. The caravan's cleared."

Despite everything, Garreth smiled. "Congratulations. To both of you. It's good to hear. But please, don't stay out in the rain. You'll freeze. We'll all freeze."

Vasch nodded, but instead of going in the house, he put his arms around Garreth in a great sopping hug. It hurt badly, but Garreth didn't push him back.

The last time Theddan had been caught misbehaving by the ancress of the women's shrine, the punishment had been that her head was shaved to the skin. The intention, she supposed, was to humiliate her. All her lovely locks taken away, as if her womanhood was made of hair. It had been fascinating. At first, her scalp had felt almost numb. She'd kept running her palms over the smooth, bare skin just for the sensual novelty of it. Then, as the fine, dark hair started growing back, there had been a hundred little surprises: drying her head by wiping the water away with two fingers, her blanket sticking to her when she pulled it over her, the coolness of the Temple's draughts against her newly bare skin. Even dressed in unflattering plainspun, she felt a little bit nude.

The ancress said Theddan had been born without shame, and the way she said it, it was supposed to be a bad thing. Privately, Theddan agreed, but in a different tone of voice.

And if the shaving of her skull was intended to make the priests less interested in her sexually, it hadn't managed that either.

She was in the common chapel digging wax out of the candle niches when Haral found her. He pretended to be examining the icons at the altar—presently Shau the Twice Born, though it had been the Three Mothers the day before—and Theddan pretended not to notice him. His shoulders were tight with distress. Once he was certain no one else was in the chapel, he moved to her side.

"You need to come with me. Right now."

"I have no choice? I don't like that. I think I'll stay here and finish my work instead." She'd always found it was very important to make sure her friends and playmates understood what they could have and what they had to ask for. Haral was usually better than this.

He took her wrist. "It isn't that. Your *friend*. She's in the storage shed. Something's happened."

"Fuck," Theddan said, then shot an apologetic look at the two-bodied god. She folded the scraping knife into the hem of her skirt, and turned toward the side door. The candles would have to solve their own problems.

The shed was gloomy and it stank of dirt, but it was dry. The rain pounding on its roof was deafening. Elaine huddled at the back, half hidden among brooms and boxes of soap and polishing wax. Her skin was pale, and she shook so violently Theddan thought at first it was for show.

"Elly," she said, swooping down to Elaine's side. "What's the matter? What happened?"

"I can't stay here. They're hunting me." Her words shuddered and slid. Theddan's alarm shifted in her throat.

"Who is hunting you? Elly? Who's hunting you?"

"My coachman, because of Ausai, I think. Or…or I don't know. There were two of them. The one with the sword had Garreth," her cousin said. Her voice broke on the words. She was cradling one arm, and her shoulder was at an unnatural angle. The bruise forming on her neck was deep and bloody. Theddan touched her gently at the collarbone, and Elaine flinched. "I can't stay. I have to go."

"If you go, you'll die," Theddan said. "You're hurt. I think you've broken a bone or worse. You'll walk out in the rain, go maybe a hundred more yards, and the cold will kill you. I'm going to keep you safe. We'll move you someplace even your coachman doesn't know about, and you'll be safe."

"I won't be."

Theddan took her cousin's cheeks in her palms and guided her eyes toward her own. When she was sure Elaine saw her, she said, "I will keep you safe."

She felt the little sob more than heard it. Elaine's mouth turned down and she started to cry like a heartbroken child at the end of its strength. Theddan started undoing her cousin's dress, stripping her naked before the sopping cloth could leach any more warmth from her. Elaine made a weak attempt to push her away.

Haral shifted his gaze elsewhere, embarrassed. "I'll get the healer."

"You will not," Theddan said, pulling off her own skirt and draping it over both of them like a blanket. She wove her legs in with her wounded cousin's, curling their bodies together. Elaine felt as cold as a corpse. "You will get me four thick wool blankets, the little iron brazier from Nual's cell, and the basket of herbs the ancress gives the girls for their cramps. The red one, not the green."

Haral nodded. Theddan pulled Elaine closer, trying to put as much of her own skin against the freezing girl as would touch. Elaine mewled, as quiet as a kitten. The weakness of it filled Theddan with black dread. "And once you've done that, find her boy. I have questions."

It was morning after a long, terrible night when Garreth reached the private chapel. It was a tiny room at the base of the Temple with a door that led out to the streets. It and the others like it had been commissioned by some family or brotherhood or guild in a show of piety, sometimes generations before. The yearly fees paid to the Temple were small and the embarrassment of defaulting on the gods themselves kept the spaces dedicated even when the impulse behind them had gone. This one had been tiled with thousands of shards of mother-of-pearl and built around an altar carved from granite into the double curve of the holy numberless. A butter lamp burned on the altar, but not as part of any ritual. It was the only light. The bedroll spread out on the floor was green wool.

Elaine lay curled on her side, her head resting on a pillow made from a folded blanket. Her face was taut with pain. The side of her neck was swollen and angry with bruises. And still, when she saw him, she smiled.

"You're alive," she said.

Garreth sat beside her. He wanted to cradle her head, to touch the wounds. She saw the impulse and the holding back. She put her hand out to him, and he laced his fingers with hers.

"You are too," he said.

"You sure? I don't feel well."

"Time and rest will fix the worst of that," he said with more confidence than he felt.

"Pity I don't have more of those," she said dryly. Then, "She let me go. She could have killed me, and she let me go."

"Why?"

Elaine started to shake her head, then stopped. "I don't know. There must have been a reason, though. I don't know who they were. What about yours?"

"He didn't let me go," Garreth said. "I didn't let him go either. He's dead, and my family's slightly more upset with me than they were before."

"I'm sorry."

The ridiculousness struck him. The prince's daughter, wounded, hiding, and at risk, apologizing that his father was miffed. The shaven-headed girl—Theddan—sat forward on the front pew, resting her elbows on her knees. "Were they really hunting her?"

"They were," Garreth said. "And they knew where we were going to be."

"The coachman," Elaine said. "I thought maybe my coachman. Unless you told someone?"

"I didn't, but some of the men I work with, I've known my whole life. They might have guessed it. I don't think they would have been part of this."

"Maybe they didn't mean to," Theddan said. "Everyone gossips. That, and an interested ear at the taproom, is all it would take."

"Or the barracks," Garreth said. "Not every bluecloak is honest at heart."

"I could have been followed from the palace," Elaine said.

Theddan made a small, impatient sound. "You know the obvious suspect is me, yes? I helped arrange it. I knew when and where and who. If anyone had everything it took to sell you to an enemy, it was me."

"You wouldn't, though," Elaine said.

"Well, I know that, but *you* don't, Elly. Not really. That there aren't any knife-wielding assassins here at the moment is a decent argument for my innocence, but if there's an ear at the Temple and I slipped, then coming here was reckless. You have to start being more careful."

Elaine laughed, then winced, but to Garreth the truth in the girl's argument was like a stone in his throat. The relief at seeing Elaine alive was fading like a dream already, and behind it: the nightmare.

"You can't go back to Palace Hill," he said.

Elaine made a sound of protest as she sat up and leaned her back against the dusty altar.

"He's right. Somewhere along the journey, you must have asked the right questions," Theddan said. "And most of the questions you asked, you asked of someone up there."

"I can go to Kint. Or have my father go to him."

"Which assumes he's not behind this."

"Kint could have had me killed at any time."

"Not without someone asking why you died under his protection," Garreth said. "If you'd died in Riverport, no one would look at him. Waiting for a chance outside the palace could be good strategy. And if he tried and failed, that may change his calculations. He might be less cautious next time."

"She can't stay here," Theddan said. "I mean, you can, Elly. But we can't keep her hidden for long, and priests can't keep secrets to save their lives. Even if none of them are specifically corrupted, enough of them are just generally corrupt that word will spread."

When Elaine spoke, her voice was grim. "We don't know who sent the killers. Anyplace we go, we might be walking into their hands. Nowhere's safe."

"Your father's the prince," Theddan said, and it meant *There has to be a way for his power to protect you.*

"My father's a man," Elaine said, and it meant *He can die too.* "I have to leave the city." She shifted, caught her breath in pain, and leaned back against the altar as if making the argument against her own plan. "What about your winter caravan? They aren't part of the city."

"A known, new ally of my family? That's where I'd look for you first if I were hunting you down," Garreth said. "Give me a day. You need to rest anyway. I'll find someplace."

He was sure she'd argue back, but her eyes were already half closed. "Just one," she agreed, then lowered herself back to the bedroll. "I'll be better by then."

Theddan tapped Garreth's shoulder and nodded to the back of the chapel. He almost refused, but Elaine's eyes were closed. He kissed her cheek, then let the other girl lead him out. The chapel door opened to a thin, winter-killed garden. Beyond the garden wall, the eastern wall of the city—the edge of Kithamar—loomed like a dark horizon. Beds of brown sticks that would leaf out in the spring were cased in ice now. Low clouds slid across a pale sky like the storm had exhausted them and left them hollow. The cold bit. Garreth coughed and the pain radiated through his ribs like he'd been stabbed.

"The fever?" he asked.

"Comes and goes," Theddan said. "The bone's not right. She can't travel."

"I know."

"Do you?" Theddan said. "She needs rest and a healer."

"I'll do what I can."

The woman crossed her arms and scowled up into the sky. "There's a conversation we need to have, you and me."

"About?"

"I don't know you, but I know men and women. What we are together and what we aren't. There's a version of this where you were just looking for something warm and pleasant and got more than you hoped for. I wouldn't blame you for regretting the choice."

"I don't think that—"

"No, I'll finish, thanks. My cousin is a difficult woman. She's angry and rough, and when she's in a mood, she can vanish up her own asshole like no one I've ever known. She doesn't have many friends, and the ones she does, she doesn't always know what to do with. But she's been kind to me when no one else was. You understand me? She was good to me. And no one else was."

"I understand," Garreth said.

"Things like the one between you two bloom and they disappear. I'm not saying you have to live your life and die by her side, but if I ever find out you've been needlessly cruel to her, I will spend the rest of my life destroying the rest of yours."

She took half a step back, her chin lifted in defiance. When he was very young, he'd seen a drawing in some book his mother had read to him or to Vasch of a mouse in a warrior's armor facing a swarm of evil rats. The memory of it made him smile.

"I didn't know who her family was when I met her," he said. "I like her. I like who I am when I'm alone with her."

Theddan's gaze shifted from defiance to something more present, more thoughtful. "What'd you be willing to give up for her?"

"What do you want?"

Theddan looked into his eyes, made a small, satisfied sound, and turned back toward the Temple. Garreth settled himself more deeply into his cloak and turned west. Walking made his sides hurt, but everything did. This at least gave him some sense of being able to anticipate the pain.

The wind wasn't high, but it was vicious. His earlobes ached, his nose ran. An old man with a ragged cart and an old mule clattered down the street before him and turned south. Garreth was more than half tempted to follow him and let the curving, tight streets of Longhill break the air. A crow jeered at him from the rooftop.

Somewhere far ahead, across the still-frozen Khahon and up the face of Oldgate, people were starting to realize that the prince's daughter had gone missing. Some of them would be the people who cared for her or for the role she played in the life of the city, some might be the people who had sent the assassins, and Garreth didn't have any idea how to tell one from the other. Elaine couldn't remain where she was. She couldn't go back where she'd come from. She couldn't flee the city. In his memory, the dead man said *She's dead if you stay.* But she was dead no matter what, and every path he reached for, every hope he tried to construct, blew away in the knife-sharp wind of Kithamar. He didn't know—couldn't know—who or where their enemies were. No ally could be trusted...

His steps slowed without his noticing. He found himself standing in the middle of the street, hands at his side, staring at the filthy, ice-laced cobblestones as if he were reading an answer written on the skin of the city. He looked back toward the Temple, south toward Longhill. *What'd you be willing to give up for her?* He pulled his hands deeper into their sleeves, trying to find warmth as he turned for what had once been home.

When he reached it, the sun had already passed its midpoint. The ice in the streets was thin, cracking, and rotten. He walked to the door that had been his once and knocked on it twice. His breath was quick, but not from exertion. The door opened on Serria, and he watched the pleasantness fall from her when she recognized him like she'd been wearing a mask.

"You're not coming in this house," Serria said. She stood in the doorway with her arms crossed and glowered at him like the storm that had just gone by. "It's not a day since you humiliated this family. Not a day. And you expect welcome? You're mad."

"I'm not here to see you," Garreth said.

"Your father is at the warehouse. Find him there if he'll see you."

"I'm here for my sister."

Confusion flickered in Serria's eyes, but only for a moment. The wariness that took its place was well enough deserved. Garreth waited a moment before he went on.

"If you want me to stay here on the street while you tell her I'm here, that's fine with me, but it will mean more people wondering why I've come."

Doubt warred with spite, and spite lost. She stepped back and gestured him curtly in. "You can wait in the lesser hall. If she doesn't want to speak with you—"

"I'll go. I'm not here to make trouble."

Serria walked with him as if he were a new guest who needed to be shown the way and closed the door behind her when she left. Garreth stood quietly to the count of twenty, then went out to the corridor and back toward the main stairs and the family's floor. The footsteps coming down toward him as he rose up were his mother's.

She looked thinner than she had in the summer. There was

a touch more grey in her hair, but it seemed thicker and less constrained than it had, as if her time in the north had remade her into a slightly wilder version of herself. She slowed when she saw him, then stopped. It had been almost a year since she'd first left. He was a different man than he'd been then. For all he knew, she might be a different woman.

"You and I need to speak," she said.

"This may not be the time. I have urgent business with Yrith," he said. "I'm fairly sure Serria's sent for Father, so I only have until he comes back and throws me out."

Mother considered this, but only for a moment.

"She's in my drawing room with Vasch," she said, and then continued down the stair. Garreth took the rest of the flight two at a time.

Yrith and Vasch were at the low table, sitting on two sides of a corner. The contract they were reading through was slanted between them. Garreth pulled out a chair and sat across from Yrith. He didn't remember her being as calm or as amused as she seemed now. Her hair was braided back in a style that spoke more of Kithamar than the north, and she wore a dress that was cut in a swooping style that made reference to Inlisc clothing without being mistaken for it. It was a little shock to realize she was beautiful.

"Garreth?" Vasch said. "What's the matter?"

"I need to ask for a huge favor with some real risk to it that I don't deserve."

"Anything," Vasch said.

"That's kind, but I don't need it from you."

Yrith raised her eyebrows and pushed the contract aside. The paper hissed against the wood. When she spoke, her accent was thick, but less thick than it had been. "And what is it you would want of me and not my husband?"

"I need you to intercede for me. Plead my case."

"To whom?"

"My enemy."

Yrith walked through Longhill with a confidence Garreth couldn't match. He didn't know if it was that her face and hair folded so gracefully with the Inlisc of Kithamar, or if the wooden buildings and narrow streets were more like her home than the stucco and stone of Riverport, or—most likely to him—she simply didn't understand the danger they were in by being there. Whatever the case, he followed behind her in a brown cloak with the hood pulled up to hide his face and scanned the doorways and alley mouths and windows, ready if trouble came.

Yrith met the curious eyes with a smile and a greeting in a language Garreth didn't speak. Sometimes she would pause with some stranger and ask something in a string of syllables that he couldn't make into individual words. Most of the time, the other person would just shake their head or apologize in phrases that Garreth could follow, but twice older men answered haltingly in that same tongue of clicks and skitters. It was eerie, seeing her be so clearly a native in his own city where he himself felt so outside of it.

The clouds had thickened in the afternoon, and the air smelled of rain and shit and rot. Tiny white flecks fell from the sky, neither snow nor hail, but something of both. Yrith ignored the cold magnificently until bits of white adorned her hair like tiny pearls. It was almost dark when she paused outside a doorway with a bright yellow banner. The cloth was marked with Inlisc characters, and Yrith knocked at the door, then stood back and waited. An ancient man with stick-thin arms and wisps of hair still clinging to his scalp opened the door and squinted out.

Yrith spoke in her language, and the man's eyes widened. He

answered her in the same tongue, and fluently. Yrith smiled, and pointed to herself and then to Garreth as she answered back. The old man shook his head not in negation but amazement. For a minute or more, the two traded words back and forth, their inflections of warmth and pleasure more telling even without knowing what exactly they said. Yrith asked a question, and the old man's face fell into sudden distrust. His answer was short and sharp. Yrith pointed back at Garreth, and the old man squinted at him uncertainly. For a moment, they were all silent, then the man pointed down the street, said something more, and curved his hand. Yrith bowed to him, then rushed up to kiss his cheek before turning south and walking away. Garreth had to trot to catch up with her.

"Did that work?" he asked.

"We will go and find out."

They made their way along the sinuous, narrow street. Garreth felt the weight of attention from the windows they passed. A bluecloak alone in Longhill was an invitation to trouble, but he wasn't a bluecloak. Not right now.

Yrith turned down an alleyway that seemed made more from shadows than wood. Her steps became less certain, and she looked back past him as if watching to see if they were being followed. Garreth ached between his shoulder blades and at his jaw. She stopped at a door with a splintered wooden handle and hinges on the inside.

"Are you certain?" she said. "We can leave now with nothing, but this is the last time that will be true."

"I don't have an option," he said.

Yrith knocked smartly at the door and spoke in her language for what felt like an hour or a few seconds. Garreth's heart was tapping against his ribs and he had to fight to keep from reaching for his blade. When she was finished, she took a coin from her wallet, leaned down in the muck and filth, and slipped it under the door.

Nothing happened.

Yrith stood, wiping her hands on her cloak, and peered one way down the alley, and then the other.

"What happens now?" Garreth said.

"There will be an answer. It may come now, or later. We can wait here or go back to—"

The door opened. The man who stepped out was Inlisc, broad across the shoulders, and hard at the eyes. He looked at Yrith, then at Garreth, then back to the woman. "Stay here," he said, and retreated, closing the door behind him.

"You can go," Garreth said. "I can do this part alone."

"I explained before, brother. The walking-away time isn't now and won't come again. What's begun is begun."

Garreth took a deep breath, crossed his arms, and regretted that he'd ever had the idea to come here. Above them, the strip of pale sky grew darker. The sound of the wind humming and whistling through the city was louder and more violent than the thin breeze he felt in the alleyway. Cold seeped into his feet and his fingers until he had to start pacing to get full feeling back. Yrith seemed calm, but maybe that was only fatalism. Once the die was cast, there was no point shouting.

The door opened again, and the man stepped out. The Inlisc woman who followed him had a scar down one side of her face and one milky eye. She wore pale canvas trousers and a shirt with a workman's vest over it. Her hair was black and cut close to her scalp. This time, there was no blood on her hands.

Yrith dropped to her knees and bowed her head. A beat later, Garreth followed her lead.

"Stand up, child," Aunt Thorn said to Yrith. "You have my attention."

Yrith stood as she'd been told. Garreth tried to think how he'd move if the big man tried to force her through the door. Or if Aunt Thorn tried to hurt her.

"Thank you, Aunt, for hearing me."

Aunt Thorn waved a hand like she was shooing away a gnat. "I'm surprised to find a daughter of the north in Kithamar. You came with the caravan?"

"The caravan came to me, and to my husband. And my new family in Riverport."

"Plots within plots within plots," Aunt Thorn said, and smiled. "And now you have a favor to ask from me. No, wait. Uyllif says you have an injured woman who you want me to care for, protect from her enemies, and release unharmed and without fetter when you come back for her or when she wants to go. Is that right?"

"It is."

"But it's not really *your* request, is it. It's his. You're spending your birthright on a Hansch boy?"

Yrith looked at Garreth where he still knelt. "He is my husband's brother, and so my brother as well."

"So you feel obligated to do as he tells you? That's thin soup, child."

"I am repaying my debt to him," Yrith said.

"Your debt?" Aunt Thorn said. "And what do you owe this one?"

"He saved me from a bad marriage."

Aunt Thorn made a low, amused sound and turned to Garreth. Her one clear eye met his and narrowed. "I know you. Why do I know you?"

"We met," Garreth said. "You told me how much you respected rules."

Her eyes widened and a cruel smile plucked at her lips. The tightness in Garreth's back turned to an ache.

"The bluecloak boy. You killed one of my crew."

"Respectfully, he was trying to gut a friend of mine when I did."

"And yet you ask me to take this woman in. Why?"

"Desperation," Garreth said. "You and the one who stole from you showed me the way. He came to us because he knew we weren't you. There are forces at work against the woman we're discussing. I don't know who they are, but I know they aren't you. That makes you the only safe place for her now."

"Well, she's fucked, then, isn't she? What's her name."

Garreth shook his head. "Do you agree to the terms?"

"I could just kill you both where you stand."

"Could," he agreed. "But you still wouldn't know her name."

For an eternity, Aunt Thorn looked at him with her attention elsewhere. It was like she was listening to music that only she could hear. She took the coin that Yrith had passed under the door and pressed it back into the girl's palm. "This isn't enough. Money won't buy this one, not even for a child of the north."

Garreth's mouth went dry. "What, then?" he asked.

"Owe me a favor," Aunt Thorn said, locking her one good eye on him. "Just one, but no question or hesitation from you when I demand it. Anything I ask of you, when I ask it. That's the price."

"Done," Garreth said.

Aunt Thorn's smile was almost pitying. "Oh, it's like that, is it? Well, we're all idiots sometimes." She turned her attention back to Yrith. "We're agreed, daughter. I'll take her in, look after her, keep her safe from anyone, and let her go free without even my smallest hooks in her when you reclaim her or when she asks to go. Now, tell me where my men can find her."

In her dream, Elaine was pulling worms out of her neck. She could see them just under the skin from an angle that her actual, waking eyes couldn't have done without a mirror. When she went to pinch at them, her skin gave way under her fingertips like she was made of soil. The worms were thicker than earthworms and yellower. The segments of their bodies were hard, like they'd just started growing shells and weren't very good at it yet. When she caught one, she drew it out slowly, feeling it lose its grip in the depths of her flesh. It was the same bright pain and shuddering pleasure as pulling off a scab. Then she'd lay the dying worm in a row with the others she'd harvested from her wounds and go back to pluck another one out. She knew it should have been horrifying, but with the logic of dreams, she felt only a kind of growing physical satisfaction.

She caught one and knew without knowing how that it was the last. As she drew it out, her eyes opened.

Her head felt clear for the first time since the attack at House Left. Her neck and shoulder ached, but they didn't throb. An older Inlisc woman with a green lacquer box was sitting beside her cot. The light came from a pair of candles in a glass box on the table. It took Elaine a moment to remember where she was and how she'd gotten there.

"Still warm, then?" the older woman asked. Elaine had heard her name before. Erja.

"I am," Elaine said, reaching for her shoulder and neck. There was a thick bandage there and a warm feeling on the skin beneath it.

"Well, the fever's not broken, but we have the rot stopped. Don't worry at that poultice. I'll come and change it out tonight when my work's done. Until then, drink water until your piss is all the way to clear and sleep as much as you can."

Elaine nodded, and the grinding feeling under her skin felt less than before. Not gone, but less.

As Erja packed up the contents of her box, pulled a cask of water up next to the bed, and prepared to leave, Elaine lay back. "I was dreaming about worms in my skin. I was pulling them out one at a time. I don't know what that meant."

"It's just a dream," Erja said. "Dreams don't mean shit."

Her room was small. The walls were a baked clay brick with iron hooks thicker than her wrist set in them at off intervals. The floor was fresh rushes on stone, the cot rough canvas on a frame of wood and iron. When Erja left, it was through a brick archway without a door or even tapestry to pretend at privacy, just an iron chain strung across it at waist height. Elaine's world was this room, a wide, squat hallway beyond it, and a private bath where cold water ran from a pipe in the wall and into a drain in the floor, the arrangement serving as night pot and shower both. Sometimes voices echoed from deeper in the halls.

She knew she should be afraid, but at first she hadn't had the energy to feel anything deeply, and as day slid into sunless day until she couldn't say if she'd been there for a week or a month, she'd become almost used to her situation. They hadn't killed her, and they could have. She had to assume they didn't want to.

Her memory of coming to the hidden rooms was fragmentary. She remembered being in the private chapel, the pain in her shoulder and neck slowly spiraling up again, and a fever blurring the line between daydream and nightmare. She had a strong impression of Theddan speaking, and a man's voice answering back something about Garreth. After that, there was a discontinuity. She remembered being carried in an open litter, with drops of freezing rain tapping her face. She'd felt too cold and too hot at the same time. She remembered someone shouting and a dark alleyway with a hidden stairway leading down into the earth. Her mother had been there wearing an old-fashioned white death shroud like an ancient drawing. Elaine figured her recollection wasn't entirely to be trusted.

She'd come to herself on this cot, in this room, with Erja ministering to her broken shoulder. Erja and Aunt Thorn.

She tried tentatively to sit up. She had more strength than before, she was sure of it. When she lifted her arm, it wouldn't go up as far as her shoulder, but it was better than it had been. There was no mirror for her to know how the bruise on her neck had changed, and so there was no way to have a sense of how long she had been underground. She was sure it had been days at least, but how many was beyond her. The room was silent and she made herself rise and pace out its length ten times, then twenty. At thirty, she began to shudder and sat back on her cot. The canvas creaked under her like it was inviting her down. She had to get her strength back, had to make her way to her father and tell him what had happened. Had to warn him. Even exhausted as she was, her mind was less fogged. It gave her hope.

She lay down, curling her one good arm under her head as a pillow. Her eyes felt very comfortable closed, and she felt no impulse to move. Shifting her weight would have taken a great deal of effort, and stillness was comforting. She was going to have to explain to her father everything that had happened. That meant the night at the boathouse, sneaking into Ausai's study, Garreth's appearance at Tenth Night, and their meeting at House Left. She felt like she was already telling him, sitting in the garden of their old compound—the one they'd given away—while he ran a length of chain clinking through his fingers.

A man said something, not in the dream. Elaine was vaguely aware of two people standing silently at the archway. She felt their attention without fully registering who they were. They turned back, leaving the iron chain swinging in the air. Elaine closed her eyes, willing herself back to sleep. But sleep didn't come. Instead, her mind sharpened, and the dream receded. She brought herself back to consciousness. When she sat up, her shoulder hurt worse. The poultice was losing its power. Still, she could stand. She could walk. She could hear two voices, and she knew them both.

Moving as quietly as she could, she let down the iron chain that was her door and followed the sound down the hallway and into a corridor she hadn't passed down before. A woman speaking to a man, the man replying.

"...told you she would come to me," the woman said. Aunt Thorn. The Inlisc criminal lord who Garreth had bargained with for Elaine's safety, such as it was. Elaine moved down the dark hall toward her voice.

When the man spoke, she knew him, but couldn't say how. Not until she reached the end of the hall and caught sight of him. "And you're right. That is definitely her. I hate leaving things like this to fate. It makes my teeth itch," Elaine's tutor said.

They were in a small chamber piled with crates marked with script from Imaja and tuns of beer. Aunt Thorn leaned her stool against the wall, its front two feet a few inches off the ground. She was peeling an orange, and the air smelled of citrus and mildew. Elaine's tutor—wiry white hair, permanently amused eyes, and dressed in rags like a wild man—paced thoughtfully through the widest part of the room, moving in and out of the light of a single candle. Elaine pressed herself against the wall, trusting the shadows to keep her hidden.

"It's how we found out about the Bronze Coast boy," Aunt Thorn said. "His mother came to you. And Shau's girl, the one of them."

"Doesn't mean I like it," her tutor said. "I thought the book would bring her in."

"You thought a young woman in the middle of a thousand changes to her life would focus on her scholarship," Aunt Thorn said. "Did she even read it?"

The man chuckled. "Well, when you say it like that, it does seem naïve. But she's here now. That's good."

"It is, but thaw's almost on us, and that's bad. There isn't time. We should kill Karsen."

"We don't need to. It doesn't know what he is, and even if it found out, what would it matter? Any proof it brings forward spills all its secrets too."

Aunt Thorn dropped a curl of peel to the floor. "It was supposed to be dead. The thread of Kithamar was supposed to be cut, and I was supposed to have the knife in my keeping. The plan's failed."

The thread of Kithamar. Elaine caught her breath when the woman said the words, but neither of them seemed to have heard her. The impulse to inch forward, to see and hear them better, warred with the voice in her head telling her to run.

"It hasn't failed yet," the man said. "We still have beads on the board. But it hasn't gone as well as I'd hoped."

"If we lose this, we won't have another chance for centuries. If ever."

Her tutor stopped. In the candlelight, he looked ancient. More than that, he looked fearful. "I know," he said.

They paused and faced each other: the man with his cloud of pale hair, the woman with her dark, close-cropped halo of black. In that instant, Elaine understood who and what she was looking at.

The fear was like being washed away by the river. She took a step back, rolling her weight carefully from her toe to her heel, suddenly petrified that they would hear her. Aunt Thorn said something, but the only sound Elaine could hear was the rushing of blood in her ears. She wanted to run, but she knew that she shouldn't. Fleeing from wolves begged the chase. Her breath was ragged, her hands trembling. The weight of stone and brick became a grave. The air was too thick to breathe.

She regained her little room, sat on the cot with her hands clasped in front of her like a child in prayer. She forced herself to breathe. With her good hand, she pulled the bandage off her neck and shoulder, wiping the thick, stinking poultice off with it, and threw it to the floor. Her injured skin felt new and raw. She knew that the shuddering in her body was fear, because no other feeling made sense. It had to be fear, no matter how much it felt like anger.

It was some time before the woman came. Aunt Thorn, so called. She had a tin plate of fish and beans in one hand, a glass bottle half filled with water in the other. Her one milky eye stared at nothing while her real one found Elaine.

"Well," Aunt Thorn said. "Look who's feeling herself again."

"I want to leave," Elaine said, biting each syllable as she said it.

Aunt Thorn shrugged and put the food and water on the cot by Elaine's right thigh. "I have sworn to release you when you want to go. If that's now, that's now. But I wouldn't recommend it. Your wounds were bad, and there's still some healing you can do. And you don't know who sent the thugs that tried to kill you."

"You know, though. Don't you?"

The Inlisc woman smiled. Her scars twisted the expression into something unreadable. "I have a guess. My guess is you'd still be wiser staying put."

"But you would let me go? If I got up now and walked back to the streets, you and yours wouldn't stop me."

"It's what I said I'd do."

They looked at each other until the silence seemed to fill the room like smoke. Aunt Thorn folded her arms across her chest, her lips pulling into the ghost of a scowl.

"You aren't a woman," Elaine said.

Aunt Thorn laughed. "If you're asking to see something personal, we're going to have to know each other much better first."

"You're a god. You're Lady Er. The other one, he's Lord Kauth. You aren't people, you're something else. Aren't you?"

Aunt Thorn's scowl softened. She didn't speak, and so she didn't deny it.

Elaine nodded as much to herself as to the thing that looked like a woman. "What's the thread of Kithamar," she asked, "and what does it have to do with my family?"

PART FOUR

SPRING STORMS

Kithamar is not what you think it is, because the world is not what you think it is, and we are not what you think we are. If you ever loved me, trust me now. Flee the city before hope and time are lost. We are not strong enough to stand against gods.

—From an undelivered letter from
Theyden Adresqat to Daos a Sal
prior to his coronation

Many, many generations ago, there was a man, and his name wasn't Kauth. And there was a woman whose name wasn't Er. The time they lived in, there wasn't writing yet. There weren't farms or cities or forged steel, but there were people, and people don't change much over the generations. So this man and woman fell into company. They loved each other. They were loyal to each other. They were better for knowing each other. The spirit of their shared attention was deep, and the people around them noticed it.

That was you? You and the other one?

Be patient. I'm telling you this for a reason. They honored each other, these two. And they honored the union between them as a thing in itself, and so that union became a little stronger. A little more itself. Its own thing that was more than the two taken separate. When they got old and frail, younger people came to them and asked how they might be able to find someone for themselves and forge a new connection like the one these old people had, and the old bastards did what they could. The secrets they could tell people, they told freely. The ones that couldn't be told, they wrapped in fables like they were putting a green leaf around a rice cake to keep it fresh until someone who could benefit from it came along. When they died, the same people who used to come to them for advice still came. They left little offerings to the memory of two people who had done something difficult well, and hoped that it would help them do the same. And sometimes it even did.

A few generations later, the story of the two of them was confused with a bullshit history about two tribes who'd tried to make peace by intermarrying, and they got the names Lord Kauth and Lady Er, only those weren't the names. He was Casson Kaualdana and she was Cassonai ab Uermatoth. A few centuries wore the edges off that.

The fables changed and grew and people made them their own, seasoned by the other versions of the history. Every now and again, people asked for help from the two of them, and answers came in their dreams. Things that might have only been coincidence started to seem like messages, like Lord Kauth and Lady Er were taking a hand in the world. Changing it. Little shrines appeared, and people started catching glimpses of the two of them, you understand? Seeing them like they were there, and so they were there. A little at first, and then more, and over time, there came to be a hand inside the glove.

That little spark that had begun as something between just two people—something specific to them that no one else would ever really understand—had layer after layer after layer of legend and belief and miracle painted on it. That little spirit grew like a pearl. Another set of stories about a warrior queen and her poet love started being told with their names and echoes of their traditions. Our traditions. We grew harder and stronger and more capable of shaping people and coincidences and the base clay of the world until Lord Kauth and Lady Er walked the world and ate honey bread and planned crimes to bring comfort to the oppressed and pain to the oppressors. We took on aspects of vengeance and sacrifice and magic. Peace but also war. What we are began with the love between two people.

And what we did with love, the thread of Kithamar did with hunger.

Aunt Thorn or Lady Er or whatever she truly was sat with her back against the wall, one leg stretched out before her, the other bent with one arm resting on it. Her gaze was set on something Elaine couldn't see, memory or vision or private regret.

Elaine couldn't have said what about her seemed inhuman. She had seen Aunt Thorn more than once, though it had been through a fever. She told herself she would have noticed or known even if she hadn't remembered the altar mural from the first time she'd gone to Theddan, even if Aunt Thorn and her wire-haired tutor hadn't been talking about a book of heresy, even if things had not been what they were.

"The Adresqat girl didn't understand everything, but she caught enough to see what was happening. It didn't save her.

"We all begin. That's our secret. There is an event, a moment, a coming together of something that managed to keep from turning back into air. Pick any quarter. The Smoke, maybe. Or Newmarket. Look at all those people moving through their lives. Someone loses their temper at a stranger. Someone falls in love. Someone grieves for the dying. Small moments, but the ones that echo a little. They have depth. Your mother died birthing you, but there was a moment when you were both breathing air. Maybe it was short as a relay runner passing the stick. That wasn't just another bit of time, same as any other, not for her and not for you. It was important."

"I don't want to talk about my mother."

"You do if you want to understand me. When you and she were together, there was a spirit there too. A little one, maybe. Powerless and blind as a new kitten, unaware of itself or of you or her, but it was there. It still is. It shapes how you live and how you remember her. What remnants of her still bend history."

She turned her one good eye to Elaine and leaned a little forward. "That happens with everyone. It happens all the time. There are gods in the streets, and most—the vast most—will disappear like snow in sunlight. But a few don't. If all the stars in the sky were gods, one of them would shape the world in a way that made it a little stronger, a little better able to feed itself, to grow, to matter to more people. That's what happened with this one. The thread. A city was born, and a little god, hardly more than an ambition, came into being. It was hungry. It still is."

"What does it want from me and my father?"

"The same thing it's taken from every prince this city has had. Skin to live in and the path to eat your children after it's done with you," Aunt Thorn said. "Gods find their fingerhold in the world anyplace. A song. A shared look. A speech repeated after the man who wrote it was killed for saying what he said. Pick your poison. Anything can become a god if you let it fester long enough. Kithamar began with the city."

Elaine willed her heart to slow, her breath to grow deeper, calmer. The fear was worse because there was no way to flee, no one to fight. She squeezed her fists until her knuckles were bloodless and pale. "I'll find a way to stop it."

"We've been trying that for generations. We're as close now as we have ever been, but the fucker's good at what it does, and what it does is survive. I thought we had it dead, but it came back. I can feel it like a hand on the back of my neck."

Elaine tilted her head, remembering something she'd heard said. *The Temple brings all traditions together and weaves them into one thing, and that thing is Kithamar.*

"It's eating you too, then. The way that the other stories and traditions and versions of Lord Kauth and Lady Er folded into you as you've become, it's turning all of you into aspects of it."

"You're very clever."

"The high priest of the Temple told me. I just didn't know what he meant until now."

"Yes, we are all becoming its creatures. We fight back where we can. Inhabit the parts of the city that are least like it. Longhill still has a tradition of remaining itself despite Kithamar's rule. The Silt is wild land. We're like cornered rats, and every generation there's a little less of us and a little more of it. Unless we can break its power. And so far, we're not doing very well with that. I think it's winning."

Elaine didn't mean to rise to her feet. Didn't know she had until she'd already done it. "Are you telling me it's my father? When I talked to him, was that . . . ?"

Aunt Thorn chuckled. "That much, we managed to keep from it. But it was supposed to be dead and fading, and it isn't. Somewhere in the city, it's wearing a human face, and I don't know which one. Even if I did, it's died before. Your father's not safe, and neither are you, though it's a little more complicated than it seems."

"Take me to the street. I have to go."

"To warn your daddy about it? He knows. He's been keeping it from you. Oh, don't look at me like that. My guess is he thought that if you didn't know, you couldn't accidentally alarm it. Make yourself look like a threat. He's been standing between you and its teeth."

Aunt Thorn frowned and looked over to Elaine, sizing her up like a woman trying to pick the best apple from a market stand.

"What?"

"His plan didn't work, though," the god said thoughtfully. "Kithamar's not trying to keep you where it can use you. It wants you off the board."

"That's not as comforting as you think."

"It's figured some things out I was hoping it might not," Aunt Thorn said, rising to her feet. "If it knows to kill you, it's farther ahead of us than I'd thought. That's not good. And with thaw here…I should have put that together earlier."

"Why do you want to kill Halev Karsen? Is he working with the thread?"

The god turned her full attention on Elaine, and for a moment it was like staring into the midday sun. Elaine flinched back, her eyes dazzled by something that wasn't light and her legs weak beneath her. She sank back down to the cot.

Anger radiated from Aunt Thorn in waves, but when she spoke, her voice was tight and controlled. "That kind of question is why he tried to keep you out of this. Eavesdropping on your host is bad form, and my hospitality is what's keeping you out of the river."

"I'm sorry," Elaine said. It was instinct and fear. She made herself look up, meet Aunt Thorn's malefic gaze. "But is he?"

Aunt Thorn shook her head, but Elaine couldn't tell whether she meant *No, he isn't* or *No, I won't answer that.*

"You should rest, little kitten. You're not as strong as you think."

With the words, Elaine's eyes closed. She felt herself folding down to the cot like it was happening someplace very far away, and even when the canvas held up her body, she kept falling. A deep and dreamless sleep descended on her.

When a hand stroked her cheek, she had the sense that a great deal of time had passed. Her mind slowly came back together. Her eyes found the woman sitting on the stool beside her cot with the green lacquer box open on her lap.

"Erja?"

"Look at you. Drowning in sweat, aren't you? You slept like a beast," the older woman said. "And you took my poultice off."

"Did I? I'm sorry. I was dreaming something. It was about Aunt Thorn and... my old tutor?"

"You and your dreams. Sit up, if you can. Let's have a look at you."

Elaine shifted. She was weak to the point of shaking, but there was a clarity as well. Like a swimmer, exhausted but safely on the shore. She turned her head one way and then the other, stretching the muscles and tendons carefully, ready for her flesh to object. It didn't hurt as much, and it creaked like leather. The older woman's eyes widened in surprise, and she leaned close, probing Elaine's wounded shoulder with her fingertips. The pressure ached a little, but the pain didn't sing.

"Well, you're a fast healer, aren't you? Let me check your pulses."

Elaine held out her wrists, and the woman took them, laying her fingers across the pulse points on both of them and closing her eyes as she felt the rhythms and strength of Elaine's blood. A mark caught Elaine's attention. A dark circle on her left forearm that hadn't been there before, and then a pale echo of it on the right.

Erja let her wrists go with a sound of satisfaction, turning back to her lacquer box. Elaine rubbed at the marks, but they were deep in her skin. They reminded her of something she couldn't quite place. Figures on an altar? The memory was just out of reach, receding like a mirage even as she felt herself on the edge of recall.

She held her arms up for Erja to see. "Are these . . . What are these?"

Erja glanced over and shrugged. "You've been blessed."

"I have?"

"Yeah. Touched by the gods, you," Erja said, and the tone in her voice might have been pity.

The city changed at first thaw. It was the same every year, and every year, it still managed to be a surprise. A morning came that didn't feel like the ones before. Cold, still—even biting—but with a sense of promise like the world itself had taken in a breath. The sun pressed a little more firmly against the city, and by afternoon, there was a sound that Kithamar hadn't heard in months. Instead of the mute silence of snow or the killing roar of freezing rain, the city began to murmur to itself in the language of meltwater. Snow that landlords had failed to clear from roofs shed little tapping drops to the cobblestones below. Small stone channels that had been covered by ice and snow burbled like little streams as they ran down toward the Khahon. In the streets and alleyways, trash and shit that had been hidden under weeks of snow were uncovered like the evidence of old sin, and the guard walked the streets charging fines for anyone with a private yard who didn't clean it fast enough.

Finches—red and orange and yellow and blue—that had been gone since the crows had descended to claim the leavings of harvest appeared again like a street magician's trick. The few trees that pushed their stubborn way toward the light started reaching out a little farther with meek, untried leaves and the tentative bumps of green that would become buds and then flowers and then plums or apples or cherries unless a late freeze came and killed them all.

And behind it all, like the voice of a giant restless in its sleep, the river groaned. Every year, a few people—children or young, foolish men—trusted the rotting ice more than it deserved. Every year, the murmuring of the river was ignored one time too many by someone who thought that they could get across to the other bank without paying the bridge tolls just one more time. Everyone knew that water was hungry. When the ice broke under them and they were lost, it was a shock and a surprise to the families every time.

For Garreth, the moment in the city's yearly cycle was filled with memories of checking the warehouses for loss, inspecting the ships that had wintered over in the boathouses of Kithamar being repaired or at least kept from the crushing power of the ice. The spring salads of dried fruit and fresh herbs that Serria grew in window beds so that she could harvest them sooner. His parents holding dinners for the allies of the house and attending guild meetings with their rivals. Vasch's nameday would be coming soon, and his own not long after that. The memories were bright and alive and a little bit wistful because they were only memories now.

It should have felt pleasant.

It felt like a smile with a knife behind it.

"You have to watch yourself in Seepwater," Old Boar said, but not to him. "Seepwater has the stage and the university and the brewers and the canals, but don't let that fool you. At heart, it's just Longhill's prettier sister. You can't trust it."

Carrig nodded once and swept his gaze across the street like an army of knifemen might be hiding in the doorways. He rested a hand on the pommel of his sword in a way that was probably supposed to look casual. Old Boar faked a yawn and leaned behind the new guard's back so that Carrig wouldn't see the wink he gave to Garreth. Garreth forced a smile.

Carrig was new to the guard. From what Garreth had heard, he was the son of Captain Pavvis's cousin, and looking for a life outside his family's home in the Smoke. He had the wide shoulders and callused hands of someone who'd grown up doing forge work, but he also seemed younger than his years. Garreth didn't know if that was more about Carrig or who and what he himself had become.

They'd taken the morning patrol, the three of them leaving the barracks before dawn. There wasn't a particular set path or schedule. If there had been, the thieves and pickpockets would have known it and planned their days around it. So instead they picked a general route, a general time, and let the city itself tell them where they should be.

There were two south gates on the east side of the river, and that morning they had made their way along the border between Longhill and Seepwater toward the southeastern gate, walking in the middle of the road and letting the thin traffic make its way around them. The sun had caught the top of Palace Hill behind them and then tipped up over the horizon and spilled its light through the streets. When they reached the gate, they stopped for a time, talking with the crew who were collecting taxes and letting the guard look over the new recruit, then when Old Boar decided it was time, turned into Seepwater proper. They'd walked past the cheap buildings and half-covered yards of the university where it was still too early for lecturers or students. When they reached the hospital gate,

Garreth assumed they'd turn back north, crossing the wooden footbridges over the canals, and be back at the barracks by midday. Every step they took brought Garreth closer to the end of his day's duty and the beginning of the work he needed to do.

"Hold up," Old Boar said as they entered a little square where three streets came together by a cistern. He pointed down to the west with his chin. A half dozen doors down, two carters had stopped their teams and were talking with an intensity that looked like the prelude to a fight. "Carrig. Go pour a little water on that fire, why don't you?"

"Just me?" the new boy said.

Old Boar winked. "You can handle it. And anyway, me and Garreth want to talk about you behind your back."

Carrig's smile meant he didn't know if it was a joke. Without any real option, he stepped out toward the carters like a child playing at being a guard. Odd how recently Garreth had been in that same role, and how young the new recruit looked to him now.

"You all right, Left?"

"Oh, are we really talking behind his back? I thought you were just cracking his ass."

"I'm doing that too," Old Boar said. "But the question stands. Are you all right? Because you seem . . . impatient."

A spike of fear ran through him. He felt exposed, and covered it with a laugh. "Sorry. I'm a little out of sorts. Ribs are getting better, but they still hurt."

"Cracked ribs are slow. That's all it is?"

"Looking forward to being paid, but just that. Sorry if I've been bad company."

"No, it's just first time out with the new puppy here, it's important to make him feel like the streets are our streets. When we're walking here, we're in our house, and the barracks are just one room. You know better, but I don't want him to think of patrol as something to rush through like a chore, yeah?"

"I hear what you're saying," Garreth said.

"Knew you would, knew you would. And here's our conquering hero now. What was that shit about, Carrig my boy, and how much did you fine them?"

They moved on, passing through Seepwater, seeing and being seen like justice made flesh. Or if not justice, at least law. Garreth let the cool air bite at his cheeks and the sun warm him, and pretended to be simply a bluecloak and not a man divided. When they made their way back to the barracks, he made himself banter and laugh with Old Boar, setting the new guard at ease and putting him on notice at the same time. He recognized the tactics. It hadn't been many months earlier when they'd been used on him.

"You should get to training," Old Boar said as they reached the yard. "Beren's working focus."

"Focus?" Carrig said. And then, "Yes sir. On my way."

As the recruit made his way to the mud and ice of the training ground, Garreth and Old Boar walked toward Captain Senit's office. Two other patrols had come in before them, but the bluecloaks hadn't scattered. Garreth caught sight of Kannish and Maur standing by the door of the common room, their heads bent toward each other.

"I see it too," Old Boar said. "Something's happened."

"Any idea what?"

"If it's ours to worry about, we'll be told."

In the captain's office, Senit had a strongbox open at his little desk, the same as he did every week. He counted out Old Boar's coins and then Garreth's before he scowled and looked past them to the doorway. "You had a third man, didn't you?"

"Sent him to the training field," Old Boar said with a grin. "Figured he could get some of the stupid knocked off him."

"Get him back," the captain said, and Old Boar's smile faded. "Meet me in the common room with the others. There's a conversation we need to have."

A fire was burning in the common room grate, but it was redundant. The press of bodies was enough to make the room stifling. The morning's patrols were all there, and the afternoon men not yet gone out. For an hour, though it didn't know it, Kithamar was ungoverned. All of its guards were in the barracks, looking one to another with concern. Kannish and Maur were standing side by side next to the pegs on the east wall, and Garreth tried to make his way to them, but the crowd was thick, and Captain Senit came in before he was more than halfway there.

The captain motioned that the door be closed behind him. The smell of bodies and other people's breath filled the room. Captain Senit waved a hand, and a little space opened around him. He hooked one of the benches with his ankle, dragged it to him, and climbed up to look out over them, a lighthouse before a sea of heads.

"We have a problem," he said. "And the first problem all you fuckers need to fix is keep your mouths shut. The way I figure, this won't stay quiet long, but if the one who starts singing it is from this barracks and I find a name, you'll wish your mother had died a child, understood?"

He swept an angry look across them. Garreth's stomach felt like someone had filled it with sand.

"All right," the captain said. "I've had word from Samal Kint. The prince's daughter, Elaine a Sal, has gone missing. She's been missing for a bit, but the palace has been playing coy about it. Now they've decided we might be useful, so now is when we're hearing of it."

Garreth glanced to the east wall. Kannish and Maur were both looking at him. He shook his head once, then looked away again and prayed they'd stay quiet.

"According to her coachman, she'd been taking religious instruction at the Temple on a fair regular basis, so she's been spending time on our side of the river. The day she went missing, she got dropped in Riverport. When she didn't come back to her carriage, the driver figured she'd found her own way home and headed back to Palace Hill, or that's his story. If he's lying about it, Kint will let us know. If he's not, that means she went missing"—the captain pointed to the ground below his feet—"right fucking here."

The room exhaled like all the guards had become a single being. Fear slid through Garreth's belly, and he tried to keep it off his face.

"She's a woman grown. We don't know for certain that anything unfortunate's happened. She may be locked up with some cult preacher, calling for the Faceless to fill her with the spirit. She might be hiding in a bedroom with a boy and a bottle of wine. Or something that *is* our business may have happened. So starting now and going until I say different, your first job is to look for any sign of the heir to the fucking throne of Kithamar. Your second job is to keep your mouths shut about what you're doing. Any spare time you have after that, enforce the law. Questions?"

Garreth felt Kannish and Maur's attention like a weight on his back, but he held steady until Captain Senit stepped down, turned, and marched out of the common room. The silence broke like river ice, the grind was a hundred conversations all going at once. Kannish and Maur were already making their way to him. Neither of them spoke or asked anything. They didn't need to.

"I just got my wage," Garreth said. "Maybe a private room at the baths, just the three of us? I'll pay."

The private rooms were along the north side of the bathhouse, the water connected to the larger pools by channels like the canals of Seepwater and the Smoke, like a map of the city seen in a dream. The basin was cut from granite, smooth on its sides and roughened on the stone benches under the water's surface. A stone brazier in the corner could have warmed the air or burned incense, but for now it was cold. Garreth hadn't picked the spot for its comforts but the privacy that the distance from the open pools and the constant muttering of water afforded.

Kannish and Maur sat across from him. Months in the guard had changed them. He could remember being boys with these two, playing at swords with boughs they stripped off of trees. He remembered Marsen from back then, Kannish's bluecloak uncle with stories of violence and adventure. They'd become the man he was then. Even Maur was thicker with muscle and roughened by sun and wind. Garreth didn't feel older or wiser, though.

"The prince's daughter," Kannish said. "You know something about this?"

"I do," Garreth said. "Not everything, but... You have to swear that this stays between us."

They nodded, Kannish angrily and Maur with a thoughtful frown, but they nodded. Garreth leaned forward and clasped his hands together under the warm water's surface.

"It goes back to before I joined the guard," he said.

He began with the night they had raided Ognan Grimn's boathouse, but then found he had to go back and explain Yrith and the caravan and all the things that had been in his mind back then. When he got to the part where he'd helped the girl escape them, Kannish's expression closed, but he didn't interrupt. Garreth thought he saw disbelief in Maur's eyes while he told about the night he and the woman who'd turned out to be Elaine a Sal spent together, and how it had made marriage to Yrith feel impossible for him, but the skepticism faded when he reminded them of the moment on the bridge when he'd learned who she was. If they hadn't been on duty and seen her with their own eyes, they would likely have dismissed everything he said as bragging or madness.

They knew about his taking Old Boar's shifts in order to work Tenth Night on Palace Hill, and when he related what Elaine had said—Ausai and the strange books and Karsen's plotting for Green Hill blood and her father's odd behavior—Maur tilted his head and pursed his lips. Kannish was unreadable.

"The day I was attacked at my family's house? She was there with me. They were hunting her."

"Who was?" Maur said, speaking for the first time.

"I don't know. The two that broke in, but somebody sent them, and I don't know who or how they knew to find us. She got hurt and badly, but she got away."

"And you know where she is," Kannish said.

Garreth didn't register the warning in his voice. "She's safe. As safe as she can be, which isn't very. If she'd been strong enough, she could have left the city, but I made a deal to keep her hidden and seen to. Whoever's trying to kill her, they won't find her." He couldn't bring himself to say Aunt Thorn's name, not even now. "We need to find out who the assassins were. Who sent them."

"We?" Kannish said. Maur glanced over at him, and Garreth felt the first touch of unease.

"I don't trust anyone besides you two."

"What you need to do," Kannish said, "is march straight back to the barracks and tell all this to the captain."

"Someone in the guard may be part of it. I don't remember if I said anything about where I was going that day. Something's rotten in Palace Hill, and if it's got roots here—"

"Then it's the captain who'll pull them up," Kannish said. "We're guard. We're bluecloaks, or at least I am. I'm not sure what the hell you are anymore. Why did you even join up? Just so you wouldn't have to marry someone? You've been sitting on one cheek since you started. You're supposed to be the law in Kithamar, and you're spending your shifts thinking about old books and how to trade up to palace guard and how to see this girl—this girl who isn't, I'll just point up, someone you can possibly be with. You're guard as a way to pass time until you can get back to what you actually care about."

"That's not fair," Garreth said.

"Right now, our whole barracks is out trying to find a girl when you know where she is. And all the effort they spend trying to find her, they're not spending on something else. How many are going to have what's theirs stolen because of you, eh? How many people are going to get beaten because the captain put this thing first? Will someone get killed for something that you could end right now if you trusted us? You may not think the guard's work matters, but I do, yeah?"

"If the guard's compromised—"

"Maybe the girl's compromised. Have you thought of that? Maybe she's the problem, and you're the one with his head on backward."

Kannish turned to Maur like he was looking for support, but the smaller man was deep in his own thoughts. Kannish slapped the water.

"You tell the captain because he's the *captain* and we're *guard* and that's how it *works*," Kannish said. "If you don't, I will."

Kannish rose from the basin, grabbed his towel, and stalked out, his face a mask of rage. Garreth turned to Maur, panic like a stone in his throat.

"It's a puzzle, isn't it?" Maur said. "The one you killed. They took a mask of him, yeah? We should find that."

The face was cast in cheap plaster, and it didn't look to Garreth much like the man he'd killed. Death or else the mask softened the mouth, the eyes. He'd heard from the older guards about the changes that water made on the bodies of the dead, the way the river slipped inside the flesh, widening faces and fingers, swelling feet and hands, deepening the sockets of the eyes until even someone's nearest kin weren't always perfectly sure that the corpse was one of theirs. This wasn't quite that, but the gist seemed the same. The dead body had been translated by water or clay into something similar, something related, but not the same thing. Not the same person.

The Stonemarket barracks showed their history as a stable in the height of the walls and the arrangement of the rooms. Their common room was wide and tall, with great wooden beams that time and smoke had turned so black they looked burned. The southern wall was a single huge gate that could open to the wind and the faint, distant stink of a launderer's yard or else pull closed. The floor was stone and still bore the ruts where decades of carriage wheels had worn it down. The fire grate had a vertical line of odd-colored stone at the back that marked where some long-forgotten wall had been taken out. Garreth and Maur sat at a low carved-oak table with the dead man's face looking up from it like the wood was water and the man drowned.

The woman sitting with them was thick across the shoulders and jaw. She wore her blue cloak and badge of office like a butcher wearing a leather apron, the tools of a bloody trade. She picked up the mask between two red, callused fingers, shifting it one way and then another. Garreth pinched his wrist under the table to keep his impatience at bay.

"In Riverport, this was?" she asked.

"House Left," Maur said.

"Don't know 'em," the woman said. "But… maybe. There's one named Ullin who hasn't been around for a while. He's trouble, and sometimes he's other people's trouble for the right price. He stays at a bunk house when he's between women."

"He's been missing, then?" Garreth asked.

The woman made a vast shrug. "I haven't seen him, and that's my patrol. Wouldn't be the first time he's had something pull him away for a few weeks and then he pops back up like a stray cat, but this one has the right kind of ears and the nose looks like his. Mouth's wrong, but it's hard to judge those. Skin is too soft. The plaster presses it out of shape. Noses and ears, that's what you look for in a death mask."

Maur nodded once, and Garreth could see his childhood friend folding the insight away in his mind for some later use.

"Is there anyone this Ullin worked for on a regular basis? Someone who might have sent him to Riverport? Maybe some connection to Green Hill?"

"Depends who you ask. There was a story that his father was

an Abbasann and his mother was a servant girl who got kicked out when his wife found out about her, but that might have been bullshit. If you want to hire a knife, there's a hundred of them. Decent people, for the most part, but short on coin, and work is work. Ullin wasn't one for the little shit, not the kind that grabs and runs at the market. He always had money, though. If he had a regular source of coin, I wouldn't be at all surprised. There was one time I heard him say something about a scarred man that made me think he'd been hired more than once."

"A scarred man?" Garreth said.

"If this is Ullin." She put down the mask with a click. "Like I said. Hard to know. You might try the Smoke barracks."

"They sent us here," Maur said. "To you, actually. They said if anyone had a full catalog of the quarter, it was you."

The big woman smiled back, flattered despite herself. "I'll keep an ear up. If I see him or else hear anyone lamenting their long-lost Ullin, I'll send word. Maur Condol, you said?"

"If you need a favor from east of the river, I'll owe you," Maur said. The talk of favors owed made Garreth tense, but if Maur or the woman picked up on it, they didn't let it show. She rose up and trundled away as Maur wrapped the plaster mask back in its cloth and tucked it into his satchel. Garreth stood up, paced for a moment, then leaned against the table, almost sitting on it.

"What do you think?"

"I think *she* thinks it's this Ullin," Maur said. "Which is interesting."

"Is it?"

"It leans into the idea that they were hunting—" Maur broke off before the name escaped his mouth. "That they were hunting her. If someone hired a knife from the other side of the city, they didn't want him recognized easily. That's strategic thinking."

"What about the Inlisc girl?"

"You didn't know her. Even if she's not from Stonemarket, I'd bet you a week's wages she's not Riverport." Maur stifled a yawn. "We should start back. I've got patrol this afternoon."

They had left the Newmarket barracks long enough before sunrise that the eastern horizon had still been as black as the west. They'd taken a small cart from the stables, the groom blinking away sleep and the pair of horses radiating an attitude of long-suffering patience. The nearly nighttime streets were touched only here and there by candles and lanterns and the laughter of girls and children carrying water from the cisterns and small fountains. The bridge that crossed from Seepwater to the Smoke had been empty in a way it almost never was, and the always-burning forges on the western side of the water only looked out onto pavement.

They had reached the little barracks at the Smoke with dawn broken and Palace Hill glowing gold before a vastly blue sky. Garreth had lived his life in Riverport. The Smoke and Stonemarket were, for the most part, names. Driving through the streets and squares with Palace Hill lower than it usually was, the slope of it gentler, and on the wrong side of the sky felt like being in a foreign city.

It was close to noon, and the streets were full now. Carts and pedestrians and dogs and carriages sometimes clogging the way until Maur and Garreth had to stop and wait or else stand on a driver's bench and threaten fines if the way wasn't cleared for the city guard. A warm wind was starting to kick up, raising little waves on the surface of the river that travelled across it from east to west, ignoring the deeper flow. The bridge back to Seepwater was full and slow. If it had been as empty as the night, they would have been back at their barracks in only a few hours. As it was, they both knew that Maur was going to be late for his patrol.

Garreth was certain that Maur's quiet and thoughtful look masked irritation and dread at the consequences of his lateness until the smaller man spoke. "Would you say that you love her?"

Garreth leaned forward, his gaze fastened between the ears of the horse before him. "Yes. I would."

"What's that like?"

Garreth shrugged. "Being in love with a girl?"

"That."

"You've been in love. What about that summer with Dannia Ferrish?"

"I liked her," Maur allowed. "And I thought she was pretty. She seemed to like me, and the sex was pleasant in a messy kind of way. But when she broke things off I felt... fine? I acted like I was heartbroken and losing sleep because that's what everyone else did when something like that ended, but the truth was I slept just fine."

"But at the start of it?"

"It started that way too, really. What is it like for you? Is it just wanting or is it something different?"

Ahead of them, a carter started shouting at a carriage that was coming the other way. Garreth couldn't make out the words, but the tone was angry enough. He could have dropped off their little carriage and run forward to break up the altercation, but it would only have been a way to avoid answering.

"Different. I mean, the wanting is there. It's part of it. But it's like when I'm with her, when we're just the two of us in a room, the room becomes a different place. It's like everything else is a play we're acting in and the city's the stage where we all say our lines, and when we shut the doors, we're not our parts anymore. We're just us. It's a different city, and there's only two people in it. And it's a good place. I like it there."

"Why? I mean, what makes it better than—" Maur gestured

at the bridge, the water, the boats and quays and buildings stretching out to their left. He gestured to Kithamar.

The carriage driver had stopped now, and was stepping out on the yellow brick of the bridge, gesturing at his team. Other carts were going around the arguing pair, but slowly so that everyone had a moment to watch.

"It's simpler. It's purer. I like who I am when I'm there. And she's . . . I don't know how to describe this. She's perfect? Not like she's a paragon and what everyone should want to be or be with. She's spiky. Sometimes she's even a little mean, and sad. She's sad in ways she doesn't know about, but I can see them."

"And you want to fix that," Maur said.

"Yes," Garreth said. And then, "No. She's not broken. She's just who she is, and it fits with who I am. Or I feel like it does. Or like it should. She feels . . . important."

Maur lifted a hand that Garreth should wait. He leaned out and shouted, "City guard! Both of you get back to your work and clear the traffic or you'll be lucky to get by with just fines. Don't fucking look at me like that, you. I'll crack your ass the other way." He took his seat again and nodded like nothing had happened. On the bridge, the fighting men left off their battle and started their horses moving again. "That fitting with someone? I don't think I've had that experience."

"Never?"

"I don't think so. I say that I've loved people. I love you and Kannish and my brothers and sisters. My parents. I said I loved Dannia Ferrish, but I don't think now that I was using the word correctly." A gust of wind pressed against them and was gone. "I understand that sense of being apart from the city, I think. But I can't imagine being there with someone else. It just doesn't make sense."

"I'm sorry."

"I'm not. I had an uncle who couldn't tell green from blue. He said they were the same color, and I always wondered what he was seeing when he put a leaf against the sky. If it was all what I'd call green or all blue or something different altogether. It's like that. I'm curious how the world's different for you, but I am what I am."

They reached the eastern shore and turned the horses north along the broad path through Seepwater. The midday traffic was thick on the roads and on the canals. Flatboats with tuns of beer from the brewers ready to cross the river or be hauled up to the port or float down past the bridge and south into the villages and towns. Carts bringing in sacks of barley and wheat and carrying out expended mash as food for pigs at the farms outside the city walls. A thick Inlisc girl at a cart sold fish and spiced rice in cones of waxed paper, and she looked away when she saw Garreth looking at her. It was only a little thing, a moment of fear from a stranger who saw his cloak and his badge before she saw him.

The wind pushed, ruffling his sleeve and pressing his cloak against his side. The noise of it made talking difficult. Maur kept the horses moving at a fair pace, but the streets only allowed so much speed. Garreth had the chance to look now, to notice the expressions of the people they passed, and it seemed to him that the girl wasn't the only one who flinched away, though she might have been the worst at hiding it. A Hansch boy with maybe eight summers behind him chased a running cat into the street, then scuttled back when he saw Garreth. An old Inlisc woman stopped at a corner and looked down as they passed so that Garreth saw the red cloth that covered her hair more than he did her face.

A few smiled, but there was an unease in the smiles as well, and while their way was often blocked, the other carts and hand wagons and people walking on foot cleared the way for them as much as they could. He had the sudden, visceral memory of being on shit patrol and whipping a man for moving too slowly. *Could be worse. You could be one of the men who enjoys it.*

Maur reached the turn, and the horses took them into a narrower street with wooden buildings and a sinuousness that made him think of Longhill. A sinuous street built to defy the power and noise of the wind.

"Do you think Kannish turned me in?" Garreth asked.

"There's a reason I wanted to leave early," Maur said. "I don't know if he will or if that was just the anger talking."

"I didn't mean to make him angry. I just... I wasn't sure that she'd be safe with the guard. I trust you and I trust him, but there was someone—"

"Wait. You think that's why he's angry?"

"Isn't it?"

Maur pulled the horses to a stop. The shoes clattered against paving stones, and the lighter of the two sighed in what sounded like frustration. Maur shifted on the bench, swinging a knee up and resting his arm against it. His voice was soft and calm, which made it worse. "We were new guards. Senit gave us a joke duty to put us in our place, and we could have turned it into a victory. If we'd caught the prince's daughter in that boathouse, it would have been kept quiet, and we'd have been the ones with our lips shut as a favor to Palace Hill. Me, Kannish, and Tannen. And instead, we got a minor noble girl who no one really cared about and a dozen drunk idiots whose families didn't thank us for the embarrassment. A take like that on one of our first patrols would have made us look better than good, and we lost it because you took it from us."

"It was just that Tannen—"

"Tannen picked at me because he thought I was the weakest,"

Maur said. "That's the kind of man he is, and there are plenty like him in the guard. They fit here. And there are some like Kannish who make the guard their whole lives and selves because past that, they don't have much else. They fit here too. He was so happy when you joined up because he thought it meant you'd be one of us and he'd still have you by him. You told him yesterday that you'd betrayed us, and you didn't even know you were saying it."

Garreth felt the words like they'd hit him below the ribs. Maur's smile was soft and sorrowful.

"Fuck," Garreth said.

"It's all right," Maur said. "Just understand Kannish is going to be mourning a bit. I don't *think* he'll really bring the captain in. I hope he doesn't. He'll feel bad about it later if he does, but that may not be enough to stop him in the moment, if you see what I mean."

Maur started the horses moving again with a flick of the reins. The carriage lurched under them. The wind whistled and shrieked, but it didn't reach them there in the valley of the streets. A bone-and-iron cart stopped before it crossed into their path, its grey nag looking weary and sullen. The man waved them forward, giving them the street in a voice like gravel and soot, and smiled like he could will their good opinion.

"What about us?" Garreth said. "Do we fit?"

"I don't fit anywhere," Maur said. "I'm odd."

The horses didn't need to be led to the stables. They knew quite well where they were going, and Maur gave them free rein to get there. The wind was stirring up bits of hay, twirling them through the air and dropping them again as they drew close. A groom with grey hair and a stoop came out, and the horses whickered in recognition and pleasure at the sight of him. Garreth clambered down off the bench as soon as the carriage stopped. Kannish was standing in the shadow of the feed stall, his arms crossed. Now that Garreth knew to look for it, he saw the hurt in the other man's shoulders and the way he held his jaw.

Kannish lifted his chin to Maur as he walked forward. Maur came close, and the three of them stood almost shoulder to shoulder. Something about it felt melancholy.

"It wasn't the guard that set them on you," Kannish said.

"I know you believe in them," Garreth said. "Us. I know you believe in us—"

Kannish made an impatient cutting gesture with one hand. "You're not listening. It wasn't the guard. These people, they didn't know who you were. They were hunting her, and they knew your name, but they didn't know who you were."

"What are you talking about?"

Kannish smiled tightly. "You're not the only ones who ask questions in their off hours."

Serria sat in a cell where a prisoner would usually be. He recognized her shirt—thick linen with a bit of embroidery at the collar. The skirt and rope sandals told him that she'd been going to the market as clearly as if someone had spoken. The leather satchel she used to carry eggs and herbs and fresh meat wasn't there, though. Garreth wondered what had become of it. Whether Kannish had let her drop the food off with the other servants before she came with him, or sent it along with some streetbound as likely to keep the food as see it delivered, or something else. His pang of guilt was unexpected, as was the nostalgia that followed. Once, he'd shared a house with this woman, and lived close enough beside her that he still knew her going-to-market clothes. It was like smelling a dish from his childhood and being transported for a moment back to the boy he'd been once and never would be again.

At first, she looked uneasy, perhaps even frightened. He saw the moment of recognition. Her eyes cooled, her chin rose, and a little hard smile pressed her lips back against her teeth.

Knowing that he was involved made her inconvenience, her confusion, her humiliation all make sense.

Maur came in last, closing the door behind him and sliding the bolt home. The three of them—guardsmen in the city blue—stood before the stool where she sat, and Garreth couldn't shake the memory of the same three standing at her kitchen asking for a little snack of fruit and bread when they had been small and her hair had still been dark.

Kannish crossed his arms and nodded toward Garreth and Maur. "Tell them what you told me. About the girl."

Serria sighed and shook her head. Garreth had time to wonder what detail about his time with Elaine was about to be hauled out before Serria spoke.

"The Inlisc girl? She was nothing very much. Plain as paper. She was trying to hide it, but she didn't know how."

"Hide what?" Garreth asked.

"Her belly," Serria said, and her voice was all contempt. "She wasn't showing yet, but I know how a girl holds herself when she knows it's not only her heart beating. And after how you treated Miss Yrith. Good enough for a quick time in some side alley, but too base for your marriage bed."

Garreth spread his hands, ready to profess his innocence, but Kannish stepped between them.

"You're saying an Inlisc girl came to the house looking for Garreth."

"Yes. I told her to come here. He made his choice, and his problems weren't ours. Not any longer. Told her to try the barracks."

Kannish and Maur both raised their eyebrows. A rush of panic was rising in Garreth's chest. "That's not... There isn't—"

"When was this?" Kannish said.

"I told you all this."

"Tell it again, when was it?"

"Midwinter. Not long after the caravan came. I didn't mark it. I didn't have reason to."

"What was her name?" Garreth asked.

Serria coughed out a laugh. "I didn't ask, and I didn't care. How many more should we expect? She was young, if that helps narrow the field for you."

"How did she ask for him?" Kannish said,

"By name."

"His full name? Garreth Left? Or just his first."

Serria's contempt spread to Kannish. "Is that the argument? She was at our house looking for someone else? In case we had some other young master Garreth stowed in a cabinet? This is ridiculous, and it's nothing to do with me. Not anymore. I want to go home now."

She started to stand, but Maur went to her side and pressed her gently back in place. "Not just yet, please," he said.

"I have nothing to add," Serria said. "Whatever your problems are, I can't help with them and I wouldn't if I could."

"Just a few minutes more," Maur said with a disarming smile, and Serria lapsed into a frustrated silence. Kannish pulled the bolt and the three stepped out into the wind.

"There's no girl like that," Garreth said. "I haven't been with anyone. I mean, but her. There's not—"

Kannish crossed his arms and leaned against the door. "There were two of them. One a Hansch man who sounds like he might have been the one you killed, and this Inlisc girl. The story changed every time they went. Sometimes it was they owed young master Garreth money, sometimes it was that he was holding a bag of wheat for them. Or he'd told them to stop by and look at a horse. I've found half a dozen people who had visits like that, and I'll bet you a week's fines I haven't got them all."

"Young master Garreth," Maur said slowly, like he was trying the words for the first time.

"Exactly. Just the one name, and that he was our age. Whenever they were told they had the wrong house, they apologized and moved on. Except when they found this one who told them to clear off."

Maur's eyes shifted like he was reading the air, and he started to grin. "Everyone here knows who Garreth is. No reason to hunt all through Riverport for him."

"I think they knew he was city guard too, but they didn't come here. They were looking for his family home. Where he came from."

"Where I was going to meet with..." Garreth said.

"Which they knew. And there's my point." Kannish turned to Garreth. "These two knew what no one in the guard knew and didn't know what all of us already did. Whoever set them on you? It wasn't us."

Garreth took a long, shuddering breath. "Then who was it?"

"Not a hint," Kannish said, "but there's a good way to find out. And get her safe. And stop wasting the guard's efforts. I'm going to get the captain. You know you can trust him now. There's no reason not to tell him, yeah?"

The idea of telling the full story to Captain Senit was like looking over a cliff, but the only argument Garreth could find against it was his own dread. Kannish was right. Whoever wanted Elaine dead, it wasn't the guard. Garreth made himself nod.

Kannish turned, and Garreth caught his elbow before he could walk away. The little flare of anger in Kannish's eyes might have been Garreth's imagination. It might not.

"I'm sorry."

"It's fine. You were just being stupid careful."

"Not just for that. For all of it. I was thoughtless."

Kannish looked up, squinting into the wind. "Say it to Tannen," he said. And then a moment later, "Don't worry about it. It's all right." The flatness of his voice meant it wasn't and that it wouldn't be.

Garreth let go of his arm and the friend he'd known from childhood walked away. The ache in his stomach could have been a dozen things—was probably all of them—but one for certain was the echo of Kannish's disappointment. Across the yard, Beren was drilling half a dozen of the others on disarming tactics. Old Boar swaggered out of the common room with a woman Garreth didn't recognize beside him, laughing at something he'd said and then turning serious. A gust stung Garreth's eyes with grit, and he tried to rub the pain away with the heel of his palm. Maur looked into the distance.

"I'm going to—" Garreth said, and pointed to the cell door.

"Yeah," Maur agreed. "I'll wait here. If you need me, just call out."

"Aren't you going to miss your patrol?"

"Seems like," Maur said.

Garreth pulled the door open and stepped back into the cell. Serria looked at him coolly as he latched the door. He didn't throw the bolt. It felt different being there with only her and not Kannish or Maur or any of the other guard. Garreth had his blue cloak, his blade, his badge of office. They were the real thing, taken in exchange for his oath, but they felt like a costume. He crossed his arms, and that felt awkward too.

"They're doing well, you know," Serria said. "Your brother and his wife? They're doing very well. The magistrate found in their favor. All the contracts were allowed. The house is on better footing now than any time in the last decade."

"Good to hear."

"Is it? I thought you'd be disappointed."

"Please, Serria. I don't want—"

"You showed the family nothing but contempt, after all. Your father built a life for you. A good life. And you walked away from it the moment he asked you to sacrifice anything for it. You wouldn't do for them what your father did for you every day of your life. Every day."

The words should have hurt. The gods all knew Garreth felt raw enough. Instead they punched him like a puppy trying its strength for the first time. He looked at Serria, not seeing the woman who'd run the small points of his home or his father's mistress either, but only the person sitting before him. The age in her skin, the whiteness of her hair, the rage that brought color to her cheeks and squared her mouth.

"Your father is a good man, Garreth Left. He's a good man who cared for you, and you treated his home like a brothel."

I wasn't the one fucking the help, he thought, but he didn't say it. It would have been empty. There was no heat behind it.

What would it be like to be the secret lover of a powerful man? How many years had Serria shared his father's body and his night, and then spent her days as his servant, excluded from his business, unwelcome at his dinner table, less than him in every way? He saw the bitterness in her, and it spoke to him of years spent being reminded that she was beneath him. The swelling in his chest wasn't anger, it was pity. Someone bound by the heart to a lover whose full life she couldn't share except as a servant.

Put that way, her burden wasn't so different from his.

"Does he treat you well? Tell me at least that he loves you."

"Of course he does," she snapped. "You can hate me all you like. You can hate him and look for ways to embarrass him by running away to play at city guard. It won't matter. I love him, and he loves me, and he has a bigger soul than you ever will."

"He doesn't," Garreth said gently. "In fact, he's more than a little cruel."

"Wash the lie off your tongue. Mannon is the best, kindest man I have ever known. You aren't half of him."

"All right," Garreth said. The confusion in Serria's eyes was heartbreaking. "If you say so, I believe you. You know him better than I do."

"Robbson and that woman are always trying to undermine him. I was more a mother to you than she ever was. I was the one who saw you fed and washed your clothes and put salve on your scrapes. You can call that servitude. You did, you all did, but I did what a mother would do. That was me." The words were coming out of her now like water spilling from a broken cask. Her eyes held a horror that she was speaking these things aloud, but now that she'd started, she didn't seem able to stop. "He stands by me. We are what we are in front of the world because we have to be, but now that the business is saved, now that he doesn't need her..."

She snapped her mouth shut, her lips pale from the pressure.

"He'll leave Mother and marry you," Garreth said. "I hope you're right. I hope he does." He was almost surprised to realize he actually did.

The flash of darkness in Serria's expression was enough to show that she didn't believe he was sincere. Or that his father was.

"You were always kind to me. That's true," Garreth said, and the latch clicked. The door swung open behind him. Captain Senit strolled in, thumbs tucked in his belt and a scowl drawing the corners of his mouth down toward his jawline. Kannish came in behind him, and Maur in the back.

"Left," the captain said, then turned to Serria. "Ma'am, I apologize for the wait. Kannish Wellis wants me to ask you about some Inlisc girl that this one drew into shame. What've you got to tell me?"

Serria gathered herself, dabbing tears away from her eyes, and told her story again, voice low and eyes downcast. When she was done, the captain opened the door for her. She left with her shoulders forward and her arms crossed in front like she was trying to protect herself from a blow.

The captain took her stool, dragged it to a space beside the wall, and sat with the front two feet off the floor and his back resting on the stone.

"Wellis," he said. "This is where you tell me why I give a wet slap about that woman, her story, or who Left here's been spending his playtime with."

"Good questions, sir," Kannish said, and told what he had to tell. He could have started with Elaine a Sal and Garreth's undermining them at the boathouse, but he didn't. He worked backward, giving as much justification for Garreth's silence as he could before the blow inevitably fell. It was a kindness and a loyalty Garreth didn't expect and wasn't certain he deserved. He felt his heart beating faster, harder, fluttering behind his ribs as Kannish came closer to the central fact of his connection to the prince's daughter. And as he reached it.

The captain's scowl softened and slowly vanished. The stillness that took its place was worse. He lowered the stool so that all four feet were grounded and leaned a degree forward, listening to Kannish with the intensity of a man in a knife fight.

"Elaine a Sal went missing the day that Garreth killed that man at his house," Kannish finished, "because she was there. She was the one they'd come to kill."

The silence was profound. After a moment, Captain Senit shifted his eyes—just his eyes—to Garreth. Garreth nodded. It was all true.

When he spoke, each word came out on its own like beads on a necklace with little silences between them. "You didn't think it wise to tell me this at the time?"

"I did, though," Garreth said. "You asked who the girl was, and I said it was her. But you thought I was joking, and then my father came, and I started thinking about who might have... how they knew..." He trailed off and looked at the ground. For a long moment, the muttering of the rising wind through the door was the loudest sound.

"Where is she?" Captain Senit asked.

"She's safe."

"Did I fucking ask if she was safe? *Where is she*, Left?"

Garreth imagined saying *I gave her to Aunt Thorn* and all that would come after. "I don't know, and that's intentional. If the Inlisc girl and her friends found me, they could torture me to death, and I wouldn't be able to tell them. But I can call her back to us." *I hope I can call her back to us.*

"Fucking Kint and his palace intrigues," the captain muttered, then drummed a finger against his leg. "All right. Who else knows about this?"

"There are two people at the Temple," Garreth said. "Friends of Elaine's. They'll keep it to themselves."

"Sure they will," he said, but the sneer was perfunctory. His mind was elsewhere. "You three go put on your civilian clothes. Half an hour from now, you're going to go reclaim the girl. I'll have half a dozen shadowing you in case we're needed and as much of the barracks as I can muster in earshot of the whistles."

"I'll have to go to Longhill," Garreth said.

The captain's scowl returned.

"My contact is there," Garreth said.

"You've got contacts in Longhill?"

"Through family."

The captain considered that. "We'll do what we can. I don't need to start a riot, but . . . You talk to no one, yeah? Do what needs doing to get her back to the barracks, and then we'll see where we stand."

"The palace?" Maur said. It was the first time he'd spoken since the captain had come.

"Someone's trying to kill the prince's daughter. I wouldn't tell that sack of rats my mother's name if I thought someone could squeeze a coin out of knowing."

"It was the same for me, you know," Garreth said, a little too quickly. "I had to know it was safe first. Before I could tell anyone, I had to know who was safe to tell."

"It ain't the same."

"But—"

"I'm me, and you're you," Captain Senit said. "That makes it not the same."

The pounding on the door was sudden and violent. All of them started, even the captain. Then, hand on the pommel of his sword, the captain stood. "Who is it?"

"It's me, Captain." Beren's voice came muffled through the door.

"I'm in the middle of something."

"Let it stand, then. I think we've got a problem."

The captain growled, "I think we've got several," and headed out. Garreth followed close. In the yard, the men who'd been drilling were still standing shirtless and sweating, the wooden practice blades in their hands. A handful of other people—men and women both—had paused in the street and were shading their eyes as they stared to the west and Oldgate. Garreth thought they were looking at Oldgate or else Palace Hill at its crown. He didn't think to look higher until Maur spoke.

"That's not a cloud, is it?"

Against the wind-whipped blue, a plume of grey-white stretched, thinner at the top and thickening as it disappeared behind the broad walls of the palace. Smoke. Something was burning. Something large.

"Is that the palace?" Kannish asked.

"Palace or else Green Hill," Garreth said. "Shit. It looks big."

"Right, then. New plan," Captain Senit said, then put his hands to his mouth and shouted, "All you bastards get your blades and come with me right now. Anyone not with me on the count of ten works the shit cart for a month. Ten! Nine!" The guards scattered and he took Garreth's arm. "We're getting her. We're getting her now, and we're getting her in force. I don't know what the hell's going on, but looks like it's already happening."

She should have felt buried alive. Days came and went—or she had to assume they did—without even a ray of sunlight. Her time was measured in sleep and food, visits from Erja and Aunt Thorn, poultices that heated her flesh and poultices that cooled her. Her shoulder still hurt sometimes, but so much less that she could mistake the ache for painlessness. When she slept, her dreams were wild and vivid. She felt herself changing, though she couldn't say what she was changing from nor what she was changing into. She only knew that some part of her was hungry for it.

Erja didn't talk about the world aboveground. Her only concern was Elaine's recovery, and she seemed pleased by it more often than not. She'd helped Elaine bathe the first few times, and while Elaine had often been attended in private moments, it still felt awkward being naked in front of Erja. As soon as Elaine's shoulder was loose enough that she didn't need the help, she didn't accept it. Erja had covered her amusement, but not well.

Aunt Thorn, by contrast, brought news of Kithamar and of her father. The plague in Stonemarket seemed to be subsiding without spilling over to the rest of the city. The iron workers' guild was putting together a fund to dredge the canals that ran through the Smoke. Byrn a Sal had missed his third day of audiences from the public, and the palace guard was spread thin looking for the missing heir. House Abbasann was vying to take the lead position in the summer games. The milk-eyed woman rattled off bits of gossip and telling detail like she was throwing a handful of gravel at a wall—one, then one or two others, and then a dozen things all at once. Elaine had the sense that she was being tested somehow, but she didn't know the purpose.

She'd just finished a bowl of beef dumpling soup when her host arrived. At first, Elaine was pleased for the company, anticipating another report from the sunlit world. Instead, Aunt Thorn tossed her a bundle of cloth and leather.

"Time to get presentable," Aunt Thorn said.

The bundle resolved into a pair of leather-and-canvas trousers, a thick shirt, boots, and a belt with a thin steel dagger in a cheap sheath. Elaine's first thought was that someone was coming, and she was being hidden in among the toughs and hired knives who peopled the corridors.

"It's been strange," the criminal prince of Kithamar said. "I trust you'll remember me kindly when you're back sleeping on silk."

"You're sending me out?" Elaine said. "I thought it would be when I asked."

"You or him," Aunt Thorn said. "Well, it's him."

"Garreth?"

"And we'll call it his honor guard. Get dressed. This is all going to go better if you look like you're nearly one of mine."

She almost asked what would go better, but she was already

stripping off her sleeping shift and pulling on the new clothes. Garreth was here. He'd learned something about the killers. Or about why the killers had let her go. Or anything, really, because he was here, and knowing it made her want to go up to the open air more than anything ever had. She told herself that the trembling, vibrant joy in her body was only excitement at the report he was bringing her, and even she wasn't convinced. Garreth was here, and even if everything wasn't all right, it was better. It would be better.

The path through the dim brick hallways was shorter than she'd expected. All the uncountable hours she'd been underground, the way up had been less than two minutes away. Aunt Thorn preceded her up stone steps worn smooth by generations of boots, down a short corridor, and to a wooden doorway that a huge, scar-pocked man with an uneasy expression pulled open for them.

The light blinded. Elaine stumbled, but Aunt Thorn caught her elbow and kept her steady. The twinge at her collarbone was the faintest echo of what the wound had been. As her eyes adapted to the brightness, men were murmuring. A voice she didn't recognize muttered an obscenity with an awe that made it sound like prayer.

More slowly than she liked, shapes began to form. A space of relative darkness before her became a wooden wall. The unbearable white above her took on the dirty blue of a hazy sky. Men in the blue of the city guard coalesced out of light into shape and form and solidity. There had to be a dozen of them, and Garreth was at the front beside a wide-bodied man with the oversized silver badge of office that meant he was captain of a barracks. She'd met him before. Senit, she thought, and then Garreth took a step toward her. Moving into his arms was as effortless as falling. Any thought of discretion or station or the avoidance of gossip was blown away in the wind that washed through the alleyway. She put her head in the curve of his shoulder and his neck and breathed him like he was perfume.

"I missed you," he murmured. "I was so worried she wouldn't really let you go."

Behind Elaine, Aunt Thorn chuckled. "I believe in following rules."

"You'd say that even if you didn't," the captain said, the buzz of violence in his tone. "Nothing helps a liar like a reputation for speaking truth."

The tension in the air plucked at Elaine, and she stepped back from Garreth. The guardsmen were all still and ready for violence. At the other end of the alley a handful of solid, angry-looking Inlisc men watched the proceedings with swords in their fists. Aunt Thorn stood in the door to her private world, smiling and apparently at ease, but her casualness raised more alarms than all the high-strung men put together.

Elaine stepped between the captain and Aunt Thorn like she was taking a stage. "Captain. What's going on here?"

"Nothing good," the big man said.

A familiar young bluecloak cleared his throat, made a little bow in Elaine's direction. "Forgive me, but before you were attacked at House Left, by any chance did you mention Garreth to anyone by name? Just his first name? Not his family?"

"This isn't the time, Maur," the captain said, but Garreth caught her gaze and nodded.

"I . . ." She pressed her hands to her head. The wind muttered and hissed. "I think my cousin? Andomaka?"

"Andomaka Chaalat," the one called Maur said. "Next in succession. This is a coup."

"Yes, you're very fucking clever," the captain said. "We're all impressed. Now shut the fuck up. Miss, what you need to do right now is make your way over to me and mine." He locked eyes with Aunt Thorn. "And no one so much as blinks until she does."

Aunt Thorn sighed and crossed her arms. "If I wanted her dead, she'd be dead."

Elaine took a reflexive step, then stopped. "What's a coup? What's going on?"

"We're not sure," Garreth said. "There's a fire. Maybe the palace, maybe Green Hill. But your cousin was the one who wanted you dead."

Elaine felt herself thinking without being sure what she was thinking. It was like hearing a fire in the next room, feeling its heat against the door. The back of her mind was churning, and she wasn't sure why. Not at first.

"The thread of Kithamar will not sever."

"I don't know what that means," Garreth said.

"Miss," the captain said through gritted teeth. "If this is what it seems, you're in danger. We need to get you someplace a thousand times safer than where you are right now. Just please step over to me."

She turned almost against her will. The scarred woman with the white eye was looking at her with something like compassion. Elaine had the sudden, powerful memory of falling into the river, fighting to get back to the surface before her air ran out. She was aware that this moment was as dangerous as that had been. She turned back to the guard captain. "Your duty isn't to protect me, it's to protect the city. Right now, the city is my father. We're going to the palace."

"Fine, good," he said. "Come, then. We'll get carriages. Horses. Be on our way, just come with me."

"Crowded streets and bridges," Aunt Thorn said. "Crawling up Oldgate like a spider. You won't be there before dark."

"Stay the fuck out of this, you," the captain snapped, but Aunt Thorn was smiling now. Elaine turned to face the woman and the doorway that still hadn't closed. Garreth was a warmth at Elaine's side, and she was glad to feel him there.

"There are other roads," Aunt Thorn said. "I can't go with you. I'm yoked to a different plow. But I can open a way, if you're brave enough."

The woman stepped to the left. The wooden door stood open, and the darkness beyond it seemed deeper than when Elaine had walked out of it.

"That is a fucking trap," the guard captain said. "Miss, you need to come back away from her and that place. You were lucky to get out once. You won't get out again."

The bluecloaks shifted, spreading in the alley like a cat pulling into a crouch. At the far end of the alleyway, the Inlisc men paced but they didn't come closer. Not yet. The promise of violence filled the wild air like smoke.

When Aunt Thorn spoke again, her good eye was fixed on Elaine, but her words were for the captain. "Hear me on this, Divol. We aren't allies and never will be, but today, your enemy is the same as mine. I can't promise you and yours will live to see morning, but I give you my word that I won't be the one who kills you."

"Go piss up a rope," the captain replied.

Elaine turned to Garreth, but not, she realized, for an answer. She knew in her bones that this moment was hers and hers alone. All he could be for her was a place that didn't pull her, a garden without wind. His eyes were soft and as lost as she was. He looked older than he had that first night. Or no. That wasn't right. He looked vulnerable and distressed. He looked to her how she must have looked to him with the river still in her hair and her sandals drowned and gone. He hauled in a great breath, about to speak, and she knew that if he told her what to do—if he commanded her—something precious would break.

"What should I do?" he asked, and the storm at the back of her mind settled.

"Come to me," she said. "I'll see you safe."

Elaine ab-Deniya Nycis a Sal walked to Aunt Thorn, chin high and shoulders relaxed. The older woman's smile could have meant anything. "Free passage for me and mine to the palace. I have your word?"

"Yes," Aunt Thorn said.

"Done. Captain! Bring your men." She stepped forward into the darkness without waiting to see if her command was followed. Erja was waiting in the corridor with a hooded lantern and an expression of surprise. The footsteps that came behind her were Garreth's. She knew them without looking back.

"This way, then," Erja said, but Elaine lifted a finger, waited. More footsteps came. Boots tramping up behind her and the tapping of scabbards against legs. The guard. Elaine nodded, and Erja turned, lifting the lantern, and led them forward and down. The brickwork walls broadened. They passed decorated niches that Elaine recognized as arrow-slits. After the wind-battered air above, the underground felt unnaturally still. Maybe it was.

They passed down a ramp as wide as a street, past dark galleries and halls. Inlisc faces watched them from the shadows, impassive or surprised or angry. Like a dark city underground, this inverted Kithamar accepted them. The guard captain was murmuring something under his breath, a single phrase repeated over and over. She thought it was *I fucking knew it* but she wasn't sure what he meant. The walls changed from brick to stacked stone and old timber. The air grew wetter, thicker. The smell of the river washed over them as Erja took them forward.

The passage opened into a wide room, tall as a warehouse, where a huge wheel turned and creaked, driven by a thick belt of what looked like woven leather that entered from and disappeared into a wide black tunnel. Five people—three men, two women, all of them round-faced and curly-haired Inlisc—were dragging a wide, low sledge with wheels on its runners to the mouth of the tunnel.

"Get on," Erja said.

"What is this?" the smaller guardsman—Maur—asked in wonder and fear.

"The king of all smugglers' tunnels," the captain answered.

"Get on it or walk the whole way under the river," Erja said. "The sledge won't come back soon." Someone echoed *under the river* in a voice of regret.

Elaine stepped onto the sledge. It was made of wide oak planks, aged almost black with pale scrapes and scars that exposed new wood. The guards clambered up beside her like little boys going on a raft for the first time.

Erja handed the lantern to Elaine. "There'll be someone on the far side to take you to the stairs. Don't run up. It's a long climb and few enough places to rest. But they'll get you where you need to be."

"Thank you," Elaine said. "For everything."

"Pay me back," the Inlisc woman said. "Win."

The last of the guards took his place at the rear of the sledge. When Elaine held up the lantern, light spilled down into the tunnel before her and failed into darkness. Garreth put a hand on the sledge's side to steady himself.

The guard captain loomed up on Elaine's other side. "I'll be back here one day. I will clean all of this out. You watch me."

"Let's make it through today first," Elaine said.

The scowl faltered and something like a smile but without

the pleasure took its place, however briefly. “You make a fair point.”

“Hold steady!” one of the Inlisc men shouted. “It’s a hard start. Might you should sit down so you don’t fall off.”

Behind her, the guards crouched on the dark oak. She held the front of the sledge in one hand and the lantern in the other as Aunt Thorn’s people took leads from the front of the sledge to the belt, a huge iron hook wider than a man’s shoulders at the end. With the dexterity of long practice, they fastened the hook to the moving belt, and the sledge bucked under her. The rooms and Erja and the eastern half of Kithamar fell behind her like she was being pulled by a team of horses at full gallop. The wheels beneath her juddered and clacked. The speed was a wind in her hair. The tunnel fell past her, stone and wood with strange arches of blue and jade that they passed under too quickly for her to make sense of.

And under the rattling of the wheels and the creaking of the belt, a deeper, softer sound filled the air like a god exhaling forever. Above her, the Khahon ran in its bed, vast and heavy as a city. Garreth was looking up at the ceiling as it sped by. The dread in his eyes echoed her own.

“What do you think happens if this starts leaking?” he asked.

“Nothing good,” she said.

“Yeah, that sounds right.”

Elaine let go of the sledge, trusting to her balance, and shifted the lantern to her left hand. She found Garreth’s fingers with her own, and like the figurehead at the prow of a ship, they stood together and sailed into darkness.

The Daris Brotherhood burned.

Public temple and private, halls, cells, storerooms, stables. All of it in flames. The reek of smoke filled the air of Green Hill, Palace Hill, and Stonemarket. The sunlight was ruddy with it. Lines of men and women hauled water from the canal to sluice the neighboring buildings in hopes that the fire might not spread.

The beast that called itself the thread of Kithamar walked in the flesh it had taken from Andomaka Chaalat. It felt the tightness in the woman's belly, the nausea of fear, slightly different in every body it had occupied. It held its head high to disguise its fright and balled handfuls of its robe in fists at its sides to keep the cloth from billowing. Its belt—and more to the point its blade—was gone.

There were half a dozen great compounds that the different religious brotherhoods kept, but Daris had been its home and shelter, the sanctuary to which it could run if anything went wrong at the palace. Something had gone very wrong at the palace, and the brotherhood, and now in the street where its enemies had found it, stolen from it, and made it vulnerable again in ways it hadn't anticipated.

Had it been arrogant? Had the flesh of the secret child it had used as refuge poisoned it with the risk-blindness of youth? Had Andomaka Chaalat left behind her own prejudices and certainties along with her skin and blood? It wanted to believe that the fault was its own, because then it would be in its power to correct.

"My lady," the head cook of the kitchens said with surprise in his voice.

"Lemel Tarrit," the thread of Kithamar said. It had known him since he was a child washing plates. This was the third pair of eyes it had looked on him with. "I'm sorry to intrude, but I was hoping to find my servant Tregarro? Have you seen him?"

"I'm sorry. No, my lady. We don't have many people here. I sent them all out to the fire. Are you all right? I could make you a cup of tea. Something soothing."

It smiled gently and shook its pale head. Tregarro was too good an assassin to be seen making his approach. He had been Andomaka's best ally and servant, but it had transformed him into Byrn a Sal's death. It wanted him back, wanted someone who understood the situation at its side. But Tregarro was an arrow loosed. It couldn't call him back.

"I can only hope he escaped the fire," it said, knowing already that he had. If he wasn't in the palace at that moment, it was because he'd already put his plan in motion and fled. The death of the prince. Lemel touched the thread's arm, offering comfort. It was both a gentle, human moment and an affront. The thread of Kithamar smiled gently with Andomaka's lips and headed into the halls and galleries it had built over centuries. Like a fish swimming against the stream, it moved in as the guards and servants and courtiers streamed out to battle the fire. The stink of smoke reached into the dim, thick-walled corridors that had once been its fortress. That still were. That would be again.

Kithamar slipped through close, dark halls, down a spiral stair, and through a doorway that hadn't been opened in a generation to the private chapel where Daos a Sal had once communed with the spirits. It walked to the silver altar, tarnished now almost to blackness, sat, and swung its legs up. Fear made it difficult to think, but it had to think. It had to plan.

The blade was gone, and with it the ritual that let it slip from the far side of death into the rich saltwater of living flesh. If it died now, who would there be to save it? Its enemies were everywhere. If it stumbled again, the great long game would be ended. It pushed the thought away. This was no time to dwell on failure.

There were two heartbeats that kept it from its place at the head of the city. The false-blood prince and his daughter. Byrn a Sal was dead, or as good as. Elaine a Sal was in hiding. So that was its focus now. Finding the girl and killing her...But the blade was gone. It looked up into the thickness of cobwebs and dust and remembered when the stones there had been clean. It felt the deep roots and cold of the palace like it was feeling its own flesh. It reached for a calm, for an option, for a way to be safe and whole again. A way to keep eating all that it needed to eat. Not an end to hunger, but the permanent cultivation of longing.

There had been a first time. A time before blade and blood and water when—small and weak as a tadpole—it had first found its way into the living flesh of the city. It was so long ago, and it had been so young, so much *less* than it had since become, it was easy to forget.

So there *was* another way. Even if Andomaka was killed. Even if Elaine a Sal took her dead father's place, there was a way. It would mean losing a great deal—memory and power and the deep history. To some degree, even its sense of itself. It would be a second first time, a refounding of the city within itself. Beginning again where it had started so many generations before with a new bloodline to rule the city for another thousand years.

It wouldn't be the full casting out that it had managed with Andomaka and Ausai and Airis and Daos. The thread would be reduced again to only a voice, an influence, a foreign impulse, but one that could whip Elaine a Sal from the inside, drive her where it needed her to go.

The plans cascaded in its mind, old memories like the glimmers of childhood recalled in great age. It would be such a loss to be so small again, such a profound setback. There were things it would need, but it could be done.

It could be done.

The thread of Kithamar rose, its route through the palace already clear in its mind. Its enemies had managed more than it had imagined they could, but there were few things as dangerous as a wounded god.

Time became very strange in the underground. The passage under the city must have taken hours, but Garreth couldn't say how many. Two seemed as likely as four or eight or that they had fallen into the darkness in some other life and were in the eternal dark with the memory following behind them like a mirage.

The stairs rose in darkness, sometimes carved out of the native granite of the land, sometimes constructed from ancient wood.

The path up followed no pattern that Garreth could understand, but wove in one direction and then another, turning sometimes in a tight rising spiral, sometimes flattening into a gently rising corridor with only five or six steps in it. It reminded him of the wandering paths worms and termites ate in old wood. The air was still and stank of mold and age. Every hundred yards or so, they passed niches in the walls with ancient iron mechanisms in them slowly bleeding into rust. Garreth couldn't imagine their function or the history that brought them there. The lantern in Elaine's hand threw a small bubble of light in the vast and twisting darkness. He didn't want to think what would happen if that brightness failed.

Behind them, the guard marched, footsteps in a deep, rolling rhythm that set the pace. Maur and Kannish and his uncle Marsen. Old Boar and Frijjan Reed. Beren and Nattan Torr and men who'd expected to spend the day drilling their swordplay instead of this. No one spoke, and the weight of stone and soil around ate the echoes of their passage. Garreth felt safer with them there. As though, since none of them had refused, the thing they were doing couldn't be as mad as it seemed.

The walk was like a forced march up the face of Oldgate, and he felt it with every step. Hard, yes, painful, yes, but not worse than the long run that Beren meted out as a punishment for sloth. Before Garreth had joined the guard, he couldn't have done it. Maur couldn't have. Kannish might have been able, but it would have left him spent. Now, it was a hard day with worse waiting at the end, but it wouldn't stop them. Elaine wasn't guard, didn't spend her days in training. It had to be worse for her, but she didn't slow, and he wasn't about to suggest that she should.

The stairs turned again, this time curling up to the right in a wide, swooping spiral that evened out into a hallway. The air smelled different here. She felt it too, but only hesitated for a moment before striding forward. A wide doorway made from oiled pine loomed up on the wall. When she paused beside it, Garreth put his hands to it and pulled. The wood bent, and for a moment he thought it was locked or frozen in place by decades. Then it shifted.

Captain Senit stepped to his side, his hands beside Garreth's. "On three," the older man said, and counted down.

The door shrieked. The wood bit into Garreth's fingers as it yielded, but it yielded. The room beyond it was blacker than night, and Elaine walked into it, lantern high. Garreth was carried along with the press of guards anxious not to be left in the darkness. Leather-bound chests huddled against stone walls. Low wooden shelves piled with sacks and boxes and pottery jars filled the center of the room like an abandoned store that sold curiosities and minor wonders. The guards—Maur wide-eyed among them, Kannish trying to look unimpressed at his side—walked through the room with hands on their swords. The sense of having stepped into a nightmare was clear on all their faces.

"I know where we are," Elaine said. "This is the south side of the palace. The old armory should be right above us."

"Kint'll be there," Captain Senit said.

"I can go to him," Old Boar said. "I know enough men in the red that he'll see me."

"That ain't the question," the captain said, his eyes locked on Elaine. Her lips thinned and she looked down.

After a moment, she shook her head. "We are the only ones we trust. Us and my father. We can bring others in once we know that they're on our side of the fight."

"A dozen of us against the whole palace guard," Beren said. "Doesn't seem fair."

"We could use blunted swords," Frijjan Reed said.

"Cut the chatter," the captain barked, then turned back to Elaine. "Where should we find your father?"

"I don't know. His rooms or his study, most likely? But if he's been attacked—"

"Marsen. You take Frijjan Reed, Beren and his crew. Find the prince's rooms. If he's there, his daughter sent you to protect him, and you don't fucking leave his side until I'm there to tell you to. If that means sticking a knife in our red-cloaked brothers, try not to be the one that starts it."

"Understood," Marsen said. In the lantern's weak light, his face was ashen.

"The rest of you, with me and the lady. We'll try the study. We don't know what we're heading into, we don't know who our allies are or who's the enemy, but the goal's easy. Find the prince. Keep him safe. And if you come across Andomaka Chaalat, take her into custody. If she fights that—"

Captain Senit paused, his mouth open, as he realized what he was about to say.

"Kill her," Elaine finished for him.

"You heard it. Kill her," the captain said, though he seemed less certain than when he'd started. "Miss, if you could see us as far as daylight."

"This way," Elaine said, turning toward the far side of the storeroom.

Garreth started after her, but Captain Senit took his arm, squeezing it hard enough to hurt. "You're with me, Left. Either I'm about to watch somebody gut you, or we'll be having words when this is done."

"I did what I had to do," Garreth said, and the captain released him with a grunt.

"You did what you picked."

○ ○ ○

Elaine moved through the thick-walled corridors and dark, heavy rooms of the palace with a certainty born of her weeks of wandering. As they reached the open air, the reek of smoke was strong, but not choking. The flames that she'd feared didn't flicker in the windows and doors. The fire hadn't taken the palace, but it was nearby. The sun had turned red with it.

The shortest path to Ausai's private study took them through a servants' hall that the palace guard frequented. With Garreth and his two friends, the captain, and half a dozen more bluecloaks beside her, she'd look like an invading force. *I am the daughter of the prince*, she thought. *Stand down and let us pass.* She practiced until the rhythm of the words and the rhythm of her stride became one thing. Her whole self, bent in a single direction and tight as a bowstring. *I am the daughter of the prince. Stand down and let us pass.* She felt the exhaustion in her flesh, but at a remove. The fear and anticipation of violence lifted her up like a hot wind.

"There may be trouble ahead," she said as they turned the last corner before the hall.

It will be all right Garreth said at the same moment the captain said *Understood.* She took more comfort in Garreth's answer.

The hall was wide, low, and dark. Centuries of soot from the fire grate had stained the walls too deeply for scrubbing to wash entirely away. Heavy wooden tables and benches filled the center of the room, leaving just enough space behind them for the servants to carry in plates of food and tuns of beer and wine. They were empty. Elaine's steps faltered.

"What is it?" Garreth asked.

"There's always someone here," she said. "This feels wrong."

"Seems like luck to me," Garreth's friend Kannish said. She

didn't know whether the discomfort in his voice was his or something that her own ear supplied. She shuddered and pushed forward. The study was two buildings over, and up one shallow flight of stairs. They were almost on it.

But.

Motion caught her attention, and she shouted by reflex. A servant girl with a thin face and curled hair—as much Inlisc as Hansch—peeked back around the corner before coming in. Her gaze flickered around at the guards and landed on Elaine, and she bowed.

"Miss," she said. "I'm so glad to see you back. Everyone was so worried with you gone. What can I do for you?"

"Where is everybody?"

"At the fire, miss."

"What fire?"

The servant girl looked up in confusion. It was as if Elaine had asked whether the sky were up from here or down. "The Daris?"

"The Daris Brotherhood is burning?"

"Burnt, for the most. Caught flame earlier today. They've been hauling water from the canal for hours. Everyone from the palace and the compounds around it. Reyos. A Jimental. They've been pulling water from the canal with bucket lines. Three different ones. One of the buildings came down an hour ago, and the others...they're gutted. I only came back because Master Allysin needed fresh cloth for one of the girls who got burned."

"What about my father? Do you know where he is?"

"I'm sorry. I don't."

"Go, then," Elaine said. "I need nothing. You should go."

The girl bowed again, turned to leave, and then paused. "It is good to have you back, miss," she said, then hurried away. Gareth's eyes were wide.

"That's hers. Andomaka Chaalat's. Would she burn her own compound for a distraction?" he asked.

"If she did, she's an idiot," the captain said. "But she wouldn't be the first idiot I've heard of."

"Or else we have allies we don't know about," Elaine said. "It doesn't change anything we have to do. Follow me."

The empty passages both within the buildings and between them seemed more ominous now. A distant sound, too faint for direction, worried at her. A crackling and hissing like rats chewing through wood. Her mind kept trying to make it into the voice of the flames consuming the Daris Brotherhood or else spreading to other buildings in Green Hill or the palace, but the smoke was no thicker. There were no voices raised in alarm, just the soft, uncanny noise.

The complex iron door—Ausai's door—stood closed. When she pushed it, it was like pressing against the wall. There was no sign that it had ever yielded to her hand, nor that it ever would again.

"We can ram it," the captain said.

"There's another door," Elaine said. "I had just hoped that..."

She lost track of what she was saying, her eyes on the iron figures worked into the door. The man with the doubled swords and the wolfskin. Oumlish, his name was. His battle with the great bird, the symbol of the Inlisc warlords. The images of him standing above his own shadow-soul and at the old Hansch altar of consecration. They were scenes from the founding of the city. The birth of Kithamar, worked in iron that hadn't rusted in centuries. Even the rising beasts and the falling angels were symbols of the turn of one age to the next that the new-made city had marked. It had all been opaque to her before. Now it was clear as good glass. The sculpture was like poetry without language, and it took her breath away.

How do you know this? she thought, rubbing unconsciously at her wrists where they itched. *You didn't know this, and now you do. How did you learn all this?*

"Elaine?"

Garreth was beside her. It was such a relief to see him. But of course, he'd been with her all along. She put her back against the door and her palms against her temples. The sense of disorientation faded a little.

"Are you all right?" he asked.

"Fine. It's that noise. It distracted me."

He frowned. "What noise?"

"The..." She lifted a fist, like she was grinding a handful of gravel together. "You don't hear it?"

Garreth frowned and tilted his head. "Maybe? A little."

"I don't hear anything," Maur said.

The captain put a hand on her shoulder. "We need to keep moving. Tell me how to find this second door and I'll leave you a bodyguard."

She shrugged his hand away. The sound was louder now, and there was a rhythm in it, like waves that slowly built and receded. She had the sense of being close to something vast, like the vertigo of looking out from the top of the palace into the wide air over the city. Or up into the vastness of the sky. She swallowed.

"It's just down the corridor here."

The air seemed to resist her as she walked, like she was trying to make her way along the riverbed, the air around her suddenly thick as water. The men walked beside her, and she had the sense that her force was larger now. That they had been joined by someone else. When she tried to count, it was just the ones who'd been there since the captain had split the forces, but she was certain that when she didn't count, there were more. The world seemed to have more depth than it should.

She led her uncertain host down the dark corridor to the new door, the passage that her father had called for, ready to confront the guards there, ready to pry open the lock or break the bar if she had to.

Two red-cloaked palace guards lay on the stone, their eyes focused on nothing. The door stood open, and a flickering light came from it. The noise that poured out from the study was so overwhelmingly loud she almost didn't hear the captain speak.

"Blades at the ready, boys. Follow my lead."

Garreth's fist ached around the sword's grip. Captain Senit moved first, entering the flickering hallway with his teeth bared somewhere between a threat and a grin. Garreth stayed close behind him, then Kannish and Maur and Old Boar. Elaine was someplace behind that, but all his attention slid forward into the light. The sound that Elaine had talked about was just on the edge of his hearing now. A hissing, clattering like hard rain or a pot at a boil. Something energetic and destructive.

The room they entered was in chaos. Books lay scattered and torn, ankle deep on the floor like a snowstorm made from pages. It was a small space, almost too close to swing a blade. Golden runes had been fashioned into the stone, but Garreth didn't know what they meant. Something swirled through the space, violent as a storm, though the air was still. Two people were in the center of the room. The one standing was a pale woman in a robe tied with a length of rope instead of a belt, her face contorted with more than rage. The one on his knees before her, blood running from his mouth and eyes unfocused and failing, Halev Karsen.

"Hey!" Captain Senit barked. "Step back from that man and keep your hands empty!"

The pale woman turned, and behind her, Karsen slumped to the ground as if her attention had been the only thing supporting him. Her eyes had a flat, fish-like brightness as they clicked from one to the other of them. When she scowled, she seemed to have too many teeth. Garreth heard Maur as if he was half a mile away, whispering *That was a bad idea.*

Captain Senit moved toward her slowly, his sword before him. Maur and Old Boar tried to follow, and Garreth meant to go after, but the room felt as if it had tipped under them. Moving forward, even a step or two, was like climbing a steep hill. The captain slipped on the ripped pages of a book and sank to one knee, his blade waving toward the floor like it had become unbearably heavy. Behind him, Kannish paused, his chest working like a bellows, the few steps toward the pale woman a greater effort than the whole march through the buried city under Kithamar.

Elaine's voice came from behind him, cutting through the roar like they were happening in different worlds. "Where is my father?"

No, Garreth tried to say. *Don't let it know you're here. Run. Don't stop running. Never stop running.*

It was too late.

The weird, fish-flat eyes shifted, and the pressure pushing him back ebbed a little. Kannish sank to his knees, and the captain coughed once and deeply. When the pale woman found Elaine there among them, she smiled. It was horrible.

"What did you ask me, cousin?" Andomaka asked through her teeth.

"Where," Elaine said, then paused for breath. "Where is my father? What did you do to him?"

The pale woman spread her hands in mock innocence. "Something's bothering you? Please, come tell your cousin Andomaka all about it."

"Don't," Garreth tried to shout, but it came out less than a murmur. The roaring, screaming, burning, chewing sound throbbed, and there were lines in the noise. Little black threads that connected the thing in the center of the room to each of them. To everything. Not a web, but the strings of a marionette that was the city and everybody in it. He felt something damp happening in his eyes, and he thought he was weeping until he touched his cheek and his fingers came away red. He heard Elaine's footsteps moving toward him, toward the beast in its almost human body, and his sense of loss was wider than the sky and deeper.

Elaine walked past him on his right, her spine straight, her shoulders unbowed. Maur shrieked with raw effort, trying to rush ahead of her, his blade high, so that when he fell maybe it would reach the target. Andomaka Chaalat didn't even shift her attention as Maur collapsed. He didn't try to catch himself, and his head struck the floor with a sound like a dropped melon. A moan came from one of the men behind them, only a few steps away and farther than the city walls. The room was small, and Garreth could no more cross it than he could fly.

Elaine stood before the god-monster, her face twisted with pain. Garreth's heart labored, ached, stung.

And another thread suddenly *was*. It was so small, so thin, so fragile, he almost overlooked it. Faint as a spider's web, it ran between him and Elaine, red and pulsing gently with his heartbeat.

The thing shaped like a woman reached out a hand, wrapped fingers under Elaine's jaw. *What am I going to do with you?* But Garreth put all his attention into that one red thread, and he found that it let him move forward. Just a little. A lessening of the invisible storm that pushed him back or a strength to defy it, he couldn't tell which. He didn't care.

He gathered himself. His muscles ached. His eyes swam with blood and tears. A deep, terrible nausea was rising in him. He ignored it all.

Elaine cried out in pain, and there was a darkness around her head that didn't come from the pale woman. Garreth felt a brightness in his own mind, glowing in him like a tiny candle. A distant star. The brightness screamed *Now*.

"Watch your *head*!" Garreth shouted as he lunged. The beast turned, lifting a warding arm, but too high. He pushed the blade into the soft place under its ribs, driving the sword deep and deeper until it caught against something.

The thing shaped like a woman released Elaine, who stepped back, unsteady as a drunk. It grabbed Garreth's sword hand with both of its own, and the touch was like being bitten. Its wide, dark eyes locked on him and he imagined he saw outrage in its barely human expression. It squeezed until something in his hand cracked and grated. Garreth threw himself to the side, twisting with all the power he had left as he fell. His hand bloomed with pain, and the sword turned, widening the wound. As he landed, the brightness in him guttered and went out. The air of the palace settled on him like a boot on his neck.

Dimly, he was aware of Elaine's foot not far from him. The little leather boot she was wearing had a tear just at the back, and the roughness there had left an angry spot on her ankle. He reached out with his broken hand, his fingers resting for a moment against her skin, the soft hair at her calf, the warmth of her body. And barely audible under the cacophony, the hush of his fingertips caressing her. That single fraction of an inch of his skin against hers, and the memories of a wilder, freer, more beautiful moment.

It was enough.

Garreth closed his eyes, and his mind fell into darkness.

○ ○ ○

The thread of Kithamar had ridden enough bodies down to death that it recognized the feeling. The bluecloak shouldn't have been able to reach it, but somehow, he had. Bad luck or some little oversight, and now the life it could have lived as Andomaka Chaalat was measured in minutes. Such a waste of good skin. Such a waste of time and years and effort.

Blood dropped out of its side like a fountain, drowning its books in red so deep it was black. Inking over centuries of its words and thoughts and insights with the lifeblood of this one insignificant woman. The pain was deep and rich and powerful. And behind the pain, the fear. And behind the fear, the hunger. The need. The unending, driving want for more life.

Elaine a Sal, the twice-false heir to the throne, came back to her senses enough to look down at the man grabbing her foot. She didn't say his name, but the shock and fear were enough. Her lover in the city guard. Her Garreth. She should have died in his arms before and saved them all the trouble. The waste of it. The depth of all that it would have to rebuild because of this giddy, idiot girl and her cuckoo's egg of a father. It was so pathetic it almost laughed, but laughing hurt worse.

It reached out with its will. Not as strong as it had been, but enough. It didn't need much more. Elaine a Sal shifted back to look at its eyes. Was there terror in her? It thought there was. It tasted like blood.

Blood.

And here it was. No blade, no blood, no water. Neither name nor deathmark. None of the tools it had built. Nothing but the will and the hunger that had created it from the first. And this was the ground. Before there had been walls, before they had laid down the stone and mortar that cut it off from the wind and the sky, this was the place. Like an old man recalling the taste of a peach eaten before he'd learned to walk, it knew that night, those stars. The Inlisc surrender. The Hansch triumph.

The moon had been at a quarter full, and growing. Afternoon rain had cooled the grasses that still grew on the hilltop back then. The enemies had come together under the flag of peace that was also the flag of surrender, and founded the city that the city would become. It could almost see their faces, could almost hear their voices speaking in accents that time and generations had erased.

Kithamar had been born on this ground, and would be reborn here too. The guards lying prostrate and dying before it would witness its rebirth and not know what they had seen. Elaine a Sal with her pretty eyes and defiant mouth would carry this new city within her like a tapeworm.

Something shifted in its belly, deep and low. The wave of pain that followed brought its mind back to the moment and the awareness that its moments were slipping away. It stepped forward, its books rustling under its feet like autumn leaves. Elaine a Sal steeled herself for a fight that wasn't coming, and the thread of Kithamar put a bloody hand on the girl's shoulder.

The hardest thing was letting go. What it had become was too large to fit the work that lay before it now. The power, the reach, the depth, all that it had acquired held it back now. Steadying itself on the girl, it let go. The city walls like skin of its body, it released. The streets and quarters of the Temple, of Seepwater, of Longhill, it released. The permanent fires of the Smoke and the constant bright, chattering dogfights of Newmarket and Riverport. It felt the Silt, which had never entirely belonged to it. But what there was, it released. Kithamar's soul washed in and up, leaving not a city but stones and wood and shit and food. All the pieces that had made it, without the animating spirit. The corpse of a great city. The thread contracted.

Stonemarket that still had streets that followed paths shepherds had made when it had been a grazing field fell away. Green Hill where the first poverty-drunk beggars had put their tents outside the walls of the ancient Hansch fort. Oldgate with its maze of war tunnels and echoes of old violence. The thread of Kithamar let it all fall away until it was only aware of the palace that had been its first city, its walls against the raiders, its protection in the wilds. Andomaka's body lit with pain, and there was more than blood spilling from its wound now. A loop of intestine, carried by the flood. The foul stink of shit complicating the smell of salt and iron.

The thread of Kithamar made itself small as a gnat. Small as a spore. Thin and slight and floating, insubstantial and unkillable as an idea, a story, a wisp of song that intruded in the mind and wouldn't let go.

As the body failed, it released that too, and pressed itself across the ocean of air between the mutilated corpse of Andomaka Chaalat and the bright, fresh new body that called itself Elaine a Sal. There was barely anything left of it. An impulse to land in the soft, warm young mind, an anticipation of the pale roots that it would press into that conscious flesh. The endless, patient, vegetive ambition of the seed.

It entered Elaine like a sickness. Like a plague too early even for the fever to present. It spread into her—

And something pushed it out. It had an impression of a thin-faced older woman who looked like Elaine a Sal might when she grew older. Or of a dark-haired Inlisc with a bad eye. Or of a maiden whose name it had known once and forgotten, rich with life and the promise of life.

The thread of Kithamar, bare in the empty world, glowed

with something that wasn't light and faded to something that wasn't grey. It was so small, so diminished, that it took every bit of complexity and energy that remained just to think *What are you?*

Not yours, came the answer. *What I am is not yours.*

But the thread of Kithamar had already been severed.

Elaine a Sal lay on stone. It was cool against her back. There was no cushion under her head, though someone had thrown a blanket over her. If she turned her head to the side, she could hear the grit grinding in her hair. Her clothes were stiff with blood. All of it felt more comfortable than any bed she could remember.

The great black wooden beams that supported the ceiling seemed as far above her as the moon. She smelled vinegar and honey and blood and smoke. The hall was filled with voices and footsteps, the creak of wooden litters that carried the wounded, and the splash of water in bowls that people were using to wash wounds. It should have been loud, but that other, deeper, angrier noise was gone, and it made the pandemonium feel quiet. She would have slept if she hadn't been so tired.

"Oh," a woman's voice said, and she felt like she should know it. She opened eyes she didn't remember closing, and the historian was there. Mikah Ell. It was strange to see her.

The older woman looked around as if trying to find someone that might help her with this surprising moment, then gave up and sank to her knees beside Elaine. Her smile seemed genuine, if a little uncertain.

"I didn't know you'd come back," she said. "All of this. All these people. Were they...did you get hurt fighting the fire?"

The question seemed to demand an answer, so Elaine elbowed

herself up high enough to look. Men in the blue cloaks of the city guard, some bleeding from the ears and eyes, were laid out side by side across the floor of the hall. The captain. The one they called Kannish. There, under a blanket with his chest rising and falling and his shut eyes bruise-blue with exhaustion, Garreth.

"Yes," Elaine said. "That's what happened. The fire."

"That's very brave," the historian said, and then seemed to run out of words. Her hands fluttered a little at her waist and she looked around again. "I'll find someone to take you to your rooms, shall I?"

"No," Elaine said. "I'm fine here."

Mikah Ell shook her head as if Elaine had given the wrong answer to her tutor. "It's not a problem. I can just—"

Elaine made the effort to sit. Her body hurt from skin to sinew. Dried blood cracked and tugged as she moved. She noticed without any real surprise that the marks on her wrists were gone. "I have work to do here. Thank you, though."

"Of course. Yes, of course." Mikah Ell regained her feet, made a bow, and almost turned away. Then, "Welcome back, though. You were missed."

When she was gone, Elaine waited, gathered her strength, and stood. It was easier to walk than she'd expected, and her mind seemed to be putting itself back in order. Even just the few steps to Garreth's side left her more wakeful. More herself. His eyes opened as she lowered herself beside him. He looked around them, confused.

"Someone bandaged your hand," she said.

"Someone tore it up." He reached out his left, uninjured hand. "This one's all right. Where is everyone?"

Elaine wove her fingers with his. "Here, I think. The wind's died down," she said, and her voice cracked on the words. She wept without knowing what she was weeping for, except that she was too full, and everything that was in her—fear and relief and confusion and triumph and sorrow—had to find its way out, and this was the one her body had chosen. She bowed her head, her eyes closing, and he rose up.

"It's all right," he whispered, his living breath warm against her ear.

I'm being silly. We won. I'm home. There's no reason for this. I shouldn't be doing this.

"Let it free. It's all right. You're safe here."

And that was all it took. Something wide opened in her chest, and she sobbed, taking fistfuls of his cloak and pulling him in against her like she was a child again, and he was the nurse set to comfort her. The tears stung at first, but there were so many that they washed themselves away. When she looked up, the others in the room were carefully not seeing her. She and Garreth were alone in the middle of the crowd, and she discovered that she wasn't ashamed. She was too tired for shame.

At its worst, the grief or exhaustion or other nameless raw emotion transported her, letting her forget herself in the ocean-wide swell of it. And then, slowly, by degrees, the storm passed. She leaned on Garreth, her breath shuddering. He smoothed her hair with his good hand and cooed softly, like he was gentling an animal. Elaine felt hollow in the best possible way. The emptiness didn't hurt.

When she sat back, Garreth's eyes were red and wet as her own. She hadn't even noticed him crying with her.

"It's been a strange day, yeah?" he said.

"Might need some time to recover before we do this again." His chuckle was rich, warm, low in his throat. She wanted to kiss him, but she had to gather some energy first.

The voice that came from behind her was as familiar as her

own name, and it took a moment to recognize anyway. "Please excuse me. I need to speak with you, Elaine."

Halev Karsen stood almost at her back. His skin was waxy and grey. He swayed a little as he stood.

"It's fine," Garreth said, but not to Halev. To her. "I'll be all right. I'm here if you have need of me."

Elaine let him go. Halev put out a hand to help her up, but she didn't reach back. It seemed more likely that she'd topple him. Her hip ached when she stood, but not so badly she couldn't ignore it. Halev turned and started off to the north, leaving the room of injured behind and stepping into the narrow darkness of the old corridors. Toward her father's rooms.

"What is it?" she asked.

"Not here."

"Is something wrong with my father?"

Halev was quiet long enough she thought he wasn't going to answer. And then, "We need to have an unpleasant conversation."

By the time Captain Senit had gathered them all to the stables, the sun had fallen behind the walls of the palace. The sky overhead was still blue, though it was darkening to indigo in the east. The first stars would press past the smoke haze and the high, reddening clouds before long. It would be full dark before they reached the foot of Oldgate.

Maur lay in the cart, as still as death. The bruises around his eyes were almost black, and his nose was thick and wide and misshapen. His eyes were closed. Kannish and Old Boar sat beside him, and Garreth stood at the cart's side, leaning against it to look in.

"He was a good man," Kannish said.

"Died following his oath," Old Boar agreed, nodding.

"Fuck you both," Maur groaned.

"The way he charged that woman," Old Boar said, looking at the sky in mock piety. "We all knew she was wielding deep magics. But brave little Maur, he thought, maybe if I run at her real fast. That should work."

"It might have," Maur said. "I wanted to see."

At the front of the cart, Marsen clambered up to the driver's box, though he didn't take the reins. "There's a great spiritual power in running real fast. The priests all say so. The way to reach God, they say, is you *rush* him."

"How is what I did any different than Garreth?"

"His worked," Kannish said, laughing.

Maur didn't open his eyes, but lifted his hands, fingers spread in supplication to the gods of putting up with bullshit. The courtyard was in shadow, the heat of the day radiating back up from the stones. The red-cloaked palace guards had returned, burns on their hands and arms, soot darkening their cloaks. There was laughter and exuberance. Someone had brought two thick-bodied barrels of beer, and the palace servants were handing out cups of it to everyone. It was the joy and laughter of danger that had just gone by. Every man and woman there had faced catastrophe in the hours since sunrise. They'd survived, and they were all drunk on that fact as much as on the beer.

Garreth looked back at the darkening stone buildings, squat and thick, and hoped to see her particular face again, but Elaine had been called away hours ago. However much he wanted to see her, talk with her, hold her, this was the palace, and she was the prince's daughter while he was city guard at most. There were other obligations that demanded her attention not by anything she'd chosen. It was just the way the world was ordered.

Still, he watched and he hoped.

Across the courtyard, Captain Senit was standing with Samal

Kint of the palace guard. They were both smiling, but very differently. Kint was canted forward, pressing for something. Senit leaned back, enjoying the act of withholding it, whatever it was. Garreth's own smile faded.

"Give me a minute, boys," he said. "I'll be right back."

He stepped away, navigating a path across the courtyard with his thumbs hooked in his belt. A young man in a servant's robe offered him a tin cup of beer. He drank half of it in a swallow and wished it were stronger. Kint glanced at him as he came close, but Captain Senit didn't look over.

"Once we figured it, we got her out of the fish and brought her back home."

"An air fish," Kint said.

"Yeah," Captain Senit said with palpably false innocence. "Use 'em in Bronze Coast all the time. They've got a bladder in 'em that pulls the good air right out of the water, and you steer 'em from the inside just like you were driving a mule. God knows how long the poor girl had been going up and down the port trying to catch someone's attention."

"And nothing to do with Andomaka Chaalat," Kint said.

"Just happy timing. I'd have waited on you, but I sensed you were busy with shoveling mud onto embers and all that. What the fuck do you want, Left?"

"Needed a word, sir."

Captain Senit rolled his head over to stare at him, then shrugged. "Fine. Excuse me, Samal, but the children are calling, yeah?"

Kint raised a cup of beer in salute and turned away, shaking his head. Captain Senit started walking briskly toward the path that led down to Oldgate. Garreth had to trot to catch up.

"Air fish, sir?"

"It's the third story I told him. With any luck, when the real thing gets back, he'll think it's just another something I made up. Which, when you look at it, an air fish ain't that much less likely. What's on your mind?"

Garreth swallowed, and they passed through the iron gate and through the short tunnel to the top of the switchback road that led down to the Khahon, far below. "I want you to know how much the guard means to me. You took me in when I needed a place and didn't have one. I know the city now in ways I never would have."

"But," the captain said.

"When I took Elaine a Sal to Aunt Thorn, I had to strike a bargain. I owe Aunt Thorn a favor. And...I don't think I can do that and still be in the guard."

Captain Senit sighed and looked out over the eastern half of the city. The shadow of Palace Hill and Oldgate was clear from here, stretching out across the river, Newmarket, Longhill. The Temple and Riverport were still bathed in the light of the falling sun, and to the south, a strip of Seepwater glowed gold. Kithamar the way a bird might see it. The tall air made the city beautiful and alien and vast.

The captain swung his arm around Garreth, massaging his shoulder like a baker kneading stiff dough. When he spoke, his voice was genial and warm.

"Son, I know boys your age don't always listen, but I want you to try now, yeah? You gave the daughter of the prince of Kithamar over to the worst Inlisc crime boss there is. You betrayed me and mine as deeply as it's possible to do. Hush, hush, hush. This is listening time. Don't talk. The idea that you still have a place in my barracks to give up is the most sweetly naïve thing I've heard all day. You aren't guard. You were never guard. You were a spoiled merchant brat throwing a fit because he didn't like what his family wanted from him. You joined because your friends had done before you, and you didn't have a thought of your own."

"I don't think that's—"

"I don't give half a shit what you think, Left. I'm older than you, I'm smarter than you, and I've seen better than you come and go. You put a knife in Chaalat, so you're the hero of the hour, but that hour's ending. The only reason you're not swimming in a sack full of bricks tonight is that you've spilled a little salt with likely the most powerful woman in the city. But once we cross that bridge down there, you're just another turd on the street to me. Your life's work now is staying out of my sight. If our paths cross again, I'll see to it no one finds your corpse. Clear?"

"Clear."

Captain Senit clapped him twice on the back and turned away, rolling back toward the palace and the cart and the guards in the blue or else red, humming a cheerful tune. Garreth stood quietly. He tried to feel shame, and he did, a little. But also relief. He picked up a bit of gravel and tossed it down the steep face of the hill where it wouldn't hit the road. The tick, tick, tick sound as it bounced away was beautiful in its fashion. Part of him wanted to walk away now, to vanish down into the city and not have to face his friends, knowing that his time with them was over. But it would have been rude to Kannish and Maur, and he'd done enough of that for one lifetime. He tossed one last little stone, and when it was silent, turned back.

He knew as soon as he passed into the courtyard that something had happened. The laughter was gone, the smiles vanished. The cups of beer were still in people's fists, but no one was drinking. He went to the cart where Kannish still sat, his face ashen.

"Hey. What's the matter?" Garreth asked.

"The prince is dead."

There's a stairway that runs along the outside of the house, so you can come and go as you like, even when the shop's closed," Yan said. "The only other thing on the hall is a storeroom, but sometimes my cousin will sleep there. I'll let you know when he does, but it's not often. Eight coppers at the start of the week. One silver if you want breakfasts and dinners with it, but I just make a little more of whatever I'm having. I don't take orders."

"I don't give them," Garreth said.

The room above the tailor's shop was smaller than the bedroom he'd grown up in, more than his bunk in the barracks had been. He didn't know where to put it in his mind. The wood had been neglected at some point, and grey streaks showed the damage of time even though the walls had been oiled. A small window with a better view than he'd expected of the rooftops to the east. A bed with a mattress that was worn, but clean. A table with two stools and a little earthenware vase with a sprig of rosemary in it. Yan looked around it with him, nodding as if her approval might be contagious.

Garreth had expected to feel shame being here, to feel lessened by the loss of his place with the guard. With his family before that. It was a surprise that he loved the room, and he didn't understand why his affection for it was so sudden or so profound until he realized it was the first bed that would be entirely his. Not his father's, not his captain's. As long as he kept the payments, the little room with its tainted walls and warped floor was his. He hadn't known he was so hungry for that.

He sat at the table and counted eight coins from his wallet. They all had the likeness of Prince Ausai on them. Byrn a Sal hadn't lived a full year on the throne. If there were any coins with his face on them, they were very new, and Garreth hadn't seen them.

"Frijjan Reed says you're good people, or I wouldn't be doing this," Yan said as she took the coins. "You know my husband is out of the city for a time. The door at the end of the hall..."

"Leave it barred. That's fine. There's water at the fountain down by that one wool shop? With the purple doors."

"I'd go a little farther. There's a cistern two streets farther north. It's a longer walk, but the fountain water tastes funny."

"I'll be fine," Garreth said. "After my last year, I just want to spend a little time being where I am."

Yan weighed the coins in her hand, then tucked them clinking in a pocket. "Going to watch the funeral procession?"

"No," Garreth said. "I saw the last one. It was enough for a lifetime."

Yan nodded, gestured to the room, relinquishing it, and went out through the inner door. After it closed, the bar scraped into place, keeping him from the rest of Yan's home, and her footsteps receded. Garreth closed the bar on his side too, awkwardly with his left hand.

His bag had everything he owned now. Two changes of clothes, a nicked dagger that Maur had given him "for protection," a little yellow bag with the money he'd saved up during his time as a guard, a leather flask, and a length of boiled cotton. These last two, he took out and placed on the table, then the night pot. Carefully, slowly, he unwrapped his wounded hand.

It was swollen badly at the knuckle of his index finger, and three wide, deep cuts marked where Andomaka Chaalat had gouged him with her nails. One of the wounds had started to scab over, but the others were still bright and raw. The bandages had less blood on them now than the last time he'd changed his dressing, though. When he opened the flask, the smell of alcohol and herbs filled the room. When he poured it over the open cuts, it stung. He let it dry before he bound his hand in fresh cloth. With only his off hand to work with, the wrap looked messy and terrible, and before he could manage to tie it off with his teeth, he heard footsteps ascending his stairs. It couldn't be Elaine, but his heart leapt anyway. A tentative knocking came at the outer door, and then a voice he hadn't expected.

"Hello?" Uncle Robbson said. "Is anyone there? We're looking for Garreth Left."

"Here," Garreth called out. "The door's not locked. You can come in."

The door from the stairs scraped, and the floorboards in the hall creaked. Mother came in first, with Uncle Robbson behind her. Her hair was free, wild and wiry, and she wore a wide skirt and linen blouse like they were armor. She looked around the room once, then settled on the edge of the bed, one leg tucked up beneath her. Robbson's angry scowl was like an old friend come for an unexpected visit. Garreth pointed toward the one empty stool in invitation.

"The man at the barracks said you were living here," Robbson said as he sat.

"That's only been true for a few minutes, but yes."

"It's... Well. We have something to discuss with you. A proposal."

"It's good to see you too," Garreth said. "I'm glad you're healthy."

Robbson grunted, but his mother smiled. "Kannish told us you'd split with the guard," she said. "Whatever the details are, the timing of it might work to all our advantages. Vasch is leaving."

"Leaving?"

"His new wife is hauling him out to the wilds."

"Yrith thinks it would be best if he went to the north and met her family in person," Mother said. "The caravan was a strong move. It cleared our obligations. But it could also be a path toward a very lucrative future."

"Plus which, it gets them out of the house for a few months," Robbson said.

"Seems wise," Garreth said. "But I don't see what it has to do with me."

"We need a supervisor for the warehouse," Mother said. "Your father and I think there would be some advantage to having it be someone that the carters already know."

Garreth leaned back on his stool, resting his back against the wall. He needed money, and so a part of him jumped toward the thought of working. A warehouse man could make more than enough to keep a room like his and live decently. But another part of him cringed back from the idea.

Robbson took a thin leather wallet from his belt and put it on the table. "It wouldn't be coming back to the house, and you wouldn't want that anyway. Things have been tense with your father, but you won't have to deal with him directly. Just send the daily records to me."

Garreth considered the wallet, thought of the thin pile of

coins in his bag and how few weeks they'd last him. "I don't think so." Uncle Robbson's face flushed and his jaw went tight as Garreth pushed the wallet back across the table. "No offense meant, but I think I need to find a path. Being given one..."

"Your brother misses you," Mother said. "I do too."

"Is he happy?"

Her eyes softened. "He is."

"Take a day," Uncle Robbson said. "If you come to your senses, you can send word. After that, I'll have to find someone else."

"I understand," Garreth said. "Thank you for thinking of me. Really."

Robbson stood, straightened his jacket, and held a hand out to Mother.

"Why don't you go ahead, Robb," she said. "I have a little more business here."

"Genna—"

"Please," she said, but she said it like a command. Uncle Robbson took the wallet, fitted it back over his belt, and turned toward the door. The floor creaked under his weight, and then the slow, steady tramp of his feet going down the stairs. Mother waited in silence until he was gone, then unfolded herself, took two steps to cross the room, and sat on the stool her brother had left. Her time in the north had darkened and roughened her skin. The white in her hair made Garreth think of drawings of lions. She gestured to his injured hand, and he passed it to her.

"I meant to talk with you when I got back," she said as she began unwrapping his awkward bandages. "Your father told you about our compromise, mine and his."

"That was a long time ago," Garreth said. "I'm not the same person I was then."

"I didn't see any reason to tell you or your brother about that part of our lives, but since your father did, I think you should have some perspective about it." She looped the cloth around her arm, considering it as she did. "I did love Mannon when we started. The worst years were when I was trying to get past that. I had an image of what a man and a woman were to each other—a husband and a wife—and it hurt me that we weren't that. Your father is a terrible husband. From what I've seen, I think he's probably too cruel to make a good lover either."

"Serria doesn't seem happy."

"She isn't," Mother said, and the last of the bandage fell away, leaving his hand exposed. She made a little sound of sympathy and turned his wrist one way and then the other as she examined the wounds. "But he's the best business partner I could have wished for. He respects me. Yes, you can laugh. It's all right. But I can travel for months, and he doesn't complain. I don't need his permission to sign a contract in the name of the family. Whatever choices I make, he supports. He knows how I think, and when it comes to money, he trusts my judgment. When it comes to money, I trust his. I've taken risks that didn't pay out, and he never used it as a weapon against me. If I do something he disagrees with, we have our quarrel in private, and he defends me before the magistrates and guilds and the other families as passionately as if he'd made the decision himself. He is the most important person in my life outside you and your brother, and he has given me the space to create a life of my own that I actually quite enjoy. We aren't two true hearts beating together, and we don't have to be."

She pressed the swollen knuckle, and looked up at Garreth, a question in her eyes. He shook his head. It ached, but the pain wasn't unbearable. She began to carefully rewrap the cloth, a little tighter than he'd had it since she had both hands to work with.

"Vasch has it," Garreth said. "Doesn't he?"

"Which it?"

"The thing you wanted."

Mother's chuckle was low and short, but also warm. "Maybe. I think so. Those two seem to genuinely enjoy each other. I'm a little envious sometimes, but not so much I can't be happy for them. Is this too tight?"

"It's fine."

"It's the dream of it that cuts. You start off with an idea of how it's supposed to be, and then when it isn't that, it hurts. That's not the world's fault. That's yours. Ours. Mine. But when you let go of the dream and look to what's actually possible... there's a way to be honest with your life that the stories and expectations and wedding oaths don't tell you. Ways of being with someone that people outside the two of you won't understand even if you try to tell them, and that's all right. They don't need to. We're deeper than the dreams they give us, if we let ourselves be. We can be faithful to something different."

She tucked the last bit of cloth into place. The bandage was firm and tight without turning his fingers dark. When he tried to ball his fist, the knuckles were stiff and painful, but stable in a way they hadn't been. "That's better. Thank you," he said.

"You're my son. I'm glad you let me help."

"I'm not going to take the warehouse job."

"I know."

She touched his cheek, smiled, and then left. Garreth sat alone at his table for a while, looking out at the street.

The funeral carried the body of Byrn a Sal to the Temple unseen by Garreth. He knew it had passed when people started appearing in the streets again. He made his way down the stairs. Newmarket was mostly closed for the day, but here and there, a few enterprising stalls had their signs out. He spent a few of his remaining coins on a bowl of chicken and barley mash that he ate sitting on a stone bench, then half a loaf of apple bread for the morning. Then he spent another hiring a boy to carry a message to Haral Moun at the Temple.

As the sun fell behind Palace Hill, he thought about going to a taproom or baths, but found himself watching a magician on the street corner as she conjured little orbs of light and made them dance on her fingertips. He put one coin in her beggar's box because it would be rude not to, and then another one for luck.

The Inlisc had a name for the night between the funeral of one prince and the coronation of the next. *Gautanna*. It was supposed to be the moment when the partition between the normal world of bricks and stones and trees and water and the stranger one of gods and spirits was easiest to cross. He didn't remember the night after Prince Ausai's funeral being much different than any other. As twilight fell, though, the sense that there were gods in the streets grew. The breeze that passed through Newmarket rattling the shutters and whistling past the eaves seemed to have words in it. The whole city seemed balanced between fear and a kind of wildness that forgot consequences. Or, Gareth supposed, that might just have been him.

The darkness came more slowly than he expected. Voices rose from the street. Two dogs argued or played until a man's voice shouted at them, and they faded into the distance. It only seemed silent because he'd grown used to the press of the barracks. The presence of family and servants before that. Yan might be in the shop below him or she might have gone out into the city on business of her own. Either way, it was the first night in his life he was genuinely alone.

He hadn't thought to buy a candle or a lantern, so nightfall was simply itself. He undressed in darkness and lay on the mattress though he wasn't sleepy. His injured hand throbbed under its wraps. The building creaked and muttered to itself, every sound seeming louder because it was new to him. A carriage drove by, horses clopping and wheels rattling, and didn't slow down. He wondered where Elaine was, and what she was doing. If, caught up as she must have been in the business of the city, she would think of him. He let himself imagine her footsteps on the floorboards of the hall. It was an empty wish, selfish and unlikely, but it brought his heart to his throat all the same.

The moon rose over the rooftops framed by his little window. The pale, milky light gave his room a softness. Garreth's mind wandered, shifting from one thought to the next like bubbles rising in still water. What work might he be able to find, how would Vasch get along with Yrith's people, were Maur and Kannish and Old Boar and Frijjan Reed patrolling or keeping to the barracks during the eerie night between one prince and another, how had Byrn a Sal died and could they have saved him if they'd made some different decision. Each interrupted the one before it until he wasn't thinking at all so much as being carried along by his untethered mind. The image of Andomaka Chaalat with her evil, hungry, flat eyes rose up before him, and he pushed it away with the memory of the thin red thread between him and Elaine.

Dreams began to form, shifting his daylight thoughts into stranger places and memories of things that he knew hadn't happened. He drifted down the soft river of his own sleep. The world faded.

The knock at his door brought him awake with a start, his heart tapping fast as a drummer against his ribs. He reached for the little dagger with his bandaged hand, only managing to knock it clattering to the floor.

"Who's there?" he said into the blackness.

"How many people did you invite?" Elaine a Sal replied.

When he opened the door, she was alone in the hallway. Her hair was down, and her cloak was a simply cut wool that the moonlight made colorless.

"Are you alone?"

"I have a guard outside in a carriage. This isn't new for him."

Garreth stood back. Her cloak rustled softer than leaves. When she spoke again, the weariness in her voice was thick. "I'm sorry about this. You shouldn't have lost your place over me."

"I lost it honestly. I wasn't a good fit."

"Still, they should have—" she began, and he stopped her.

Her mouth was sweet, like she'd been eating caramel. Her breath warmed the skin at his throat. They stood still together in the darkness, leaning in like two drunks outside a taproom propping each other up. Her hair smelled like smoke and incense.

"I need," she said, lost herself, and then returned. "I need to be selfish with you tonight."

"Whatever my lady—"

"No. Don't do that. Not even joking. I don't want to be her when I'm with you."

"Then you aren't. You're just you. I'm me."

"That has to be all right. Is that all right?"

"Yes," he said. He felt her nod against him. He moved his hand. She caught her breath, stiffened, softened as she exhaled. "Now, just the two of us, and no one else in the world? Show me who you are when you're selfish."

Afterward, they lay in the bed, side by exhausted side. He traced his fingers along the skin just under her ribcage, feeling the gooseflesh that rose there more than seeing it. The moon had shifted, and the light from it was a small bright square on the floor by the table.

"You're beautiful naked," he said.

"You are too," she said. "You should get candles. Or a lamp."

"I was thinking the same thing," he said. And then, "Are you all right?"

"Do we talk about that? Isn't that against the rules?"

"It isn't," he said. "I don't want to know how the prince of the city is. I'm asking about you. That makes it different."

"It does, doesn't it."

"You were at your father's funeral tonight. That has to weigh something."

She was quiet for a long time. His left hand hushed along her thigh, and she turned, moving closer to him. "I'm sad. And angry, but it's complicated. There are things I'm not going to tell you about. I know it's not fair, but—"

"It's policy," he said. "I understand that. My whole childhood was built around policy. But there are limits to policy."

"Are there? How does that work?"

She moved against him, pinched gently, and he chuckled. "It doesn't work like that. Not if you want me to keep thinking straight."

"Fine. I'll show restraint."

"What your business needs, your business needs, and your work is the whole city. I don't care. I don't want to know. But how you are? That, I do. If you're frightened, I can be frightened with you. If you're tired, I can help you rest. You're more than the roles you play."

"That's a sweet thought."

"It's truth."

She took his uninjured hand, guided it. Her eyes were very clear in the near-dark. "Yes?" she asked.

"Yes," he said. "But one thing first. Whatever the answer is, I'll be fine with it, but I do have to ask."

"Now?"

"Now," he said. "That first night, you said you didn't have room in your life for me, and I told you I didn't have room for someone like you. And it's a hundred times more complicated for us now. Tomorrow you're prince of Kithamar, and I'm going to look for a job."

"I know," she said.

"Is this the last we have?"

She propped herself up on an elbow. Her hair spilled across her face, and he stroked it back, tucking it behind her ear. "The last we have?"

"After tonight," he whispered, "are we finished with each other?"

The silence as she considered lasted a breath. It lasted a lifetime.

"No," she said, her voice certain and calm. "We're not."

I'm pregnant."

Elaine, halfway to fastening a necklace of white Caram gold and black Bronze Coast pearls, stopped. "You're what?"

"Pregnant," Theddan said again. She was wearing a cloth-of-gold gown of the same cut and design as her plainspun. It was special for the coronation, but the contrast of humble design and gaudy cloth seemed implausible. When she took the sides of the gown, pulling them back to show the contours of her body, there was a low little bump just below her navel that hadn't been there before. Elaine shot a glance back down the private chapel. Statues of a dozen gods looked out from the walls and the little crèche by the door, but no other novices or priests were there. Even so, she whispered when she spoke.

"What are you going to do?"

Theddan let the cloth fall back to its usual drape. "Make a baby, Elly. That's what pregnant means."

Somewhere just outside this windowless room, the sun had risen, washing the streets and windows and doors of Kithamar with fresh light. The grey cloth that had decorated the path that the black cart had followed was being replaced with bright streamers and banners. Bleakness followed by joy. The flowers strewn at yesterday's funeral procession wouldn't have lost their petals yet, but the world was supposed to have changed. Which, in fairness, it had, but Elaine couldn't help feeling rushed by it all.

Maybe the day would have been easier if she'd slept for more than a few minutes. Tradition and ritual required that the new not-quite-prince spend the last night of their freedom in meditation and purifying prayer. Her father had done, though she didn't think it had meant much to him besides sleeping in a different building. Looking back at the previous generations, it might have had a deeper use for the thing that had held the city's throne. Some consolidation of the new body it had taken possession of that the rest of the city had understood as piety.

Ever since Halev had explained all of what they'd discovered in the secret library, Elaine had found herself understanding things differently. Andomaka Chaalat's interest in her, the wis dom of how the prince's throne changed the men and women who sat on it, the tradition of keeping the servants and staff of the palace rather than bringing the ones from the family compound along. A thousand innocuous details and customs that she'd considered trivial to the degree she'd considered them at all suddenly became ominous. And so she didn't have any particular compunction about breaking them. Especially the one that said she should remain at the Temple and not go to Garreth Left.

She more than half wished she was still there. Bathing in the scented waters that probably symbolized something important, having servants braid her hair with ribbons of silver and gold, donning a gown of Gaddivan silk with thousands of hours of embroidery stitched on it, the thing that kept occurring to her was how much she would rather have been asleep, sprawled naked on a cheap mattress in Riverport.

She imagined waking late, with the sun spilling over the half-rotted wood, and sharing the apple bread and water with Garreth, and then maybe going down to the street or maybe not. But instead, she was being given the greatest honor her city could bestow, and being entrusted with the power of life and death over its citizens.

It left her cranky.

"I know what pregnant means. I didn't know that religious novices are welcome to carry their toddlers around to prayers. Aren't you supposed to be celibate? Is that a miraculous baby conceived by prayer and the will of the gods?"

"Haral is a sweet man. But no. Not a god," Theddan said, and shrugged. "I'll be kicked out. He will too. We've talked about it. I think we'll go run a farm. Father has a dozen west of the city. Not directly, but he has merchants who run them and they all trade money and favors. Beautifully corrupt, all of it. Anyway, Haral grew up on a farm and knows how they're managed, and I think I'd make a simply splendid farmer's wife and mother."

"Do you?"

Elaine returned her attention to the necklace, placed it around her neck, and Theddan leaned over to fasten it for her.

"I do, actually. Strange as it sounds. I love *feeling*, Elly. Everyone thinks I love sex, and I do, but it's because it's so rich and full. I think this will be too. Differently, but that's the joy of it. It's a way I've never been, and maybe it's time to be. I don't know how you people live your whole lives in your head and never get out as far as your skin."

Elaine considered herself in the mirror. There was a little darkness under her eyes, but that was the only sign of the exhaustion she felt. A little paint, and she'd be a fine and proper prince. "I don't always live in my head."

"That's my influence."

Elaine paused. "*Fuck*," she said. "So it is."

"You'll talk to my father, then?" Theddan made an exaggerated grin, toothy and hopeful and falsely innocent.

Elaine couldn't help but laugh. "Yes, I will take the throne and immediately compromise my influence and reputation by talking your father into giving his twice-disgraced daughter yet another chance at a halfway respectable life."

"I knew you would. I love you, Elly."

"I love you too," Elaine said. And then, looking seriously into Theddan's eyes, "I love you too."

For a moment, Theddan's frivolous mask slipped, and the two women were there together. Elaine could see the worry and sorrow and defiance in her cousin's eyes and the set of her mouth. The price that being herself despite the rules of her society demanded, and the strength she had to pay it.

She couldn't guess what Theddan saw in her, but her cousin said, "I don't know whether to be happy for you or sad."

"I'll take both," Elaine said, and the door opened behind her. Two other novices—these with much longer hair than Theddan—bowed their way in carrying half a dozen pairs of shoes that the new prince might choose to wear for her ceremony before the great altar. Three more followed with the paints for her face and gloves, if she wanted gloves. Theddan retreated, giving space to the great theater piece that was power.

Elaine surrendered to the process. Servants and novices and priests fluttering around her like agitated birds. Then, the grand ceremonies before the court and then the public. Audiences of congratulations and welcome with the heads of the great houses who had all had audiences of condolence with her yesterday. The tour of the city if she wanted it or the return to the palace that was hers now. After that, weeks and months and years of the slow, grinding work that Garreth called policy. It had been her nightmare when her father took his place. It should have been worse now that it was hers. But as they tried different shoes, different earrings, different shades of paint to warm her cheeks and lips, she noticed that the dread was less.

Strange as it seemed, she was less oppressed by her elevation now than she had been. Her other self—the Elaine a Sal that the court bowed before, that acquaintances pretended intimacy with, the one that grew up and around her like a shell on a crab—was stronger than it had ever been. But she had Theddan as her friend, Garreth as her lover. She had Halev Karsen—she still couldn't bring herself to think of him as anything but Halev Karsen—as her advisor. Three people who knew her for who she was and who she wasn't. And they were enough. And her father...

She wasn't ready to think about her father.

"We have to hurry, miss," the girl with the face paint said. "We don't want you going out to the altar with your eyes half done."

"Of course not," Elaine said.

Three people were enough, and there weren't only three. She wouldn't be spending time with them any longer, but there was Erja, the criminal and medic. Aunt Thorn, who Elaine was technically supposed to hunt down and kill for her crimes. There was her own mother, more fairy tale than memory, who she'd always imagined like a scowling angel looking over her in disapproval. She didn't see that now. Elaine ab-Deniya Nycis a Sal, second of the new princes of Kithamar, didn't have very much about her for a mother to disdain. When she pictured the woman standing there in the room with the servants and the gods and the high, shadowed vault of a ceiling, Elaine could only imagine her proud. Her daughter was, after all, the girl that a god couldn't kill.

"Please, miss. Try not to smile. I'm almost done."

"You know," Elaine said, stopping the girl's hand. "I'm really quite tired. I'd like a cup of tea. Could you go ask for one for me?"

The girl's eyes went wide with confusion and distress. She looked from the wooden palette smeared with flesh tones to the door behind her to Elaine's face again. "Yes," she said. "Of course."

As she scampered away on her new mission, Elaine spread her arms to all the others bustling around her. "In fact, if you could be so kind as to give me the room for just a few minutes. Once I've had my tea, we'll finish up, yes?"

They hesitated and filed quietly out, closing the door behind them. Elaine leaned back in her chair, alone with the gods. She picked out Lannas, with his feline head and golden eyes. Adrohin with his blindfold and sword. The Three Mothers huddled together in one corner, Lord Kauth and Lady Er in another. Twice-born Shau and the abstract symbol of the Faceless. In the steady light of the candles and lamps, a host of gods and mysteries, but not Kithamar. Kithamar was a city broken from the reins of godhood, and so it could become anything. For the first time since its founding, Kithamar was free. And because she was its prince, so—in her limited, constrained half-manner—was she.

The great secret of noble blood, she thought, was that it didn't give you everything, but neither did it have to take everything away.

The door opened, but instead of a servant with a cup of fresh tea, the high priest came in wringing his hands. She remembered sitting in his study that first time she'd come looking for Theddan. He seemed less certain of himself now.

"My lady a Sal, your city awaits you."

"It does," she said. "Let it wait half an hour more."

Here ends the second book of the Kithamar Trilogy,
where love, like a weed between bricks, endures.

ACKNOWLEDGMENTS

First and foremost, I would like to thank Jayné Franck, who was my collaborator when the city of Kithamar was first built. Without her dedication and invention, this project would have been something very different.

I would also like to thank Danny Baror and Heather Baror-Shapiro at Baror International, Inc., for having my back, the whole team at Orbit (particularly the saintlike patience and vision of Bradley Englert and Tim Holman), and the small council of Ty Franck, Kameron Hurley, Paolo Bacigalupi, Carrie Vaughn, and Ramez Naam, who were a comfort in dark times. And more than ever, my gratitude goes to my family for their love, support, and occasional intervention when I'm not entirely on the rails.

Any failures and infelicities in the story are exclusively my own.